The Crown of Dalemark

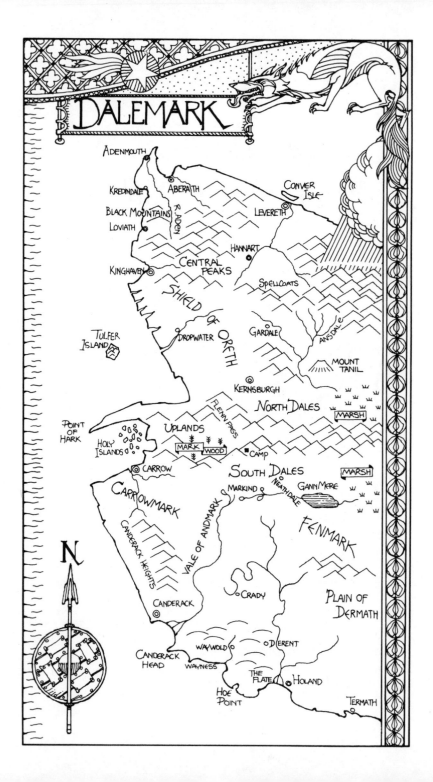

Diana Wynne Jones

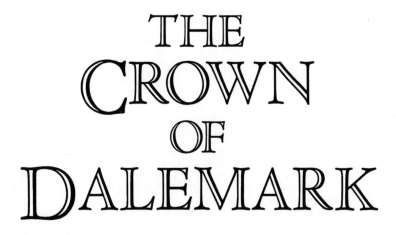

THE CROWN OF DALEMARK

Greenwillow Books, New York

Map by David Cuzic
First American Edition
1   2   3   4   5   6   7   8   9   10

Library of Congress Cataloging-in-Publication Data

Jones, Diana Wynne.
   The crown of Dalemark / by Diana Wynne Jones.—1st American ed.
      p.   cm.— (The Dalemark quartet ; bk. no. 4)
   Summary: The Countess and Lord Keril send Mitt to kill
a young woman, Noreth Onesdaughter, who claims to know
where the lost crown is hidden.
   ISBN 0-688-13363-0.   [1. Fantasy.]   I. Title.
II. Series: Jones, Diana Wynne. Dalemark quartet ; bk. 4.
PZ7.J684Cr   1995   [Fic]—dc 20   94-17936   CIP   AC

For Rachel

CONTENTS

:∥ PART ONE ∥:

Mitt

:‖ 1 ‖:

THE EARL OF HANNART arrived in Aberath two days before Midsummer. He was bringing the Countess of Aberath a portrait of the Adon to put in her collection. As this was a state visit, he brought his son as well and a string of his hearthmen, and his arrival caused a rare bustle.

A tall man dressed like a shepherd watched it all from high in the hills where the green roads ran. He had an excellent view from there, not only into the seething courts of the mansion but of the whole town, the cliffs, the bay, and the boat sheds. The Earl was easy to pick out among the hurrying figures, because he was with a servant carrying the picture. The man watched them go straight to the library, where he knew the Countess was waiting to receive the Earl. Almost immediately the servant was sent away to fetch someone else. The watcher could see him pushing his way, first to the stables, then to the dining hall, and finally to the hearthmen's quarters, where he fetched out a large gangly person and pointed to the library. The gangly one set off there at a run, on long, gawky legs.

The watcher turned away. "So they did send for this Mitt," he said as if this had confirmed his worst suspicions. Then he looked up and round and over his shoulder, clearly thinking that someone else was standing nearby, watching, too. But the green road was empty. The man shrugged and set off walking swiftly inland.

About the same time as this man left, Mitt arrived at the top of the library steps, trying not to pant, and pushed open the creaky door.

"Oh, there you are," said the Countess. "We want you to kill someone."

She was never one to beat about the bush. It was almost the only thing Mitt liked about her. All the same, he wondered if he had heard her right. He stared at her long, bony face, which was set slightly crooked on her high shoulders, and then looked at Earl Keril of Hannart to make sure. Mitt had been ten months now in Aberath, but the North Dalemark accent there still sometimes made him hear things wrong. Earl Keril was dark, with a long nose. Everyone said what a likable man he was, but he was looking at Mitt as grimly as the Countess.

"Didn't you hear?" Earl Keril asked. "We want someone dead."

"Yes. Is this a joke of some kind?" Mitt said. But he could tell from their faces that it was not. He felt cold and disgusted, and his knees shook. "I gave up killing—I told you!" he said to the Countess.

"Nonsense," she said. "Why else do you think I had you trained as my hearthman?"

"*You* would have it that way, not me!" Mitt said. "And I never kidded myself you made me learn all that out of love for me!"

Earl Keril looked questioningly at the Countess.

"I warned you he was rude," she said. She leaned toward him, and they murmured together.

Mitt was too disgusted to try to overhear. He looked beyond their two implacable faces at the painting of the Adon propped on an easel behind them. The light was across the canvas from where Mitt stood, in a bluish haze, but the painted eyes caught his, like dark holes in the haze. They looked ill and haunted. The famous Adon had been far from handsome, sickly-looking, with lank hair and crooked shoulders. Near on a cripple, like the Countess, Mitt thought. She and Earl Keril both descended from the Adon. She had the shoulders; Keril had the Adon's long nose. Earlier that day Mitt would have been thoroughly disappointed to find that the Adon looked like this. Since he came to Aberath, he had heard story after story of the Adon, the great hero who had talked with the Undying and lived as an outlaw before he became the last King of Dalemark several hundred years ago. Now he looked from the painting to the two living faces leaning together in the twilight of the library, and he thought, Fairy stories! Bet he was just as bad as they are! Well, I ran off from Holand, so I reckon I can run off from Aberath, too.

Just then he caught a murmur from Keril. "Oh, yes, I'm sure that he is!" *Sure I am what?* Mitt wondered as they both looked at him again. "We've gone into your history," Keril said to him. "Attempted murder in Holand. Successful murder in the Holy Islands—"

"That's a lie!" Mitt said angrily. "Whatever you think, I never murdered a single soul! And I gave up trying long before I came here."

"Then you'll have to force yourself to try again," said the Countess. "Won't you?"

"And you came on here by boat," Keril went on, before Mitt could speak, "with Navis Haddsson and his children Hildrida and Ynen. In Aberath the Countess took you in and had you educated—"

"For my sins," the Countess said unlovingly.

"So you see the North has treated you well," Earl Keril said. "Better than most refugees from the South, in fact, both you and your friends. We found Navis a post as hearthman to Stair of Adenmouth, and we sent Hildrida to study at the Lawschool in Gardale. Have you ever wondered why this was?" As Mitt wondered about it, Keril added pleasantly, "Why the four of you were separated in this way, I mean."

It was a pleasantness that made Mitt feel like a sack with a hole in it. Everything trickled away through the hole, and his knees almost let him down. "Where's Ynen then?" he said. "Isn't he with Navis?"

"No," said the Countess. "And we are not telling you where he is."

Mitt watched her long jaw shut like a trap. "I used to think," he said, "that the earls in the North were good. But you're as bad as the ones in the South. Go to any lengths, all of you! You're telling me to kill someone for you or my friends suffer. Right?"

"Let's just say—if you want to see your friends again," Keril suggested.

"Well you're wrong," Mitt said. "You can't make me do anything. I don't care two hoots for any of them."

The two implacable faces just looked at him.

Mitt managed a careless shrug. "We happened to ride on the same boat, that's all," he said. "I swear it."

"You swear it? By which of the Undying?" Keril asked. "By the One? The Piper? The Wanderer? She Who Raised the Islands? The Weaver? The Earth Shaker? Come on. Choose which and swear."

"We don't swear like that in the South," said Mitt.

"I know," said Keril. "So it won't hurt you to swear to me by the Earth Shaker that Navis and his children mean nothing to you. Just swear, and we'll forget the whole matter."

Their faces tilted toward Mitt. Mitt looked away, at the dark painted eyes of the Adon, and tried to make himself swear. If Keril had chosen any other of the Undying, he thought he could have done it easily. But not the Earth Shaker. And that showed how frighteningly much Keril knew. Even so, perhaps he could swear about Navis and Hildy and let on he meant Ynen, too? Navis, cold fish on a slab that the man was, still didn't seem to like Mitt particularly, and as for Hildy, after her last letter, Mitt could almost swear he hated her. But he had shown he was worried about Ynen, like a fool, and there was no way he could even pretend to dislike Ynen or let these two earls hurt him.

"Is Ynen all right?" he said.

"Perfectly, at the moment," said the Countess. She never told lies. Mitt was relieved, until he realized that she and Keril both had the same look, satisfied and unsurprised. They knew he had given in. They had expected it.

"I warn you," Mitt said, "if there's murdering needing doing, I can see two ripe cases for it here in this room. So who do you want killed? What's so special that you need to go to all this trouble with me to have it done?" Keril's eyebrows went up. The Countess seemed surprised. Good, Mitt thought. *Find out how important it is from how rude they let me be.* "Do you take me for a fool?" he said. "If it was lawful, you both have lawyers to burn, and if it was ordinary, you've hearthmen to do it by hundreds. And I'd lay good money you have spies and murderers better than me any day. So it stands to reason it must be politics— you wanting to lay this on Southern scum like me."

"You said it, not me," Keril replied. "Politics, it is. We want a young lady out of the way. She's very charming and much too popular. The whole of the west coast, including Dropwater, will follow her as soon as she gives the word."

"Flaming Ammet!" protested Mitt.

"Be quiet!" said the Countess. "Listen!" She said it like the snap of a steel trap. End of rudeness, thought Mitt, and swallowed what he had been going to say. It hurt, as if he had swallowed an apple whole.

"Noreth of Kredindale, known as Onesdaughter," Keril said. "I expect you've heard of her." Mitt shook his head, but it was from amazement, because he had indeed heard of Noreth Onesdaughter. The story of the One's only human child was one of the many, many stories he had heard round the small coal fires in Aberath this last winter. He had thought that like other stories, it was from times long ago. But Keril, in the most matter-of-fact way, went on to speak of Noreth as alive here and now. "Unfortunately," he said, "she's extremely well connected. The Kredindale family go back to the Adon's daughter Tanabrid, whose mother was of the Undying. Noreth is cousin to Gardale and Dropwater—though Stair's wife at Adenmouth is the aunt who brought her up—and she's a distant cousin of mine, too—"

"And mine," said the Countess. "Pity the girl's mad."

"Mad or not," said Keril, "Noreth claims that her father is the One himself. As her mother died when Noreth was born, there's no one to contradict her, and this claim gives her a huge following among the ordinary people. She makes no secret that she thinks she's born to become Queen of all Dalemark—North and South."

"And that fool in Dropwater backs her," said the Countess.

So that's it! Mitt thought. They're scared for their earldoms. So they get me to stop her and then blame it on the poor South! "Just a minute," he said. "If she's who she says she is, no one can do a thing about it. And someone who's from the Undying on both sides isn't going to be easy to kill either."

"Quite possibly," Keril said. "That's why we were so interested in what we heard about you from the Holy Islands. Reports from there suggested that you could well ask the Undying to help you." Mitt stared at him, shocked at how much Keril knew and how coldly he was prepared to use that knowledge. Keril leaned forward. "We don't want yet another false king and yet another ruinous uprising," he said. Mitt saw he really meant it. "We don't want another war with the South. We want Noreth quietly stopped before she can lay her hands on the crown."

"The crown?" said Mitt. "But nobody knows where that is. They tell stories here about how Manaliabrid hid it."

"She did," said Keril.

"Noreth," said the Countess, "says that the One will show her where it is." Mitt looked from one face to the other and suspected both of them had a fair idea where the crown was hidden. "The girl claims the One talks to her," the Countess added disgustedly. "I told you she was mad. She says the One has promised her a sign to prove her claim and that this year at Midsummer she will become Queen. Silly nonsense."

"She's in Dropwater at the moment," Keril said, "acting as law-woman for her cousin, but our information is that she'll be going to her aunt in Adenmouth for Midsummer to drum up support there. We're sending you to Adenmouth, too."

"And," said the Countess, "you're to go there and stop her. But don't do it there. We want this quiet."

"We advise you to join her as a follower—you shouldn't be noticed among all the others—and then look for a suitable opportunity," Keril said. As Mitt opened his mouth, he added, "If you want to see Hildrida and Ynen again, you will."

"But Midsummer's the day after tomorrow!" Mitt protested. A stupid thing to say, but he had been looking forward to the feasting in Aberath.

"It's an easy day's ride," said the Countess, who rarely went anywhere except by carriage. "I shall give out that you have my leave to go and visit Navis Haddsson in Adenmouth. You will go first thing tomorrow. You may go away and pack now."

Mitt had been taught that you bowed on leaving the presence of an earl, but he was too disgusted to remember. He turned and blundered his way across the dimness of the library, past the books and the glass cases that held the Countess's collection: the necklace that was supposed to have been worn by Enblith the Fair, the ring that once belonged to the Adon, a flute of Osfameron's, and the withered piece of parchment that went back to the days of King Hern. Behind him he sensed the two earls drawing themselves up in indignation.

"Mitt Alhamittsson," said Keril. Mitt stopped and turned round. "I remind you," Keril said, "that a man can be hanged when he is fifteen. They tell me your birthday is the Autumn Festival. Noreth had better be dead before then, hadn't she?"

"Or we may not be able to avert the course of justice," added the Countess. "You have nearly three months, but don't cut it too fine."

So there was no possibility of putting things off. "Yes," said Mitt. "I get you." He looked past them to the harrowed, ill-looking face of the Adon. He could see the portrait better from here. He pointed his thumb to it. "Miserable-looking blighter, isn't he?" he said. "It must be giving him a right bellyache having you two as descendants!" Then he turned round and walked to the door, rather hoping he had been rude enough to be thrown into prison on the spot. But there was no sound behind him while he opened the door, and no sound but the groan of the hinges as the door shut on his heels. The man on guard outside straightened up guiltily and then relaxed when he saw it was only Mitt.

Mitt marched away down the steps without speaking to him. They really meant him to kill this girl. Even the Countess had not told him off for his rudeness.

His knees were trembling as he came out into the courtyard. He almost wanted to cry with shame. It was the way Keril had muttered "Oh, yes, I'm sure he is!" that seemed to have got to him most—sure Mitt was a guttersnipe, a Southerner with no feelings, the first person earls turned to when they wanted dirty work done. Mitt had known such a person and vowed never to be like that, but fat lot those two cared!

Someone shouted to him across the courtyard.

A knot of people stood there, all about his own age. Earl Keril's son, Kialan, was one of them, and the others were waving to Mitt to come over. Mitt had been rather anxious to meet Kialan. Now he found he could not bear to. He ducked sideways and turned along the wall.

"Mitt!" shouted Alla, the Countess's bronze-haired daughter. "Kialan wants to meet you!"

"He's heard all about you!" shouted Doreth, the copper-haired daughter.

"Can't stop! Message! Sorry!" Mitt shouted back. He did not want to meet the daughters either. Alla had jeered at him for being so miserable when Hildy was sent away, until Mitt got mad and pulled her bronze hair. Then Doreth had told the Countess on him. Mitt had been quite surprised not to be sent away then, too. But that must have given them proof that

Mitt did care what became of Hildy. Flaming Ammet! The Countess and Keril must have had this planned for months!

Kialan was now shouting himself. "See you later, then!" Mitt had a glimpse of him waving, tawny and thickset and quite unlike his father—but quite certainly not *really* unlike, not deep down where it counted. Mitt put his head down and sped along by the wall, wondering if Kialan saw him as a dirty Southern guttersnipe, too. Kialan would certainly see a lot of lank hair and two spindly legs and shoulders that were too wide for the rest. Mitt kept his face turned to the wall because that was the real giveaway, a guttersnipe face that still looked starved even after ten months of good food in Aberath. He told himself Kialan wasn't missing much.

He plunged through the nearest door and kept running, through rooms and along corridors, and out again on the other side of the mansion, to the long shed on the cliffs above the harbor. That was the best place to be alone. The people who were usually there would all be rushing about after Keril's followers or getting the Midsummer feast ready. And he was having to miss that feast. Hildy had once said that misery was like this: Silly little things always got mixed up with the important ones. How right she was.

Mitt rolled the shed door open a crack and slipped inside. Sure enough, the place was empty. Mitt breathed deep of the fishy smell of coal and of fish oil and wet metal. It was not unlike the smell on the waterfront of Holand, where he had been brought up. And I might just as well have stayed there for all the good it did me! he thought, staring along a vista of iron rails in the floor, where tarry puddles reflected red sun or rainbows of oil. He felt caught and trapped and surrounded in a plot he had not even noticed till they thrust it at him this afternoon. Everyone had told him that the Countess was treating him almost like a son. Mitt had been pretty sarcastic about that, but all the same he had thought this was the way people in the North did treat refugees from the South.

"Fool I was!" he muttered.

He walked along the rails to the huge machines that stood at quiet intervals along them. Alk's Irons, everyone called them. To Mitt, and to most people in town, they were the most fascinating things in Aberath. Mitt trailed his fingers across the cargo hoist and then across the steam plow and the thing that Alk hoped might one day drive a ship. None of them worked very well, but Alk kept trying. Alk was married to the Countess. It was the only other thing Mitt liked about the Countess, that instead of marrying the son of a lord or another earl who might add to her importance, she had chosen to marry her lawman, Alk. Alk had given up law years ago in order to invent machines. Mitt dragged his fingertips across the wet and greasy bolts of the newest machine and shuddered as he imagined himself pushing a knife into a young woman. Even if she laughed at him or looked like Doreth or Alla, even if her eyes showed she was mad—No! But what about Ynen if he didn't? The worst of this trap was that it pushed him back into a part of himself he thought he had got out of. He could have screamed.

He went round the machine and found himself face-to-face with Alk. Both of them jumped. Alk recovered first. He sighed, put his oil can down on a ledge in the machine, and asked rather guiltily, "Message for me?"

"I—No. I thought nobody was here," Mitt said.

Alk relaxed. To look at him, you would have thought he was a big blacksmith run to fat, with his mind in the clouds. "Thought you were calling me to come and run about after Keril," he said. "Now you're here, have a think about this thing. It's supposed to be an iron horse, but I think it needs changing somewhere."

"It's the biggest horse I ever saw," Mitt said frankly. "What good is it if it has to run on rails? Why do your things always run on rails?"

"To move," said Alk. "Too heavy otherwise. You have to work the way things will let you."

"Then how are you going to get it to go uphill?" said Mitt.

Alk rubbed an oily hand through the remains of copper hair like Doreth's and looked sideways at Mitt. "Boy's disillusionment with the North now complete," he said. "Taken against my machines now. Anything wrong, Mitt?"

In spite of his trouble, Mitt grinned. Alk and he had this joke. Alk himself came from the North Dales, which Alk claimed were almost in the South. Alk said he saw three things wrong with the North for every one that Mitt saw. "No—I'm fine," Mitt said, because the Countess had probably told Alk all about her plans anyway. He was trying to think of something polite to say about the iron horse when the door at the end of the shed rolled right open. Kialan's strong voice came echoing through.

"This is the most marvelous place in all Aberath!"

"Excuse me," Mitt muttered, and dived for the small side door behind Alk.

Alk grabbed his elbow as he went. He was as strong as the blacksmith he looked like. "Wait for me!" he said. They went out of the side door together, into the heap of coal and cinders beyond. "Taken against the Adon of Hannart, too, have you?" Alk asked. Mitt did not know how to answer. "Come up to my rooms," Alk said, still holding Mitt's elbow. "I have to dress grandly for supper, I suppose. You can help. Or is that beneath you?"

Mitt gasped rather and shook his head. It was supposed to be an honor to help the lord dress. He wondered if Alk knew.

"Come on, then," said Alk. He let go of Mitt and lumbered ahead of him through the archway that led to his apartments. Alk's valet was waiting there, with candles lit and water steaming and good clothes hung carefully over chairs. "You can have a rest tonight,

Gregin," Alk said cheerfully. "Mitt's going to clean me up today. Part of his education."

Even if Alk did not know he was doing Mitt an honor, the valet certainly did. His face was a mixture of jealousy, respect, and anxiety. "Sir," he said. "The coal. The oil." He started to back out of the room as Alk waved him away, and then came back to whisper fiercely to Mitt. "Mind you don't let him stop you scrubbing him when he's still gray. He'll try. He always does."

"Go away, Gregin," said Alk. "My word by the Undying that we won't let you down." Gregin sighed and went away. Mitt got down to the hard work of scrubbing Alk clean. "Do I take it you've had another of your disagreements with my Countess?" Alk asked while Mitt labored.

"Not . . . the way you mean this time," Mitt said, rubbing away at one huge hairy arm.

"Her bark is worse than her bite," Alk observed.

Alk had to think that, Mitt supposed. He must have had a lot of illusions about the Countess to have married her at all. "Keril's worse," he said. "He's all bite and no bark, as far as I can see."

"So Keril's in it, too?" Alk said musingly. He took his arm away from Mitt, looked at it, and gave it back, sighing. It was still gray. "Now I see you're in no mood to agree with me, but Earl Keril's a good man, shrewd as he can hold together. Knows all about steam power, too. They have a steam organ at Hannart, did you know? Huge thing. But he's not the man to get on the wrong side of if you can help it."

"Well, I have," Mitt said bitterly. "I was on his wrong side before he even set eyes on me."

"Now why was that?" wondered Alk.

He was obviously waiting for Mitt to tell him, but Mitt found he could not bear to, any more than he could bear to go near Kialan. He finished scrubbing Alk's left arm and began on the right, even blacker and larger than the left.

"Something's up," Alk said at length, "that I don't know about, I think. And it can't be quite legal, or she would have told me. Did they tell you not to tell me?"

Mitt looked up to find Alk staring shrewdly at him across his lathery arm. "No," he said. "But I'm not saying. They knew I wouldn't, too, for fear you'd be disgusted and kick me out. How do you like being washed by the scum of the earth?"

Alk frowned. "You scrub even brisker than Gregin, if that's what we're talking about." He said nothing else for a while, until Mitt had scrubbed him to clean pink blotches and was starting to help him into good clothes. As his head came out through the neck of the white silk shirt, he said, "See here. I was only a poor farmer's boy before I came to be a lawman. Keril's Countess Halida was nobody much either, and she was from the South like you." Mitt had not the heart to answer this. It was kindly meant, but so wrong.

"Hmm," said Alk. "Wrong track there." As Mitt helped him force his arms down the sleeves, he added, "And it's maybe the wrong track, too, if I was to mention that you're much better placed than you were when you came? You can read and write and use weapons now. They tell me you learn good and quick, and you've brains to use what you learn—well, I know you've got brains. My Countess has not treated you so badly—"

"And that's a lie!" Mitt burst out. "She did it all for a reason!"

"As to that," Alk said as Mitt threaded golden studs into his cuffs, "*you've* not gone out of your way to make her love you, Mitt. And everyone always has a reason for what they do. It's only natural."

"Then what's *your* reason for trying to cheer me up like this?" Mitt retorted.

"Easy," said Alk. "I can't abide misery, and I hate mysteries. Anyone taking half a glance at your face could see something was wrong. And cheering up often brings things to light. I found *that* out when I was a lawman, the first time we had a man accused of murder." Mitt winced at that and nearly dropped a stud. He knew Alk noticed, but Alk only said, "Want me to talk to my Countess about this?"

"No point. Wouldn't do any good," Mitt said. Everyone knew that Alk never went against the Countess. He turned away and got Alk's vast brocade trousers. "Look, I don't want to talk about this no more," he said, helping Alk step into them.

"I see that. And I think you ought to," Alk said.

Mitt obstinately said nothing while he buttoned the trousers round Alk's bulging waist and then fetched the huge embroidered jacket. Alk backed into it with his arms out, like a bear. "Nothing you want to say, then?" he asked.

"Nothing, only a question," Mitt said, meaning to change the subject. "Is the One real?" Alk turned round with the jacket half on and stared at him. "I mean," said Mitt, "I never heard of the One, nor half the other Undying either, until I came here. We don't take much note of Undying in the South. Do *you* believe in any of them?" He went round Alk and heaved the jacket onto him. Then he bent down to help Alk with his boots.

"Believe in the One!" Alk said, and trod into the right boot. "It would be hard not to, here in Aberath, at this time of year, but—" He trod into the left boot and stamped down in it, thinking. "Put it like this. I believed in my machines when they were just a notion in my head and nothing I could touch or see. Who's to say that the One isn't as real as they were in my head—or as real as they are now?" He flipped the fastening at the neck of his shirt to see if Mitt had tied it securely and tramped to the door. "Coming?"

Supper would be ready in the great hall. It came to Mitt that it would be his job to wait on Kialan at table. He could not face it. "I got to polish my gear and pack now," he said. "I'm off to Adenmouth tomorrow."

"Are you now?" Alk turned round in the doorway

:⊪ 2 ⊪:

Mitt had to set out for Adenmouth without seeing
Alk again. The Countess had obviously given strict
orders. He was roused before dawn, and fed, and
pushed to the stables as the sun rose, where he found
the armsmaster waiting for him in a very bad temper.
Mitt sighed and watched every buckle, pouch, and
button being checked, and then every scrap of tack on
the horse. He had had some idea of hanging his belt,
with the sword on one side and the dagger on the
other, up on a nail and then forgetting it accidentally
on purpose. But there was no question of that with an
angry armsmaster standing over him.

"I'm not going to have you let me down in front of
potty little Adenmouth," the armsmaster said as Mitt
mounted.

Mitt rather hoped the horse would try to take a bite
out of the armsmaster, the way it always did with
anyone else, but of course, it did not dare, any more
than Mitt did. "I wish you'd let me take a gun," Mitt
said. "I can use a gun. I'd let you down with a sword
for sure."

His idea was that it would be much easier to shoot this Noreth from a distance than to get close up the way you had to with a sword. But that idea died at the look on the armsmaster's face. "Nonsense, boy! Guns here have to be smuggled in from the South. Think I'd trust you with something that expensive? And sit up straight! You look like a sack of flour!"

Mitt straightened his back and clopped angrily through the gate. He *could* use a gun, and care for it, too. Mitt's stepfather, Hobin, made the best guns in Dalemark. But nothing ever seemed to convince the armsmaster of this. "Yes, sir, good-bye, sir. Good riddance, sir," he said, raising one smartly gloved hand when he was too far away to be caught.

He clopped through the streets of the town, all hung with decorations for the feast he was having to miss, and up along the top of the cliffs, where the sun was a gold eye opening between heavy gray eyelids of sea and sky, and looked down on the boat sheds at the cliff foot as he went. One of those sheds hid the battered blue pleasure boat they had arrived in: Mitt, Hildy, Ynen, and Navis. Ynen's boat. And the Countess had started plotting from that moment on. Today Mitt found he was angry about it, very angry. And the odd thing about being angry was that it seemed to break through the walls that had seemed to hem him in yesterday and give him space to hope. He was going to see Navis. Navis was Ynen's father and a cool customer, and he would think of something. Navis was used to dealing with earls' plots, being the son of an earl himself.

Thinking of Navis, then of Ynen, Mitt rode between the sea and the steep fields on the hills above, where people were scrambling to scrape in a crop of hay despite its being a feast day. Ynen was younger than Mitt, but Mitt had nevertheless come to admire him more than he admired anyone else. Ynen was—steadfast—that was the word. His sister, Hildy, on the other hand . . .

After first Navis, then Ynen had left Aberath, Hildy and Mitt had been together there another short month, while Hildy was coached by the Countess's lawwoman in law, geometry, history, and the Old Writing, so that she could pass into the great Lawschool in Gardale. That way, as she told Mitt, she could always earn her living. Nobody was more respected than a lawyer. Hildy was inclined to patronize Mitt, just a little, as Mitt struggled simply to read and write along with all the other duties of a hearthman-in-training. "I'll send you letters," Hildy had promised, when she went away, "to help with your reading." The trouble was, she kept her promise.

Her first letters were carefully printed and quite full of news. The next few were dashed off, with an air of duty about them. Around then Mitt had learned enough to be able to write back. Hildy had answered several of his letters with one of her own, carefully, point by point, but she had been quite unable to resist correcting his spelling. Mitt had kept writing—there had been a lot to tell—but Hildy's letters had become ever briefer and farther apart, and each one was harder to understand than the last. Mitt had waited well over a month for Hildy's latest letter. And what came was:

> Dear Mitt,
>   This grittling the boys on fayside were at trase with peelers, would you believe! They had sein right, too, so it was all kappin and no barlay. We only had mucks. But Biffa was our surnam and you should have seen the hurrel. Now highside is doggers and we have herison from scap to lengday, and everyone looks up to us although we are to be stapled for it. In haste to trethers.
>   Hildrida

It was like a message from the moon. It hurt Mitt badly. Hildy and he had had little enough in common anyway, and now Hildy was making it clear that this little was gone. After that letter Mitt had told himself he did not care what became of Hildy, and then Earl Keril came along and forced him to behave as if he did care. As he rode on, he tried to tell himself that he was being noble about Hildy. This was not true. He did not want Hildy hurt, not when she was evidently having fun for the first time in her life.

The sun came up higher. People began passing Mitt on their way to the feasting at Aberath, calling out in the free way of the North that Mitt was going the wrong way, wasn't he? Mitt called jokes in reply and urged his horse on. The horse, as usual, had other ideas. It kept trying to go back to Aberath. Mitt cursed it. He had a very bad relationship with this horse. His private name for it was the Countess. It held its head sideways like she did, and walked in the same jerky way, and it seemed to dislike Mitt as much as the real Countess did. They came to the place where the road forked, a rutty track going along the coast to Adenmouth and a wider and even ruttier one winding back right into the mountains at the heart of the earldom. People were streaming down this wider road and turning along the way Mitt had come, and the horse tried to turn back with them. Mitt wrestled its head round onto the Adenmouth road and kicked its sides to make it go.

"Going my way, hearthman?" somebody called after him.

Hot and annoyed, Mitt looked round to find a boy on an unkempt horse turning out of the main road after him. Another hearthman, by the look of the faded livery. Mitt did not feel like company, but people in the North never seemed to feel you might want to be alone, and it was a fact that the Countess-horse went better for a lead. So, as the two horses slid and stamped in the ruts, Mitt said a little grudgingly, "Going to Adenmouth, hearthman."

"Good! Me, too," said the lad. He had a long, freckled face with a sort of eager look to it. "Rith," he introduced himself. "Out of Dropwater."

"Mitt," said Mitt. "Out of Aberath."

Rith laughed as they set off side by side up the narrower road. "Great One! You've come even farther than I have!" he said. "What's a Southerner doing this far North?"

"Came by boat—we went where the wind took us," Mitt explained. "I think we missed Kinghaven in the night somehow. How come you knew I was a Southerner? My accent that bad still?"

Rith laughed again and pushed at the fair, frizzy hair that stuck out all round his steel cap. "That and your looks. The straight hair. But it's the name that's the clincher. Dropwater's full of Southern fugitives, and they all answer to Mitt, or Al, or Hammitt. I'm surprised the South's not empty by now, the way you all come to the North. Been here long?"

"Ten months," said Mitt.

"Then you've had one of our winters. I bet you froze!"

"Froze! I nearly died!" said Mitt. "I never saw icicles before, let alone snow. And when they first brought the coal in to make a fire, I thought they were going to build something. I didn't know stones could burn."

"Don't they have coal in the South?" Rith asked wonderingly.

"Charcoal—for those that could afford it," Mitt said. "At least that's what they used in Holand, where I come from."

Rith whistled. "You *did* come a long way, didn't you?"

By this time Mitt had forgotten he had wanted to be alone. They rode with the sea sparkling on one side and the hills climbing on the other, under the douce Northern sun, talking and laughing, while the Countess-horse followed Rith's travel-stained little mount as smoothly as its jerky gait would allow. Rith was good company. He seemed genuinely interested to know what Mitt thought of the North now he was here. Mitt was a bit wary at first. He had found that most Northerners did not like criticism. "It's this porridge they all eat I can't stand," he said jokingly. "And the superstition."

"What superstition?" Rith said innocently. "You mean, like the Holanders throw their Undying in the sea every year?"

"And you lot put bowls of milk out for yours," said Mitt. "Believe anything, these Northerners! Think the One's a pussycat!"

Rith bowed onto his horse's neck with laughter. "What else do we do wrong?" he said when he could speak. "I bet you think we're inefficient, don't you?"

"Well you are," said Mitt. "All runabout and talk and do nothing when a crisis happens."

"Not when it matters, though," said Rith. "And?"

And he went on coaxing Mitt until Mitt at last came out with the real cause of his disappointment with the North. "They told me it was free here," he said. "They told me it was good. I was badly enough off in the South, but beside some here I was rich—and idle. People are no more free here than—than—" He was trying to find a proper description when they came round a bend to find the road blocked house-high with earth and boulders. A stream sprayed from the top in a raw new waterfall and ran round their horses' hooves. "This just about sums it up!" Mitt said disgustedly. "And your roads are all terrible!"

"The Southern roads are, of course, all perfect," Rith said.

"I never said—" said Mitt.

Rith laughed and dismounted. "Come on. This is hopeless. We'll have to lead the horses uphill and come back to the road where it's clear."

Mitt slid down from the Countess-horse and discovered he was more than a little saddlesore. Ow! he thought. I wonder my pants aren't smoking! But he did not like to confess this to Rith, who had ridden all the way from Dropwater and was obviously a seasoned hearthman. A small, tough boy, Rith. When they were both on their feet, Rith only came up to Mitt's shoulders. Makes me look a big booby if I moan, Mitt thought, and he set off dragging the Countess-horse up the hill after Rith. Both horses were huge, heavy, and reluctant. Their hooves slid in the slippery grass. Mitt's horse put its ears back and tried to bite him.

"Stop that!" Mitt slapped its nose aside. "You Countess, you!"

Rith broke into a panting laugh. "What a name! It's a gelding. O-oh! Piper's *pants*!"

Mitt dragged his horse up beside Rith's. The hill, in the mysterious manner of hills, was twice as high as he had thought. Beyond and above them, it was a huge triangle of earthy boulders and trickling water, which had slid down across the road, blocking it for as far as they could see. At the lower edge of it, the sea twinkled, flat and impassable.

"We'd better go up over the hill," Rith said. "I know the way. It'll mean fording the Aden after we cross the green road, but it won't be deep this high."

So they struggled on upward, about twice as high as they had already come, until they left the landslip behind and reached a squishy yellow-green shoulder, where Rith said they could ride again. Mitt nearly yelled as he kicked his way into the saddle. He was raw. But he did not like to mention it. He simply bore it, all the way through a long, marshy valley and then up an endless firm green slope, where they came to one of the things the Northerners called waystones. It was round, like a roughly shaped millstone set up on one edge, with a hole in the middle. Rith leaned over and slapped the thing.

"For luck," he said, grinning. "I'm a superstitious

Northerner. I may ask the Wanderer's blessing, too, just to annoy you. There's the Aden down there. What do you say we stop for some lunch?"

Mitt was only too glad to get down. He helped himself off by hanging on to the waystone, which was a way of touching it without seeming to. He knew he could do with some luck. And once he was down, he was so sore that he had to concentrate on small things, like stripping off his gloves and tucking them into the proper place on his belt, and hitching his horse to the waystone, where someone had tied a piece of red twine through the middle for the purpose. Then, moving in a careful, stiff-legged way, he unbuckled his baggage roll and got out the food they had given him. By then the agony had gone off enough for him to sit down beside Rith, bat the Countess-horse's nose aside as it tried to eat his bread, and look at the view.

There were hills all round, yellow and green, with sunlight scudding over them in patches. The green way stretched from the waystone, very level and firm and dry, leading south into the mountainous heart of Dalemark, and the Aden rolled parallel with it about a hundred yards downhill from where they sat. It was a fine big river, wider than any Mitt had seen, and the way it rolled quietly along among all those reeds and willow trees suggested that it might be pretty deep. Mitt hoped Rith knew what he was talking about when he said they could ford it. He leaned back and sniffed the smell of the river and willows mingling with the damp wild smell of heather and rock, the smell of the North, which Mitt still thought of as the smell of freedom in spite of his disillusionment with the North. Perhaps, he thought, not very hopefully, he would be stuck this side of the river and never get to Adenmouth at all. But that would be the worse for Hildy and Ynen.

"You look pretty gloomy!" Rith said, laughing.

"Just thinking," Mitt said hurriedly. "What *are* these green roads? Who made them—really?"

"Kern Adon," said Rith. "King Hern. They're the roads of his old kingdom. That's why they don't go to places where people live anymore. They say that Kern Adon set up the waystones and told the Wanderer to guard the roads, and if you follow them right, they say you arrive at King Hern's city of gold."

"I heard them called the paths of the Undying," said Mitt.

"Oh yes. They're called that, too," said Rith. "My old nurse used to tell me that the Undying sit in the hole in the waystones. What do you think of that?"

"They couldn't!" Mitt said unguardedly. "Not unless they shrunk."

Rith got very interested in this idea. "Then how big do you think the Undying are?" he kept saying, in the same coaxing way he had tried to get at Mitt's opinion of the North. "I've never been able to decide. Do you think they're made of something that isn't as solid as we are, so that they can be of any size? Or what?"

These Northerners! Mitt thought. Rith was laughing, but he was serious, too. They finished eating, and Mitt got up, rather reluctantly, to untie the Countess-horse.

"What size do you think?" Rith said, leading his horse downhill to the river.

"If you must know," Mitt called over his shoulder, "they're people-sized. It stands to reason." He dragged the Countess-horse round to follow Rith. "How could—" He stopped and blinked.

There was no wide rolling river anymore. Rith was on his way down to a sunken crease in the hillside that was choked with small oak trees. Mitt could hear water rushing among the trees.

"You're probably right," Rith called back, "though some of the things they do make them seem smaller. Come on. It really is quite shallow here."

Mitt slowly followed him down among the oaks, wondering just what river it was that he had seen. There was no question in his mind that the real Aden was the yelling, stony stream in front of him now, glinting bright coins of sunlight under the trees. Rivers in the North always seemed to crouch like this one along dips in the hills. And he had not seen a single willow tree since he left the South. Shivers ran down his back, and he approached the brawling little Aden very cautiously indeed.

So did the Countess-horse. At the edge of the water it put its ears back, braced its hooves, and refused to move. Mitt called it names.

"I'll give you a lead," said Rith. He stepped into the shrilling water, which proved to be only a few inches deep, and waded carefully, watching the stones in the bottom, until he and his horse had become dark shadows, patterned with sun between the oak leaves.

At this point the Countess-horse found it preferred not to be left behind and took off suddenly after Rith, dragging Mitt in sheets of bright water. Mitt kept hold of the reins and managed to stay on his feet until he was halfway across, where his foot turned heavily on something that flashed in the sun.

Rith called out, *"Look there!"* in a surprisingly deep, strong voice, and dived toward Mitt.

It was all sun-patterned wet confusion. Both horses got away, and Mitt sat down with a splash. Rith plunged his hands down where Mitt's feet had been and stood up triumphantly holding something that shone. Water poured off his elbows as he held it out for Mitt to see.

"Look at this!"

Mitt floundered to his knees. The thing had evidently once been a little statue—a figurine, Mitt thought the word was. As Rith turned it round, Mitt could see traces of a face and the folds of a robe on the side that was green with river slime. The other side was grated and scratched all over, and that side shone a pure buttery yellow. Mitt in his time had worked enough inlay into gun handles to know what that meant. "It's solid gold!" he said.

"I think it is," Rith said. He sounded awestruck. "Who found it? You or me?"

"You picked it up," Mitt said. "I only stepped on it."

Rith turned the dripping statuette round again. "I wish I could be sure— Look, may I keep it for now and give you your share when I've got it?"

If Mitt had not been so saddlesore, he might have argued. But the cold water was smarting him like acid, and he could think of almost nothing else. "Fine," he gasped, and splashed his way across to the far bank, where the horses were standing head to tail, looking pleased with themselves. Rith followed, stowing the wet figurine in the front of his jacket.

"You're being very generous," he said several times, as they mounted and rode on. "You really mean I can keep it for now?" He was evidently feeling a strange mixture of doubt and elation, but then anyone would, Mitt thought, who had just picked up a pound of solid gold. He thought Rith was nice to be so bothered about it. All through the next hour or so Rith was either exclaiming at the amazing chance that had led them to that spot or asking Mitt if he really minded waiting for his share. "If it hadn't been for that landslide," he said, "we'd never have come this way. Look, are you really sure?"

Mitt got increasingly gruff with him. Mitt's leathers were wet through and rubbing his soreness until he was convinced he was being flayed. Besides, he thought angrily, the way he was caught in the earls' plotting, he couldn't see himself having much use for gold or anything else shortly. He wished Rith would shut up. By the late afternoon, when the sea came into view again blue and crisp to northward, Mitt was wanting to scream at Rith, and he might have done had they not come out on a headland overlooking Adenmouth to find themselves looking down on an accident.

A Singer's cart had overturned on the bridge below. The bridge had no sides, and the horse that had pulled the cart was dangling struggling in the Aden. Mitt saw someone pulling uselessly at the horse. A girl lay on the bank as if she might be dead.

"Come on!" shouted Rith, and his shaggy horse was off down the hill as if it was aiming to end in the river, too.

Mitt followed as fast as the Countess-horse would let him, which was not very fast. The hill was extremely steep. Even Rith slowed down halfway, but this was probably because he could see that help was on its way. They could see into a long green valley to one side, where a party of people were running from one of the farms. More people were running across a second bridge, from Adenmouth itself, and a horseman was galloping ahead of them.

Everyone converged on the bridge, but the horseman got there first. He was a hearthman in Adenmouth livery. As the Countess-horse slithered cautiously down the last slope, Mitt saw the horseman leap to the ground, thrust his reins into the hands of the redheaded Singer's boy, and run toward the struggling horse. There he took one look, cocked his pistol, and shot the horse through the head.

Mitt and Rith came down to the bridge while the horse was still jerking. The bang rang in Mitt's ears like the memory of his worst dreams. The white staring face of the Singer-boy looked just like he felt.

"Anything we can do?" called Rith.

The hearthman turned from slashing at the traces that held the dead horse. Mitt almost laughed. It was Navis. It would be. "Hello," he said.

Navis nodded at him in his cool way. "You see to that girl," he said to Rith. "I think she's alive. Mitt, you help me cut this horse loose."

As the two of them dismounted, Mitt noticed the Singer himself wandering about on the bank, carefully laying out musical instruments from the overturned cart. A dreamy-looking fellow with a gray beard. Mitt ignored the Singer as useless and hobbled over to Navis, while Rith sprinted to where the Singer-girl was sitting up, holding her head.

"Get your knife out and cut here, then here," Navis said. He did not seem in the least surprised at seeing Mitt there. His attention was mostly on the accusing yellow-white face of the Singer-boy. "Your horse had broken two legs—look," he said to the boy. "There was nothing else to be done."

"He was blind in one eye," the boy said. "He walked off the bridge."

"I just wish mine would do that, too!" Mitt said, to make him feel better. "Mine's a right brute."

The boy simply stared at him. "Southerner," he said. "You both are." He turned his back and led Navis's mare to the other side of the road.

Navis glanced at Mitt. "There's a lot of prejudice," he said. "Now cut here." Mitt slashed away angrily. Cool, cool Navis. He had forgotten just how cool.

By the time they had cut the horse loose, the people from the farm and the town had arrived. There was a lot of typically Northern milling about and talking. The chief talker was a lad from the farm, who wanted everyone to know how quickly he had gone for help to the mansion and what the lady Eltruda had said to him. But amid all this there was unnoticed efficiency. In less than a minute many hands had heaved the neat green cart upright and Mitt was able to read the gold lettering on its side.

"Hestefan the Singer."

"You want me?" Hestefan asked.

He was standing beside Mitt with a cwidder in one hand and a fife in the other. Mitt was embarrassed. He had only said it aloud because he still found it easier to read that way. Now he felt he had to say something. "How did you get past the landslip on the road?" he asked.

"Landslip?" said Hestefan. "What landslip?"

Mitt gave him up again and turned to Rith, who said in a worried whisper, "I think that girl, Fenna, has really hurt her head. Can you help me get her on a horse?"

The Countess-horse was at that moment demonstrating that it was not carriage-trained. They had tried to back it into the shafts of the cart, where it divided its attention between trying to take bites out of anyone near and attempts to kick the splashboard in. Mitt ran and hauled it clear. "You good-for-nothing Countess, you!" He dragged it over to the injured girl, where the Singer-boy held it while Mitt and Rith heaved Fenna into its saddle. The chattering crowd seized Rith's horse and backed that into the cart instead. Nobody thought of using the beautiful mare that belonged to Navis. Typical of Navis, that, Mitt thought, taking the reins from the boy. The lad looked as ill as Fenna. "Want me to boost you up behind her, Moril?" Mitt asked. He had gathered the boy's name was Moril.

Moril simply turned away and walked to the cart.

"All right. *Be* like that then!" Mitt said to his back. All this running about made his backside feel as if it was on fire. It got worse when he set off leading the horse into Adenmouth. Fenna had to nudge him with her foot before Mitt noticed she was trying to speak to him.

"Er—young hearthman. Sir."

Mitt looked up. She was pale, but she was dark and pretty, and she spoke with just a trace of a Southern accent, which made him try to smile at her. "Sorry. What?"

"Don't think too hard of Moril, sir," Fenna said. "He loved our old horse. And I heard tell he had another horse killed by Southerners last year."

Well, he's no call to take it out on me! Mitt thought. But he said politely, "Heard tell? I thought he was your brother."

"Oh no, sir," Fenna said. "Moril is Clennen the Singer's son. He'll be a great Singer himself before long."

Rith grinned at Mitt round the nose of the Countess-horse. "These artists! You can tell what they're like from the red hair. Sit straight, Fenna, or you'll fall off."

It was not far to Adenmouth, just across another bend in the Aden, which then poured noisily past low gray houses crowded at the edge of a cove. Mitt was glad. By the time they had gone up the main street to the mansion, he was not sure he could have walked another step. Their arrival caused much confusion, for a good hundred more people came out of the houses to see what was wrong and then followed them into the courtyard of the mansion, where rows of trestle tables that had been set up for the Midsummer Feast all had to be moved to make way for the cart.

Lady Eltruda was out on the hall steps, bellowing instructions in a voice like the armsmaster's. "Navis!" she yelled. "Get that thing through to the stables!

Spannet, fetch the lawman! You!" she screamed at Mitt. "You in the Aberath livery! Bring that poor girl to me!"

Before Mitt could move, Rith was dragging Fenna and the Countess-horse toward the steps, zigzagging between tables and shouting back. "Aunt! Aunt! I'm here! I got here, and I got my sign!"

At this Lady Eltruda dashed down the steps, yelling, "Noreth, my dove! Noreth!" and flung her arms round Rith.

Mitt stared. He felt terrible.

:| 3 |:

THE CONFUSION CLEARED UP surprisingly quickly. Mitt was almost alone in the yard, wondering what on earth to do now, when Navis put a hand on his shoulder.

"Come to my room," he said. "Tell me your news there."

Funny, Mitt thought, staring slightly downward into Navis's cool, clear-cut face. I don't remember him being that small. Maybe I grew. "I would if I could walk," he said.

Navis smiled a little. "It's not far. But I can't carry you."

He turned and led the way. Mitt hobbled after him, protesting, "I do know how to ride! It's just that I never did it for a whole day before!" They went through the hall, big enough, but a dark little place compared with the one at Aberath, and up a shallow flight of steps. Navis had a comfortable paneled room beyond, as good as one of Alk's. Typical, Mitt thought, looking round. He must be well in with Lord Stair. "How did you know I got news?"

"Hush a moment," Navis said. Two servingmen came into the room. They were grinning rather and carrying a large bowl of something sour and strong. They dumped it where Navis pointed and then hung about, lingeringly, as if there was some joke. "Thank you," Navis said, "but we'd like to be private now."

"What is this?" Mitt said suspiciously as the men left, still grinning.

"Vinegar," said Navis. "Take your leathers off and sit in it. Go on. It works."

Slowly, with misgivings, Mitt did as Navis said. He sat. Yelled. Tried to get out again and found himself held down by Navis's unexpectedly strong hand. Vinegar spilled on the rugs, and Mitt went on yelling, even though he was sure the two men were standing outside the door loving every shriek. "Flaming Ammet!" he roared. "Are you trying to kill me?"

"No," said Navis, and he went on holding Mitt down until Mitt's yells had given way to gasps and then to miserable panting. Then he let go and went to the half-open door. "That will be all," he said, and closed the door.

Mitt heard footsteps retreating. "Can I get out now?"

"The longer you stay in, the sooner you'll be able to ride again," Navis said. "Tell me your news to take your mind off it." It was on the tip of Mitt's tongue to tell Navis he was as bad as Earl Keril, but he did not say it because he suddenly realized it was true. Navis, in his way, could be quite as ruthless as Keril.

Earls' blood will out! Mitt thought. He was wondering
if he was going to be able to tell Navis anything after
all when Navis added, "They wouldn't have let you
leave Aberath without very good reason, I'm sure."
Very strong bitterness came through his coolness.

He feels just as caught as I do! Mitt thought. "Well,
before I start, do you know where Hildy is?"

"In Gardale," said Navis. "Though, from the one
letter she deigned to send, I wondered if she wasn't in
the moon."

"I got one of those," Mitt said. "Total gibberish.
And Ynen? You have any idea where Ynen is?"

"No," said Navis. There was a cold little silence
before Navis said, "No. No one has bothered to tell
me that. Is that why they let you see me? To bring
me a threat?"

"That may be part of it," Mitt said. "They must
have reckoned I'd tell you. Navis, they want me to
kill that girl Noreth. And I tell you I rode most of the
way here with her and she's no madder than what I
am!"

"Sit still," said Navis. "You'll get vinegar everywhere." He drew up a chair and sat facing Mitt in his
bowl. "Tell me this carefully. *Who* wants you to?"

"The Countess and Earl Keril," said Mitt. "Talk
about your past catching up with you! They found
out all about me."

"Keril," said Navis. "Keril. Then, Mitt, you are not
the only one whose past has caught up with him. I

once risked a good deal to send a message to Keril to warn him that his sons were prisoners in Holand. He must have taken it as a threat. What did he say?"

Mitt sat in his bowl and told Navis everything, including his ride with Noreth. The only thing he left out was the way he had thought the Aden was a mighty river. He was not sure he believed that himself now. He found he felt a little tearful as he talked, not for obvious reasons but because Navis was listening and not treating him as the scum of the earth.

"That statue," Navis said. "You were a little overgenerous there. Can you persuade her to give you your half?"

"Chop it in two? Why?" said Mitt.

"Because if it *is* solid gold," said Navis, "neither of us need depend on the charity of earls. We could leave tonight. Mitt, I don't like this at all. You hear a great deal about Noreth here in Adenmouth. She is much loved. If anything happened to her, there would be an outcry all down the coast dales as far as Kinghaven. You are an obvious Southerner. Yet they send you after her in full Aberath livery. What are they playing at? Everyone will know Aberath had a hand in it, however villainous they say you are."

"I'm not doing it," said Mitt. "I can't. That's final. But what do we do?"

"We leave," said Navis, "as soon as I think of an excuse, with your share of the gold if possible. We look for Ynen and we cut short Hildrida's education and we hope we can get to them before Keril finds out." He sighed. "Then we all go into hiding again. Meanwhile, keep sitting. You have to be able to ride."

Mitt sat for another hour. During that time the big paneled room darkened, and drops of rain patterned on the tall window. Lady Eltruda's voice was heard bawling for Navis to see about awnings over the yard. Navis hurried away. He came back only to be called away to see about candles. By the time he was back from that, the clouds had passed and red-gold sunlight was slanting into the room. Lady Eltruda bawled that it was going to be fine after all, and Navis hurried off to have the awnings rolled away. Mitt saw why Navis seemed so well in with Lord Stair. People welcomed a little Southern efficiency round here. He grinned as he watched Navis come back and dress for the feast, with the same efficiency, in a ruffled shirt and blue-green Adenmouth livery. You wouldn't think, to look at him, that Navis must have been dressed by a valet all his life until these last months.

"You can get out now and wash," Navis said.

Mitt did so. He was not sore anymore, not even tender. In fact, he was as smooth and leathery as his own buff and gold Aberath livery. "You pickled me!" he said.

"That was the idea," said Navis.

They went out into the hall, which was full of cooking scents and people standing about waiting for Lord Stair to arrive and start the feast. The big doors were open, blowing in a chilly wind. A lot of noise came from the yard, where everyone else in Adenmouth was gathered at the tables drinking beer until the food arrived. Mitt stood, a little lost among all these strangers.

"Oh, *there* you are, Mitt!" said Rith's voice.

Mitt turned and found himself facing an elegant lady. He was utterly dismayed. The only thing that was the same about her was the longish, freckled face with its eager, cheerful look. But that was surrounded by clouds of fair, frizzy hair, done in a most fashionable style, and she had on a slender dress of gray-blue that hung in sheeny folds round a thoroughly female figure. Mitt could see now she was a lot older than he was— eighteen or twenty at least—and that was enough to make him feel a fool. But the thing that dismayed him most was the fact that Noreth was alive, utterly alive, and warm, and a person.

"Come on!" said Noreth. "Where's your tongue?"

"Er," said Mitt. "Your ladyship—"

"I told you," she said, "to call me Rith."

"Yes," said Mitt, "but . . . what were you doing, letting on you were a boy?"

"I always travel like that," Noreth said. "It's far quicker and safer than a carriage, and I don't need to bother to take a guard. My cousin lends me the livery. And I can use the weapons, too. You learn to, during grittling. But listen—" To Mitt's consternation, Noreth reached out and took hold of both his hands. Her hands were strong and warm, but so small they made Mitt's feel like great cold paws. "I'm very nervous," she said. She was. Mitt could feel her hands trembling. "There's something I have to do. Do you know how it feels to do something that means your life will never be the same again?"

"Don't I just!" Mitt said. He sensed that Navis had come up behind him and was watching Noreth coolly. That reminded him that he had to ask for his share in the statue, but he was too confused to know how to put it.

"I had a feeling you did," said Noreth. "Listen, could you—" There was a bustle up on the dais. Someone was calling for lamps to be lighted. Noreth looked round. "Oh, here comes my uncle," she said. "Drunk as usual. I must go. If you could just bear witness about that statue when the time comes?"

"Sure," said Mitt, "but—"

Noreth let go of him and hurried away. Everyone was surging toward the long tables to sit down. Navis beckoned Mitt to a place beside him, just below the important table on the dais. Mitt found there were advantages to being sent to Adenmouth after all. At Aberath he would have been waiting at the tables with the other boys. Here he was a guest, and he could sit and let boys wait on him. He settled down to enjoy himself. The food was good, though Mitt found he did not much care for the traditional Midsummer sausage. Like so much of the food in the North, it seemed to be mostly oatmeal. But there was venison and pork and chicken and beef as well, oyster patties and plum-and-mutton pies, strawberries, raspberries with sylla-bub, and sweet soda bread. Ale and spirits were passed round the whole time. The sound of voices became a cheerful roar that almost drowned the even greater din from the yard outside. Mitt ate hugely and became very friendly with the hearthmen at his table. There were a great many jokes about vinegar.

Lord Stair was indeed drunk. It was impossible not to notice. He was a large, sallow man, and he sat sprawling in his chair, eating very little and shouting for more drink. Every so often he complained loudly about the food. Nobody took much notice. If people needed to have orders about anything, they asked Lady Eltruda. It looked as if Lady Eltruda, short and fat and loud as she was, had the same power here that the Countess had in Aberath.

"Indeed she does," Navis told Mitt. "I owe my position here to Eltruda. I imagine Noreth does, too."

Lady Eltruda was obviously very fond of Noreth. She kept smiling at her proudly.

The feast drew to a close in sweet cream cheeses and sugared fruit, which Mitt was too full to touch. Lord Stair began to get impatient. His voice roared something about "those idle flaming Singers!" and there were terrific clatterings and scrapings from the yard, where the tables were being moved aside. Hestefan got up from a table near the end of the hall and went to stand in the great doorway. With him, to Mitt's surprise, came Fenna and Moril.

Navis frowned. "I don't think that girl should be here. Nor the boy. They both look ill to me. But I suppose they have to earn their keep."

His voice was nearly drowned in cheering and clapping. Nobody else cared two hoots how the Singers felt, for there was going to be dancing. Tables were pushed aside in the hall, too. Hestefan slung a narrow drum round his neck, looked to see if Fenna was ready on the portable organ and that Moril had tuned his cwidder, and struck up a strenuous jig. Outside and inside, everyone grabbed a partner and danced.

The dancing went on and on. Mitt at first leaned against a table, feeling a little out of things and watching Navis being whirled about by Lady Eltruda. But at the next tune he was grabbed by a young lady in scarlet ribbons, and from then on he danced with the rest. The hall whirled around him, hot and riotous. He kept catching glimpses of Navis dancing with Lady Eltruda, which bothered him slightly, since Lord Stair simply sprawled in a chair and went on drinking. But once or twice he saw Navis dancing with Noreth, in a very courtly way. Mitt would not have dared dance with Noreth himself. He knew absolutely none of the dances. The young ladies squealed with laughter and pushed him into the right places, and he kept going wrong. Every time his desperate, ignorant caperings got him into a real mess, he seemed to catch the eye of Moril, tirelessly playing his cwidder in the doorway, and there was malicious amusement in Moril's look. It began to annoy Mitt.

It took Mitt unawares when the Singers suddenly changed to a slow, haunting tune and everyone stopped dancing. For a moment Mitt was the only one capering. Moril grinned. "What's this tune, then?" Mitt gasped.

" 'Undying at Midsummer,' of course," said the girl in scarlet ribbons. "It's nearly midnight."

Around him dancing partners were breaking apart and the servers were going round with bottles of rare white wine, Southern wine, to welcome midnight with. Someone put three mugs of it down on the steps for the Singers.

Navis bent over his mug, sniffing deeply. "Now this I *have* missed," he said to Mitt. "Grapes don't ripen this far North."

They exchanged a little smile of pride in the South, even though it had turned them both out. Mitt said wonderingly, "That can't be the only thing you miss!"

"I think it is," said Navis. "Life's never dull up here." Saying this, he thrust his mug into Mitt's free hand and dived toward the doorway. He was just in time to catch Fenna as she dropped the heavy organ and passed out. Everybody stared in shock as Navis turned to Hestefan with Fenna draped over his arms. "What were you thinking of, letting this girl play tonight? Couldn't you *see* she was ill?"

Hestefan gave him a slow, worried look. "She swore

she was well, sir, and we needed her part on the organ. I thank you for catching her so quickly."

Navis looked at Moril. "And you? Are you quite well?"

Moril's face did not have much expression, but Mitt could tell that he would not have admitted it to Navis even if he had been playing with all ten fingers broken. "Perfectly, thank you," Moril said.

Here Lady Eltruda raised her voice. Two women came and took Fenna quickly away. Someone shoved the heavy little organ to the side of the doorway. It was almost midnight. A running crowd of men and women were carrying every lamp and candle in the place and putting them down on the ground in two long lines leading from the gates of the yard, through the yard, up the steps, and into a circle in the middle of the hall. It was good luck to place a candle, so everyone fought for the honor except for Lord Stair— and Mitt and Navis, who did not know the custom.

"Let in the Undying!" everyone shouted as the last candle was put in place.

Silence fell, expectantly. From the yard came a strong grating sound as the two big gates were pushed open. At Hestefan's nod, Moril again played the slow, haunting chords of "Undying at Midsummer." To Mitt's ears he seemed to be playing now in an odd, different way. At any rate, there was a queer humming building under the notes. A damp breeze blew in from the yard, where it was probably raining again, bending all the candle flames. A great wavering shadow advanced across the floor and grew up the wall beyond.

Flaming Ammet! Mitt thought, with shivers spreading up his back. I think something really *is* coming in!

But the shadow shortened and fell, and Mitt saw it had been caused by Hestefan advancing up the lane of lights, carrying a small treble cwidder. When Hestefan reached the circle of lights, he turned round and called out, "Welcome the Undying to this house, for this night and the coming year!" Then he played the same slow tune on his cwidder. Mitt wondered why it sounded so much more ordinary now.

A growl of voices welcomed the Undying, too. The custom seemed to be to tip your mug and let a few drops of wine splash on the floor. Navis looked at Mitt. Mitt shrugged. And they both spilled some wine as well, with a private murmur to Libby Beer. After that the feast broke up into groups loudly wishing one another luck for the year. It looked for a minute or so as if things were nearly over.

But suddenly everyone was shouting, "Noreth! Noreth! Noreth, has your sign come?" as Noreth came to stand in the circle of candles beside Hestefan. She was carrying the golden statue, and she held it up for everyone to see.

"Here is my sign," she called out.

Navis murmured to Mitt, "You can say good-bye to your half of it, I think." A number of people were cheering, although Lord Stair was saying loudly in the distance, "Is that girl up to her nonsense again?"

"*Hush!*" someone said.

Noreth called out again. "Will my uncle's lawman please come and stand by me? I wish to make a statement in the proper form of law."

There was a lot of grumbling from the back. One of the men who had been at the high table, rather unsteady on his feet and very embarrassed, came and joined Noreth. She left the circle of light and walked down the lane of candles with him to the door. "I want everyone to hear," she explained to the lawman as they came past Mitt. "Tell me if I say anything wrong." Mitt could feel her shaking with the importance of what she was going to do. It made his stomach give a cold jerk.

"You know ash mush law ash me," the lawman complained, but he went and stood by Noreth as she took up a position in the doorway where she could speak to the people outside as well as those in the hall. The two of them pushed Moril right back to the side of the door. Mitt could see him there, looking awed.

Noreth said, loudly and slowly, "I, Noreth of Kredindale, do this night state and affirm that I am the rightful Queen and heir to the crown of Dalemark, over both North and South and the peoples of both."

It really is true, Mitt thought sadly. The lawman leaned across and murmured to Noreth.

"Oh yes. Thanks," said Noreth. "And over all earldoms and marks therein, not excluding the earls of those marks and the lords under them. This claim I make through my mother, Eleth of Kredindale, descendant in direct line from Manaliabrid of the Undying, and also by right of my father, the One, whose true names are not to be spoken, and from whom all Kings descend. In proof of this my right, my father promised me a token at Midsummer this year, and this promise he kept. This is the token." She held the golden statue up over the nearest lamps so that it could be seen. "Who witnesses," she called out, "that the river Aden today gave me this golden image of my father, the One?"

Mitt jumped and looked round for somewhere to hide. But Noreth turned and looked at him as she spoke. He sighed and pushed his way to the doorway. "If I'd known what you meant when you asked," he said, "I'd have gone straight back to Aberath."

The lawman said, "Do you witnesh thish?" and swayed a little.

"Sure," Mitt said bitterly. If Keril and the Countess had arranged personally for the landslip, they could hardly have pushed him into this any deeper. "I trod on the statue halfway across the brook. She picked it up. That do?"

Noreth replied with an eager, flustered smile. Her hands were still shaking as she held up the statue. She was truly nervous. She was not doing this because she was mad but because she saw it as her duty, as perhaps it was. Mitt felt himself bound to give her a smile in return before he edged away. Beyond Noreth he could see the Singer-lad staring at him resentfully. *Now* what does he think I've done? Mitt thought irritably.

"I call on you all," Noreth said, "to support me in my right. Today at dawn, its being Midsummer Day, I go to ride the green roads until I come to where the crown is hidden, and there I shall be crowned Queen. Let whoever wishes to ride with me and support my claim meet me at the waystone above the quarry at sunrise today."

There was another silence, which was followed by a surge of murmurs, half doubtful, half enthusiastic. Navis whispered to Mitt, "Well, there seems only one thing we can do now." Mitt nodded, but his attention was on Moril in the doorway. He could almost feel the boy making some kind of decision. Sure enough, Moril put his hands to his cwidder and struck up the tune called "The King's Way." Hestefan looked surprised but took the tune up on his cwidder, too, and walked between the two lines of guttering candles to join Moril. Moril, leaning over, plucked once again in the odd and different way. The humming gathered and gathered behind the tune, until it had become more than simply a rousing song. Mitt could quite clearly feel a serious purpose booming behind the notes. Everyone sang:

"Who will ride the King's Way, the King's
          Way?
Who will ride the royal road and follow with
          the King?"

There was a certain amount of muddle as about half the people tried to sing "Queen" instead of "King," but the singing was truly lusty. It seemed to affect Mitt's head, either the singing or the queer boom of Moril's cwidder, and his memory went a bit faulty after that. He remembered Noreth, glowing in the doorway, holding the glinting statue for everyone to see as they sang. He remembered glancing uneasily at Navis because this song was banned in the South, and finding, to his confusion, that Navis was singing with the rest. Mitt knew the song because he had been a freedom fighter, but Navis was an earl's son, for Ammet's sake!

Next thing he knew, he was back in Navis's room, where Navis seemed to be persuading him to get into bed. Mitt interrupted what he was saying—he seemed to be repeating with great earnestness, "This is serious, Navis, she was serious!"—in order to protest that he didn't need to sleep.

"Please yourself," Navis said. "It's only a few hours to sunrise anyway." Mitt had a confused notion that Navis went away then, saying he had a lot of things to do, and he knew Navis did not come back until the next thing he knew, which was Navis shaking him awake in gray dawn.

"What is it *now*?" Mitt said.

"Time to get up," Navis said. "You and I are going to ride the green roads with Noreth."

"Whatever for?" protested Mitt. "I told you I—"

"Can you think of a better way to keep Hildy and Ynen safe until we get to them?" Navis asked. "You were told to join Noreth. Keril will assume you are doing what you are told. Now get up."

Mitt got up—luckily he still seemed to be dressed—and shortly stumbled out into old food and beer smells in the hall. His bedroll was on the nearest table alongside one for Navis. Navis was just beyond, with his arms round someone, evidently kissing that person good-bye. For a moment Mitt thought it was Noreth and was outraged. Then the girl—no, woman, no, *lady*—stood back with her hands on Navis's shoulders, and Mitt saw it was Lady Eltruda. He stood there in even greater outrage. How *could* Navis! An elderly woman. A married woman. Taking advantage of Lord Stair's being a drunk!

"Take care of my girl for me, love," Lady Eltruda said to Navis. "I trust her to you. She's the only child I ever had."

"I'll look after her, I promise," Navis said, and smiled in what Mitt thought was altogether too loving a way.

At that moment Noreth herself rushed into the hall, once more dressed as a hearthman. "Aunt, where's my bedroll? Aunt! Oh!" she said as she saw how her aunt was occupied. She made a face at Mitt that showed that she felt much the same as he did about it. "I'd better go and look in the stable," she said. "I don't think I ever unpacked. Are you riding with me?"

Mitt nodded.

"Oh good!" Noreth said, and raced away outside.

PART TWO

Maewen

:‖ 4 ‖:

MAEWEN CAME BACK to the present with a jump. For a moment there it had seemed as if the noise of the train was not the beat of wheels on tracks, but the sound of water rilling over stones. She had almost seemed to see young leaves rustling overhead, casting a mix of sunspots and shadow on the racing water. In the confusion of glints she could have sworn there was a brighter glint, hands diving for the brightness, voices, and then the brightness taking the form of a dripping golden statuette.

Nonsense, of course. She must have dropped off to sleep while the train was rushing into this deep green cutting—such a deep one that there was no sign of the mountains beyond—and the glint had to be the gold buttons of the guard, just passing on his regular walk down the corridors. The guard smiled gravely at Maewen with his head cocked to one side. Was she all right?

Maewen managed a sort of smile, and the guard passed on. She prickled all over with embarrassment again. It was too bad of Aunt Liss. Mum would just have given Maewen a vague kiss and waved good-bye, but Aunt Liss, being the practical sister, had had to collar the guard and explain loudly and at length. "This is my niece's first-ever train journey. She's going all the way to Kernsburgh to visit her father and I don't like to think of her going all that way without *someone* to keep an eye on her. *Could* you make sure she's all right? *Can* I leave her in your tender care?"

And so on for five minutes, while Maewen wished she were anywhere else and hoped the other four passengers in the carriage were all deaf. As if she were ten years old instead of nearly fourteen! The worst of it was that the guard was quite young and rather good-looking. He probably did think Maewen was only ten. She was unfortunately small for her age. He listened seriously to Aunt Liss and eventually took his cap off, baring his beautiful white-fair curls, and bowed slightly.

"Thank you, madam. You can safely leave your niece to me."

Looking back on it, Maewen wondered if the guard hadn't been making fun of Aunt Liss, but it hadn't seemed like that at the time, and Maewen had spent the entire space between Adenmouth and Kredindale trying to hide her hot face and squirming all over.

The silly part was that Maewen usually got on with Aunt Liss, better than with Mum. Aunt Liss was the one who cared. While Mum wandered in her studio covering her strange gawky statues with metal rags and splashes of bright color, deaf and blind to the world, Aunt Liss made sure Maewen had meals and clothes and—most important of all to Maewen—a horse to ride. Aunt Liss earned day-to-day money by running a livery stable. When Mum sold a statue, she earned big money, but that only happened—

"Are you traveling far, young lady?" asked the passenger opposite, making her jump again. He must have got on the train at Orilsway or somewhere. She looked at him, trying to remember, and decided she must have been asleep when he got on because she had certainly not noticed him before. He was one of those wide kind of old men who are almost bell-shaped sitting down. He had a sheet of wriggly gray hair on either side of his wide, plump face. Maewen was not sure she liked the way his eyes were half hooded in fat eyelids—it made him look cunning and rather cruel—but his question had been perfectly polite, and she supposed she had better answer.

"Just to Kernsburgh."

"Indeed?" he said. "And where did you get on?"

"Adenmouth," said Maewen.

"From the farthest north," said the old man, "halfway down the country to King Hern's city of gold. That is a momentous journey, child. At one time it was the royal road to the crown of Dalemark." He chuckled in a windy, breathy way. "And what brings you on the paths of the Undying?"

What a silly way to talk! Maewen thought. There

are people who travel between Adenmouth and Kernsburgh every day of the week. "I'm going to visit my father," she said. Up to this moment she had secretly thought this was the greatest adventure of her life, but thanks to this old man, it was suddenly ordinary and boring. "For the holidays," she added drearily.

"Your father," said the old man, in a breathy sort of pounce, "works away from home? In Kernsburgh? Eh?"

"Yes," said Maewen.

"You travel to see him often?"

"No," she said. "This is the first time I've been." And she wished she could end this conversation. She did not like the old man's voice. There was something odd about it.

"Ah, I see. He's only just gone to work in Kernsburgh, is that it? Eh?"

"No. He's worked there for the last seven years." What *was* so odd about his voice? It almost seemed as if the sound was not coming from the old man at all but from somewhere else quite a long way away. Perhaps he was one of those people who had had surgery on his larynx and had to use a false voice box, in which case he was unfortunate and she ought to be polite to him. Maewen tried to explain without giving away her entire family history. "I haven't seen him since I was— was a lot younger." She really did not want to tell him her age, which he would know if she told him her parents had been divorced when she was seven.

"Now why is that?" the old man asked. "Do your parents perhaps not get on? They seem to have lived a long way apart for most of your life."

Cheek! Maewen thought. It's none of his business. "My mother," she explained haughtily, "is a sculptor who prefers to work near the stone she uses. And my father is a very busy man. He's head curator of the Tannoreth Palace."

"Ah," said the old man. She really did not like his half-hooded eyes. She looked away. "So you are truly on your way to the royal palace?" he said. He seemed very pleased. "And traveling all on your own until we met, eh? Now you can travel with me." He leaned forward. The carriage seemed full of his wheezing breath, as if it were coming from outside into him, instead of the right way.

For one horrid moment Maewen thought he was going to pat her knee. She surged herself right to the back of her seat, but that did not seem nearly far enough away.

"I will be with you from now on," he said, leaning at her. "Think of me as a friend."

No! Help! Maewen thought. She looked at the other passengers. Three were asleep, and the other was deep in a book. She thought of putting her feet up and kneeling sideways out of reach of the old man's fat hand hovering to pat her. And the guard only just went past, she thought, so it'll be hours before he comes back again.

"Look at me in the eyes," said the old man, "and tell me you think of me as a friend."

His face seemed to be right in front of hers, filling all she could see. Maewen shut her eyes. Let the guard come! she prayed. Let somebody help!

And here, like a miracle, the carriage door was sliding back and the guard's solemn good-looking face was leaning round it. "Are you all right in here?"

"I . . . oh . . . yes . . . no . . . he—" Stop stammering and say he tried to pat your knee, you fool! "He—" Maewen turned to point at the seat opposite and found herself stammering again, this time with astonished embarrassment. The seat was empty. A quick look round the carriage showed her that there were only four passengers, three asleep, one reading. "But he . . . there was . . . I thought an old man . . . I mean—"

The guard shifted his head to look gravely at the empty seat. "I don't think he'll bother you again," he said, perfectly straight-faced and polite, and he shut the door and went away.

Maewen sat back hot and squirming, worse than before. If one more thing happens with that guard, I think I shall *die*! She must have fallen asleep and dreamed the old man. What had possessed her to have a sinister little dream like that? Probably, deep down, she was terrified of seeing Dad again. Determined to stay awake from now on, she sat looking out at the mountains, dun-colored shoulders, green steeps, black crags, and blue jagged distances, spinning past as the train thundered through the center of North Dalemark. She thought firmly of Dad, to conquer her nerves. He had written over and over again to ask Maewen to visit him. He must really want to see her. But Mum just said irritably that she was not letting Maewen go until she was old enough to take care of herself. "Because he's quite likely to forget you exist after half a day," she said. "You'd starve or worse." She went on to a tirade about how wrapped up Dad was in his work.

Maewen grinned. That, coming from Mum, was rich. But it seemed to have been the main reason for the divorce. Dad just kept forgetting he had a wife and daughter. She felt that if Dad turned out to be a male version of Mum, she could cope. She was used to it. It was worth it for the chance of living in the royal palace of Amil the Great in the middle of the capital city. But what if Dad turned out *unpleasant*? Maewen had always found it hard to believe that you could divorce someone just for being vague. After all, she had never felt the slightest desire herself to divorce Mum. That made her grin again.

By the time the train slowed and rolled creaking into Kernsburgh Central Station, Maewen was feeling quite cheerful and poised. But that was in her mind. Her body persisted in thinking it was very nervous, and her arms felt like string as she tried to heave her suitcase off the train. It was blocking the door, and she could sense the crowd of passengers behind getting more and more irritated. But just as she was getting truly flustered, here was the polite, attentive guard again, giving her a serious smile and picking up her case for her.

"Let me carry that."

He set off into the station, and she pattered after him, grateful even though he was looking after her like a baby. The station was much larger than she had expected, high and ringing with announcements and people's voices and feet, and full of big red pillars that made all the parts of it look the same.

"My father is meeting me," she began defensively.

She saw Dad as she said it, coming through hordes of people going the other way. He was reading from a bundle of notes in his hand, and it was clear that the other people pushing past just did not exist for him. The sight took Maewen instantly back seven years. It was a pure delight the way Dad stood out from everyone else by being so trim and clear-cut—but not for being tall, she realized as Dad came close. He only came up to the guard's shoulder. So that's where I get my smallness from! she thought, and for one mad moment she wondered if Mum had divorced Dad because Mum herself was so tall and willowy.

Dad looked up from his notes and recognized her as if he had only seen her yesterday. "Oh, hello," he said. "You don't look a bit like this photo." He turned the bundle of notes round to show her the snapshot clipped to the front. It was one Maewen had never liked, herself all long-faced and freckled with her arm over a horse, not unlike the horse, and the horse the better-looking of the two. "I suppose that's how your aunt Liss likes to see you," Dad remarked. "She sent the photo, of course."

There was a slight awkwardness then as Dad bent a bit and kissed her cheek and did not quite give Maewen time to kiss him back. He smelled just the same as she remembered, with pipe smoke somewhere. He wheeled away almost at once to stare at the guard. "You needn't have bothered, Wend," he said. "I can be trusted to remember to meet my own daughter, I hope." He had put back his head and gone all haughty. Maewen remembered that haughtiness well. Was it the haughtiness that had caused the divorce, really?

"I was supposed to take care of her, sir," said the guard. "Or so I thought."

Maewen turned to stare at him. She had thought the uniform he was wearing was a railway one, but now she saw it was a paler blue and that the cap was wrong. How puzzling.

"I take it you two have met," Dad said. He was still haughty. He went on with the utmost sarcasm, "Maewen, my chief assistant, Wend Orilson. Wend, my daughter, Mayelbridwen Singer." Then he swung round and strode rapidly toward the way out, leaving Maewen to dither, not knowing whether to run after him or stay with the puzzling Wend and her suitcase.

She arrived at the exit doing neither, partly chasing Dad and then stopping and turning to look at Wend, wondering if she had the nerve to ask him if Dad had really sent him all the way to Adenmouth to collect her, and then forgotten—and then not daring and running after Dad again. They arrived outside in single file, into a roar of traffic and much hotter sun than Maewen was used to. There was a vast stone, round, with a hole in the middle, upended in the traffic island in front of the station. Its huge shadow fell across the front half of the queue for taxis.

"We won't need a taxi; it's no distance," Dad said. He pointed to the huge stone. "The old waystone," he said, and set off striding into the town, "marking the start of the ancient road system of North Dalemark. King Hern, or most probably his descendants, made the roads, but simple people often thought the gods made them and tended to call them the paths of the Undying."

Maewen pattered after him up a broad thoroughfare, listening to as much as she could hear of a series of little lectures. After the waystone, it was the traffic, then the circular road system invented by Amil the Great, then the goods sold in the expensive shops she could see on either side. Somewhere along the street, Wend caught up, carrying her suitcase, and she thought he said, "I'll explain later," but she was too confused to be sure.

She forgot everything, anyway, when they came

between giant gilded gates in a high wall and she had her first sight of the palace. It was across a cobbled court, and it was majestic. Like a very graceful cliff, she thought, almost too big to take in, and all upright lines that made it look taller still. In front of it, right in the middle of the court, there was a very much smaller building. It caught Maewen's attention for being so different from the palace that it looked quite out of place. It was like a house-sized model of a fairy-tale palace, with three small onion domes and such numbers of spiral towers that it looked almost absurd.

"Whatever is that?" she said.

"That? Oh, that's the tomb of Amil the Great," her father told her, and followed this up with one of the little lectures Maewen was coming to expect. "He completed the old part of the palace two hundred years ago, quite early in his reign. That's Amil's old facade we're looking at now; those recessed arcades along the lower stories were one of his own ideas. He was always full of ideas, but toward the end of his reign the ideas got rather out of hand, I'm afraid. Amil seemed to become obsessed with death and evil. He divided his time between having this tomb built and journeying all over the kingdom to eradicate what he called pockets of Kankredin. He simply meant places where there was injustice or lawlessness, but he had become very eccentric by then, and he preferred to call them that."

"He was very old when he died, wasn't he?" Maewen asked.

:‖ 5 ‖:

Dᴀᴅ ʜᴀᴅ ᴀɴ ᴇɴᴏʀᴍᴏᴜs, spacious apartment right at the top of the Old Palace, filled with books and old furniture. The main room looked over the leads of the roof, where pigeons waddled to the windows, expecting crusts of bread for breakfast. Maewen's bedroom looked out over the forecourt and the top of Amil's mad little tomb to what seemed miles below, with a huge view of Kernsburgh beyond that, all dark trees and towers and square office blocks. The room was enormous, with almost nothing in it but a bed, a cupboard, and a great threadbare carpet that had been old when Amil's son imported it. Next door was a large clanking bathroom with plumbing so elderly that Maewen was more awed by it than anything else in the palace.

"I'm afraid I can only spare time to be with you in the evenings and early mornings," Dad said over supper. Supper was supplied by one of a bewildering set of young ladies, who all seemed to wait on Dad hand and foot and then turn into secretaries in between. Seeing them, Maewen instantly knew that Dad regretted the divorce no more than Mum did. He was entirely comfortable. After supper he lit a pipe and explained, "We're just moving into the height of the tourist season now. As soon as the palace opens to the public, I have to be everywhere at once. But I've told everyone that you can explore anywhere you want. Tomorrow I'll make sure they all know you, so there won't be any trouble."

That evening they just talked, with Dad puffing clouds of pipe smoke through sunset light slanting in across the leading. Maewen found they got on. Dad seemed to think the same kind of thoughts that she did. Next morning he woke her quite surprisingly early and they had breakfast—supplied by another young lady—with rosy light slanting the other way across crusty rolls and rich black coffee. Just as Maewen was thinking how grown-up and leisurely this was, Dad sprang up and took her on a tour of the palace.

The Tannoreth Palace was vast. Buildings of various ages rayed out around courtyards with fountains, or gardens with statues and summerhouses in them, and hedges and roses, and a small menagerie. At every huge room they came to—and on some of the stairways—at every picture or work of art or curious object, Dad gave her another of his little lectures. In between he was introducing her to bewildering numbers of people who worked in the palace: ladies in overalls polishing the long museum galleries or dusting gilded tables, security men, guides, secretaries, and Major Alksen, who was head of security. Maewen's mind began to seize up. When Dad took her outside to be introduced to the gardeners, she was thinking, I shall *never* remember all this! Our minds are not the same after all. It was too early. Even though she was used to being up with the lark in the holidays to help Aunt Liss in the stables, she could see to a horse on autopilot, half asleep. This was different. No one *introduced* you to horses or expected you to know the history of the barn.

Afterward she found the only thing she could remember from the entire tour was Major Alksen because he was so much her idea of a retired soldier. And Wend, of course. She was glad Dad had not reintroduced her to Wend. Maewen felt too much pure embarrassment to go near him.

But she felt she was letting Dad down, or wasting opportunities, or something. So when Dad had given her another of his swift, awkward kisses and rushed off, Maewen felt herself bound to go all over the palace again.

It took days. Some of the time she joined in the guided tours, having made sure first that the guide was not Wend, and the guides would give her a special smile among all the crowds of foreign schoolchildren, and ordinary families, and silk-suited men and women from Nepstan, and then go on with their spiels. She visited Amil's tomb with one such crowd, but it was a cold, boring arched room inside, with a lot of gold lettering on the tombstone, and she only went there that once. She preferred indoors.

Here she usually started her sightseeing in the Old Palace, where most of the pictures were. That was easy to find because of the art students. They lay on the floor in what had been the great hall but was now a ballroom, copying the perspective in the ceiling picture. On the walls of this room Amil the Great, with his mane of fair hair and a roll of plans trailing from one hand, supervised the building of the palace. Amil was wearing purple breeches, which Maewen thought were decidedly unfortunate. They looked worse in the copies the students made of them. On the ceiling there was the whole of Dalemark spread out, from the plains and slow rivers of the South to the mountains of the North, and full of battling figures, as Amil (in the same purple breeches) led his armies against the rebellious earls at the start of his reign.

Next door to the ballroom was a smaller room where oil paintings hung in frames. This was where Maewen's favorite pictures were. She got into the habit of stepping over the students lying on the floor and then pushing between the easels and the busy students in the smaller room in order to look at the portraits they were copying. The biggest was of the Duke of Kernsburgh, posed haughtily looking over the shoulder of a trailing crimson cape, in front of a new castle on a hill.

"Amil the Great's chief minister," Dad told her

when she asked that first evening, "and one of the most ruthless men in history."

Maewen could see the Duke was ruthless—it was in every fierce, clear line of him—but there was something familiar and almost friendly about him, too. She almost felt as if she knew him. She kept trying to decide why. He looks as if he was very nice to his friends, she decided. But if you weren't one of his friends, you had to watch it. He'd put you to death without turning a hair.

The Duke was flanked by two dismal portraits of the Adon, both much, much older, and beyond that was an even older portrait of Enblith the Fair, who was supposed to have been the most beautiful woman ever, daughter of the Undying and a famous queen. The portrait was cracked, but even so Maewen could only suppose that ideas of beauty had changed. Enblith reminded her very strongly of Aunt Liss—and no one had ever called Aunt Liss a beauty, even when she was young. I bet she *managed* people into thinking she was lovely, Maewen thought. That was all women were supposed to *be* in those days. And she pushed between easels to the portrait that truly fascinated her.

It was called *Unknown Minstrel Boy*, and she kept wishing she knew more about him. He was probably about her own age, and he had red hair—which Maewen had always secretly wished for herself—with the paleness that always goes with such hair. He was rather richly dressed in dark maroon satin, so either he was a very good minstrel or a young aristocrat posing as one. Good minstrel, Maewen decided. It was in the way his pained eyes met yours and yet looked way, way beyond, full of thoughts and knowledge and strong sadness. Someone's let him down badly, Maewen thought when she first met those eyes. She wished she knew who had and why. And kept going back to look.

She wanted so badly to know about that boy that in the end she joined the afternoon guided tour that went round the pictures. The advantage was that the students had gone home by then. The disadvantage was that this tour was always taken by Wend. It took Maewen several days to muster courage to go with it. When she did, the mere sight of Wend started her fizzing with embarrassment again. Wend saw her and gave her a polite little bow and a restrained smile. Maewen felt her face flooding with red. It was the awful way Wend never seemed to show any emotion but politeness. But she clenched her teeth and followed the other tourists.

The picture of the minstrel boy was famous for several reasons, she discovered. Nobody had ever been able to find out who the boy was, although he was important enough to have been painted by the best artist of the time. And he must have been important to Amil the Great, too, because Amil made a special bequest of the picture to his grandson, Amil II. Books had been written about the picture. Some theorists suspected the boy was Amil himself, before he won the throne. Amil the Great had also carefully preserved the cwidder that had been painted with the boy. It was obviously old, even then. The minstrel boy had his hand dreamily wrapped across the cwidder, half hiding the strange old lettering inlaid on the front. And the actual selfsame cwidder was in a glass case just beside the portrait, very fragile and cracked-looking, despite careful restoration.

"Well, fancy that!" said everyone, raising cameras and jostling for the best shot of it.

After that Wend took the party into the ballroom, where he told them that the paintings on the wall and the ceiling had been done in the time of Amil II. Nobody knew what Amil the Great really looked like, and the purple trousers were a pure invention. This so amused Maewen that she left Wend's embarrassing presence in order to go down to the hallway and buy a postcard of Amil in his breeches and write a "Wish you were here" message on it to Mum and Aunt Liss. Then she made a foray into Kernsburgh itself to post it.

The city was even more crowded than the palace, and the traffic was terrible. A very few glances into the shops as she passed showed Maewen that she had barely enough money even for ordinary presents for Mum and Aunt Liss. Kernsburgh sold things from all over the world, and it was expensive. But the distressing thing to someone who had been brought up in the country like Maewen was that the place seemed to have almost no trees once you were down on street level.

"Where do all the trees go?" she asked Dad that evening.

It was a perfect example of the way she and Dad got on. Dad knew just what she was talking about although he was busy laying out sheets of stiff paper and notebooks on the other end of the table. "In people's gardens, I think," he said. "I believe Amil the Great planned it that way, because there were no trees on the site when he started to rebuild Kernsburgh."

"Then he made a mistake," Maewen said. "It's all buildings and cars, and it makes me cough."

"You'd have coughed worse when the place was new," Dad said. "Two hundred years ago it would have been smog from coal fires. Though I'm never sure it was such a good thing when they discovered oil under the Marshes. It makes the Queen a rich woman, I suppose, but it has its drawbacks."

"Where *is* the Queen?" Maewen asked. "I've been almost all over the palace now, and—"

"Oh, she very rarely comes here these days," Dad said. "She's pretty old, you know, and she prefers the warmth in the South. She almost only ever comes to the Tannoreth for state occasions."

"And the Crown Prince?" Maewen asked, feeling rather let down.

"He lives in Hannart," Dad answered absently, busy

with a notebook. "Doesn't get on with his mother or with public events."

"What are you doing?" Maewen asked him.

"Trying to establish our family tree," said her father. "It's a hobby of mine—and damned exasperating, too. You can come and look if you like."

Maewen came and leaned on his square, warm shoulder, and he spread scrawled books and careful diagrams out for her to see. "Here," he said. "My family. As far as I can tell we go back to one of the traveling Singers. I *think* his name may have been Clennen, but Singers wandered about so and were so little documented that it's a fiendish job to find out for sure. Compared with that period, the last hundred years were a doddle, and I thought those were bad enough. And when we get to your mother's family, things get even worse. Here." Dad pushed sheets of paper in front of Maewen, hectically scrawled all over in pale pencil. "See? There's some connection with Amil II's brother Edril, but that's as far as—"

"You mean Mum descends from Amil the Great!" Maewen exclaimed.

"So do a lot of people. If you mean that accounts for your mother's standoffish vagueness," Dad said dryly, "I hardly think so. If you remember that everyone has four grandparents and eight great-grandparents, you can see that almost everyone has to be related if you go back far enough. We're talking here about doubling the number of ancestors each person has every generation, and halving—or even quartering—the number of people those ancestors could have come from. The population of Dalemark was quite small until a hundred years ago."

He was lecturing again. Maewen tried to listen. She was quite interested in the difficulties Dad had sorting out the two generations around the time of Amil the Great. School history didn't tell you half the confusions and revolutions there had been then. But there was so much of it. It had been dark for hours and she was yawning before Dad said, "Well, that will have to do for now. I've another long day tomorrow."

Once she was in bed, Maewen tried to sort out how she felt about Dad and the divorce. She was very fond of Dad—achingly, fiercely fond—but not so much when he lectured. And try as she might, she could not be upset that he was quite happy to be divorced from Mum. She had expected to feel sad—she felt she *ought* to feel sad—but whenever she passed the big busy office on the floor below and saw Dad conferring with secretaries, snapping instructions at Wend, or consulting with Major Alksen—and sometimes all three at once—she was glad she did not have to live with him and Mum at once. These were two strong-minded people who were both utterly buried in their work. And one of those, Maewen felt, was enough at one time.

Next morning, as she chucked pieces of bread onto the leads for the fat waddling pigeons, Maewen discovered that sorting that out about Dad had somehow let her off having to remember everything about the palace. As it was another baking hot day, Maewen decided to go for a swim. Major Alksen had said she could use the staff bathing pool. But he had not said where it was. She set out to find him and ask him.

Downstairs she went to the office. It was so busy that though she could hear Dad's voice, she could not see him among all the other hurrying people. And the secretary nearest the door said that Major Alksen had already gone down to his security post. Maewen went down again to the great upper galleries of the palace, which were cool and quiet and empty yet, until the palace opened to the public. These long rooms were a sort of museum, where curios and clothes belonging to past kings and queens sat in cases among statues and pieces of carving that had once been on the outside of the palace. As a lot of the things were very valuable, Major Alksen was often there, patrolling with a radio phone, checking security. As she came into the first room, Maewen could hear his footsteps ringing in the distance somewhere and his voice talking into his radio. "Coming through Gallery Two now. All secure. Over." She made toward the sound.

The person she saw when she went round the corner was Wend. Maewen stopped. How had he sounded so exactly like Major Alksen? Luckily Wend's handsome face was set intently on distance as he listened to the voice on his radio. He had not seen her. Full of embarrassment again, Maewen started to tiptoe softly round the corner.

"Don't go, Maewen," said Wend. "I'll be with you in a moment. Right. Everything in place here. Over and out."

What excuse could she possibly give for rushing away? Maewen wondered. So sorry, I need to swim this second. Forgive me, but I have to go and depress myself at once by seeing Amil's tomb. Excuse me, I must go and look at the Duke of Kernsburgh—urgently. Or she could just run away. But Wend was already turning toward her, and the only thing she could think of was to let him explain why he had been sent to meet her as if she were ten years old and get it over with.

"You must have wondered," Wend said to her.

"No, no!" Maewen said. It seemed as if she did not want to get it over after all. "No, no, I never wonder—"

"Who that old man on the train was," said Wend. "The one I sent away."

This was so entirely unexpected that Maewen said, "Oh!" Then because she could feel her face was as red as it could be, she said, "He wasn't there. I dreamed him."

"No," said Wend. "He was—well—*there*, even if he wasn't what you'd call quite real. I'm afraid he's about to become a very big threat to you unless you let me help you. *Will* you let me help—or at least let me explain?"

"I—er—" Maewen was even more flustered. She was suddenly sure that Wend was mad. This was the only explanation for his grave, polite, *sane* look and the way it made her squirm every time she was near him. "Who *was* the old man?"

"A piece of Kankredin," said Wend. "A pocket of evil. And"—he smiled—"I promise you I am not mad."

This was worse than ever. "Yes, you are! You must be!" Maewen cried out, and she knew she would squirm even harder about this when she had time to think about it. "Kankredin's just a legend from the days of King Hern—and Hern killed him, anyway, when he conquered the Heathens."

Wend looked his most serious, and there was a sympathy about him as if he understood precisely how she was feeling—which, if possible, made Maewen feel worse. "Yes, I know how the story goes," he said. "People tell it like that because it's more comforting, but it wasn't the way of it, I assure you. Hern helped defeat Kankredin, that is true, but Kankredin couldn't die because he was dead already. The only way he could be conquered was for someone to unbind the One himself. You've heard of the witch Cennoreth. She unbound the One, and Kankredin was broken and scattered into a million pieces. But he wasn't dead. He came together over the centuries—concentrated, if you like, into larger and larger pockets—and eventually he was strong enough to take over the South and divide it from the North. Amil the Great found a way to destroy quite a bit of Kankredin, but even that didn't really defeat him. He was just scattered, and some parts of him came forward in time to these days. Other parts simply stayed around and arrived here and now by keeping secret and outlasting anyone who believed he was there. I'm not sure which kind of pocket you met, but I think from the way it behaved, it was one of the parts sent forward in time."

"I don't believe you," Maewen said. "How do you know?"

Wend shrugged. "I was there for nearly all of it. Hern was my brother."

Maewen stared at him. "But that's"—she was going to say "nonsense!" but she stopped herself, because you had to be careful with mad people—"not possible, Mr. Orilson. You see, that would make you so old you'd almost be one of the Undying." And no one believes in the Undying anymore, anyway, she thought, but I'd better not tell him that.

Wend nodded. There was a sad, priggish sort of sanity to him that Maewen found deeply suspect. "I found it hard to believe, too, when two of my brothers died and I didn't even age. It is hard to admit that you are anything but mortal. But the Undying exist whether people believe in them or not. I am one. You have probably heard of me. I was known as Tanamoril for a while. Then I was called Osfameron."

Osfameron! The Adon's friend who raised the Adon from the dead! He's further round the twist than I thought a person *could* be! Maewen stared at Wend, all alone in the long empty museum room. Do all lunatics look this sane? I wish I knew. He'd look quite normal if he wasn't so good-looking. Keep humoring him until he gets called away to his duties. "What do you think this piece of Kankredin wanted with me?" Maewen asked gently.

"I think," said Wend, "that he was trying to get control of you."

Maewen's spine felt as if cold fingers were being trailed down it. She backed into the nearest glass case in order to feel safer. "Why—why would he want to do that?"

"Because you are the image of a young woman who lived just over two hundred years ago," Wend told her.

"That makes no sense!" said Maewen.

But Wend continued talking as if he had not heard her. "A very important young lady," he said. Looking at his constrained and serious face, Maewen thought that this was the heart of his mental disorder, whatever it was. She leaned on the glass cupboard and let him go on talking. "Noreth," Wend said. "Born to rule all Dalemark. My grandfather the One was her father, and she knew from her childhood up that she was to take the crown and rule both North and South. When she had it, people would have risen to her all over the country, whatever the earls had to say."

"What happened? Wouldn't she do it?" Maewen asked.

"I don't know what happened. She was willing

enough." Just for an instant Wend seemed to feel wretched about this. Then his face smoothed over. "I was guarding Noreth on the royal road," he said. "The midsummer after her eighteenth birthday, as was right, she set off from Adenmouth to ride to Kernsburgh for the crown. Nothing should have gone wrong. I was as watchful as I could be. But somewhere along the way Kankredin got to her as he was trying to get to you, and she . . . simply disappeared." Wend swallowed a little. Then, with his face all cold and smooth, he said, "That was how Amil, so called the Great, was able to claim the crown."

Maewen stayed pressed against the glass. "And," she said, gently and humoringly, "you're telling me this because I look like this lady."

"No," said Wend. "I'm telling you because I'm fated to send you back in time to take Noreth's place."

"Fated?" said Maewen. "That's a strong word. You need me to agree first, and I haven't."

Wend came nearer to laughing than she had ever seen him. "You forget," he said. "I was there. So were you. So I know I did send you." He had a funny lighthearted air to him, now that he had arrived at this point. "As I see it now," he said, "I must have asked the One to send you to the moment on the royal road when Noreth disappeared, so that you could find out what happened and tell me when you came back here."

"Oh." Maewen looked down at her two somewhat scruffy sandals planted on the glossy floor. Then I must have been—I will be—as mad as he is! Though of course, if he really *was* there, he is over two hundred years old, and that means he can't be mad. It all hung together. And she knew mad people's fantasies did often hang together. That was why they found it so difficult to get out of them. Perhaps the best way to deal with Wend was to show him it was nonsense by daring him to send her into the past. No. He could turn violent then. Best just to go. She slid carefully away along the glass cupboard and braced her sandals to run.

Wend smiled his polite smile. "Thanks. I was needing to get at this showcase. Your father wants some of the things moved."

He fetched up his bunch of keys and advanced on the lock of the sliding door. He was far too near. Maewen could feel her stomach squirming and those queer pins and needles in her back that she always got when she was about to do something wrong. Strange the way Wend always made her feel like this. She slid farther away, warily watching him as he undid the electronic lock and then the ordinary one. Any second now she would be far enough away to risk running for help.

Wend reached inside the glass cupboard and gently, almost reverently, picked up a small gold statue that was standing there among vases, salt cellars, rings and other golden objects. While Wend turned to her holding the statue in both hands—she could see it was heavy—Maewen craned to see the label it had been standing on.

FIGURE OF KING OR NOBLE (GOLD).
PREHISTORIC. ORIGIN UNKNOWN.

"This is the image of the One that my family once guarded," Wend said. The radio on his belt beeped as he spoke. He frowned. "Would you take this to your father for me? Someone wants me."

He held the small golden image out. It was the ideal excuse for going away. Maewen reached out gladly and took hold of the image in both hands. The thing was so worn and old that all you could say of it was that it had once had a face and wore a long sort of poncho robe, but the instant she touched it she had the queer doing-wrong feeling worse than before. Her teeth ached with it, and her hair tried to lift. She snatched her hands away. But by then the pins and needles were worse down her hands and legs and through her face. It seemed to affect her eyes, so that the long empty room grew foggy, and her ears, so that she could only dimly hear Wend's beeping radio.

:‖ 6 ‖:

THE FOGGINESS WAS COLD as well as thick. Maewen lost all sense of direction. She staggered and found her sandals were getting wet in short grass beaded with fog drops. It felt icy. "Oh—ouch!" she cried out.

Her voice had the unechoing clarity of somewhere outside—and high up, too, she thought, having been brought up among mountains. Anyway it was nothing like the woody, stony echoes inside the museum gallery. She looked up and around in a panic. Everything was mist, thick white mist, except for—thank goodness!—one pink streak of dawn over to the right. And there was something dark ahead through the mist. Maewen took a couple of excruciating cold, wet strides toward the dark thing, enough to numb her feet, and found the thing was a round stone a little higher than her waist with a hole in the middle. A waystone? It was only about a tenth the size of the one outside the station in Kernsburgh, but she supposed that was what it might be.

She stood shivering in her scanty summer shorts

and shirt, staring at the stone resentfully. It's real! she thought. Wend tricked me! I'm in shock! I'm going to die of exposure, and I haven't the *faintest* idea where I am! Or *when*!

Here she noticed that the pins and needles feeling was no longer with her. It had been replaced—some seconds ago, now she thought about it—by a much better feeling, a feeling that everything was going to be all right. Well, I hope so! she thought. I *could* scream, only there doesn't seem to be anyone around to hear.

She began to feel definitely warmer.

She looked down in time to see her sandals closing over and growing up her legs into stout-looking boots. Her shorts were growing downward into felty, rather baggy trousers that tucked into the boots. A faint jingling alerted her to the fact that her shirt was also growing, and multiplying, into linked mail with one thinnish shirt under it and another, thicker one on top. A heaviness on her head caused her hand to leap up there. She touched metal. She now had a light domed helmet on.

She felt a mad, hilarious pleasure. I'm a warrior maid! I'm changing into a fighting girl under my own eyes—what I can see of myself! Her feet were still frozen inside the boots, and her hands were no warmer, but she nevertheless had a warm, cared-for feeling. Something—the golden statue?—was looking after her.

There was another jingling over to the right. Maewen whirled like a wild animal. The jingling mixed with a *pruff* of breath, a sound that she knew very well. She moved warily over that way, jingling herself. Sure enough, looming out of the mist, dark against the pink stripe of dawn, was a horse, standing patiently waiting for someone. Not a bad horse, though rather shaggy, as far as she could see, and it was saddled and bridled, with a roll of baggage behind the saddle. It turned and blew steamy breath at Maewen as if it knew her.

Maewen had not realized how much she had been missing horses. Almost by reflex, she gathered in the reins, put her foot in the stirrup, and swung up into the saddle. Ouch! Effort! The mail and the boots were *heavy*. It was only when she was up that it occurred to her that the horse almost certainly belonged to someone else. What did they do to you for horse stealing? Oh well. Say I'm awfully sorry, there was this thick fog and I thought it was mine. Would that work? It felt so much better to be mounted that she hardly cared. Deal with the owner when we meet her. She reined around toward the little waystone and tried to make out where she was.

The mist was clearing gradually, downward, dropping into a valley below the stone, but that was still all she could see. "Hello?" she said uncertainly.

"Oh—your pardon, lady. I never heard you come."

Maewen bunched herself, again with wild-animal wariness, as a tall man unfolded himself from where he had been sitting against the other side of the way-stone and bowed to her, hastily and politely. When he straightened up, she saw he was Wend. She went warier than ever. His hair was a good deal longer, grown into wavy whitish ringlets that were not very well combed, which altered the shape of his face some-what, and instead of the neat uniform she had seen him in a few minutes ago, he was wearing patched and baggy woolens with an old sheepskin jacket on top. The sort of clothes, Maewen thought, that a poor shep-herd might have worn two hundred years ago. She stared at Wend, wondering if she really was in the past. And does he know me? Does he think I'm Whats-hername?

Wend stared back with the usual grave politeness. "I am Wend, lady," he said. "If you remember, we met before." So he *does* know me, Maewen thought. "And I am here to follow you from waystone to way-stone along the royal road, until you come to Hern's city of gold and claim your rightful crown."

He's briefing me, Maewen thought, and so he should—tricking me into pretending to be this Nor-theen, or whatever she's called! The trouble was Wend still made her fizz with embarrassment. He spoke in a very strong Northern accent, of the kind that Mum and Aunt Liss always objected to when Maewen spoke that way. It seemed quite natural to Wend, but she had heard him speak quite normally only a minute ago, and she could not get over the feeling he was putting on an act. It irritated her. "I think I need to know a bit more than that," she said angrily.

Wend bowed humbly, which irritated Maewen even more. "True, lady. Then I will tell you what no one else knows. I am the one they call the Wanderer, and I keep the green roads—"

He stopped talking and looked over his shoulder. There was a brisk jingling of tack below and nearby. Maewen once more bunched up like a wary wild animal and watched two more riders scramble uphill out of the fog. They seemed to bring the fog with them, fog of their own breath, fog of their horses' breath, and fill the air with their presence.

"Good morning, Noreth," said the smaller of the two. "You got ahead of us very quickly. We were hoping to ride up with you." He was riding a truly magnificent mare. His clothes were like the ones Maewen had so recently acquired, mail coat and cap and all, except that on this man they had a neater, wealthier look. Maewen was shocked to find that she knew his face. She had last seen those clear-cut ruthless features staring over a painted shoulder out of the portrait of the Duke of Kernsburgh.

It gave her a vivid, physical shock, like touching a live wire. Up to then Maewen had not really believed she had been sent two hundred years into the past. But here was a live man, breathing out warm, live, foggy breath, whom she *knew* to have been dead for well over a century. It made it real. It made it much more frightening. She looked rather frantically across at the taller rider, wondering if she would know him, too. He was young and gawky and obviously in the middle of growing even taller. His clothes, which were quite neat, too, sat on him as if they were his best clothes and he was used to wearing something much scruffier. And his horse looked villainous.

He was a total stranger, but Maewen's feelings about that changed from relief to dismay when this young one smiled at her. He smiled in a cheerful, friendly way, with just a touch of shyness, as if he knew her quite well. And she had simply no idea who he was. O great *One*! she thought. Why hasn't Wend *warned* me about these people?

She looked at Wend, waiting humbly by the waystone, but had to look back when the man with clear-cut features spoke again. "As you see," he said, "Mitt and I have come to be your followers on the royal road."

Maewen was thrown into confusion again. He sounded so sarcastic. It was just the way a man like this one *would* speak—and it made her feel about five years old. But it was a double confusion. She suddenly found she had no idea *when* this was. She had been assuming, in a muddled and buried way, that she had been bounced into this Noreth woman's place somewhere halfway to Kernsburgh. But from what this man said, she could be right at the start of Noreth's journey from the North. It gave her a low, grinding sort of worry to add to all the other things. Among the other things was the thought, If Kankredin got to Noreth *that* early, how soon will he get to *me*? And a slightly more trivial thought, but just as worrying, was that this man on the fine mare was not going to be made Duke of Kernsburgh until some years on in Amil the Great's reign. If she was Noreth and at the start of Noreth's journey, then Amil the Great was somewhere else in Dalemark and nowhere near being King yet. So this man was not Duke of Kernsburgh yet. And she had no idea what to call him. At least she now knew the younger one was called Mitt.

She gave Mitt a flustered smile and tried a stately bow on his companion. He bowed back, ironically, and raised an eyebrow at Wend. He was, naturally, one of those who could slide one eyebrow up without the other one moving at all.

"I am Wend, sir," Wend said humbly, "and I follow the lady, too."

"Well, well. That makes three of us," the man said. "How many more are we expecting?"

Maewen could not answer since she probably had less idea than he did. In fact, she had no idea what they expected her to do. She simply sat on her purloined horse and hoped that Wend would have the decency to give her a hint.

Wend said nothing. They all sat, or stood, while the horses fidgeted and the pink of the sky spread and faded toward a gray morning. Below, the mist seemed to be thinning, but not enough to show any landscape that might give Maewen some idea whereabouts they were. She began to feel stupid. This had the feeling of a party when none of the guests turn up.

The man who would be Duke of Kernsburgh obviously felt the same. "Not much sign of a mighty band of followers," he remarked.

Mitt was horribly embarrassed. "*Navis!*" he protested.

Navis! Maewen thought in the greatest relief. Or should I call him Your Grace? No. Stupid. Not yet.

"I suggest we give it till full daylight and then be on our way," Navis said.

It was more of a decision than a suggestion, as if Navis was in charge, but Maewen was simply grateful for someone deciding *something*. "Yes," she said. "That's fine."

It was the first time she had spoken in front of Navis and Mitt. She saw Mitt give her a puzzled glance, as if her voice, or her accent, or something, was not quite right. She glowered at Wend. She was angry enough to smash his smooth, grave, handsome face. He had tricked her into this, and now he was not giving her any help at all. If one of these two noticed she was not Noreth, it would be his fault, and it would serve him right.

Luckily—probably it was lucky—Mitt was distracted by someone else arriving at last. There were clatterings and a light rumbling from the thinning mist below. It could be quite a number of people. Everyone turned that way. The first thing to appear was a lop-eared glum-looking mule. Then a darkness behind it resolved into the rounded canvas cover over a cart, the whole thing painted a sober dark green. The bearded man driving the cart looked as sober as the rest of his turnout. As the cart tipped forward onto the level land beside the waystone, he looked up and reined in the mule as if he were surprised to see anyone there at all. Maewen read the name in sober gold lettering: Hestefan the Singer. Now this was interesting. Her mind shot to Dad's family tree. He could be one of her own ancestors. And she had had no idea that Singers still roamed the land as late as two hundred years ago.

"This is a surprise, Hestefan," Navis said. "Did Noreth inspire you to follow her, too?"

He was even more ironic than he had been before, but Hestefan answered quite simply, "I thought I'd come along. Yes." His voice rolled out foggy breath, full and trained-sounding, but not very deep.

"But," Mitt chipped in, "Fenna's not fit to travel, is she?"

A boy stuck his head out of the back of the cart. "We're not fools," he said. "We left her in Aden-mouth." The gathering sunlight struck red on his head. Maewen could not take her eyes off him. She knew him, too. He was the unknown Singer-boy from the portrait in the palace.

"And Lady Eltruda was good enough to lend us a mule," Hestefan said.

"Lady Eltruda is always generous," Navis said. He seemed to mean this. At least he did not sound nearly as ironic as usual, saying it. "And what of others following? Did you pass any large numbers of folk hurrying to join Noreth?"

Hestefan slowly shook his head. "We were the only ones on the road." Maewen caught the Singer-boy, and Mitt, too, looking at her as if they were afraid she would be very disappointed at this news.

Then everyone was looking at her expectantly.

"Er—" Maewen said. "Well, I suppose we'd better be getting on, then." Thinking that she had better lead the way, she turned her horse toward the green path stretching from the waystone. Then she paused. Wend was on foot. "Will you be able to keep up?" And serve you right if you can't!

Wend put a horrible old baggy cap on his head and smiled his restrained smile up at her. Maewen was growing to hate that smile. "I walk the green ways every day, lady. Unless you gallop, I shall be beside you."

I wish he wouldn't *talk* like that! Maewen thought as the small party set off.

Nobody talked much at first. Maewen was glad of the silence. She had so much to sort out. For one thing, she was still full of quivering animal wariness, first from thinking Wend was mad and then from finding he seemed to have told her the truth. On top of that was the sheer shock of being, really and truly, two hundred years in the past. And one thing sorted itself out of that: This expedition, with herself in place of Noreth, had to be very important. The mere fact that two of the people who had been important enough for their portraits to hang in the palace were on it made this certain. It was frightening—too much responsibility for an ordinary girl who just happened to look like this Noreth. Perhaps, she thought hopefully, Noreth escapes and comes back to take over later. But if that were going to happen—

Here Maewen came hard up against a question which had been nagging at the back of her head from before she laid hands on the golden statue, from the moment Wend first mentioned Noreth. If Noreth was that important, why haven't I seen her name in a history book somewhere? And I haven't, not even once. Dad never mentioned her. None of the guides said a word about her, and they were forever on about Amil the Great. The really frightening thing was that, as Maewen now seemed to be Noreth, *she* was the one who was going to vanish utterly from the face of history. She shivered and tried not to think about Kankredin.

Well, Amil the Great comes along soon. I just have to hand over to him, she thought. That was a much better thought than the idea that she was all alone here having to make history—or fade out of history permanently. I'll simply go on until he turns up. She raised her head and began trying to see where they were.

The green road curved gently ahead, sloping upward a very little, carving its way into the mountains by what seemed the easiest route. At first it ran between high hillsides of brown rock and Maewen could not see very far. The shapes of mountains do not change, she reminded herself. When I see them, I'll know. Even though two hundred years ago there was no big refinery at Kredindale, and Weaversholm was probably hardly a town, there would be something to give her bearings.

But there was nothing to see for some miles, except every so often a rowan tree, leaning like a guardian over the path, or a stream carefully channeled under it. Corners had been built up to keep the road level. Maewen wondered about this road. There was nothing like this that she knew of in her day. Did Wend *mean* it when he said he kept the green roads? She looked at him, striding beside Hestefan's mule. Two hundred years old. He had to be. He had to be of the Undying, then.

She looked round again to find the path coming out on an upland and, like a relief, blue peaks and khaki shoulders of mountains in all directions. They swung slightly right. Maewen stared at the high horseshoe top of Aberath Tor and knew at once where she was. In the far North, right up near Adenmouth somewhere. She and Mum and Aunt Liss lived—*would* live—just twenty miles west of here. But it was no good rushing off home at a gallop. She might find the house—it was old—but there would be strangers living in it. A miserable, lonely thought. And she had been right. Wend had pitched her in right at the start of Noreth's royal ride, and Noreth had been kidnapped, so she was in for *days* of this. Oh—damn!

Maewen turned another glowering look on Wend. And this made her notice that the rest of the party was not entirely happy either. Mitt and Navis rode side by side, but this was so that they could argue in low voices. As she looked, Navis snapped, "I never believed you could be such a prig!"

Mitt answered, "Call *me* names! It was you took advantage!"

"It was *not* taking advantage," Navis retorted. "Surely, with your background, you must have *some* idea of what it means to be married to a hopeless drunkard!" He turned haughtily away, found himself looking at Hestefan, and turned haughtily from Hestefan, too, as if Hestefan displeased him as much as Mitt did.

Hestefan took no notice. He just stared dreamily at the mule's ears. Probably he was a dreamy type, but just then he looked as if he was having rather bitter dreams. The boy—Moril, she had gathered his name was—sat equally dreamily beside Hestefan, plucking at his big old cwidder, but he was no happier. He did not have quite the tragic look that Maewen remembered from the portrait, but she could see he was brooding on something miserable. Whatever this was might have had something to do with Mitt. In between arguing with Navis, Mitt made various friendly remarks to Moril, and Moril either pretended not to hear or else gave a short, snide answer that stopped any conversation dead.

Nobody but Maewen seemed to have met Wend before. After their latest argument Navis tried to talk to him and ignore Mitt. Wend's replies were so polite and humble that Navis raised both eyebrows and gave up. Serve Wend right! thought Maewen. Then she thought, This won't do! What a dreadful way to start an important journey!

Angrily she turned her horse sideways to the rest of them. "What's the *matter* with you all?"

They stared at her out of a confusion of horses and mule half pulled up. Mitt's horse refused to stop and went bucking backward into the stones of the verge. He hit it. "Behave, you Countess, you!"

"Matter?" Navis said with his head haughtily up.

He reminded Maewen of someone like that, but she had not the patience to think who just then. "Yes," she said. "There are only five of you, and every one of you is deliberately annoying all the others. You're to *stop* it, do you hear! Why can't you all be cheerful?"

Mitt, who had on the whole been trying, Maewen had to admit, gave his horse another bang and said resentfully, "That's great, coming from you! Who's been off ahead the whole time, looking like a wet week?"

Moril grinned at this, as if he could not help it.

Maewen glared from one to the other. Boys! "All right. I'll try as well. But I order the rest of you to be cheerful, too!"

Navis asked smoothly, "And how do you suggest we fulfill your orders?"

"*You* can do it by stopping being so damn sarcastic!" Maewen shot back. "And you"—she pointed to Hestefan—"can come out of your dream."

This seemed to alarm Hestefan. He stared at her in a stunned, terrified way which seemed entirely wrong for the kind of person he was. Maewen did not understand, and it cooled her down rather suddenly. She had been about to go on to Mitt and suggest he made peace with Navis and then to Moril and tell him to stop the dumb insolence, but Hestefan's stare made her see that she really knew nothing about what had happened among these people before she met them. Maybe they were right and she was wrong. So she swung round on Wend, as the only one she knew. "And you're to stop being so polite all the time!"

Wend snatched off his cap and seemed about to give one of his humble bows.

"No," said Maewen. "Don't even think of it!"

Navis threw back his head and bellowed with laughter. Mitt snorted. Moril actually giggled. Even Hestefan gave a shaky smile. Maewen thought there might even have been a bit of a grin on Wend's face, too. Thank the One! Maewen heaved a deep startled breath and rode on again, staring at a large bird—eagle?—circling among the nearest mountains, to help herself cool down. How had she *dared* snap at Navis? No matter. It had worked. She could hear people talking behind her in an ordinary, cheerful way now. But she thought she had better go round each of the party and talk privately to them if she could. That way she might piece together what had made them so gloomy.

Mitt came up to ride beside her as she was thinking this. "You've got that golden statue safe, have you?" he said. "Don't forget that it's half mine."

Maewen went hunched and wary again. She had no doubt which statue he meant. The trouble was, it was two centuries away, locked in a glass case in a palace which was not built yet. "Oh yes. Safer than houses," she said, which, she thought, was certainly true.

:|| 7 ||:

HOLDING THAT FIRST conversation with Mitt was one of the hardest things Maewen had ever done. Long before they stopped for what Navis called "a nuncheon," she could feel sweat starting in beads on her face. The air grew milder anyway, warm enough for Maewen to remember that this was, after all, Midsummer Day, but it was not that. It was the sheer difficulty of keeping her end up. She kept looking at Wend, hoping he would give her a hint or so, but Wend simply strode along, easily keeping up with Navis's mare, and said nothing to anyone. Maewen took this to mean that Wend was only going to come to her rescue if she made a really bad mistake.

In a way this was comforting because it meant she had not done anything really wrong yet, but it was frightening, too. She knew her face was a mass of dots, dots of freckle and dots of sweat. She hated herself like that. She kept sneaking looks at Mitt's long, bony profile, hoping he was not too disgusted.

Mitt usually turned and grinned at her. After a while Maewen realized that he was as flustered as she was.

At first she thought it was because she was supposed to be Queen. Then Mitt said, "I'll tell you straight, Noreth. It came as a shock last night, finding out you were so old."

Old! Maewen thought. Oh, *bother* these freckles! He must be at least fifteen! How old does he think I am? Eighteen, said her memory. Noreth went on her ride the Midsummer after she was eighteen. That would seem old to Mitt. "Don't hold it against me," she said. "Please!"

Mitt laughed. "I'll try not to."

This did not make the conversation any easier. Maewen was trying to find out who Mitt was—he had a dreadful Southern accent for someone so far north—and how he knew Noreth, and how he was connected with Navis, and why Moril disliked him so, and why Mitt talked as if he lived in Aberath, not Adenmouth, and what had made him come on this expedition, and Mitt would keep talking about that golden statue. His beastly horse did not help. It kept trying to bite her leg.

Each time Mitt hauled its head round and cursed it. "Stop that! I told you, you Countess, you!"

After about the sixth time, Maewen had to laugh. "It's a gelding. Why do you call it Countess?"

"I told you yesterday," Mitt said, obviously surprised.

Help! "Oh, so you did," Maewen said hurriedly.

It was like that all the time. But Maewen kept on,

because she did need to know, feeling ridiculously flustered for someone riding in the clear open air with mountains slowly wheeling around them on all sides. And at last she seemed to have the story of the statue sorted out. Mitt and Noreth had found it together in the river Aden. Maewen frowned a little at this. There was that odd dream she had had in the train. . . .

"And I need my share of the money," Mitt told her. "I need it bad. It's to help Navis out, too, or I wouldn't keep nagging about it."

Mitt believed in plain speaking, Maewen could see. She liked that, but it made her feel dishonest. "The statue is quite safe . . . honestly," she repeated. She began to hope devoutly that the horse she was riding might have belonged to Noreth. It had been wandering by the waystone. Noreth had meant to meet everyone there, and then she had been kidnapped, so it could have been her horse, if you supposed the kidnappers had hauled her into a carriage and turned the horse loose. If that was so, then the golden statue just *could* be in the roll of baggage behind the saddle.

They stopped to eat in a grassy bay surrounded by high rocks. Maewen made haste to lead her horse to one side across the moist green tender grass, where she hunted through that baggage roll, pretending to look for food. Food she found—bread, cheese, apples, and a fine small pie—though not very much of it, not nearly enough to last all the way to Kernsburgh. She found a clean undershirt and drawers and some socks.

They were all her size, so it did begin to look as if this was indeed Noreth's horse, but there was no statue. What about this roll of blanket, then? It felt unpromisingly soft and light, but Maewen unrolled it all the same. As she did so, someone spoke, close beside her.

"You won't find the statue there. It has been stolen."

It was a man's voice, deep and rather echoing. "What do you mean, stolen?" Maewen said, wondering how whoever it was knew. She looked round, expecting to find herself talking to Navis or Hestefan. She was confounded to see Hestefan many yards away, still dreamily sitting on the driver's seat of the cart, and Navis unsaddling his mare right on the other side of the green bay. It had not sounded like Wend. Wend was anyway sitting against the wheel of the cart, fetching a loaf out of his knapsack. Mitt was over beside Navis. Moril came crawling out of the cart beside Hestefan as she looked. Everyone was too far away to have spoken—unless of course one of them was a ventriloquist. Maewen looked up at the rocks, and all round, and then bent to look under the horse's belly. There was no one else. But the blanket came unrolled as she stooped, showing that it was nothing but blanket. There was no golden statue anywhere in this baggage.

"Who are you?" she said, keeping her eyes warily on all of the other five people. "Where are you? How do you know?"

She had spoken too softly for anyone to have heard her, and none of the others moved. But the voice answered her, seemingly out of the air beside her. "I am the one who has always advised you. And I can feel the statue near. One of those five has it."

"Thanks very much!" Maewen rolled the blanket up. "I can't tell you how that sets my mind at rest!" She thought she was in a state of shock again. Her mind was whirring with it. Whoever had taken the statue could only have taken it from Noreth. Therefore, one of her companions must have helped kidnap Noreth, and that person knew Maewen was a fraud. Why had that person not said? Or was this voice lying?

"I am glad to find you so calm," the voice said. "You speak like the Queen you will be."

Calm! thought Maewen. She rammed the blanket and clothes back in the container and turned back across the grass, juggling pie and cheese and apple with hands that seemed too shaky to hold them.

Moril met her as she came. He was eating a large hunk of bread—one-handed, because his other hand was supporting that cwidder of his. Maewen had yet to see Moril put it down. It was as if it were part of him. She noticed now, without any surprise, that it was the same cwidder that had been in that portrait of Moril, the one that was in the glass case beside it. She was noticing everything just then. She felt like a hunted hare, wild big eyes staring. She noticed that Moril did have a scatter of freckles on his pale skin, rather like hers, only not so many. She noticed he was looking at her wonderingly.

"What's the matter?" he said with his mouth full. "Have you seen a ghost?"

"Yes—or I heard one at least," Maewen said. "Out of the air. A man spoke."

"I thought something happened," Moril said. "I think I need to break my rule again. Just a second." He bit off another mouthful of bread, tossed the rest down on the grass, and put both hands to the cwidder. For a moment he chewed and thought, and then he played a short run of mellow rippling chords.

Peace swept through Maewen, running like strength up her back and down her arms, and relaxing muscles in her face that she had not known were there. She found herself smiling dreamily, thinking that, whatever that voice had been, it had no way to harm her. "Thanks," she said.

Moril left the cwidder humming and looked at her critically. "It was easy," he said. "You're really quite a relaxed person." And he added, very seriously, "Things do happen on the green roads. There are lots of stories."

He bent to pick up his bread. Mitt and Navis sauntered over. Moril must have seen them out of the corner of his eye, because his face went blank and unfriendly, and he went away at once, back to Hestefan.

Maewen sat against the cartwheel to eat, looking out across broken rocks to blue-black mountains, in front of dun-colored mountains, with more jagged mountains beyond that, all under a heavy gray sky. She must get to know Moril, she thought. He had seemed to be one of those dreamy types, entirely wrapped up in himself, but he noticed things, dreamy or not, and that—whatever—he had played on his cwidder had been . . . Well, go on. Say it, Maewen. Magic. That boy is some kind of magician, and I want to know how he does it.

Far off among the mountains an indigo peak caught the sun and was for a moment yellow and green and purple.

Wend pointed a fist holding a piece of cheese. "City of gold!" He and Moril and Hestefan spoke almost in chorus. "Hern's golden city."

"Go on," said Maewen. "It *can't* be! Kernsburgh's miles south of here."

"It's what we say, lady," Wend explained, "when a peak catches the sun—to show we remember the city even though it's long ruined and gone."

"Ruined and *gone*!" Maewen said. "But—"

"It is, though," Hestefan said reprovingly from the cart above her. "Did you not know?"

"I—" Maewen craned round at what she could see of the gray beard. What did Hestefan remind her of? She should have known about Kernsburgh. All the guides in the palace had never seemed tired of pointing out that Amil the Great had rebuilt the city. But none of them had thought to say that he had rebuilt it from nothing. "Ruins and rubble?" she asked.

"More like grass and humps in the ground by what I heard," Mitt told her.

"Oh—*bother*!" Maewen said. "How am I supposed to find a crown in a place like that?"

"How indeed?" Navis murmured.

"A way will be found, lady," Wend said.

Maewen supposed Wend knew. But as they mounted again and moved off, she could not help thinking that this mission was becoming more impossible with every mile they went. She wondered if Noreth had realized and simply run away. Maewen would not have blamed her. Six people set out wandering the old roads—one of those six accused of theft by a voice in the air, too!—in search of a crown buried in a city that did not exist anymore, with no provisions and almost no baggage, and this was supposed to prove that the wrong girl was Queen. As if the earls in their earldoms would let even Noreth get away with it! Maewen uneasily remembered that earls were like little kings in those days, bad kings in the South and better ones in the North, but all of them kings. And kings always made a point of keeping their thrones.

But Amil the Great did it somehow, she told herself. Don't be too long turning up, Amil. I'll hand over to you with the greatest pleasure.

The green road all this while was taking them through another gorge, overhung by more rowan trees. Maewen found she was nervously looking at the skyline, high above, in case an earl had sent a party of hearthmen to make sure they got no farther. It must be an earl who had kidnapped Noreth. One of her five companions was in the pay of an earl.

She felt a great deal better when the road took them out onto a green plain, high, high up. Chilly reviving wind swept over her. Far below, and yet seeming to stand up into the sky, was the gray sea, chopped by white galloping waves.

"This is better," Mitt said, coming up beside her. "Maybe it's being brought up a fisherman; I always like seeing the sea. Or maybe it comes of being a Holander. Eh, Navis?"

Navis had come up on the other side. He was looking out at the sea just as Mitt was—as if it was home, really. He said, "I miss the blue of the sea farther south, but I wasn't displeased the Countess sent me to Adenmouth. Plenty of sea there. And I've never for one moment regretted leaving Holand."

It was odd to hear Navis talk without sarcasm at all. Maewen wondered how to find out what they were both doing so far from Holand, but before she could think how, Navis said to her, "You, of course, will have a special interest in this stretch of sea."

"Why? Do you know something I don't know?" Maewen shot back. A silly thing to say, but Navis had that effect on her.

"I was meaning that we must be quite near Kredindale," Navis said, "where I gather you were born, Noreth. Isn't it your cousin Kintor who's lord here?"

Maewen said quickly, "Yes, but we don't get on." That, she hoped, would stop Navis expecting her to go and visit her cousin. But he can't be right! she thought. It was miles round the coast from Adenmouth to Kredindale. It took ages, even by car. But as they moved on, she saw the long spit of green, scribbled with the ditches of a sea marsh, stretching out into the sea below, where, in her day, the big refinery stood. She had seen it from the train only days ago. It seemed that the old road had cut straight through the mountains.

"Whatever you feel about your cousin," Navis said, "I imagine you could hope to gather quite a number of followers here."

Followers! I hope *not*! Maewen thought. Whatever would I *do* with them?

"Yes, I reckon you're going to have to have an army," Mitt agreed. "Show those earls you mean business."

They were probably both right, but Maewen just could not see herself leading an army. She would feel such a fool. She rode on wondering how to get out of having one.

The coastline made a grand curve, and the road followed it, but so high that Maewen could not see the big Kredindale Valley she knew must be down there somewhere. There, as they came round the curve, was the waystone marking the way down to the valley and—horrors!—really quite a big crowd of people gathered on the clifftops beside it. As Maewen's group came into sight, there was a lot of shouting. She heard the name Noreth! over and over again, and—she couldn't help it—she pulled her horse to a standstill, terrified. Her eyes blurred, and her knees shook.

She said stupidly, "What do you think they want?"

"To talk to you, evidently," Navis replied.

He seemed to be right. A group of people, men and women, was running toward her eagerly, with one man out in front, and the crowd itself was pressing forward behind them, more slowly, in a jog-trot filled with windy wavings of scarves, hair, arms, ribbons, and some kind of long, snapping banners. Midsummer flags, Maewen thought. They must be holding their Midsummer Fair up here. She wanted to shake her horse into a gallop and leave. Fast. But the crowd was blocking the road. And they all looked so glad to see her.

Oh Noreth! she thought. Why did you have to let me in for this?

Wend strode up beside her. "May I hold your horse, lady, while you get down and speak with them?"

Mitt had seen how she was feeling. "I'll go with her. D'you mind holding the Countess, too?" he asked Wend.

"And mine," Navis said, hurling his reins over his mare's head.

Maewen was too grateful almost to be ashamed at how obvious her terror must be. It felt much better walking toward the eager man with Mitt towering slightly behind her on one side and Navis pacing sedately and briskly on the other.

"Noreth Onesdaughter," the eager man greeted her. "We heard tell you'd ride the roads this Midsummer, and you must forgive us that we lay in wait for you, in a manner of speaking, but—" Here the small group of men and women caught up and stood panting, nodding, smiling and staring. "We are all the gang heads at the mines," the eager man explained. "I am Tankol Kolsson, and I speak for the heads. Lady, will you talk to Lord Kintor, your cousin, for us? We are at our wit's end truly and truly do not mean to be lawless the way his new law-woman says we are."

At this all the others in the group burst out talking, too. "Willing workers all," Maewen heard. "The land being that poor" and "No sale in summer so he'll only pay half!" overlaid by "The mines now the main way to make a living" and "Next to nothing if you've a family to feed!" This was half drowned by someone saying over and over, "Then Lord Kintor would have to sell his horses and that we do not want," and someone else saying just as often, "Pay half for what we fetch out and put only a quarter back in winter—that's starvation, lady!" During this the entire crowd arrived, so that Maewen was surrounded and buried in people all shouting, "It's that new law-woman of his! Make him send her away!" or, "We're only miners, lady, and we don't know what to do!"

Mines, she thought distractedly. Miners. She remembered the Kredindale of her day, and the big spoil heaps that had been landscaped with grass and trees down by the coast, with the ruins of chimneys and old mine shafts farther up the hills. There was a colliery museum somewhere. Maewen remembered Aunt

Liss's saying that when she was a girl, Kredindale had been nothing but coal mines wherever you looked. It looked as if it had started being like that very early on. But she had no idea what all these shouting people expected her to do about it.

"Hold hard!" Mitt shouted. "Do you mind not all talking at once!"

Into the slight hush that this made, Navis called, "Let's get this straight. You're in some kind of quarrel with Lord Kintor, and you want this lady to put it right."

Amid the shouts of agreement Mitt said to the eager man, "You. Tankol. If you're spokesman, you tell her."

Tankol was only too ready to tell. The trouble was, he was not one of those people who could tell a thing simply and quickly. Maewen listened for a good quarter of an hour, almost glad of being surrounded by people because the sea wind was cold, even though she found the pressure of all their attention nearly unbearable. At the end of that time she had gathered that her supposed cousin had hired a new law-woman who had told him he would have to sell his horses because there was no demand for coal. There were lots of figures, too, halves, quarters, thirds, which had something to do with the wages miners earned. The main thing Maewen really gathered was that neither Tankol nor anyone else had the least desire to leave Kredindale and follow Noreth as an army.

She ought to have been relieved. She was, in a way. But she was also exasperated. If even the people in Noreth's birthplace did not consider following her, this really did make her mission impossible. But there had to be more to it than this. Mitt and Navis seemed to be following what Tankol said. Maewen turned to them. "Can you explain?"

"A rather familiar story," Navis said dourly, "one I thought I'd left behind with the South."

"Isn't it just!" Mitt agreed. "He's saying this Kintor of yours has hired the law to help him diddle the miners. Kintor's hard up, mind you, because folk can burn peat for nothing. And she's told him—this law lady—that he can halve their wages in the summer and then put a bit back in the winter, without them being able to do a thing about it. If they complain to him, it's unlawful. If they hold meetings about it, that's not lawful either. So what are they to do?"

"They seem to have been smart enough to get round the law by having their meetings as the Midsummer Fair up here, while they waited for you," Navis said. "But one does wonder how many miners' wages your cousin is paying his new law-woman."

Maewen was beginning to feel glad that she could disown this Kintor as her cousin. All the worried faces staring at her had the hollow eyes of people who never quite got enough to eat. Everyone was in holiday best, to judge from the ribbons and embroidery, but they were poor clothes, old and darned and carefully looked after. "Why don't they want him to sell his horses?" she asked.

"Famous bloodstock," Navis said. "Everyone is proud of them."

"Yeah. This is the free North," Mitt said bitterly.

"Free to some," Tankol retorted, quite as bitterly. "You're an Aberath hearthman, lad. You don't know you're born."

Because Mitt looked about to become extremely angry, Maewen said almost without thinking. "Then why don't you go on strike?"

Every face, Mitt's and Navis's, too, turned to her, perplexed. Oh help! she thought. They've never heard of strikes yet. Strikes were unheard of until industry started. And when did industry get going? Maewen wondered frantically. Not quite yet, she was sure. But wasn't it quite early on in Amil the Great's reign? Yes, because she remembered learning that Amil had encouraged industry, particularly in the North. But, oh dear, all the same. Everyone was waiting for her to explain, and she was going to have to send history in a circle, because she only knew about strikes because there had *been* strikes, probably because she had told everyone about them one windy afternoon in Kredindale, because . . .

"It means," she said, "that you all stop work until my cousin agrees to pay you a fair wage."

"But we can't. We'd be turned off work," Tankol protested.

"Oh come *on*!" Maewen said. "My cousin needs you to work the mines. If you all stop, he can't sack you all because he'd starve, too."

"But," said one of the women, "it's like Young Kol said. It's not lawful."

They were so slow and sad and doubtful that Maewen wanted to shake them. "Look. It's not unlawful if one of you is sick and can't get to work, is it?"

"No." Everyone agreed to that.

"Then you all get ill at once," Maewen explained.

This caused a startled, interested silence. Mitt broke it by pointing out what Maewen had always thought was the weak part of strikes. "They'd never get away with that in the South," he said. "The Earl would just send his hearthmen to hang the ringleaders, sick or not. Maybe your Kintor won't do that in the North here. But he'd have to do something. If he didn't, they'd *all* be ruined, him and them together. It goes," Mitt added, just as if he had read Maewen's mind, "in a circle, like."

It did. Maewen wanted to shake Mitt, too. "But there's going to be a huge demand for coal," she said. "Any day—well, any year now—in five years, anyway. I know. There'll be machines—"

Mitt frowned disbelievingly. "You mean, like Alk's Irons?"

Maewen did not know what he meant, so she turned back to persuading the rest of them. "It's true. I really do know. Tell Kintor that if he'll just pay you properly and wait, people will be yelling for all the coal you can mine, and more!"

She heard murmurs, back in the crowd, dubious and awed. "The One speaks to her. She might know, at that." But Tankol, who was clearly a more practical type, said, "You wouldn't be willing to walk down the dale and tell Kintor that yourself, would you, lady?"

"We don't get on. He wouldn't listen," Maewen said. Besides knowing I'm not Noreth, I'll bet. Great One, this is difficult! "Now what I think you should do is wait to go on strike until people start wanting coal again in the autumn, and Kintor really needs you. Then you all say you're sick and—and those that want to can come and join me at Kernsburgh and be my army."

"After Harvest," someone said. "We could, if the harvest's in."

Maewen could feel them all slowly beginning to agree. She felt warm with victory. How was that for brilliance? How was that for a way to recruit an army without having one? How was that for killing several birds with—

Navis canceled all that by asking coolly, "After Harvest? But what, may I ask, will you be doing, Noreth, for the three months in between?"

Doesn't it take that long to get to Kernsburgh then? Oh *hell*! "I shall be very busy," Maewen said.

Navis's eyebrow slid up. But quite unexpectedly Tankol came to her rescue. "Of course she will, hearthman. We all know she'll want to be searching out the Adon's gifts to take to Kernsburgh."

Both of Navis's eyebrows soared. "I beg your pardon? Adon's gifts?"

Tankol, and several other people, gave Maewen knowing smiles. "Southerner, isn't he?" Tankol said. "Knows nothing. But we all know they answer to the true Queen, and even the strongest claim *can* be stronger. Very well, lady. You've mapped us our way. We work all summer and then fall sick of starvation, and those of us still with our strength bargain with Kintor and then vanish away to Kernsburgh. What say, all? Is this what we do?"

To Maewen's considerable amazement, there were shouts of agreement. Navis was possibly even more dumbfounded, but he kept his head even though they were suddenly being jostled every which way in a cheering crowd. He seized Maewen's arm strongly, and quite painfully, just as it seemed that she might be swept away from himself and Mitt, and he shouted, in a ringing voice that came out over all the other voices, "The army is to gather at Kernsburgh. Bring weapons and food if you can. For now, will you please supply the lady Noreth with provisions for her ride."

Maewen thought that last demand was a bit much. These people were so poor. All the same, when Navis and Mitt dragged her clear of the crowd, more than half the people in it were already running the other way to see what the pens and stalls under the banners could supply.

They found Moril angrily hanging on to Mitt's

horse. Hestefan was off the cart, hauling at the mule. Wend, who had enough to do with Navis's mare and Maewen's horse, said, very irritably for him, "That vile gelding with the teeth bit the mule. Tell the boy to take care of it."

Wend doesn't like Mitt, Maewen thought. Doesn't anyone like *anyone* on this expedition?

PART THREE

Ring
and Cup

:║ 8 ║:

"CONGRATULATIONS, NORETH," Navis said as they rode away from Kredindale. Behind them Hestefan's cart was laboring and creaking with its load of provisions. "Tell me, do you intend to call for an army in every dale we pass?"

Maewen had been afraid he was going to ask her that. While Mitt and Navis had been riding about choosing cheeses and bags of oats, and rejecting numbers of skinny upside-down hens, Maewen had put in quite a bit of thought. "I don't think so," she said judiciously. "Kredindale was special. Now they know I'm calling for an army, word will get round."

"I admire your faith," said Navis. "So we—"

"And I admire the way you got all the food organized," Maewen said quickly, to stop him saying what she knew he was going to say next.

"Think nothing of it. I was an officer in Holand before you were born," said Navis. "Although," he added thoughtfully, "it was last year in Adenmouth that really taught me to do ten things at once." Then, just as Maewen was sure she had distracted him, Navis went on, "But as I was about to say, your plan is that we spend the intervening months searching for certain objects with which to bolster your claim? Just what are these Adon's gifts?"

Maewen tried not to sigh. But then people did not get made Duke of Kernsburgh by being easy to distract. The trouble was, she had no more idea than Navis did. "I think," she said, "that the best person to ask is Hestefan. Singers always know more about these things."

"I shall," said Navis. "But you are aware, are you, that none of the earls are going to take kindly to our wandering the green roads like this? Three months will give them ample time to deal with your claim."

Maewen knew he was right. She had been wondering whether to answer this one by saying piously that the One would provide, but she had a feeling that Navis would simply laugh at that. So she did the only other thing she could think of and smiled a secretive, knowing smile—or she hoped it was—and then asked Navis how he came to be in the North.

He had had an adventurous escape from some kind of danger in Holand, she gathered, though as he would only talk about it lightly, in scraps, as if it were a joke rather than a flight for his life. Maewen never quite understood what the danger had been. He had met Mitt for the first time in the Holy Islands. "Mitt appeared to be having dealings with the Undying. Quite beyond my depth," Navis said lightly.

He was so easy to distract that Maewen felt rather sad. She knew he was letting her change the subject, and that had to mean that Navis did not really care what they did in the next three months. Someone like Navis was not going to join this expedition without some other, personal reason. Maewen suspected that he and Mitt were going to leave and go off on their own as soon as that personal reason led them in a different direction.

"Don't worry, Noreth," Navis said. "I promised your aunt I would take care of you. I intend to see you right."

Maewen was still surprised by this when they stopped for the night. The road had plunged them back into the heart of the mountains again, through narrow places full of pine trees, then out again into a sort of crossroads in the green ways. It was a large, lumpy meadow among the crags with quite a number of waystones round the edge. They camped in a flat space among the lumps. People obviously used it regularly. There was a fireplace, a surprisingly clean latrine pit, and sort of caves scraped in some of the humps for sleeping in.

"Where is this?" Mitt asked while Moril was lighting a fire with the bag of coal the miners had given them.

Wend answered, but he spoke to Maewen as if Mitt was just a servitor. "This is Orilsway, lady." Orilsway! Maewen thought. But I went through this in the train. It was a *town*! "It is the northern crossway," Wend explained, pointing to the various waystones. "That leads to Aberath, and that to central parts, with Hannart at the end. Southeasterly, you may go by Ansdale and Loviath, to Gardale and beyond, but I take it, lady, we'll be wanting the way down the end there that goes south to Dropwater."

Maewen looked up at Wend's serious face. Always serious. Why can't he unbend a little? she thought irritably. "I'm considering," she said. "I'll tell you which way in the morning."

Supper was fresh bread, curd cheese, and pickled cherries. Mitt loved pickled cherries. It was not a thing he had met in the South. But Navis spit his first and only one into the fire. "I take it the cherry crop was large in Kredindale," he said. "They should have left it for the birds. Hestefan, tell us about the Adon's gifts."

Hestefan looked up from the other side of the fire. "These are well known to everyone in the North," he said.

"But not to me," said Navis. "Or Mitt."

Mitt threw a handful of cherry stones on the fire. "Speak for yourself, Navis. They're supposed to be the things Manaliabrid gave the Adon in her dowry. There's a sword and a cup and a ring, and the Countess has got the ring in that old collection of hers, back in Aberath."

"And the cup's in the One's chapel at the Lawschool in Gardale," Moril said. "I saw it when I went to see my sister."

"The sword is in Dropthwaite," said Wend. "It is well hidden, but I have seen it."

"And would they answer to the true Queen?" Navis asked Hestefan. "Tankol seemed to think they would, and he's the sort of practical man I'm inclined to believe."

Hestefan had been looking from one to the other, for all the world, Maewen thought, like a schoolmaster who had come prepared to teach and found his class knew all the answers. He had reminded her of a schoolmaster ever since she first saw him—Dr. Loviath, who taught her physics last year, that's who he was like! He said, in exactly Dr. Loviath's repressive way, "There are various kinds of hearsay about the gifts— nothing I have seen myself and nothing anyone is known to have proved."

Mitt, who thought Hestefan was a right stick, took up another handful of cherries and said, "Alk told me the ring always fits the right one's finger. He says it fits the Countess, and not him, because she's descended from the Adon. Mind you, it's a small ring. And you should see the size of Alk's fingers!"

"So that is not proven," Hestefan said, frowning. "Singers are bound only to tell the truth. I can say nothing more."

Moril seemed puzzled. "Yes, but we can tell what people *say*," he said. "And I know they *say* that only the Adon's true heir can draw the sword."

"I can say nothing more," Hestefan repeated.

Maewen tried to smooth things over by asking, "Can

you tell me something I've always wondered? Was the Adon of the Undying?"

It did not work. Hestefan stared at her rather as he had stared before, when she told him to come out of his dream. Then he said grudgingly, "I think not, though he was of their blood. He died twice, you know."

Chalk up two more of us who don't get on, Maewen thought. Hestefan and me. Thoroughly disgruntled, she got up and went to sit on top of a hump some distance away, where she watched the last of the light fading from the highest peaks. The sky was still silvery, but the mountains were bluer and bluer. Over the other way the campfire made it seem quite dark. What was the matter with her? Why should it bother her that nobody in the group got on? She was only a fraud and a substitute, who was in danger of making history go in circles after this afternoon.

That seemed to be it. This afternoon she had done something which really would affect history, and because of that, whether it was impossible or not, she wanted this mad venture of Noreth's to *succeed*. She wanted to take it and make it work. Maybe, when the time came, she would not tamely hand over to Amil the Great. That would be changing history indeed—if only she could think how to do it.

"You dealt very shrewdly with those miners," the deep echoing voice remarked in her ear. "My advice has not been wasted on you."

Maewen jumped and looked round carefully. For as far as she could see in the gloaming, she was alone on her damp green hillock. She could see Navis, Hestefan, and Wend over in the orange light of the fire. Besides, she knew their voices now, and it was none of those three who had spoken. Moril's voice was still a husky treble, and Mitt's tended to crack and rumble. It was that ghost again. Ghosts cannot hurt one, but Maewen did not like the bluish wafts of mist that were gathering in the spaces between the hummocks. She got up casually and started to go back to the fire.

"Now you must acquire the Adon's gifts," the voice said, still at her ear. She walked faster, but it was still at her ear, sending deep, deep vibrations through her. "Find the Adon's gifts. They will prove your claim. They will also give your followers a purpose, and your search will confuse the earls."

This was exactly the idea that Maewen had been fumbling for in her own mind. Perhaps this voice *was* part of her mind. That made it worse. "I'll consider it," she said, and fled.

By the fire everyone seemed to be getting up and settling for the night. But there was no sign of Moril. Moril was the one Maewen wanted. She needed some more magic from that cwidder. She thought she heard it, twanging gently, beyond one of the hummocks to the right. She swerved and ran that way, over a hump and down the other side, where she very nearly trod on Mitt, sitting rather as she had been sitting herself.

Mitt sprang up with a hoarse squawk. Maewen yelled.

"Thank you very much!" Mitt said. "That's all I need for a perfect day!"

"Is anything the matter?" Navis called from the fireside.

"Nothing," Mitt called back. "Just saddlesore. Vinegar!" he said disgustedly to Maewen. "He made me sit in vinegar. Maybe I'd be worse without it, but it doesn't do your temper any good, I can tell you! And then you come charging over this mound. What's up? You seem a bit off from yesterday."

"I was wanting Moril," Maewen said.

"He's off over here somewhere," Mitt said. They wandered that way together, between two lines of vague dark mounds. "Looks a bit like a street," Mitt remarked. "I shouldn't wonder if this wasn't a town once. What do you want Moril for?"

It was soothing wandering between hummocks with Mitt. Maewen found it much easier than she had expected to say, "I'm being haunted. A ghost keeps speaking to me, and Moril helped last time."

Mitt was truly puzzled. "What do you mean, a ghost? Last night you were saying it was the One, your father, who spoke to you. Or is this another voice?"

Help! thought Maewen. Why didn't Wend *tell* me?

"It's—it's always very alarming when he does," she said.

"That's the Undying for you," said Mitt. "What did he say?"

How can he be so matter-of-fact? Maewen wondered. Even for two hundred years ago. But she remembered what Navis had told her. Mitt knew what he was talking about. "He said I ought to have the Adon's gifts," she said. She wanted to ask Mitt if he thought the voice was really the One's, but Noreth seemed to have told him already that it was, so she could hardly do that. Instead she said, "If this is Orilsway, Aberath is only a little way to the north. I can go and get the ring from there tomorrow."

Mitt laughed. It was a hacking, unhappy noise. "You'll be lucky! They'd cut your throat on the spot, girl. I know. I *know* that Countess."

Maewen began, "But—" Then she saw that Mitt, once again, probably knew what he was talking about. Two hundred years before she was born, people really did cut throats. Earls could get away with it then. She changed her objection to "But I need that ring. What should I do?"

"I'll get it for you," said Mitt. It seemed obvious to him that this was what Noreth was angling for. And it ought to be child's play. "I was looking at that ring only two days ago," he explained. "I know just where it is. If I go off now, I can sneak in while it's dark and pick it up with no one any the wiser."

"But you're saddlesore," Maewen protested. "And your horse isn't fresh."

"Teach that horse a lesson," Mitt said blithely. "And I'm not that bad. I was just having a moan."

He was lying a bit about the soreness. Ouch! Flaming Ammet! he thought as he mounted the surprised and reluctant Countess-horse. But he kept his mouth shut. Noreth's face, which he could see as a pale, anxious oval, was lifted toward him from beside the hummock he had used to mount. She was worrying, anyway. As he set off beside the half-seen waystone that marked the road to Aberath, he thought that she would have to give over this habit she seemed to have of worrying about everyone. She'd go off her head with it if she got to be Queen.

The green road, as they all seemed to be, was level and smooth and surprisingly easy to follow in the dark. The Undying did a good job, Mitt thought, if it was them who made the roads. And he was pleased to find that after years of indoors work, he had not lost the knack he had learned as a fisher lad of finding his way in the night. You did it the way they said bats did, mostly. Sort of by feel. Whenever the road turned, he could feel the air pressing off the bigger bulks of rock, and he knew to veer left or right, even when he could not see the pale grayishness of the track. The Countess-horse, to be fair to it, had the same knack, when it consented to go.

It made quite a fuss at first. After a mile of head tossing, loitering, and pretending to go lame, and hearty cursing from Mitt, it chose to surprise him by consenting to go. They thudded on at a fair pace. Mitt, in order not to think of the trouble he might be in if he got caught at the mansion, tried to work out why he was going off to get this ring for Noreth.

It might have belonged to the Adon, but whatever Alk said, Mitt was fairly sure it was just a ring. The Northerners could believe in these things if it made them happy, but Mitt had been brought up by the practical Hobin, making guns for a living in Holand, and he knew that the only virtue that ever got into a piece of metal was fine, careful workmanship.

Right. That was the ring. Did he believe the One wanted Noreth to have it?

Mitt had a little more difficulty here. He had never met this One the Northerners made so much of. Or had he? Mitt narrowed his eyes into the mild wind of the night as he remembered finding the golden statue and that great deep voice crying, *"There!"* That had surely not been Noreth shouting. Well, keep an open mind there. But would the greatest of the Undying be that bothered about a ring?

You could say it was Mitt himself bothering. If he took this ring, it would prove to the Countess that Mitt was not her hired murderer. That could be true. But it was fairly clear to Mitt that he was riding through the night like this simply because Noreth thought she needed the ring. That nervous, freckly look of hers made you want to do things for her. So you did them. And then trusted to Navis to get them all out of the consequences, Mitt added to himself as he came out beside the waystone above Aberath.

The Countess-horse knew where they were. It slithered gladly down the raked track to the town. Mitt was almost sorry for its disappointment when he dragged it over to the woods beyond the first fields and—to its incredulity—left it tied to a tree. It made its feelings plain, quite loudly, and several other horses answered it from stables in the town.

"Shut *up!*" Mitt told it. "Be quiet or *I'll* bite *you* for a change!"

He ran away round the fields toward the cliff. Reproachful horse noises followed him for a minute and then stopped with a sigh Mitt could hear even at that distance. He grinned and ran with long strides. His legs ached from being wrapped round a horse so long, and it was good to stretch them in spite of his soreness. He supposed he had vinegar to thank that he could run at all. He only stopped running when he was looking down at the pale heaving sea. There he paused to speak to the Undying he did know.

"Alhammitt," he said. "Old Ammet. Do you hear me? I'd be much obliged if you and Libby Beer could keep an eye on me in the mansion. If I get caught there, quite a few people are going to be in trouble."

There was no sign from the glimmering sea, but Mitt felt better as he hurried along the clifftop to the place where all the children regularly scrambled round the wall. He nipped round, quietly and carefully, and there he was out in the space by Alk's shed. It was so easy Mitt could hardly believe it.

It went on being easy. Mitt slithered in among the buildings of the mansion, from well-known spot to well-known spot, and not a person moved or a sound disturbed the place except for the faint crunch of his own feet when he crossed the gravel court in front of the library. There were one or two dim lights in some of the upper windows. Otherwise he would have thought the place was empty. It reminded him of times in Holand when he sneaked into strange places with a forbidden message. In fact, it was too much like that. The mansion did not feel like anywhere he had ever lived anymore. Nor was it now, he thought ruefully, as his feet carefully inched through the dark archway and met the flight of stairs up to the library.

At the top his hand met the door and found the handle. Gently, gently, he turned the great latch ring and pushed the door open on the woody, booky mustiness inside. It was so dark in there that he realized he was going to have to find the glass case where the ring was by memory and feel. But since he was going to have to break the glass and someone might hear, he shut the door behind him as gently as he had opened it. He took a step into the room.

Cree-eak.

"Flaming Ammet!" Mitt muttered. "Wish I'd remembered how *noisy* this dratted floor was!"

Light came on, blindingly, with a metal clapping sound.

:∥ 9 ∥:

Mɪᴛᴛ ᴅɪᴅ ɴᴏᴛ ᴇᴠᴇɴ feel despair. He felt dead. He was caught, as he had always known he would be one of these days. He simply stood, blinking to see through the light, wondering if it was only the Countess lying in wait for him or Earl Keril as well.

The light was a dark lantern standing on the selfsame case he had intended to rob. When Mitt tore his eyes sideways from it, he could see the bilious visage of the Adon's portrait, still on its easel. Beside that, in a big dark wood chair, Alk was sitting, bulky and blinking. Either the light had blinded him, too, or he had been asleep—asleep was most likely, because Alk yawned before he spoke.

"I told you," he said, "not to do anything stupid until you'd talked to me. Did you shut the door?"

Mitt nodded.

"Then come over here," said Alk.

Mitt went, still without any word to say, over several miles of violently creaking floor, until he was beside the table and the glass case, and in front of Alk's chair.

Alk put out a beefy hand and carefully closed down the iron shutter of the lantern until the library was nothing but shadows all round them.

"Now stand over there," Alk said, pointing the other beefy hand.

Mitt moved, regretfully, away from the table and the glass case, and stood at the edge of the pool of light, beside the easel. Alk was alone, but this was no comfort. Mitt knew very well how quick and strong Alk was. Alk had put him where it was impossible for Mitt to get to the door before Alk did.

"Doing a bit of studying tonight," Alk remarked, yawning again. "Or so I told my Countess. I had a bit of a conversation with her, like I told you I would, and I wasn't pleased with what she had to say at all. To put it bluntly, as soon as Keril was out of the way, we had words—which is not a thing we've ever had before." He blinked at Mitt, as sleepy and glum and grim as Mitt had ever seen him. "What do you think about that? You being the cause of those words."

Mitt cleared his throat, which had somehow closed solid. "I'm sorry."

"Glad to hear it," said Alk. "So then I had a think. And it seemed to me that in your shoes I'd be trying ways to wriggle out of the bind they'd got you in. Am I right?"

Mitt cleared his throat again. His voice still came out hoarse and desperate. "I'm not doing any killing!"

"So I should hope!" said Alk. "But I'm glad to hear you say it. What's she like, this Noreth?"

"Freckly," said Mitt. "Full of life. I took her for a boy at first. She's all right. She's got her head screwed on more than you'd expect, considering."

"Has she, now?" said Alk. "Then what's she up to, riding the King's Road with you for a follower? That doesn't sound too clever to me. There's more earls around than Keril and my Countess who'll want to put a stop to that."

"I know. Put like that, it sounds right daft." But daft though it was, Mitt found himself defending Noreth. "She cares about people, and she's got some good ideas. People will come to her. And she *has* got a claim."

"As to that," Alk said, "so have a lot of people got a claim. She's saying she descends from the Adon over beside you and his second wife, Manaliabrid—right? Now I've been reading up again on all that."

His big hand made a gesture, down by the lantern and the glass case it stood on. There was a spread of books there, several of them open, others with markers in. One of the markers was a shoehorn; another was a six-inch nail. Typical of Alk. Mitt would have grinned at any other time.

"My law stuff is a bit rusty after all these years," Alk explained. Mitt was not sure he believed that. "But I've been finding out that even the Adon didn't have that good a claim to be King. But he took the crown, so we'll take it from there. Now if this Manaliabrid was who she said she was, she certainly made his claim better. She claimed to be of the Undying, daughter of Cennoreth and great-granddaughter of the One. Well, no one seemed to doubt she was, so we'll give her that. Now she and the Adon had two children, a son and a daughter. And either these two were a great disappointment to their parents, or *they* weren't any too sure of their claim either, because neither of them made the least push to rule after. The son, Almet, took the kingstone, but all he did with it was go off to the South and govern a little lordship that's dead and gone now, somewhere near Waywold. And the daughter, Tanabrid, was quite satisfied to marry and settle down in Kredindale. After that there were marryings and intermarryings, the way there are, and Kredindale gets related to half the earls of the North. What I'm saying, Mitt, is that the claim's rubbish. Her cousin Kintor has a better claim, and so has my Countess or that soft-faced boy in Dropwater."

Mitt felt a bit light-headed. The last thing he had expected was for Alk to sit there talking family trees at him. He could only suppose that Alk was trying to make him feel foolish and give up the whole idea. So probably the Countess had not told him about Hildy and Ynen. "Yes, but—"

"You're going to say she says her father was the One," Alk interrupted. Mitt had not been, but he held his tongue. "Now there we're into the difficult part."

Alk leaned back in his chair. It creaked horribly. "Even King Hern only claimed the One as his grandfather—which is probably just what we say when we call the One our Grand Father." Alk tipped his face round to look at Mitt, across what had been a beautifully ruffled lawn collar but was now dirty laundry. "I've seen the One," he said, to Mitt's surprise. "Several times. Not a thing I talk about to everyone. You'd know why, if it ever happened to you. And . . . well . . . it's like coming into a shadow all of a sudden, or the shadow coming into you. A bit like this." Alk's hand went out and downward across the narrow slit he had left in the shutter of the dark lantern. A huge hand-shaped darkness swept across the floor and Mitt and the wall of books beyond. Mitt shivered. "See?" said Alk. "He's there, but not solid—but I could be wrong. And Noreth's mother's not alive to tell me I'm wrong, is she?"

When Earl Keril had said something like this, Mitt had not felt it mattered. Coming from Alk, it did. "But the One talks to her," he protested. "I think I heard him. And it scares her."

"I don't doubt you," said Alk. "That's the most difficult part of the difficult part. If the One has an interest in all this, us mortal folk had best tread very wary. You don't cross the One. I wish my Countess would see that. But that Keril's one of your new, reasonable folk, and the Undying are just out-of-date beliefs to him. And she listens to him." He leaned his massive arms on top of the books and pondered glumly.

After a moment Mitt said, "Were you expecting me

. . . to come back here?" His voice was still annoyingly hoarse.

"After a fashion. It was one of the options," Alk replied. "I was here on the off chance you'd take the option of going along with this Noreth and helping her claim. I knew I was right when that nag of yours started sounding off in the meadows. Woke me up. Probably woke the dead, too. She's after the Adon's gifts, isn't she?"

Mitt's heart sank. He felt himself sag slightly.

Alk noticed. He never missed much. "I thought so. She knows, and you know, she's got no real claim. You were going to pinch this ring here, weren't you?"

Mitt managed a small, throaty "yup."

"And I thought you never believed it answers to the right blood!" Alk smiled slightly, his face all slabs of shadow and curves of light. He shook his head. "I wish I knew how the man who made it *did* it. I've tried all ways to catch it changing size, but I never can pin it down. And my Countess can put it on any finger and both her thumbs, and it'll fit her. I made Gregin try it, and it fell off him. So I've no doubt it would fit your Noreth whatever size her hands are."

"Small." Mitt's eyes went longingly to the glass case, where the ring picked up gleams of light underneath the lighted pane of glass, as if it were underwater. It looked as always very big, nearly big enough to fit one of Alk's massive fingers. If it did not fall straight off Noreth, it would be a miracle indeed.

"But it's a stupid way to get out of a mess," Alk

said. "And I know you're in a mess, Mitt. Take this ring, or put a foot wrong any other way, and my Countess will have you—or Keril will. My sense is, they don't mean you to live too long. Or maybe they mean you to spend the rest of your days as their hired murderer. My Countess wouldn't admit to one or the other, but it has to be that."

Mitt nodded. He had worked this out, too. He tried to imagine Alk twisting the information out of the Countess, and he just could not see it. It was like imagining one of Alk's engines running straight up a house.

"And the only way you can keep out of that," Alk continued, "is to stay completely lawful and not give them a handhold. If you do that, I'm on your side. Will you promise me you won't murder or steal or anything like that?"

Alk didn't understand. It was clearer than ever to Mitt that the Countess had not told Alk about Hildy and Ynen. "What else *can* I do?" Mitt said, trying to talk round it.

"Uh-uh," said Alk. "Promise, I said."

"I'd rather not," Mitt said. "Something might come up."

"Fish feathers," said Alk. "I put it to you, you've done nothing outside the law yet. You went off to visit Navis Haddsson. You came back to have a chat with me."

"I came to pinch that ring," Mitt said, looking at it gleaming below the glass.

"But only I know that, and you're not going to," Alk said. "Whatever threats they made to you, I'll stand by you if you give me that promise."

Whatever threats? Perhaps Alk did know about Hildy and Ynen then. Mitt looked searchingly at Alk's big shadowy face. It gave nothing away. "What can *you* do against Keril?" he said.

"Hold him to the law," said Alk. "I don't know! Everyone round here seems to have forgotten I used to be a lawman once upon a time! And the law's the same whether you're an earl or a fisherman. Are you going to give me that promise?"

"I—" Mitt was not sure he dared.

"I'll make it easier for you," said Alk. "You didn't come here to steal that ring. You came here to ask me to *give* it you."

"*What?*" It was odd how the library seemed to be a brighter, warmer, freer place all of a sudden. "You couldn't do that," Mitt said, trying not to laugh. "She'd notice."

"I made a copy," Alk said, "trying to get it to change size the same way. And I couldn't do it. It's just a ring. But it looks just the same. Now what d'you say?"

"I promise," Mitt said. "You won't know me, I'll be so lawful."

"That'll be the day!" said Alk. Smiling a little, he fetched out a small key that was marking a place in another of his books and stood up to move the lantern and unlock the glass case. The dim light swept around the room, and his vast shadow blotted half the library into darkness. "Remember," Alk said as he turned the key, "that the One has an interest in this, and don't go forgetting you promised."

Mitt looked at that vast shadow and shivered. "I'll bear it in mind."

Alk lifted the glass lid, fetched out the ring, and held it where the light from the lantern was strongest. It was a plain heavy ring, made of gold, and its only ornament was the big seal carved out of some kind of red stone into the haggard-looking profile of the Adon. Alk's huge, deft fingers twiddled it. "Safest way to carry it is to wear it," he said. "Put your hand out."

Mitt spread his long, bony hands into the light. Alk tried to slip the ring on the ring finger of Mitt's right hand. It stuck at the knuckle. "I got big lumps there on all my fingers," Mitt said.

"You put it on then," said Alk.

Mitt took the heavy ring and, still barely able to believe Alk was letting him have it, tried it on finger after finger. Each time it slid only as far as Mitt's first knuckle. The only finger it would fit, and only with a struggle, was the little finger of his left hand.

"Well, at least it won't fall off," Alk said. "Off you go then, and give it to your Noreth. And if she wants you to do anything else unlawful, you say no. Understand? And I'll back you up."

"Thanks," Mitt said. It was truly heartfelt.

He was not any too clear about much of the journey back. He scrambled back round the mansion wall.

That took concentration because it meant balancing on the edge of the cliff above the sea. After that some kind of reaction hit him. Things came and went. He remembered getting onto the Countess-horse, because it tried to bite him as usual, and—dimly—going up the rake to the green road, because that took all the concentration he had left. But as soon as the horse was on the road to Orilsway and there was nowhere else it could go, Mitt was probably asleep in the saddle. He thought he dreamed that Alk had given him the Adon's ring. It had to be a dream, he decided, waking up about a hundred yards from the camp, because it was just not probable that Alk would do a thing like that. Why had he woken up? He thought it was the Countess-horse, which had gone from a stumbling plod to a much more eager pace. No, it seemed to be because something was wrong with his left hand.

Wrong! That was an understatement. He felt as if his little finger had been clamped in one of Alk's vises. And someone was still twisting the vise. Throb, throb, throb. Mitt could *feel* his finger swelling. He dropped the reins and wrenched at the ring. It would not budge. Flaming Ammet! He could have pulled his finger off sooner than moved that ring! He had to have light—help—something! He shot down from the horse and rushed toward where he thought the camp was.

Maewen sprang up. She had been half listening, not really asleep, hoping she had not got Mitt into trouble with this Countess of his. She heard mad, blundering footsteps, followed by a cracking voice swearing and then demanding, "Where *is* this flaming camp then? They *can't* have all gone off and *left* me!" Maewen ran in that direction. And there was Mitt, a demented leggy figure in the near dark, racing toward the southernmost waystone, apparently wringing his hands.

"What's the matter?"

Mitt rushed up to Maewen and towered over her, still pulling at his finger. "I got you the ring. The flaming thing's stuck on my finger! I think I'm in it for life!"

Maewen seized the hand he flapped in her face. She could feel the ring, a tiny metal waist in a finger that seemed as large and hot as a fresh-cooked sausage. "Oh my lord!" She tugged. Mitt yelped. It was most well and truly stuck. "Don't you know any better than to put on a ring that's too small for you?"

"How should *I* know? I never wore a ring in my life!"

"Well, you should have *thought*! People were small in the old days!" But this *is* the old days. *He's* not small. Never mind.

They bent over Mitt's hand, both of them in the same panic. "I'm stuck in this thing for*ever*!" Mitt squalled.

"Lick it. See what lots of spit does," said Maewen. "Or soap." There had been no soap in her baggage roll. But surely soap *was* invented by this time? No one struck her as *that* dirty. "Or—water—water might cool your finger down."

"I've got some soap," Moril said from beside them. "Shall I fetch it?"

"Yes, and a light, too," said Maewen.

Moril dashed away. Mitt put his hand to his mouth and slobbered on it mightily. Maewen helped him spread the spit up and down the swollen finger. Then she pulled. Mitt pulled. Neither of them had budged the ring one fraction by the time Moril dashed up again with a piece of soap and a lighted lantern from the cart. By the light Moril looked both awed and scornful.

"That's the Adon's ring?" he said.

"Yup," said Mitt, soaping for his life.

"It only fits people with royal blood," Moril pointed out.

"I know *that*!" Mitt snarled. "I only wore it not to lose it, you stupid little—"

"Cool it, cool it," Navis said, arriving with a slopping leather bucket.

"Oh no!" said Mitt. "Keep him away from me! He'll try to boil it off or something!"

"It's only cold water," Navis said. "Put your hand in it."

"Yes, that should take the swelling down." Wend agreed, coming, yawning, up beside Navis.

Mitt plunged his hand in the bucket. Took it out, soaped it, hauled on the ring, sighed, and put his hand in the water again. He did this four more times. "I'll bring this water to the boil, at this rate," he grumbled. As he plunged his hand in for the sixth time, Hestefan arrived, yawning, rubbing his beard and wanting to know what the fuss was about. By this time it was plain to Maewen that she could not have kept the theft of the ring secret, as she had meant to, any more than if she had shouted it from the top of the nearest mountain.

As Mitt took his hand out of the bucket for the seventh time, Wend said wearily, "Here. Let me." He seized Mitt's bony wrist in one hand and the ring with the other. And dragged.

"*Yow!*" said Mitt. "Leave me my hand!"

But the ring was off. Everyone was silent while Wend held it under the lantern light, where they could all see the red stone flash, and then passed it to Maewen.

She felt sweat popping out among her freckles. "This is the Adon's ring," she said, making a clean breast of it, "that Mitt very kindly—er—obtained for me. I intend to collect all the Adon's gifts. Tomorrow we're going to Gardale."

"How convenient," Navis murmured to Mitt. But Mitt was watching Maewen across the finger he was sucking. They were all watching.

Maewen realized there was no way she could distract them. She was going to have to put this ring on, now, under the light, and it was not going to fit. It was huge. Mitt's fingers might look long and bony, but each of them would have made two of hers. If Dad was right, she told herself, Mum does go back to Amil the Great somewhere. But she was afraid that drop of royal blood had got very watered down by the time it came to her. She took a deep breath—and an even deeper risk—and slipped the wide gold band round her right thumb, this being the only place it had even a chance of fitting. And it fitted. Everyone sighed.

"I'll see to your loathsome horse," Navis said to Mitt. "You get some sleep."

:‖ 10 ‖:

I⟨T TOOK SOME DAYS⟩ to get to Gardale, even straight through the heart of the mountains. Long before they got there, everyone except Mitt was heartily sick of pickled cherries. Mitt was simply sick with himself. The Countess-horse was tired and subdued, and he rode slackly at the rear, watching clouds come down and stream like gray scarves below spiky black mountain peaks, and then seeing those mountains wheel aside to show more and yet more ranged behind, and clouds stream against those mountains, too. It seemed as if the green road was gradually rising to take them through the central heights of the North.

Mitt supposed it was all very beautiful and grand, though it was not what he was used to. It was harsher than the sea and even more obviously cruel. And empty. One of the times they stopped, Navis remarked that they had not met another soul on the way. "Everyone is at home celebrating Midsummer, I imagine," he said. "It makes this the best time to travel and not be found."

Mitt simply grunted, "Good." His mind would not seem to let go of that promise he had made to Alk. In a way it was a weight off his mind. That worried him. It seemed so feeble to shelter behind a promise. Smug. Now I can do no wrong, you said, and ended up doing nothing, like a total failure. At the same time he had a gloomy feeling that the promise clamped him round as tight as that ring had, and that meant doing nothing, too, and total failure *that* way. It was worse than Keril and the Countess.

Maewen kept rubbing the red stone of the ring on her thumb. It became quite a habit. The voice had told her to get this ring, and she had got it. Somehow that made her uneasy. She had the same fizzing, doing-wrong feeling about it that Wend had given her in the train and in the palace. Without exactly admitting it to herself, she was careful never to be alone somewhere where one of the others could not hear. She suspected, again without admitting it, that the voice would only speak to her when she was on her own. And that was all mixed up with a nasty suspicion that the voice was part of her own mind, perhaps something to do with being sent back in time. It was bound to make your mind play tricks on you.

She would have liked to talk to Mitt or Moril about it. But Mitt either rode glumly on his own or else made the kinds of jokes that meant he did not feel like talking, and Moril was usually inside the cart, playing scales and pieces of tunes on different instruments. When

Moril did emerge, it was to drive the cart while Hestefan sat with his legs hanging over the tailgate, practicing different instruments, too. Their small procession went to shards and trills of music most of the time, higher and higher into the central peaks. The clouds came damply about them. It was never easy to sleep at night.

Maewen stayed with Navis. She liked Navis. He was so efficient and imperturbable. It fascinated her the way he never let an evening go by without polishing his mare's tack and his own boots. In the mornings he brushed his hair and his clothes, and then, unfailingly, he shaved in whatever water was going, usually icy cold from a mountain stream. And he was so sharp, too. One morning Navis cut himself shaving. He exclaimed with annoyance and tried to keep the blood from running into the collar of his shirt. Wend, without a word, produced a clump of cobwebs from somewhere.

Navis said, "I thank you," gratefully. But as he pressed the cobwebs to his chin, Maewen saw his eyes go narrow and turn for just an instant to Wend's smooth chin. After that Navis's countenance was as bland and composed as ever, but Maewen knew he was wondering why Wend, a grown man, never seemed to shave or grow a beard either.

It interested Maewen, too. Maybe this was a sign of the Undying. But she did not like Wend enough to ask him.

From that day on, the green road was up in the clouds. Everything was moist and white. As Mitt rode in the rear, everyone ahead had turned into quiet gray shadows. A dewdrop gathered on his nose.

"I hate this!" he told the Countess-horse. It was the sort of remark he knew it would agree with.

Moril hopped out of the cart and walked beside Maewen's horse. She did not blame him. It was warmer walking, and no one was going fast in this fog. After a while she dismounted herself, and they walked side by side, talking, leading her horse. Maewen was surprised and glad at how ready Moril was to talk. He told her how it felt to lead a Singer's life, and the new way he wanted to treat the old songs, and about his plans for the future. She encouraged him. Ever since she had seen that portrait, she had had an ache somewhere about Moril. And without putting it to herself that she was once again trying to change history, she wanted badly to comfort him. It would be wonderful if she got back to the Tannoreth Palace to find that the portrait smiled instead of looking wretched.

Coming behind, Mitt honestly tried not to hear what was obviously a private conversation. He wondered about pushing past and riding on ahead where he could see the sketchy gray bulk of the cart, but the road was in a narrow ravine here, with wet black rocks close on either side, and it would have meant forcing his way through beside Moril or the horse, which would remind both of them that he was there, overhearing. He could see Moril's pale face turned eagerly to Noreth, as he told her about the dangers in the South, where Singers were often called upon to carry illegal messages. Noreth certainly had a way with her, Mitt thought ruefully. *She drew me out the same way.* Now Moril was telling her how he had come North last year after his father had been killed.

Moril's voice cracked a little. Mitt reined back the Countess-horse and tried to keep well behind. He knew that if he were to tell Noreth about *his* father, he would want no one listening in. But the horse had a long, rangy stride, and he kept catching up. He was up close behind again in time to hear Moril explaining that Hestefan was no relation. "He came to Hannart while I was there," Moril said. "And I asked him to take me with him. We went off secretly because I knew Earl Keril wanted me to stay."

Keril's name was enough to send Mitt backward again. This time he dismounted and walked, too. It was warmer that way, as well as slower. He tried to keep the three shapes ahead looking like pale gray shadows, out of hearing and almost out of sight. But Mitt's stride was as long and rangy as the Countess-horse's, and somehow, before long, he was able to overhear again.

"I told Hestefan I'd follow you on my own if he didn't want to come," Moril was saying. "But he said he'd better come because great events afoot need a Singer to record them. I'm sorry he's so neutral. I'm not. I think it's like the time Osfameron followed the

Adon. Did you know Osfameron was my ancestor? My big cwidder used to be his."

Something about this seemed to make Noreth modest and uncomfortable. Mitt could hear her trying to change the subject. He waited for them to get ahead again. The mist seemed to be thicker here, perhaps because the ravine had widened. They were going past a chain of dimly seen lakes, each one like faintly rippled milk under the fog. Mitt thought he kept well behind while they passed three of these lakes, but he must have caught up again gradually, because he was able to hear Moril's voice then, evidently in the middle of something upsetting.

Noreth's answer floated back clearly. "But Navis couldn't possibly have known about Olob when he shot Dapple. Be *reasonable*, Moril."

"I know," Moril answered. "I didn't say it was reasonable. Anyway, he's Earl Hadd's son, and I hate him for that."

"He couldn't help being born," Maewen said patiently. "And Mitt's definitely not a noble, and he *didn't* shoot your horse. You can't just lump him in with Navis like that."

"Can't I just!" Moril said. "I hate all Southerners." For a while neither of them said anything else. Mitt, walking on the soft grass beside the milky lake, thought they had gone out of hearing again. Then Moril said, "I'll tell you why I really dislike Mitt. He makes jokes all the time—about serious things."

I do not so! Mitt thought indignantly. It occurred

to him that though Noreth might have forgotten he was there, Moril probably knew perfectly well.

"A lot of Southerners do that," Maewen said. "It doesn't mean they aren't serious."

"Mitt's *never* serious," Moril said contemptuously. "Look at the way he joked when he was bearing witness about the One's statue. That made me so angry I broke my rule. I told you how I swore not to use the power of my cwidder. Well, I knew it was *serious* that you'd been given a sign to set out on the King's Road. So when you told everyone to follow you, I started to play the song with the power, to show people that it was important and they shouldn't follow you unless they really meant it."

Noreth, Mitt noticed, did not point out that the song seemed to have misfired a little. She said, "That was nice of you." And Mitt wondered if perhaps Moril did not know he was just behind them after all.

"You should watch Mitt," Moril said. "He's trying to suck up to you, the way all Southerners do. But he's shifty, too. He may even have been sent North as a spy."

Right! Mitt thought. That does it! Moril knew he was there. He had no doubt of it now.

Maewen said, "Now you're being ridiculous, Moril. I shan't listen to you if you're going to talk like that."

Mitt thought it was nice of her, but he was not in the least mollified. As the mist began to thin to a moist yellow, and Navis shouted back that there was a good place to stop for a nuncheon, Mitt thought, If that little sneak says *one more thing*! He towed the Countess-horse out of the mist to find everyone else sitting on wet rocks unpacking bread, cheese, and pickled cherries. Here, the ravine with the lakes had opened into what was almost a meadow. The horses moved about in it, trying to crop the grass, half hidden in golden shifting mist that might have been the top of a cloud.

The bread was stale. Everyone ate quickly and packed up again. "We're at the highest point the green roads go, lady," Wend told Maewen. "From now on it is down toward Gardale."

"Oh good," she said. "Real food. If I eat one more pickled cherry, I might scream. Or does anyone know a way to cook them to make a change?"

"I might have a notion," Mitt said. "On a skewer, like, with cheese and a bit of that bacon."

They were all moving about, getting ready to go on. Moril gave Maewen a meaning look as he went toward the cart. "See what I mean? Sucking up to you."

Mitt went after Moril with giant strides, roaring, "You take that back, you little slime-bag!"

Moril turned round against the tail of the cart. He was prepared. He was holding his cwidder in front of him like a shield. "What should I take back?" he said coolly. "*Didn't* someone order you to suck up to her?"

There was enough shrewd truth in this to make Mitt even angrier. The cwidder made a poor, fragile shield, but a year in Aberath had taught Mitt the value of a beautiful old instrument like that. He knew it was less of a sin to break Moril instead. "You little coward!" he said, grabbing for Moril's arm.

Moril swung aside and tried to pluck a chord on the cwidder. Mitt's hand, lashing out in what was now the wrong direction, hit the strings as Moril's fingers plucked them. The cwidder boomed. It was a mighty chord, and it seemed to boom on and on. Mitt felt the hairs on his outstretched arm stand upright. What Moril felt he had no idea, but he felt something strongly. There was shock all over his white face. To Mitt it was as if he had just punched a cwidder made of solid granite.

Then they were both in rushing cold water up to the shoulders.

The other four travelers scrambled for the panicking animals. Wend seized the mule's bridle on the other side from Hestefan, and together they hauled mule and cart through the rushing shallows and out onto the strip of turf beside the rocks. The three horses were all farther in. Maewen was soaked all over as Mitt's horse floundered past her and galloped away down the bank, but she managed to catch her own before it followed Mitt's. Navis was just beyond her, soothing his mare while he dragged her through rolling stones and racing current. Maewen and he made it to the cliffside almost together, where they turned, both dripping, and stared at a sudden mighty river where there had only been grass before.

The river was a good half mile wide and one of those tricky, spiteful stretches of water, full of upreared rocks and vicious back eddies, flowing with a force that made it hard to stand up in. Mitt and Moril were a long way out in it, much farther away than Maewen had expected, staggering this way and that and, as far as she could see, still screaming insults at one another in spite of it. At the moment when she looked, they were submerged to Moril's shoulders and Mitt's chest. Moril had his cwidder held high in both hands. He was raising a bubbling wave of water under his chin as he pushed and surged, and almost fell sideways into a hidden pothole, trying to make his way to the nearest big rock. She could hear Mitt's voice faintly through the incredible noise of the water, roaring at Moril.

"Stop them, somebody!" she said.

Mitt surged after Moril, grabbing angrily. The result was that Mitt went sideways into the same hidden pothole and vanished underwater. He emerged almost at once, flailing sheets of spray and yelling with rage.

"A bit hard to do anything from here," Navis observed.

Moril made it to the rock. He put the cwidder carefully down on a dry space and, scrabbling and hauling, managed to drag himself onto the rock, too, brown and skinny with wet as a drowned weasel. Mitt was still in the water with a white wave frilling round his neck. Moril knelt on the rock and called down at him derisively.

"If you want to stop this," Hestefan said, coming up beside Navis, "someone must go and take that cwidder away. It's a thing of great power. Moril ought not to be trusted with the thing."

Navis shrugged. "Really? I should never have guessed. And how do you suggest we remove the cwidder? But while you consider that problem, please do not underestimate Mitt. I have reason to believe he can call on power of his own."

Maewen thought both of them were being utterly unfeeling. She looked at Wend for help. Wend was pale, subdued, and awe-stricken. "It's not for any of us to interfere, lady," he said. "They have put themselves in the hands of the One himself."

"O-oh!" Maewen said. *"Fiddlestick!"*

She looked helplessly out at that distant rock.

Out there, up to the neck in racing river, Mitt said, "What do you mean, look what I made you do? Of all the feeble, wingeing things to say! It's *your* flaming cwidder that did this!"

To his surprise Moril seemed quite ashamed. But his white face remained mulishly set. "I meant the rest of it," he said. "You try to get on this rock, and I'll kick you off!"

"And a fat lot of good it's going to do us, each squatting on a different rock!" Mitt bawled up at him. "We got into this river together. It stands to reason it's going to take both of us to get out."

Moril looked from bank to bank of the improbable

river. Mitt had already looked. He knew water. He had been brought up with it, both fresh and salt, and it was kind of instinctive with him. He hoped what Moril saw would bring him to his senses. Wisps of fog hung over the shrilling water, making it hard to see far, but it was possible to pick out a sheer, dark cliff on either side. Trees clung to niches in the cliffs here and there, so high that at first glance they looked like bushes. And those were the only other living things in sight. There was no sign of Navis, Hestefan, and Wend, or of the horses and the mule. As he discovered this, Moril's face unbunched into wide-eyed alarm.

Good, Mitt thought. His teeth were beginning to chatter, and this river scared him badly. He knew it. He had seen it before while he sat with Noreth by the waystone above Adenmouth. This one had the same smell, the same feel to it, and the thing which scared him most was that it did not seem to exist. "Listen," Mitt called up to Moril, "I'll give you my life history if it makes you feel better. I know you hate us Southerners—I heard what you said to Noreth—but I swear to Ammet you got no reason to hate me!"

Moril went on hands and knees and leaned down to look at him. Mitt actually had hopes that Moril was going to help him scramble up, until Moril said, "Yes, I knew you'd listen in. I was trying to annoy you."

Mitt roared with frustration. "Flaming Ammet! What's wrong with you? I think your *mind's* mixed up! You behave like the whole world's out to get you!"

That got home to Moril. He was pinched and staring and hurt for the time it took to draw breath, but then he went calm again. "And you're jealous," he said. "I meant you to be."

Jealous? The word seemed to take all the heat out of Mitt's body. He felt as cold as the water rushing round him. An instant later the heat came back, tenfold. He could feel his face burning above the frill of water round his chin. He was surprised the frill didn't start to steam. He tried to tell himself that he hadn't a clue why one word should affect him like this, but if one of his own words could affect Moril as badly, why not? Moril's mind *was* mixed up. And Mitt had a thousand clues about his own condition: Rith's cheerful freckly face and man-to-man way of talking and then Noreth, the young lady in the fashionable dress who was so nervous about what she had to do, and then the girl trying to hold them all together on the road. As soon as he picked up these clues, Mitt could look up into Moril's pinched and greenish face and see that some part of the mix-up in Moril's mind was the same thing. The same clues were there. They had both been unhappy. They had both fallen at the same young lady's feet. Both of us! Mitt thought bitterly. How flaming *stupid*!

"All right!" he shouted up at Moril. "So I am jealous! So are you! Calf love, they call it. And it's not going to get either of us *anywhere*!"

A surge of pink swept across Moril's face. He blinked. "I . . . wasn't only angry about that," he said.

"Neither was I!" Mitt shouted back. "Let me come up, and let's have it out, shall we?"

To Mitt's extreme relief, Moril at last held out a thin wet hand to help him up. Gripping it, Mitt hauled himself upward, skidding and slipping and clawing at the rock with his other hand. His boots weighed like lead, and the sodden leather of his clothes seemed to have the whole river in them. As Mitt floundered onto the top of the boulder, dripping and panting, Moril hurriedly crouched in front of his cwidder.

"Don't get it wet!"

That made sense. If the cwidder was spoiled, they would be in this for good. Mitt stood at the edge of the rock and let the water course and sluice and trickle off him where it did no harm. He was freezing, but to his surprise the air was warm. He could see himself beginning to steam as he said, "Well then. What's biting you?"

Moril bent his head and fiddled with some pebbles lodged in a crack of the boulder. "I— It's not that I *think* the whole world's out to get me. I *know* the whole South is. I . . . killed an awful lot of them last year."

"What? With that cwidder?" said Mitt.

Moril nodded. "When they tried to invade the North. It can move mountains. I closed Flennpass."

"You did Noreth a favor then," Mitt said. "In advance like. They can't get at her till she's ready, and from what I heard she can come down at them on the sheep tracks whenever she wants."

He looked down at Moril's head, wet and brown,

feeling almost sympathetic until Moril said, "You don't understand. I don't dare go near Dropwater—it's so full of Southerners—and I've no proof that you and Navis haven't been sent to kill me. Almost the only person I can *trust* is Hestefan."

"Get away!" said Mitt. "I heard you tell Noreth what friends you are with Earl Keril. That's what got me mad."

"Yes, but he treats me like—like a child," Moril said. "And I'd done something so . . . awful I needed to go away and work it out for myself."

"Just as long as you don't have your workout on me," Mitt said. "You don't look much of a child to me if that's any comfort to you. How old *are* you?"

"I shan't be thirteen for another month," Moril said regretfully. "How old are you?"

"Fifteen come Harvest," said Mitt.

"I thought you were more than that," Moril said, marveling. "You come from a slum somewhere, don't you? You've got that old-and-young look they all have in Holand and places. But I thought you were at least as old as my brother."

"Comes of earning a living as soon as you can walk," Mitt answered. "But then I reckon that applies to both of us."

From there it was the most natural step for Mitt to sit down on the edge of the boulder and swing his soggy boots above the streaming water while he told Moril about his life in Holand and his journey North and then about the Countess and Keril. Moril frowned at this. "I like Keril," he said, dubious and thoughtful. "Could he be up to something deep?"

"No," said Mitt. "No deeper than he wants Noreth out of the way before she can get to be Queen."

Moril's face came alight, the way it had when he talked to Noreth in the fog. "She *must* be Queen! It's like the old stories, like Enblith and Tanamoril. I want to help her. I know the old things are still true."

"Well, well," said Mitt. "You make me feel old. Here was I going to say that the country needs bringing together because the North is poor as an empty barrel full of mice—let's face it—and the South is rich—or it would be if those earls didn't take it all. Noreth wants to do that, so I'm for her. Very dull and political."

Moril laughed. "So you ride off in the night, like an old story, to steal her the Adon's ring."

"As to that," Mitt said, knowing his face had gone hot, "it proved I wasn't going to stick a knife in her, didn't it?"

"That made me jealous," Moril said frankly. "You must let me steal her the cup. Anyway, I'm dull and political, too. She said she thought the Singers ought to be paid by the Queen to stay in one place and make better music than they can going round in a cart. A royal academy, she said. I like that idea."

"She's got good ideas," Mitt agreed. "I really loved the way she settled those miners. All right. So we're both on the same side. Are you feeling happy enough about it to think how we get out of this river?"

11

Moril picked up his cwidder, carefully so as not to wet it on his clothes. "Can you read what it says on the front of it?"

There were swirls and dots there, made of mother-of-pearl, inlaid on either side of the strings. Mitt recognized it as the Old Writing, but that was all. "Not me," he said. "It takes me all my time to read the usual stuff."

"I can't read it either," Moril confessed. "But I was told that one bit says, 'I sing for Osfameron'—and that's *my* name, along with Tanamoril—and this other bit says, 'I move in more than one world.'"

"What's this?" said Mitt. "You mean we're in another *world*!"

"I . . . don't know," Moril admitted. "You always have to tell the truth with the cwidder. It works on how you think when you play it."

"Then let's get at what we were both thinking," Mitt suggested. He looked at the water boiling round the front of the boulder. "You were thinking I want this Southerner drowned deep. That right?"

Moril ducked his wet head uncomfortably. "Not quite. At least, I was probably meaning the sea. I was thinking, Let this Southerner go back where he came from, and I knew you came by sea—"

"How?" Mitt demanded.

"I heard about you in Lavreth last spring," said Moril. "It's all round the North that a Southerner came north by the wind's road with the Undying before and behind to guard him. Singers call the sea the wind's road in a lot of the old songs."

"I never knew *that*!" Mitt said. "And it's true, too, in a way!"

"They told me in Adenmouth that you were the one," Moril told him, "and I didn't like you because I could see you had something bad on your mind."

Mitt shivered. He was beginning to feel awed by Moril's perceptiveness, not to speak of that cwidder of his. A dangerous enemy, Moril, if they hadn't both chanced to get themselves into this mess together. "Stuck out like a sore thumb, did it?" he said ruefully. "You'd think I'd do better than that after a lifetime of guilty secrets. All right. So you wanted me back at sea."

"And you hit the strings, too, and we were both in this river. What were you thinking?" Moril asked.

Mitt stood up and scowled at ribbons of foam tearing backward from the nearest jagged rock. He was fairly sure that he would not have been so blindly furious with Moril if he had not been feeling so trapped himself. Then Moril had brought it all to a head by asking,

"Didn't someone order you to suck up to her?" That had brought two pictures into Mitt's mind. One was of the Countess, sitting upright in her chair, making it clear that Mitt had to do what Keril wanted. The other was of Alk, bulging out of that selfsame chair, turning the whole thing round with that promise, making Mitt feel just as trapped, because the One was supposed to have an interest.

"In a funny way," he said, "I may have been thinking about the One. That's where I was at when my hand hit, anyway."

Moril tipped his face up. His eyes were squinted with dismay. "You were? Then we've gone back into the One's river, before he destroyed Kankredin. I hope he's not too angry."

"You mean we're back in history?" Mitt demanded. "Or dead, really?"

"More like . . . the place in the stories where the One really is, I *think*," Moril said doubtfully. "It's hard to explain, but the other world the cwidder moves in is the place where the stories are."

Mitt looked again at the torrent tearing past their boulder and thought that he had seldom seen anything more real. Equally real were his steaming, clammy clothes. He had a notion that the One was taking the opportunity to point out that *he* was real, too. No wonder Alk had been so cautious. "Then we get back by apologizing and asking the One to let us go?" he said.

Moril nodded, looking as sober as Mitt felt. "I'll ask, if you like, because I know the way. You get ready to hit the strings in the same place as you did when I nod."

"I don't know where I did hit!" said Mitt. "And it won't do to get it wrong, will it?"

"You hit the lowest string," said Moril. "This one— it's always the dangerous one—and I wasn't touching it, because I didn't want to kill you or anything, but I heard it sound. Just pluck it, with one finger when I say."

Mitt put forth one doubtful finger and knelt ready. Moril seemed to settle himself—no, it was not simply that. Mitt could feel the power building in the cwidder. It hummed along his shaking finger. He felt even more awed by the thing.

Moril drew a big breath and spoke in the strange formal way that Hestefan had used to invoke the Undying at Midsummer. "Great Grand Father of the golden bonds, Unbound and Undying, understand my asking. Hear and help. History's flood took us and tore us from our traveling. Restore us to our own realm out of the river you made. Mitt and Moril ask this by Manaliabrid most humbly, and by Cennoreth, Clennen's son begs you cast aside your anger." He nodded at Mitt: *now*.

Mitt's finger twanged the thickest string heartily. He thought he saw the way of this speech, and he could not resist doing it, too. "By the Adon and Alhammitt and his *all*-fruitful lady," he said as he twanged.

Moril's fingers made the rest of the sound. It was a many-toned roaring.

It seemed as if the sound of the river had increased, almost unbearably, to a sound that fogged their eyes as well as their ears. They felt the river was now thundering over a cliff in a waterfall, whose thunder gradually faded to a long, deep chord, and then a growling vibration. As the sound faded, it seemed to carry the river away with it. The water became foggy and quiet. The golden whiteness of the fog spread to the very riverbed, and for a second or so it was the great transparent ghost of a river, silently rushing over green ground. At the instant that Mitt realized that the green was really grass, the river was gone, except for the faintest vestige of that chord, still sounding and dragging on him like a current. During the next instant it took him to realize that the dragging was taking *all* the river with it, including the water that filled his boots and soaked his clothing. He was dry. So was Moril. Moril's hair went from draggled brown to true red again. And though they were dry, though there was a little feeble sunlight on them, the air was so much colder that they were both still shivering.

From Maewen's point of view, the river vanished as suddenly as it had come, leaving Mitt and Moril crouched on an outcrop of rock just across the green road. She was not sure whether to cheer or to run and shake them. It had been maddening watching them. All they seemed to do was sit on that rock in the river and talk for an hour. Maewen kept shouting to them. Navis had shouted, too, after he had rounded up Mitt's horse, but the boys had taken no notice. Hestefan and Wend maddened her almost as much. Both shook their heads and said, "They'll not hear from where *they* are."

Moril and Mitt climbed off the rock and crossed the road, both looking self-conscious.

"So soon?" said Navis. "We were expecting to wait all night."

Mitt tried to give him an explanation. It sounded lame and stupid to him, and he was glad when everyone was distracted from it by Hestefan. Hestefan seized Moril by one shoulder and ranted at him. He began in a low, penetrating voice. "This is neither the time nor the place for such tricks. We have a journey to go on, fellow travelers to consider, and a performance to give in Gardale." His voice gradually increased as he went on to, "You could have spoiled your cwidder, or—worse!—lost it. You nearly stampeded the horses. You could have drowned us all!"

Everyone listened uncomfortably. Moril was staring at Hestefan as if he had never heard anything like this in his life, and that made it clear that this was not just a master giving his apprentice a dressing-down, but something more. Maewen could see that Hestefan had been terrified by the sudden river, and she supposed he was working it off on Moril. Then Hestefan's voice increased again.

"Now give me your cwidder at once, and I shall

lock it in the chest until you are old enough to be trusted with it."

Moril clutched the cwidder and stepped backward. "No. You've no right—"

"I have every right!" Hestefan enlarged his voice as only a Singer could. It rang in the rocks. "My apprentice has been fooling with something too powerful for his years. You have no notion what that cwidder is!"

"Yes, I have," Moril said, dogged and white. "And it belonged to my father, not to you. You've no right to take it away."

Mitt felt he had better intervene. "Now look. He didn't do any harm with it."

Hestefan ignored Mitt. "Give me the cwidder here," he said, and held his hand out sternly for it.

"There's no need—" Mitt tried to say.

But at this point Navis intervened, too. He came up beside Moril and said, in his most sarcastic way, "Is it possible the master envies his apprentice? Surely not?"

Hestefan turned and glared at Navis.

Wend looked urgently at Maewen. "Lady!"

Maewen had been feeling like she did in school, watching one of the teachers tell off someone else in her class. Hestefan was so very much like Dr. Loviath that she could not help it. And of course, if a teacher decides to tell someone off, no one else in the class dreams of interfering. Wend's look made her realize that it was not like this at all. She tried to gather her wits.

"Stop it," she said to Navis. "Er—Hestefan, I'm not sure this is right. Moril told me this morning that it was your daughter, Fenna, who was indentured to you, not him. He said he came with you from his own choice. Doesn't that make him your—er—colleague instead of your apprentice?"

"Well yes," Hestefan said, very displeased. "But considering his years and his actions, common law would hardly make that distinction."

That displeased look made him so like Dr. Loviath that Maewen had to fight herself not to agree humbly. As so often happens, she found herself going too far the other way. "But I'm the leader," she said, "and I say he isn't *really* your apprentice. So I say you can't take his cwidder away even if he did something—er—rather mad with it."

"That was my fault, too," Mitt put in, but in a very gruff and unfriendly way. He was having trouble even looking at Noreth after what Moril had said.

Hestefan lifted his chin and jutted his beard at Maewen.

A black mark and detention! Maewen thought. And Mitt glowering, too. If you're a leader, everyone hates you. So will Moril after this. "And, Moril, you were trying to hurt Mitt with that cwidder, weren't you?"

Any other boy would have protested that Mitt was bigger than he was. Moril impressed Maewen by just saying, "Yes."

She felt like a beast, but she was launched on her way now and found she had to go on. "Then, until we get to Gardale, someone else is going to take charge of it. Moril, will you give your cwidder to Wend, please?"

It was hard to tell if Moril, Wend, or Hestefan was more surprised. Hestefan turned away and climbed into the cart, still jutting his beard. Moril at first clutched the cwidder closer. Then, with a glance at Mitt that certainly meant something, he passed the beautiful gleaming instrument over to Wend. Wend took it so reverently that it seemed to slide into his hands. He hung the worn leather strap across his shoulder and looked down at the cwidder as if it was a lamb he had just rescued from the snow. His left hand formed a chord on the strings as if it could not help itself. "May I?" he asked Moril.

"If you *can*," Moril said. "I'll fetch you the case."

Wend's right hand played on the strings as if it were stroking the lamb's head. He only played a sequence of chords and arpeggios, but he became a new person doing it. His face came alive, into a slight, rapt smile, full of thoughts and energies that had not been there before. The way he stood altered, to accommodate the cwidder, into the stance of someone much stronger. For the first time since Maewen had met him, he looked happy. Oddly enough, that made him look ten times more dangerous, too.

Why couldn't he be like that all the time? Maewen wondered as she turned away to mount her horse again at last. Instead of trying to pretend he was not an

Undying among all us dying-people? She tried to catch Mitt's eye to see what he thought, but Mitt was raw with shame about that word *jealous*, and he turned away quickly. Hestefan gave her an unloving look from the seat of the cart.

Two black marks and a whole week in detention! Maewen thought. She thought Navis was right. Hestefan had wanted Moril's cwidder. As they rode on, she found herself wondering why Hestefan had chosen to follow Noreth if he disliked her so much.

The handing over of the cwidder had a surprising effect on Moril. While Wend strode along, looking strong and different, Moril behaved like a boy let out of school. He went scampering along beside Mitt's horse, shouting cheeky remarks up at Mitt. Mitt answered the same way, and both of them laughed themselves silly. After a while they began taking turns to ride, with a lot more silly laughter when the Countess-horse tried to throw Moril off.

Maewen rode out ahead, feeling lonely and unloved, listening to the pair of them laughing in the foggy distance behind. I suppose owning a thing like that cwidder *is* a big responsibility, she thought, but she had a stupid, hypersensitive feeling that Moril and Mitt were fooling about because of *her*. I was *told* to come here and be the leader, she thought. No need to be paranoid.

As if that word had triggered it off, the deep voice spoke to her, at her ear in the gathering fog. "You did well not to let the Singer get his hands on the cwidder," it said.

Maewen's hands shook on the reins. She had known that the voice would catch her alone sooner or later. *Was* it the One? Somehow, because it was telling her what she wanted to hear, she doubted it. After seeing that sudden mighty river, she had a feeling that the One was more likely to tell her something unexpected that she did not want to know about at all. No. It was some kind of ghostly effect of her own mind on the green road.

"You will need that cwidder, and the Singer-boy to play it," the voice continued, "when you come to find the crown."

Maewen had not meant to answer, but she found herself saying, "And what about the cup and the sword?"

"The Southerner can steal both of those for you," said the voice.

"Oh? Can he? Just like that?" Maewen said.

"I tell you so," said the voice. "You must accept my advice or you will never find the crown. And I tell you not to alienate the Singer-boy."

"All right." Maewen was working on her horse, slowing down so that Navis and Wend could catch up with her. "All *right*. Just go away now, will you?"

She could hear Navis behind now, asking Wend how much farther it was to Gardale, and Wend answering that it would take another day. Maewen fell in on the other side of Navis, and as she had hoped, the voice did not speak to her again.

The fog thickened. By nightfall, when it was blue-dim, they stopped in another of those lumpy places that might once have been a town. There was a well-made fire pit where Moril built a cheerful coal fire. Maewen reminded Mitt of his idea for cooking pickled cherries. Mitt could not bring himself to be natural. Gruffly he borrowed skewers from the cart and kept his back turned while he stuck them with cherries, cheese, and dried meat to roast. It was terrible. Mitt tried to be polite and found himself agreeing fawningly with Noreth that a lentil stew would help. He tried to correct that and went gruff again. He could not seem to get it right. Plainly by the firelight, he could see the hurt, puzzled look among Noreth's freckles. He could feel her wondering what she had done to offend him, and of course there was no way he could tell her.

Never mind. I'll be seeing Hildy again in Gardale, he thought. For some reason he knew that would make things better.

While the lentils plopped and bubbled and turned too thick, Maewen tried to put Mitt out of her mind by thinking what she should do in Gardale. Should she make a speech? She had told Navis that her army would arrive by itself, but that was over on the coast. They were now a long way inland, where people would not know about Noreth. The trouble was that

she had no idea what to expect. She had been to Gardale in her own time. She and Aunt Liss had driven
there on a sight-seeing trip. But she had a feeling that
this was only going to confuse her.

Around then Wend politely asked Moril's permis-
sion and played the cwidder again. Lilting tunes from
the old days rang in the crags. Everyone seemed to
feel better. They ate caked lentils and Mitt's sooty
skewered things quite cheerfully, and when they had
finished, Hestefan surprised them all by telling tales.
Most of them were stories that were around in
Maewen's day, too, but she had only read them in
books. It was another thing again to hear Hestefan tell
them, gravely and plainly, as if every strange occur-
rence were the exact truth. The stories were suddenly
unknown and new. Maewen had known what was going to happen nearly every time, but it still surprised
her.

This is what it means to be a good Singer, she
thought, and he really is good!

"I thank you," Navis said when Hestefan finished.
"I have never heard those tales better told."

Hestefan bowed as he sat. "And I thank you. Never
have I told them so well for so little in return."

Navis laughed and tossed Hestefan a silver piece.
Hestefan took it with a bit of a twinkle. It looked as
if they were actually beginning to like one another.
Maewen caught a little smile on Wend's face as he
carefully put the waterproof case round the cwidder,
and she wondered.

The fog was worse in the morning. Probably they were down into the clouds again. Certainly the green road sloped gently downhill as if it were leading them back to the valleys. Before long it was branching past waystone after waystone, and Maewen was glad to have Wend striding out in front to show the right way. And this day, for the first time, there were other people using the road. It made sense, as Navis remarked. Up to now they had been ahead of or behind all the folk who had gone somewhere else to celebrate Midsummer. Now they came up with all those people returning home and also the usual traffic of people going into Gardale.

They passed riders, groups of walkers, and families with carts all coming toward them. Hestefan called out cheerfully to each. But when they passed the first person going the other way, who was someone driving a flock of geese, he said ringingly, "Hestefan the Singer here! Watch for me in Gardale."

Maewen tensed. Hestefan had to advertise, of course, but so did she. She wondered whether to call out in the same way, Noreth Onesdaughter here! and ask the gooseman—no, it was a woman all bundled up against the fog—ask the goosewoman, then, to join her at Kernsburgh. She dithered. She hated the idea, and besides, the woman might tell the Earl of Gardale. On the other hand, perhaps she *ought*. For once she would have welcomed that deep voice speaking to her out of the air to tell her what to do. But of course, there were too many people near.

Meanwhile, more and more white triangular geese kept appearing out of the fog. As Maewen, still dithering, opened her mouth to imitate Hestefan, Mitt's horse demonstrated that it considered geese a lower life-form. It began moving at them in pounces, with Mitt hauling on the reins and cursing it. After ten feet of rocking-horse-like progress, the Countess-horse won and plunged in among the geese. Mitt fell off into an outrage of honking, flapping, and running. Geese ran in all directions, except for two, which ran for Mitt with spread wings and outstretched necks. The lady driving them shouted mightily—most of it very rude things about Mitt and the horse.

Navis was into the fray almost instantly, using his riding crop on everything. The lady shouted at Navis, too. But the two geese fled, Moril caught the Countess-horse, and Navis hauled Mitt up. Everyone else chased geese for a while. By the time the flock was assembled again, Maewen's nerve was gone. Even if the goose-lady had not been so very angry, she thought, watching Navis and Hestefan being wonderfully polite to the woman, the proper time to declare Noreth as Queen was when she had reached Kernsburgh with the Adon's gifts and had something to show those earls. The decision made her feel utterly relieved and completely feeble in about the same proportions.

"I think this is yours, madam," Navis said, bowing and handing the goose-lady the stick she had dropped.

"Just keep that big looby off his back and out of my geese," she answered.

"Certainly," Navis agreed. "But I'm afraid that would mean buying him a real horse, and we neither of us have the funds just now."

At this the woman hooted with laughter. Mitt struggled back into his saddle again feeling like an utter idiot.

After that he kept tight hold of the beast whenever another traveler loomed through the fog.

:‖ 12 ‖:

W<small>HEN THEY CAMPED</small> that night, Wend said that Gardale was only a mile or so away, below in a valley they could not see.

It was odd, Maewen thought, that it had taken all this time to get that near, even coming straight through the center of the mountains. When she had driven here with Aunt Liss, it had only taken four hours, and that was with a detour on the way to look at Hannart. Her sense of distance was all confused.

Her sense of *everything* was all confused. She was dreading Gardale. Mitt was still being so distant and gruff that she knew she was not going to ask him to steal the Adon's cup for her. And Moril was younger than she was, and she was not going to ask him either. She would have to do it herself. But she still felt hurt at the way Mitt was behaving. She wanted to apologize, although she had no idea what she had done to annoy him. Perhaps they should all just go away and not bother about the cup.

No. Out of this muddle of thoughts came one thing that was clear—probably. Maewen and Aunt Liss had done the usual tourist thing and seen round the college at Gardale, where the old Lawschool was. Part of the Lawschool was the Chapel of the One. There had been—would be—a cup on the altar there, with a notice saying that this was only a replica of the cup that had been stolen two hundred years before. So it looked as if she had stolen—would be going to have stolen—the darned thing. In a mad, circular way, that meant she had to go down into Gardale and steal it because she already *had*.

It came on to rain. Oh, I give up! she thought.

Moril and Hestefan had the best of it. They vanished into the cart. The others draped the oilskin covers off their baggage over three large rocks and crawled underneath, where they spent a hot and sticky night, steamily full of the plopping and thrumming of rain. It was so uncomfortable that everyone woke and crawled out again at dawn. The rain stopped and became thinning mist, almost mockingly.

Maewen was clammy all over, and itchy, and—well—plain dirty. She could smell herself. She wanted to clean her teeth. But nobody seemed to bother about tooth cleaning any more than they appeared to worry about baths. At that moment Maewen felt she would have given her left ear and probably several toes as well for a nice hot bath full of rose-scented bath oil. And there was not even a hairbrush in her baggage roll! While Navis was shaving and Hestefan was clawing the kinks out of his beard, Maewen did what she could by taking her hair down from the little helmet, shaking it out and scratching hard at her scalp. Her hair smelled awful, of horse mostly, but dirty human hair was part of the smell, too.

"What wouldn't I give for a *bath*!" she said as she crammed the helmet back on her head.

"Me, too," Mitt said, surprisingly, looking up from tightening the buckles on the Countess-horse. This was always a wary business, of circling and darting, in order not to get kicked or bitten, and he was glad to be distracted. "I never thought I'd live to hear myself say that," he said. "But I got spoiled this last year in Aberath. Alk's got the whole place mined through with lead pipes and a furnace down in the dungeons. Water comes out boiling."

A chuckle rose up in Maewen's throat. Things were all right again. Mitt was back in form. Now she could almost look forward to Gardale.

Mitt kept talking about Alk as they wound their slow way down into the valley. It matched a tender place in his mind where that promise to Alk was. So he was not sure why he was suddenly so cheerful. Maybe it was that the fog had gone. You could see mountains navy blue against pink dawn, peak after peak, right away to far-off Mount Tanil, which had a quiet feather of smoke coming out of its pointed head. Near to, there was still no sign of a valley—only a chasm of dark blue emptiness with mist boiling up out of it as if there were a giant version of one of Alk's Irons down there.

"I hear there's this great huge steam organ they have in Hannart," he remarked, as the roiling, rising mist put him in mind of it.

Maewen nodded. She had seen the carefully pre-served remains of that organ on that trip with Aunt Liss.

Maybe, Mitt considered, it was the sight just now of Noreth with her hair down from her helmet in long, frizzy clouds. Like that, she was the young lady he had felt so respectful to in her aunt's hall, so different and so far away from Mitt that it was silly to be awk-ward with her. Or maybe he was simply looking for-ward to seeing Hildy again.

The track that led down from the waystone was nothing like as grassy and well made as the green roads. Mostly it was rubble and raw earth and quite danger-ously frayed at the edge of the great drop-off, where the mist heaved and rose. It led down in zigzags beside a furious stream of white water splayed over wet rocks, and at every hairpin bend, the cart threatened to come off and pitch into the depths. Hestefan led the mule. Everyone else took turns leaning on the outer side of the cart, boots braced in sliding gravel, either above white water or horrifying mist-filled steepness, helping to ease the cart round. When Maewen took her first turn, a nattering and honking above made her look up. There were white triangular splotches some bends overhead. The goosewoman seemed to have caught up.

The splotches and the noise came nearer every bend.

"The geese get down here more easily," Navis remarked to Mitt as they leaned side by side against the gold letters. Mitt laughed, and hoped they would not have to meet the goose-lady again.

As they slowly descended the track, the white stream enlarged into a mountain river roaring on a bed of green rocks, under a cliff hung with holly trees and small perilous rowans. The mist continued boiling its way upward as they went down. Somehow it had miraculously changed from mist to a proper cloud hovering against the upper crags. The sun caught it there and turned it to a cloud of gold film, with the green-black bones of the rock showing through. Everyone began to feel dry again at last.

About then Maewen caught sight of a woman standing on the other side of the loud green river. At least she thought she saw someone, between two of the rowan trees. But when she turned her head, there were only the two trees. She saw Mitt's head jerk, as if he had seen someone there, too. Then, as if he was struck by a sudden thought, Mitt turned his head back and up to look at the zigzags of the track above. Maewen looked, too. There was nothing up there. No gaggle of geese, no woman driving them. She could not even hear the geese chatting anymore.

They're out of sight on a bend, she thought.

Mitt thought, Libby Beer! Now what's she playing at?

Wend came hurrying down to the cart in a slide of

small stones, unslinging the cwidder from his neck as he came. "Is it all right to give this back now?" he called to Maewen. "I'll have to leave you for a while. I'll wait for you by the waystone south of Gardale Valley."

"Yes, I suppose so," Maewen said, rather taken aback. "What if we take all day, though?"

"I'll wait," Wend promised, handing the cwidder to Moril. Moril settled it on his knees, and quite a weight of responsibility with it, from the look of him. They went on down. The last Maewen saw of Wend, before a shoulder of the hill hid him, he was leaping in great, splashing strides across the river.

Going to see that lady, Maewen thought. She *was* there, then.

At the next bend of the path Wend vanished from her mind. The path came out above the great green wedge shape of the Gardale Valley, with Gardale Town nestled into the pointed end just below them, seemingly at their toes, a mass of smoking chimney stacks. Maewen was astonished. She had known the place was bound to be smaller, but not *this* small! It was more like a large village than a town.

Two more turns of the road brought them into green meadows outside the town, and Maewen still marveled. She knew it was absurd, but she had been expecting the high blocks of buildings and the tall shops she had seen on her visit with Aunt Liss. This Gardale was all low. The houses were all built of greenish stone, and none was more than three stories high. The amount of smoke from all those chimneys astonished her. The track suddenly turned into a proper road paved with the same greenish stone and took them across a bridge over the same river, now flowing quietly and more brown than green, between stone walls where small boys sat fishing.

After that they were in the main street, and Maewen could hardly breathe. It's like a foreign country! she thought. There were crowds of people. She had thought she had become used to being in the past. Now she knew she had only become used to the people traveling with her and the way those five people dressed and talked. Everyone who crowded the street here seemed to have more lines on their faces—or fewer—as if they all worried about different things from those that concerned people in Maewen's own time. This set their faces into quite another shape, like people who spoke a foreign language. As to their clothes, the hearthman's livery she had grown used to was the rarest kind here. The men wore bright wools and sober velvets in any number of styles, from tight-fitting suits with a colored blanket thing folded over one shoulder, through the looser sorts of clothes that Moril or Hestefan wore, to the elderly fellow pushing past in a long dark blue velvet robe with a jeweled chain round his neck. The women were in so many styles and colors—nipped waists, loose pleats, long flounces, calf-length gathers—that even when Maewen saw the outfit was homemade and probably redyed from another color, they still made her feel dowdy and wrongly dressed. The place smelled of people and, almost chokingly, of smoke with, underneath that, most definitely cesspits.

"It seems very busy," Navis remarked. "Market day?"

"That and more, I rather think," Hestefan said. People had seen his cart by then and were pressing up to it all round, wanting to know when the Singer would perform. Hestefan enlarged his voice, in the Singer's way, so that though he seemed to be speaking normally, his voice rang round the street. "In the market square in an hour's time."

"Oh but—" Moril started to say. Then he saw faces turning and nodding eagerly. He gave up.

"What are our plans?" Navis asked Maewen. They were down to a slow walk, boot to boot, as they pressed through the crowd.

"Go to the college—Lawschool," Maewen said.

"That suits me," Navis said, and he bent to the nearest person to ask the way.

It was out on the other side of the town. They had to go through the market square, where there was a frenzy of buying and selling going on, and such shouting mixed with smells of new bread, fruit, leather, and cattle dung to add to the cesspit smell that Maewen's stomach began to feel unhappy. Hestefan cast a professional eye over the chaos and agreed with Moril that they would have time to visit the Lawschool before people were ready to listen. So the whole party continued, out through the farther end of the market square and down another street, to where the crowds and then the houses quite abruptly stopped and the street became a white dirt road leading across more green fields. There were animals—cows, goats, and a donkey or so—tethered out in the fields, but the only other people in sight were a small party of horsemen some distance ahead on the road.

"Hannart livery," Navis said. He and Mitt exchanged a significant, worried look. "I think we'll let them get well ahead."

That suited Maewen. In these times Hannart was a name to conjure with. As everyone reined in and hung back at the mule's slowest pace, she looked anxiously at the horsemen until they vanished behind a clump of trees. "Do you think someone told the Earl of Hannart that the Adon's ring was stolen?" she asked Mitt.

"I don't *reckon* so," Mitt said, almost equally worried.

"I'll give a false name," Maewen said, "if anyone asks."

"A wise precaution," Navis agreed. "At times like this I could wish Mitt and I were not so obviously Southerners."

The Hannart horsemen had vanished by the time they came round the clump of trees and saw the Lawschool. Maewen had another moment of sheer surprise. She had known the school would have to be the oldest part of the college she and Aunt Liss had visited, but she had expected that this would be the part with all the towers and tall, pointed windows. She had not expected it would be these low, graceful greenish buildings topped with clusters of long, stylish chimneys. The windows were wide, one and all, and they had diamond panes. In the middle, an elegant archway filled by a wrought-iron gate joined two blocks of the buildings together. The rest were joined by a high stone wall.

"Looks a good place for studying," Mitt said. He tried to smile, but he knew his face had gone pinched and worried. Those Hannart riders were inside. He could glimpse horses between the bars of the gate.

By the time they reached the gate, there was nothing to be seen through it but a garden and a cobbled path leading away between lavender bushes. An official walked to the middle of the gate. Maewen bit the inside of her mouth, or she would have laughed. He was wearing exactly the same uniform that the porters at the college wore in her day: baggy knee-length breeches and tunic in dark blue, with a wide white collar. It was obviously old-fashioned even two hundred years before that. He had bad teeth. She saw them as he spoke.

"Visitors for Sending Day? Which of the scholars are you for?"

Navis hesitated a fraction because of those riders from Hannart. "Hildrida Navissdaughter," he said, with a shrug you could only have seen if you knew him.

"And I'm for Brid Clennensdaughter," Moril called from the cart.

The porter smiled at them. Maewen had to look away from his teeth. "I'm sorry for it, but you're all too early. Sending Day doesn't start till midday. Come back then, and I'll let you in with pleasure. You're not the only ones I've had to turn away. You'll find the town's full of you. But," he said to Hestefan, "you can come half an hour ahead if you want to set up to sing. The other Singer will be coming back then."

Hestefan frowned to hear of another Singer to compete with and began to turn the cart round. "Thank you. I shall only perform in the town then. But my apprentice will be back to see his sister."

Nobody pointed out that the riders from Hannart had been let in at once. Nobody even remarked that since they had been let in, this meant they were not just a chance band of hearthmen but members of the Earl's household on important business. Yet they all knew it, even Maewen. They rode back the way they had come very soberly.

The other Singer was now camped just outside the town. They saw him as soon as they came round the trees, a neat black, white, and gold cart at the edge of the wide green, surrounded by sacks and bundles of provisions. Someone—presumably the Singer—was sorting through the bundles in a rather hopeless way.

Moril, at the sight, tugged excitedly at Hestefan's arm. Hestefan whipped up the mule. The green cart, in a most uncharacteristic way, went rollicking and bumping across the turf toward the black and white one. Moril stood up on the seat, waving and shrieking, "Dagner! *Dagner!*"

The Singer, a slightly built young man with reddish hair, who looked very little older than Mitt, had just picked up one of the sacks. He turned round at the noise and let out a bellow of his own. "*Hestefan!* MORIL!" He dropped the sack and came racing over to hang on to the step of the green cart, laughing as if this was the most wonderful meeting in the world. The three of them fell into instant eager talk.

As Maewen came up with Navis and Mitt, she thought she had never seen Hestefan look so animated. They hung about a short distance away, none of them sure how private the Singers wanted to be, and admired the new Singer's turnout. The horse, which was enjoying a nosebag, was as black and glossy as the black paint on the cart, and its harness was white. The austere colors served to show up the fact that instead of a name painted on the cart, there was a large and complicated coat of arms.

Moril turned and shouted to them, "It's my brother! Isn't it wonderful! Dastgandlen Handagner!"

"Oh, I've heard of him," Mitt said, decidedly impressed. "Aberath folk said he was the best."

"Let us be introduced," Navis said.

But before they had come within talking distance, Moril had said something to Dagner which seemed to alarm him acutely. Dagner backed away from the green cart, asking anxious questions. Next moment he was running for his cart and hurling the sacks and bundles in anyhow, latching the tailgate, and running again to take the nose bag off the horse. The horse's head came up. It looked as surprised as everyone else. "Sorry, Stiles," Dagner called out. "Later." With that he was in the driving seat and untying the reins, and the cart was in motion. All in seconds.

"But what about *Brid*?" Moril yelled.

"You're here now. You can give her my love!" Dagner shouted back. "Get *up*, Stiles. I want your best pace." The horse broke into a trot. The black and white cart went in a swift near circle past Navis, Mitt, and Maewen. Dagner leaned out to call as he passed, "I'd have followed you, too, lady, if this hadn't happened!"

Maewen realized he was talking to her and managed to shoot a smile in reply. Then the horse was going faster still. The black and white cart went careering away into the distance, raising a cloud of moisture and grass seeds behind its flying wheels.

"What got into him?" Mitt asked.

"I told him Fenna was hurt," Moril said. "He's in love with her. He's going straight to Adenmouth by the green road above Hannart." It was clear Moril was very pleased by his brother's devotion.

"And why does he carry a coat of arms?" asked Navis. "It looked like the arms of the South Dales to me."

Moril grimaced. This was something which did not seem to please him so much. "It is," he said. "Dagner's Earl of the South Dales. Since last year, when our cousin got killed. He told me Earl Keril made him put the arms on his cart, but I know Dagner only agreed because it takes up less space than his names do." He looked fondly after the galloping cart. "Dagner's only proud of being a Singer," he said.

Navis had one eyebrow right, right up. "Is Tholian dead then?"

"Yes," said Moril.

"Well, well," said Navis. "One hesitates to say good riddance, since he was obviously a near relation of yours, but—"

"We have to sing in the market square," Hestefan interrupted. He was back to his schoolmaster manner.

"Well, well," Navis said again as they followed the green cart back into the town. "Tholian dead! If I had to choose between Tholian and Keril, I might, even at this moment, choose Tholian."

"Never met him," said Mitt.

"You have no idea how lucky you are," said Navis. He did not say anything else until they were in the confusion of the market again. Then he said, "Mitt, how about a decent breakfast at the inn?"

"That," said Mitt, "is the best thing I heard today."

The two of them threaded their horses between the stalls toward the large inn at one side of the square. Maewen had no money. She was watching them rather wistfully when Navis turned round and called, "You, too, lady. This is my treat."

Maewen followed gratefully. They clopped under a huge archway into a stable yard, where a boy with a raw face and yellow hair spit out the straw he was chewing and came to listen to Navis's instructions. He wanted the horses to have a good breakfast, too. Maewen patted her horse and let the boy take it away with the other two. A nice horse, she thought, as she followed Navis into the inn, but one without any character at all. If it *was* Noreth's horse, the girl must have used it like a bicycle. What *had* become of her?

The front rooms of the inn were wide open to the square, where tables were set out under a sort of covered way supported by old gnarled pillars with creepers trained up them. A nice arrangement in summer, Maewen thought. It reminded her of the pillared balconies at the front of the Tannoreth Palace. But what did they do in winter? Kernsburgh was many degrees warmer than Gardale even now. People in these times seemed to be so hardy. They lived out of doors much more than Maewen was used to.

The only free table they could find was a long way from the end of the square where Hestefan had stopped his cart. Maewen could hear his voice faintly, behind all the rest of the din, calling to people to come and listen, but any view was blocked off by a gnarled pillar and a big stall selling iron pans. It was a slight disappointment. Maewen had never yet heard the Singers perform. Still, as she agreed with Mitt, it was good to be sitting in a proper chair listening to Navis ordering food from a cheerful, hurried man in a dirty apron.

"And beer for three," Navis finished.

Help! thought Maewen. Coffee came from abroad, of course, and it was not much drunk until a hundred years later than this. She would have preferred water—except from the way this town *smelled* she was sure the water was not fit to drink. Oh well. Beer couldn't be that bad, or people wouldn't drink it. Hestefan and Moril were singing now. Maewen leaned back, trying to pick out the sound from behind the shouts, the talk, the yelling of animals, and the bonging of the pans in the ironware stall. It was not a tune she knew.

The food came promptly on enormous wooden platters, sizzling hot: bacon, kidneys, eggs, mushrooms, and hot bread to go with it, with butter and honey for the bread. With this arrived three pewter tankards of sour-smelling yellow stuff. Maewen tried it. Yuk. But she was very hungry, and all that food needed something to wash it down. She kept drinking, in valiant sips.

Mitt could no longer contain his anxiety. "They let Hannart in early," he said to Navis. "I don't like that. What do we do?"

"Play it as we see it," Navis answered. "At least we're here."

"And what's this Sending Day?" Mitt asked, wolfing down food he hardly noticed.

"As I gather, it's the day most pupils go home for the summer," Navis said. "Not that anyone thought to inform me. I asked Noreth's aunt."

"Then you can take her away," Mitt said.

"So can Hannart," Navis pointed out. He was, as usual, trying not to show his feelings, but Mitt could tell Navis was as strained and gloomy as he was himself.

There was applause from the distance. Hestefan began a new song. Maewen thought it was perfectly lovely, but it was low and sweet, and she kept losing it in the noise.

"Suppose," said Mitt, "that Hannart has been and gone by the time they let us in?"

"There's a closing ceremony," Navis replied. "Surely even Hannart can't remove a pupil before that. And of course neither can we."

"First moment we can then," Mitt said urgently.

"Whatever's possible," Navis agreed.

They ate in worried silence after that. Hestefan seemed to be telling a story. There were bursts of laughter and clapping, but Hestefan's voice was almost inaudible. Maewen was straining to hear when Navis pulled himself together and turned to her politely.

"I fear we have been leaving you out of our private

concerns, lady," he said. "As you may have gathered, we became your followers not entirely out of personal conviction."

"Speak for yourself," said Mitt. "I'm convinced." He turned to Maewen, waving a hunk of bread and honey in one bony hand. Here was something to take his mind off Hildy. "Tell us your beliefs, Noreth. Convince him."

Help! thought Maewen. She stared at the pots and pans swinging on the stall, hoping for inspiration. Mitt was leaning toward her eagerly as if he thought she really did have beliefs. Probably Noreth did have beliefs, but Maewen had no way of knowing what those were. She had simply been getting by on a messy muddle of beliefs from her own day, mixed up with what she knew had happened in the last two hundred years. Dalemark had changed, almost out of recognition, in that time, and not wholly for the better at that.

"It is possible she just follows the will of the One," Navis remarked in his usual sarcastic way.

This bounced Maewen into speaking. She did not want to let Mitt down. "I believe there has to be change," she said. A disgustingly safe thing to say. Something seemed to be wrong with her, adding to her difficulty. Her face buzzed, and the sounds from the market had gone quiet and distant. Moril was singing. She could just pick out his voice among the deep belling chords of his cwidder. She would have liked to think it was the cwidder doing this to her, but she was fairly sure it was the beer. And the way Gardale smelled like a filthy farmyard. Maewen swallowed. "There's a lot in Dalemark that hasn't come out yet," she said. "Wonderful people, and talents and richness. Some of the reason it hasn't come out is that all the ordinary people are too poor for different reasons"— am I going to be sick?—"but the *main* reason is that everybody is too busy thinking of themselves as North and South. They need to be one country and—and be *proud* of it before—before they can show what's . . . really in them." There. I believe that. Maewen pushed back her chair. She knew what was wrong with her now. A truly vicious stomachache. Nerves? Those mushrooms? She could not help it that Mitt's eager face was going puzzled and disappointed. "I'm sorry . . . I have to— Do you know where is the—"

Navis understood instantly. "It'll be round in the stable yard. First door. Women to the right."

Maewen bolted that way. She raced under the arch. And—bless Navis!—there was the door. It was dark inside, with a sticky mud floor, but she was led to the right door by the smell. Yuk! She nearly *was* sick. Inside, it was clean enough in its primitive way, with whitewashed walls and a bundle of rags instead of paper, but the *smell*! Why hadn't things smelled anything like this bad up on the green roads? Did Wend really look after that kind of thing as well as the roads?

It was not a place to stay long in. Maewen finished as quickly as she could and unlatched the door to the dark muddy passage with relief. That's better. Now I can go back and talk sense to Mitt.

A hard arm grabbed her round the throat. A hand, with the faint glint of a knife accompanying it, rose and came down, stabbing.

"*Help!*" Maewen screamed. The hard arm cut her scream off to a squawk. She struggled furiously. What an *awful* place to be killed in! I *will* not die here! She twisted sideways against the grip on her throat and kicked where she could feel legs behind her. The rest of her twisted and bucked mindlessly. It was horrible the way she could *feel* the man. Intimate. Beastly. It never occurred to her to use the knife and short sword she had just hitched aside to fasten her breeches. She kicked madly, trying to fall out of the man's grip into a sort of squat. That unbalanced him. The hand with the knife swept away sideways and banged on a wooden wall as he tried to stay upright. His arm loosed her throat enough for her to give a high, whistling scream.

"With you!" someone said. Doors banged. Wood resounded. The knife gleamed in half daylight. It had grown. No, it was a sword, being held by someone else. Maewen only glimpsed it before her attacker dropped her as if she was on fire and fled, kicking her as he barged across her, shoving the swordsman aside, and banging out through the door. Maewen could feel the pounding of his running feet as she lay on the sticky mud floor.

"Are you all right? *Noreth!* Where are you hurt?"

It was Navis. His hand was pulling at her arm. Maewen tried to sit up and found she had suddenly no strength at all. Navis hauled her upright and dragged her out into the comparatively pure-smelling yard.

"Where are you hurt?"

"I—I'm not . . . I . . . How did you— Who *was* he?"

"I wish I knew," said Navis. "It was far too dark. As I didn't see him when I came along behind you, I conclude he was hiding in there."

"What a horrible place to hide!" Maewen managed to say. "Why did you—"

"I told you," said Navis. "Your aunt told me to look after you. Let's get the horses and go out on the common. You should be safe out of the crowds. We should have stayed there as soon as we saw Hannart was in town."

:‖ 13 ‖:

Mᴀᴇᴡᴇɴ sᴘᴇɴᴛ ᴡʜᴀᴛ was left of the morning sitting on the grass outside the town, more or less where Dagner's black and white cart had been, hedged in by Mitt, Navis, and the three horses. Even this did not make her feel safe. If someone came to untether a cow, or a goat bleated, or a lark went up from the grass, she jumped and stared round, expecting her throat to be grabbed and a knife to appear. She was, slowly, beginning to feel more rational when crowds of people came streaming out of town to follow the road to the Lawschool. Maewen started shaking again.

"Nearly midday." Navis stood up and brought her horse over.

Maewen mounted, hoping she would feel better high up on a horse. It seemed to help a little. They rode sedately over to join the stream of carts, carriages, riders, and walkers on the road, and she found herself hanging back nervously.

"Get the Southerner to steal the Adon's cup for you," the deep voice said suddenly in her ear.

Maewen felt like a water bed, trembling all over from being trodden on. "Is that all you can say? Where *were* you? Why didn't you warn me?"

"You are not hurt. The Southerners were there to help," said the voice.

"Oh thank you!" said Maewen. "You're such a comfort!" She was trembling with indignation now. What use was a ghostly adviser who did not care that you might have been killed? Angrily she caught up with Mitt and Navis as they joined the busy road. They had almost reached the clump of trees before she realized that she felt much better. It made her smile. Perhaps the voice knew what it was doing after all.

Outside the gracious buildings of the Lawschool there was now a picket line set up for horses, and boys in that old-fashioned uniform to guard it. The man with bad teeth was now letting people through the gate in slow twos and threes. Mitt jigged with impatience as they joined the line of people waiting to go in, and even Navis looked anxious.

Moril got down from a waiting carriage which had evidently given him a lift and came jogging over to them with his cwidder bumping on his back. He was folding up a pie and corn cakes in an expensive-looking linen napkin and chewing as he arrived. "They gave me lunch, too," he explained. "I wondered where you'd got to."

"And where is Hestefan?" asked Navis.

Moril looked a little anxious. "He said he'd have a

rest and meet us at the waystone with Wend. I don't think his health's very good. He's looked ill ever since the cart overturned."

"You think he got hurt then?" Mitt asked.

"Yes, but he won't say," said Moril.

They came to the gate and the man with bad teeth. Moril gave him a beaming smile. "Do you think you could take care of my cwidder until I come out?" That was how he got the ride in the coach, Maewen thought, watching the porter try to pretend that no one had ever asked him such a thing and then give in and take the cwidder carefully in his arms. Singers learned to get round people.

"Through the garden and turn right to the small quadrangle," the man said, as he said to everyone.

Nobody looked at the garden. Moril and Maewen passed through on the cobbled path, trying to keep up with Navis and Mitt. They swept through an archway on the right and came to a square court surrounded by buildings. Here stood a long row of young people in gray, with broad white collars. Some were much younger than Moril; some were nearly grown-up. Most seemed around Maewen's real age. Many of them were already greeting parents and other relatives, and most of the rest were staring sideways at the archway, looking for their own families. There were no hugs or shouts and almost no jigging about. Evidently the way of this school was to pretend you were very grown-up. It made things very awkward. Mitt, Navis, Moril, and Maewen went crabwise along the line, and the ones waiting stared coolly past them, until Navis stopped in front of a thin dark girl, whose pale face seemed to be set in a permanent little frown.

"Hildy!" he said. There was delight and relief all over him. Mitt was the same.

The dark girl turned from whispering to the enormous girl bulking beside her and stared at Navis. "Father! Fancy you being here!" Her face lit up. For a moment it looked as if she were going to break out of school custom and hug Navis. Then she remembered the grown-up behavior and took hold of both his hands instead, smiling all over her face. It made her look much younger. "Father, this *is* good! Now I'll have someone to show round and shout for me at last grittling after all!"

"Are you all right? Is all well here?" Navis asked her.

"Absolutely *mountaintop*!" said Hildy. "I love it here. But this is Biffa." She turned and pulled forward the huge girl beside her. "Biffa's my besting. Do you mind if she comes round with us? She's a winthrough like me, and her parents can't afford to come today. Please. She won't have anyone if I go off."

"I shall be honored," Navis said. Huge Biffa turned pink right down to her white collar and stood bulking helplessly, smiling. She had a very sweet smile. It transformed her slab of a face and made everyone see why Hildy liked her.

"Good," said Hildy, and began to tow Navis away, ignoring the rest of them completely.

Navis hung back. Mitt said, "Hello, Hildy."

Hildy glanced over her shoulder. "Oh. Hello, Mitt." It was barely friendly. Maewen found she could not bear to look at Mitt's face. The hurt in it and the disillusionment were so huge and so plain that it hurt her, too, just from the one glimpse she had of it.

Navis firmly pulled Hildy back again. "My dear daughter," he said. "Not so hasty. Let me introduce my friends. This young lady is, ah, Ilona Kernsdaughter."

Maewen bowed, impressed that Navis remembered to invent her a false name. Hildy's eyes swept over Maewen's travel-stained hearthman's livery and back to her face, which she seemed to study freckle by freckle. Hildy's eyes were very dark, very observant, and not very warm. Maewen felt thoroughly uncomfortable. She was wondering whether to bow again, ironically this time, when Hildy seemed to decide that Maewen met some standard she approved of. The little frown cleared from between her eyebrows, and she smiled and bent her head to Maewen.

"Who is placed in my care by her aunt," Navis continued. "This lad with me is Moril, from a line of famous Singers."

Singers were obviously something Hildy respected. She bowed and smiled at Moril, who stared gravely and did not bow back.

"And," Navis finished dryly, "Mitt, of course, you know."

Mitt had his face under control by then. It still stared pale and blank, but he grafted a joking smile onto it. "Turned up again like the bad penny," he said.

Somehow this hurt Maewen more than the way Mitt had looked at first. When Hildy nodded coolly and turned away, Maewen could have slapped her. *He's* looked forward to meeting you and worried about you—which is more than you deserve!—and you do *this* to him! she thought. You little—little *cow!*

They all moved off, with Mitt drifting in the rear like a sleepwalker. Moril spoke to huge Biffa. "Do you happen to know where I'll find my sister?" He said it shyly but somehow made it plain that he had no use for Hildy. "She's called Brid Clennensdaughter."

Maewen caught a look of sheer awe above her on Biffa's face. "Brid!" said Biffa. "Is Brid your *sister?* She's Great Girl this sessioning. She won all the prizes on tally. She's somewhere about with the Adon."

Eh? thought Maewen. But the Adon's dead, centuries before this.

Hildy turned half round from in front. "She means she's with the Earl of Hannart's heir," she said. "He came to see her because she's the Earl of the South Dales' sister."

There was a reverent note to her voice that told Maewen that Hildy was a snob. This probably accounted for the way she treated Mitt. Mitt had caught the reverent note, too, and his face was worse than ever.

"They say," Biffa added shyly to Moril, "that the Adon's in love with your sister."

"*Is* he?" said Moril, as if he thought he might have something to say about that. "Where's the best place to find them?"

"Skreths—no, maybe Climbers," said Biffa. "I'll come and show you if you like."

She led Moril off, while Hildy called instructions about where to meet again and Biffa called back about when. Both of them seemed to be talking gibberish. And when Biffa had vanished round the nearest corner, Maewen realized that there were only three of them left. Mitt seemed to have slipped off with Biffa, too. She could hardly blame him. She would not have stayed to be ignored by Hildy either. No, it was worse than ignoring. It was more unkind than that. From what Moril had told her, Hildy was an earl's granddaughter, but Navis was only a hearthman now. He was not going to be Duke of Kernsburgh for some years yet. There was no reason, no *excuse* for Hildy to think so well of herself.

She gloomily followed the girl on a grand tour of the school. It soon became a great blur to Maewen, confused in her mind with tours of the Tannoreth Palace—except that this tour was strewn with other pupils in white collars leading brightly clothed relatives who all looked as bewildered as Maewen. When she thought of the visit she had made here with Aunt Liss, she became even more confused. None of it was the same. When she remembered some of the buildings, they seemed smaller or in the wrong place. And parts of it were like any old school.

Maewen's head ached, and her stomachache came back. She trailed behind Hildy and Navis, wanting to sit down, while Hildy dragged Navis along by one hand, saying things like, "and this is where hardimers set trethers. Even if you're sailing in grybo, they can make you a comedown for squarks." She never once bothered to explain. Navis looked increasingly ironic. Maewen thought, Hildy doesn't want us to know what it really means. She's one of those that like to be on the inside knowing things, with everyone else on the outside, not knowing.

Perhaps this was unkind. Maewen knew she was still feeling odd because someone had tried to kill her. She made an effort. She came politely up beside Hildy while they were crossing an enormous courtyard that did not exist in Maewen's day and tried to join in the talk. But after a very short time of politeness, she found herself saying, not altogether kindly, "Why did you treat Mitt like that? He's been looking forward to seeing you."

"Really?" said Hildy. "How stupid of him. I suppose it comes of being uneducated."

"*Is* he uneducated?" Maewen said, even less kindly.

"He's practically *illiterate*," said Hildy. "He can

hardly read." She made it sound like an infectious disease. She added, "He used to *fish* for a living." Her manner of saying it told Maewen that Hildy was quite aware of Maewen's unkindness, that she had met it often before, and that she expected it and did not care two hoots.

Hmm, thought Maewen, dropping back again. I suppose that says volumes about her early life. She has problems. Well, I suppose unpleasant people *do* have problems, or they wouldn't be unpleasant, but that doesn't mean I have to like her—*or* forgive her! And she went on trailing behind. She ached all through. Some of it seemed to be an ache of the heart about the way Mitt must be feeling.

Been here before, Mitt was thinking. It's only what I'm used to. Only to be expected, really. Hildy's back in the life she was bred for and that's that. But though this stopped his hurting—a little—he was still hurting in other ways he was not used to at all.

He had thought Hildy was his friend. He had not known friendship could be such a fragile thing. Probably Ynen, if they found him, would not want to know Mitt either. And who cares? he said to himself, sauntering behind the mountainous Biffa and the much smaller Moril. The size of Biffa made him grin, hurt as he felt. She was a good few inches taller than he was, and Mitt knew he was around six feet these days.

"My parents keep the mill over in Ansdale," Biffa was saying to Moril, "and they're both taller than me.

If you think I'm big, you should see my brother. Size runs in our family."

"It's not far to Ansdale," said Moril.

"Two days," and Biffa. "That would be four, if one of them came to fetch me. They can't afford the time. But they sent me the horse hire to come home. I don't have to stay all through the recess like Hildy does."

Mitt wondered what kind of mountainous horse Biffa would have to hire to ride home on, but the sick, choked, hurt feeling kept him from joining in the conversation.

They crossed an echoing cloister and came out into a bright, hot courtyard with steps at both ends. "Climbers," said Biffa. "There she is."

A number of hearthmen in Hannart livery were sitting on the steps opposite, indulgently watching Kialan Kerilsson walk about the court talking with a dark-haired girl in Lawschool uniform. Mitt checked a bit at the sight. He had not properly attended to where Moril was going. But of course! he thought bitterly. Kialan comes here to see his fancy, and they let him in early because he's an earl's son, and he probably doesn't even notice he's getting special treatment. There's earls for you. Mitt thought he might go away. Then his misery said, What the hell—I'll give him a rude message to his father. And he walked down the steps with Biffa and Moril.

"Brid," Moril said sternly.

The girl spun round. She was very pretty, even

prettier than Fenna, and not as old as Mitt had expected, probably only his own age. *"Moril!"* she screamed, and unlike the pupils in the sober line, she rushed at Moril and flung her arms around him. The two of them hurtled round and round, both talking at once and laughing, with Kialan throwing remarks at Moril and laughing, too. Mitt stood back, hurting.

"I only came to fetch her back to Hannart," he heard Kialan say.

Brid's voice rose in a Singer's soprano, with a good strong edge to it. "Of *course* I'm not throwing away Singer heritage, Moril, *or* law learning! But it's *my* life, and I decide it!"

"So she'll be here for three more years," Kialan said ruefully. "Satisfied, Moril?" He probably was in love with Brid, Mitt thought. See the way he looked at her. His chest gave a wrench at the thought.

Out of a further babble of talk, Moril asked, "Is your father here?"

Kialan shook his frizzy head. "No, I came over alone. Why?"

Alone except for twenty hearthmen, Mitt thought, and was taken by surprise when Moril said, "Good. Then you can meet my friend Mitt."

Mitt's chest gave another wrench, that Moril called him a friend, and then a sort of hop at the eager way Kialan instantly swung round and stared, with his head up so that his nose made him look like a questing eagle. "Mitt?" Kialan said. "From Aberath? Really?" Mitt nodded warily. "What are you doing here?" Kialan asked, no less eagerly.

Mitt intended a laugh. It came out as a hacking sort of caw. "Visiting on Hildy Navissdaughter."

Kialan's mouth bunched like a prune. "That white-faced little sow. She'll be worse than Earl Hadd before she's through; she's the image of him already! Her brother Ynen's worth ten of her."

Mitt's chest did odd things again. He was not sure what he felt, but he somehow made no protest when Kialan signaled to Brid to keep talking to Moril and seized Mitt's arm and walked him out of their hearing. It was a lordly thing to do. Mitt found he hardly cared. The way he was feeling showed him that Kialan was a lordly type who would have acted like this if he'd been born a fisherman's heir. It was a strange discovery. He faced Kialan, pricking with odd new sensitivity.

"Am I glad to meet you at last!" Kialan said. Mitt knew he meant it. "I was looking for you all over when I was in Aberath. Did you really sail north with the Undying?"

"In a manner of speaking," Mitt said as they walked up the steps together. "It was Ynen's boat, but I helped bring Old Ammet aboard."

"I want to hear you tell it," Kialan said, "but that'll have to wait." He stopped halfway up the steps and again pulled Mitt round to face him. They were near enough of a height to look into one another's faces, but

Kialan was chunkier. Kialan said, slowly and carefully, "It was lucky I didn't run into you in Aberath. I'd have blurted out all sorts of jolly messages from Ynen—or I would have until that evening. My father spoke to me before supper then and told me you weren't supposed to know where Ynen is. And of course I couldn't go against my father."

Mitt looked into Kialan's light-colored eyes, a good many shades bluer than his own, and realized that Kialan was telling him all the same. His chest did strange things again. "When did you last speak to Ynen?" he asked, testing the situation.

"This lady—Noreth—is she riding the green roads?" Kialan asked, testing Mitt in return.

"Alive and kicking," Mitt said. "She's around the school somewhere if you want to meet her."

For a second Kialan looked as if he would dearly have loved to meet Noreth. Then he shook his curly head regretfully. "My father would be furious. In answer to your question, I spoke to Ynen this morning before I set off to come here. He wasn't allowed to send his love to his sister—" He looked questioningly at Mitt.

"All right," Mitt said. "I'll tell her."

"Thanks," said Kialan. "I'd promised Ynen. And you're riding with this Noreth Onesdaughter?"

"Down to Kernsburgh," said Mitt. "I suppose."

"I'll join you there," said Kialan. "With Ynen. Wait for us if we're not there first. It's going to take a bit of planning." He swung Mitt round again, and they strolled back down the steps. "So where did you make landfall?" he asked loudly, for the benefit of the hearthmen across the courtyard.

"Holy Isles," said Mitt. "And right weird they were."

"I've heard they are," Kialan agreed. "Where then?"

"Blown north again to Aberath," Mitt said. "We never saw the coast till then. We'd no idea we'd come that far."

"Amazing," said Kialan. "Well, thanks for telling me." He let go of Mitt's arm.

"You're welcome," Mitt said, backing away. "Tell Moril I'll be with Navis when he wants us."

"Right," said Kialan, strolling back toward the others. Brid waved and called out something happy to both of them.

Mitt could not face happy scenes. He went the other way, back up the steps with long, busy strides, pretending he had something important to do. His mind was all over the place. He needed to be alone to think. But there were people everywhere, in happy, chatting groups. Back and forth went Mitt, looking as busy as he knew how, through gardens, under arches, across a wide paved court, into buildings again. And always there were people. Until at last he came out into a gravel court where there was a small separate building, a funny domed place that looked older than all the rest. Nobody seemed to be about here. Mitt went cautiously in through its arched doorway. Inside, it seemed to be a stone summerhouse with a stone table up some steps at one end. Mitt sat on one of the stone benches that curved round the walls, between bundles of twisted greenstone pillars, and gave himself thankfully up to thought.

So Ynen was in Hannart, then, right under Keril's eye. It made sense. Even Navis would hardly try to get Ynen out of there. But Kialan could. Who would have thought it? Mistrustfully Mitt tried to tell himself that Kialan had not meant a word of what he seemed to mean. He was just acting for his father, getting Mitt to betray himself. "And I did—didn't I just!" Mitt said aloud. But as the words echoed round the domed room, he knew that Kialan had been entirely straight with him. Kialan was all right. The bitter, disillusioned feeling that made Mitt not want to trust anyone was about Hildy, not Kialan. He knew very well how Kialan came to think so differently from his father. Mitt had only to recall that glimpse he had had, of Kialan shuffling through Holand, a prisoner of Navis's father, to know it. Over a year ago it had been now, but Mitt remembered it as fresh as if it were yesterday. No doubt Kialan remembered even better. Kialan knew all about how it felt to be in the power of an earl.

All the same, Kialan had no call to say Hildy was like Earl Hadd. Mitt decided he hated Kialan for that—all the more because he suspected Kialan might be right.

"Damned *earls* and their families!" Mitt said out loud, clenching both hands on the edge of the stone seat. His eyes glared ahead at the stone table and the lopsided metal cup on it. Hildy and Kialan between them had mixed his mind up properly.

His eyes suddenly told him what they were seeing. That stone table was an altar. There was an image in a niche above it of an old man lifting up a mountain. The One. That meant that the lopsided cup had to be the one Noreth wanted—the Adon's cup.

Mitt clutched the stone bench even harder. It was the perfect opportunity. All he had to do was walk over, pick the thing up, and stuff it down the front of his jacket. Noreth would rejoice. And with the school swarming with people, if somebody did notice the cup was gone and raise a shout, how were they to know which of the crowd had taken it? If Mitt took it and went *now*, through the valley and up to the green road, he could be gone before anyone could do anything. So why was he sitting here like an idiot, clinging to a stone seat until his fingers hurt?

Because it was stealing. Because he had made that promise to Alk. Because he had spoken words to Old Ammet and to Libby Beer—who had been around yesterday and today, perhaps to remind Mitt of those words. Mitt grinned, a bent, unfunny smile. Funny the way it was never enough to swear and promise just the *once*. You seemed to have to rethink and repromise every time the subject came up. Mitt's smile narrowed away. This time he would be stealing from the One, and even sane, level Alk was cautious with the One. On the other hand, Noreth was the One's own daughter, and the One wanted her to have the cup. And now, after Hildy and Kialan had mixed Mitt's mind up, he felt like doing something bad. It would be a waste not to, really.

Mitt unclenched his fists from the bench and stood up. He listened. All the voices and footsteps he could hear were off in the distance. What he could see of the gravel court through the doorway was empty. So. Get it over with.

Mitt took three long strides to the altar. There he flinched and froze. He could have sworn a shadow, like an old man with a long nose, had swung through the room as he took the third step. As if someone had flitted across the doorway. But he stood and he waited and he listened and no feet crunched on the gravel outside. The new view he had of the court from here was empty. He stretched out a cautious hand and grasped the cup round its wide, uneven stem.

The domed room filled with crackling blue light.

Mitt leaped back. One arm was over his face and watering eyes. The other hand was fizzing, prickling, and stinging, and he shook it frantically. The light was gone by then. Mitt blinked away tears and dazzle, panting. No wonder no one bothered to guard this cup. The thing looked after itself. He looked round nervously, hoping that no one had been near enough to see the One's chapel suddenly fill with light.

Somebody must have been. There were shouts outside, loud and desperate, from somebody young.

:‖ 14 ‖:

MAEWEN HAD HAD ENOUGH of Hildy by then. Navis was being far too patient with her. "Now look, my dear," he was saying, as they wandered through the garden by the gate, "it really is vital that you come away with us today. If you remain here, you're playing into Earl Keril's hands. He's using you as a hostage for my behavior—not to speak of Mitt's."

"Let's *not* speak of Mitt," said Hildy.

"All right, we'll speak of you, then," Navis agreed. "Everyone else goes away from here today, isn't that right? Surely you would prefer not to be left all alone in this place all summer."

The fierce little frown grew between Hildy's brows. "Why are you bothering now? I was alone here for nearly two weeks at spring recess—at least, Biffa was here, too, but it was *nearly* alone—and I didn't mind."

"Things have changed since then," Navis said patiently.

"What things?" said Hildy.

"Politics. I know now that you were sent to this place as part of a plan," Navis explained. "The plans I've made to counter the earls' move could make it very dangerous for you. Keril knows you are here. He has only to take you away. Anyway, the only safe thing for you to do is to be with me for the next three months. I—"

"Three *months*!" Hildy interrupted. "But then I'd miss Harvest grittling and modes *and* the start of middle vokes— *No!*"

"Well, yes, I'm afraid you would," Navis admitted. "But you'd be alive. You'd not be in prison. You can always come back next year, if things go our way."

"*If!* Next *year*! Miss a whole *year*!" It was clear Hildy could not believe her ears. "Just for politics! No *way*!" She meant this so much that she actually made an effort to explain. "Father, you're asking me to go back to junior vocation studies, just for *politics*."

Navis looked exasperated and, for him, surprisingly helpless. His eyes flicked to Maewen. Maewen realized she must be some of his difficulty. She supposed it was because Navis had told Hildy she was someone called Ilona Something and Navis was not sure he dared explain who she really was—or who Navis *thought* she was. Oh, what a muddle! Maewen was sick of this. It was with enormous relief that she saw Biffa coming towering through the garden toward them. Maewen rushed to meet her.

"There you are!" Biffa said. "I hunted everywhere.

Then I thought she'd decided to show you the One's chapel and I came this way. Have you been there?"

"Not yet," Maewen said. "Which way is it?"

But Biffa was gazing over Maewen's head. "What's wrong with Hildy? She looks near on in one of her rages."

Maewen looked back at Navis and Hildy, bent toward one another arguing, against a great bush of lavender full of bees. She saw the anger in Hildy's white face and the worry in Biffa's healthy pink one, and she wondered how Hildy had managed to be friends with such a nice girl. "Navis wants to take her away with him," she explained, "and she won't go."

"Why ever *not*?" said Biffa. "She's been right gloomy all this week, saying she'll be alone all summer here—you wouldn't believe!"

Maewen could believe. "Then go and persuade her. Navis is worried to death," she said. "Which way is the One's chapel?"

"Over there," Biffa said, pointing. "You'll just have time before grittling." She strode over to the lavender bush to loom anxiously over Hildy.

Maewen sighed as she trudged off the way Biffa pointed. She knew Biffa would persuade Hildy. She supposed it was a good thing, if Hildy *was* in danger. But the idea depressed her too much for her to bother to work out what the danger might be. There would be Hildy all the way to Kernsburgh, frowning angrily and pretending Mitt did not exist. And Mitt would have that look all the time, with that horrible jokey smile grafted on top of it. It hardly bore thinking of.

Chalk up another black mark to this Keril, she thought, as she came through the bushes and saw the One's chapel across a gravel court. It was just as she had remembered it. But she had not remembered it *here*. The buildings must all have been in different places after two hundred years. I wonder why she didn't show us it, Maewen thought. No, I know why. It's not something she can call a silly name and mystify us with. Or maybe she'd call it Wunners.

The thought amused Maewen enough to give her the courage to advance slowly and quietly toward the small, domed building. She was not happy with the idea of stealing this cup. But she did think she ought to do something for herself. And of course she was in the fortunate position of knowing that she had done it. Just rush in, snatch it, and out, she told herself as she advanced cautiously, slantwise to the door.

A funny blue flash made her jump round. The gravel crunched under quick footsteps. Maewen swung round further, almost in time. Someone muffled in a gray robe grabbed at her with one hand and raised a knife in the other.

"No, not again! *Help!*" Maewen screamed.

She went on screaming because this time he had not grabbed her throat. It was so much like last time that she was sure it was the same man. He had her arm instead of her throat, and he was trying to twist it so that she would hold still for him to bring down the knife into her neck. In spite of the way it hurt, Maewen seized the wrist of his knife hand with her free hand and frantically held it away. She could see his face over her head. It seemed to be made of gray cloth, except for his glaring eyes. The sight turned her weak. She could only push at his wrist and keep screaming, "*Help!* I'm being *killed*!"

Gravel scrunched and spurted, stinging her face. Someone said, "Flaming *Ammet!*" and then, "Drop that, you hooded horror, you!" Mitt's unmistakable large bony hand closed over the fist that was trying to stab Maewen. Everyone swayed, and grunted, and slid, in a shrill jangling of gravel. Then the attacker wrenched his hand, and his knife, free and ran, with Mitt after him like a greyhound. Maewen was left standing in a patter of small stones, still shouting.

"Oh save me, Mitt!"

She heard herself say it, as the madly running gray man plunged into the bushes and trees of the garden and Mitt hurtled after him. She stood staring, feeling a total fool. Tears were running down her face, though she had no memory of when she had started crying. How—how totally . . . *girly!* "Oh save me, Mitt!" she mimicked herself. Honestly!

She tried to walk to the chapel then, but her legs wobbled and refused to go, even though at the time they were carrying her round and round on the spot, like someone in a mad, giddy dance. She seemed to be trying to see all sides of the yard at once in case there were any more gray attackers. She made herself stop that. She managed to stand still and wipe her eyes, but that was all she could manage before Mitt came hurtling back with Navis running beside him. Both of them looked so anxious that tears came leaking down Maewen's face again.

"Bastard got away in the bushes!" Mitt said disgustedly.

"What are you doing on your own here?" Navis demanded.

Maewen swallowed. "Cup," she managed, but that was all.

"That's easily solved," said Navis. "Stay with her, Mitt."

Before Mitt could say anything, Navis had crossed the gravel and briskly vanished into the chapel.

"Are you all right?" Mitt asked Maewen. He put both hands out uncertainly, with half a mind to take hold of her shoulders. But then he did not quite like to touch her. Maewen instantly found she was hurling herself against him. She pressed her face against his chest. Through the hard mail she could feel Mitt panting and his heart thumping. She was sure she was embarrassing him horribly, but this did not prevent her from wrapping her arms round him, tightly. One of Mitt's arms came gingerly round her shoulders and he patted her back. "There, there. It's all right."

"Oh Mitt, I'm so sorry!" Maewen blurted. "About me and about Hildy—about *everything*!"

"There, there," Mitt repeated.

That was all they had time for before Navis trod briskly out of the chapel again, carrying something bundled in a large handkerchief. "Quite simple, you see," he said.

Mitt stood back a bit, with a damp spreading patch on his jacket where Maewen's face had been. "Simple?" he said. "It's got a hex on it sizzles off like a thunderbolt when you touch it!"

"This being the North, I considered that," said Navis, "and I didn't touch it. Look." He opened the silk handkerchief a fraction to show the cup nestled in it. Then he calmly stowed the bundle in one of his wide pockets. "We'd best take ourselves off to the great court," he said as he made sure this pocket was arranged not to bulge more than the one on the other side of his coat. "We must attend a closing ceremony, it seems."

They went there slowly. Maewen was still shaking, and her legs were not steady. Navis courteously put his hand under her elbow to help her along. Mitt avoided touching her. Maewen kept seeing him rubbing at the wet patch her face had made on his chest. She could hardly look at him for embarrassment.

"You persuaded Hildy to come along?" Mitt asked, rather too casually, giving his chest a further rub.

"Not yet," said Navis.

Mitt's face went tight and bony, like a skull. "She's *got* to."

"I know," said Navis. "I'm hoping that extremely

large friend of hers can make her see reason. In that hope I explained the whole situation to both of them."

"Biffa?" said Mitt. "Is that safe?"

"I trusted her," said Navis. "And this you won't believe! The girl's real name is Enblith!"

"After Enblith the Fair!" In spite of his skull face of worry, Mitt began to giggle.

"Unkind, isn't it?" Navis said. "Her parents made a serious miscalculation there. Not that she's *un*beautiful, poor girl. Just too big for one to see it."

Maewen wondered how anyone could be so cool with the stolen cup in his pocket. Mitt tried to match Navis in coolness. He said, "I found out where Ynen is. It seems like bad news, but it could just be good— very good."

"Later. Hush," said Navis.

They came round a corner in a covered walk and found themselves at the top of wide steps overlooking the biggest courtyard. People were crowded on the steps below them, serious, parently people, all looking across to the main school building, where a line of gray-coated teachers stood. One stood out in front in a blue and gray gown. In front of them the courtyard was filled with rows and rows of uniformed pupils in bright white collars.

They had missed quite a bit of the ceremony. The gowned teacher was saying, in a voice that carried almost as well as Hestefan's, "For those who now go out into the world, this is a solemn leave-taking. For those who will return here next Harvest, it is a temporary parting, accompanied, I hope, by new resolves and higher endeavors. I would like you all seriously to consider . . ."

Maewen let the strong voice fade to a drone in her ears. I don't believe it! she thought. Headmasters must have made this speech ever since schools were invented!

Something scuffled behind. She and Mitt both jumped round. But it was only Moril, tiptoeing toward them. He looked white and worried. Mitt, at the sight of him, self-consciously rubbed at his chest again. "What's up?"

"The cup!" Moril whispered back. "I went to get it and it wasn't there!"

"Never fear," Navis murmured. "The sacrilege has been committed already."

"Is that why you all look so worried? Why don't we just go, then?" Moril said.

People on the steps turned round and said, "Hush!" Navis put a finger to his lips. Maewen pulled herself together enough to take hold of Moril's arm and tow him back round the corner.

"We have to leave with everyone else or they'll know exactly who's got it," she whispered.

Moril was no fool. She saw him realize this as she was telling him. "Sorry," he said. "But I told Mitt *I'd* get it. He—"

"It wasn't Mitt. It was Navis."

This obviously astonished Moril. Well, it astonished Maewen, too, now she came to think of it. Navis was an adult and a sensible person. If he thought it was necessary to take the cup, this somehow made the whole matter more serious.

When they came back round the corner, the headmaster was saying, "We will now sing our customary prayer to the One, who is the special guardian of our school. What comes after that is something my staff and I know nothing about."

For some reason almost everyone laughed. Then the gray rows of pupils broke into song. It was a solemn and simple invocation to the One and like nothing Maewen had heard before. Mitt was as startled as she was. The song was beautiful. The strange old tune swelled and mounted, warm and chilling at the same time, and full of reverence. While it lasted, something seemed to fill the vast courtyard that was not of this world. Maewen's back prickled. Navis has done an awful thing! she thought. But Navis never turned a hair.

Moril listened critically. "I never care for those old tunes," he said. "What's going— Oh, I remember."

The headmaster and the other teachers had vanished from the front of the building as if the ground had swallowed them up, and the ranks of gray-uniformed pupils were suddenly seething. Nearly every one of them was pulling over his or her head a colored hood of some kind, and most were putting on clumsy gloves, too. Quite a number of the hoods were gray, or gray with a blue or orange tuft on top. As soon as Maewen saw them, she understood how her attacker had managed to be so thoroughly disguised. He must have raided a cloakroom. The hoods covered faces except for the eyes. Sober pupils had now become blob-faced monsters, with formless gray, green, or red heads. The sight upset her.

There was confused shouting, muffled and strange, from under the hoods. It sounded like "Bad on" and "Herry's gone."

After a second Kialan came sauntering down the steps at one side, trying, from the look of him, not to look as silly and sheepish as he felt, and stopped slightly to one side of the milling monsters.

"They always ask the most important visitor to start it," Moril explained.

"Eye, eye, eye," came the muffled shouts. "Owe it eye."

Kialan nodded. Someone on the steps tossed him a great brown ragged ball. Kialan took it in one hand, bent over sideways with it, and heaved it high into the sky. He probably intended it to come down somewhere in the middle of the crowd, but either the thing was weighted oddly or Kialan miscalculated his throw. The ball came down again almost where he was standing. Kialan saw it come and simply ran for his life.

"Nor don't I blame him!" Mitt said.

The whole crowd of monsters closed on the spot,

fighting like maniacs. Many fought with fists and feet. But weapons appeared, too, which must have been hidden under the sober uniforms. There were clubs, whips, and sticks, and at least one person was wielding a short plank. It looked as if someone would be maimed or trampled to death any second.

After a stunned minute Navis said, "This, I take it, is grittling?"

"That's right," said Moril.

"How comforting to know," Navis said, "that the South is, after all, a comparatively peaceful place. And here was I thinking that all the bloodshed happened south of the passes."

"Yes, but what are the *rules*?" Mitt wanted to know.

The rest of the spectators were shouting, "Up the reds!" and "Yellow, yellow, yellow!" as if they knew what was going on. Moril was not very sure, but he thought each of the colors was a team, and the aim was for one team to get the ball into its own special place round the edge of the big court. There were lots of places. There seemed to be at least seven teams. The fight rushed this way and that.

"I hope they don't make a mistake and score with someone's severed head instead of the ball," Navis murmured. "How long does it usually take, and how many deaths result?"

"I don't know," Moril confessed. "Brid doesn't do it."

It seemed to take hours. Hours of yelling, battling,

and thwacking, of giant surges and furious counterattacks. Long before it was over, Maewen was hiding her eyes. The sight of all this fighting, after someone had twice tried to kill her, was just too much. She wanted to leave. But as she had sensibly told Moril, they dared not leave.

Moril was not happy either. "It reminds me of Flennpass," he said.

Mitt, on the other hand, had discovered that it was easy to pick Biffa out in the fray, and he was yelling with the rest. "Come *on*, Biffa! Hit him! Ammet, that girl's strong. Go to it, Biffa! Go it!"

And eventually the ball went into someone's goal area in a tumble of gray bodies and a great deal of shouting.

Shortly after that Hildy and Biffa joined them on the steps. They were both dangling blue hoods and were very flushed. The hoods were padded all over, particularly across the nose, and they must have been boiling hot in them.

"Well?" said Navis. "Did you win?"

Hildy's chin lifted haughtily. "*Of* course. You must have seen."

"I saw murder, mayhem, and confusion," Navis retorted. "Are either of you seriously maimed?"

"Of course not—not with Biffa as our surnam," Hildy said.

"It was great!" said Mitt. "Don't mind him. Hildy, Ynen sends you his love."

Hildy glanced at Mitt as if it were very tiresome to

have to answer. "Thanks," she said, and turned back to her father. The look settled on Mitt's face again. It was not so much hurt as mortally wounded, Maewen thought. She wished someone *had* maimed Hildy.

"Father," Hildy said, "I've come to a decision. I intend to be a really good law-woman and—"

"An excellent intention," said Navis. "Is this recent? Did it come upon you during the grittling?"

Hildy stamped her foot. Maewen hardly blamed her. Navis could be maddening. "Oh, I wish you wouldn't be so—so *unserious* all the time! You always try to stop me doing things by making me look silly!"

"Let us get this clear, Hildy," Navis said, almost angrily. "I have never, ever wanted to prevent you being a lawyer. I am not trying to stop you now."

"Yes, you *are*!" Hildy cried out. "If what you told me goes wrong, then we'd be on the run and I'd *never* get back here. I'd have to sacrifice what *I* want to politics, just like I have done all my life! I'm not going to. I refuse to come with you. I'm staying *here*!" She spun round and marched away down the steps, angrily swinging her blue hood.

Navis watched until she was lost in the surging, mingling crowd. His eyes were narrowed. He looked vicious and wretched.

"Excuse me, sir," Biffa said, looming shyly over him.

Navis jumped and looked up at her. "Didn't anything I said get through to her?" he asked Biffa.

"Not really," Biffa admitted. "But it got through to

me. That's what I wanted to talk to you about. I know she ought to be away from here, somewhere where no earls will think to look, and I thought— Anyway, if I asked her to come home to our mill with me for the summer, I *know* she'd come, and no one would expect that, because we're poor. But—but the trouble is I only have the hire for one horse."

Navis's face relaxed. "May the One bless you, my child!" he said. "That would solve the summer. But I was talking about an autumn campaign, if you remember. Can you think of a way to stop her coming back here?"

Biffa shyly twisted her hood. "That's the other thing I wanted to tell you, sir. We get the autumn storms real terribly in from the Marshes, over in Ansdale. Sometimes you can't get down to the valleys until weeks after Harvest. I was over a month late getting here last autumn. That's how I came to know Hildy. We were both latecomers, as well as on scholarships. But Hildy came a month after me, and she won't know."

"Aha!" said Navis. "This is deep cunning, my dear!" Biffa went very pink and shot a flustered smile at Mitt, then at Maewen and Moril. "Well, if you think you can keep my thankless daughter safe," Navis went on, briskly undoing his money belt, "here is the hire of a horse for her and money for her keep. Is this enough?"

Biffa looked at the pile of gold coins he pushed into her hand, and her eyes went large. "It would do me a year, sir—or two, if I went steady. I'll give it Hildy now, not to be tempted. That's the third thing I wanted to tell you: We ought to go *now*, in among everyone else, so that when those Hannart people look round for Hildy, she's gone. Wouldn't you say so, sir?"

"Absolutely right," said Navis. "Biffa, you are an extremely intelligent young woman."

Biffa went an even brighter pink. "Yes, I know," she said. "But me being so big, people never think of me as clever. I trade on it quite a lot." Everyone laughed. It was too much for Biffa. She turned and ran.

"Quite a character," Navis said.

"Do you *trust* her?" Mitt said.

"I think it's all right," Moril said. "She sort of worships Hildy—you know the way girls do."

"But all that money!" Mitt muttered as they joined the shuffling mass of people trying to get through the garden and out of the school gate. "I wouldn't trust *myself* with that lot. And she said she traded on her size."

It was a nerve-racking time. They shuffled and stopped and shuffled again, and the garden lawn got trampled under many feet. They were too far from the gate to tell if the cup had been missed, or if the many holdups were because Hannart hearthmen were waiting at the gate for Hildy or Maewen. And that gate was the only way out.

"I think it's merely the confusion of so many departures," Navis said. He was completely cool. He seemed to be one of those people who just got cooler the more danger there was.

As they shuffled nearer the gate, it began to look as if Navis was right. The opening was crammed with parents and pupils and younger brothers and sisters, all with luggage and lunch baskets. Pupils kept forgetting things and shoving back into the school to find them. Many families had hired porters to carry the pupils' trunks, so the way was constantly being blocked by men with handcarts, shouting, "Porter for Serieth Gunsson!" as they came in and, "Por-ter! Mind your backs!" as they shoved their way out again.

After a while Moril said quietly, "Biffa and Hildy are in the crowd behind us."

Maewen wished she was taller. It took her five minutes of twisting and standing on tiptoe to see the two girls. Both carried bulging bags. Very sensibly they had mixed themselves up with a family of tall men who were fetching home a boy pupil even taller than Biffa and were talking busily with them as if they belonged.

"A relief," Navis said, after he had turned casually and seen them, too. "So young Biffa *is* honest then."

They reached the gate at long last. People were just shoving their way through without being stopped but without any order either. The man with bad teeth was standing to one side. He stopped Navis.

"Excuse me, sir." Everyone waited for the worst. "Excuse me, one of your party left a cwidder with me."

Moril shoved his way through, while the rest of

them tried hard not to look as relieved as they felt. The man turned and fetched the cwidder out of his cubbyhole beside the gate.

"Here you are. One cwidder, safe and sound. Is it you the Adon's waiting for?" He pointed sideways through the opening.

There, beyond a confusion of carriages and carts, the Hannart horsemen stood in a huddle. Kialan was in the midst of them, looking bored and impatient.

Moril took it in without a blink. "No. It's my sister. She's always late."

"No, lad, she's out there," the man said.

They could all see Brid as he spoke, on a horse beside Kialan.

"Well, it's not me. I don't live in Hannart," Moril said. "I expect they're waiting for Hildrida Navissdaughter. Isn't that so?" he asked Navis.

"My daughter," Navis said, looking quite at ease, "is even more inclined to be late than your sister."

The man laughed a mouthful of bad teeth. "Women!" he said, handing Moril the cwidder.

They went out through the gate. Mitt and Maewen felt weak at the risk of it all, but Navis and Moril wandered nonchalantly along the line of horses and Navis gave Moril a leg up to ride double with him until they came to the cart. As he arrived on top of the mare, Moril gave Kialan a friendly wave. Kialan waved back. They saw him scan the three horses and try not to look puzzled.

Moril giggled. "Expecting Hildrida to be with us and all set to pretend he didn't see," he said as Mitt and Maewen mounted. "Now he can't think what's going on. Good. It distracted him beautifully."

Mitt batted aside the Countess-horse's biting mouth. "What do you mean?"

Navis set a sedate pace round the walls toward the main part of Gardale Valley. It was sensible, although Maewen could see the cup flopping heavily in Navis's pocket and the sight made her want to gallop. "Moril means," he said, "that while he was waving to Kialan, Hildy and Biffa came out and almost instantly cadged a lift in a carriage. If that carriage takes them into town and they hire horses at those stables in the first street, they could be away almost as soon as we are."

"And Kialan can't tell Keril," said Moril. "Keril's rather good at getting things out of people."

"I believe you," said Mitt.

As their three horses rounded the corner of the school walls, Maewen had a good view of a man in Hannart livery pushing his way out through the gate and running toward Kialan, shaking his head. Before they were quite out of sight, Kialan was giving a genuine display of someone annoyed and baffled and at the end of his patience. As the walls hid them, the Hannart horsemen were turning to ride off the other way.

Miraculously, nobody at all seemed to have noticed the cup was missing.

PART FOUR

Sword
and Crown

:‖ 15 ‖:

Weariness hit Maewen as soon as they were well away from the school. The Gardale Valley was as beautiful as she remembered from her visit with Aunt Liss, and much the same except there were far fewer houses. They took narrow lanes where wild roses grew in the hedges, miles of them, that blurred in her mind. She was so tired she almost missed seeing Hestefan's cart and would have ridden straight past if the others had not stopped.

The cart was parked on a triangle where three lanes met. The mule was hitched to an oak tree almost the same color as the cart and dozing on its feet. Moril jumped off the mare and went racing anxiously over, with the cwidder bumping on his back. He looked over the tailgate and came back. "It's all right. He's asleep inside." The relief in his face was mixed with worry. "I don't think he's well."

"He's not a young man," Navis said. "And I'm sure he was injured, or shocked at least, when your cart overturned."

"Let him sleep," Mitt suggested. "They say sleep cures."

Moril unhitched the mule, which was not anxious to move, and drove the cart behind the horses. Hestefan did not stir. The miles went by slower still. Moril was white with worry.

"And no wonder," Navis murmured to Mitt. "What becomes of him if Hestefan dies?"

"There's that brother of his," Mitt said stoutly. "He's fond of the old lolly, that's all. Worry about Hildy instead. And I'll tell you about Kialan now."

The two of them talked in low voices. Maewen continued to ride in a daze, long, long lanes through the valley, a long, long haul up a slanting track into the hills beyond. After what seemed an age, her horse humped itself onto level green turf at the head of the track, and there was the waystone casting a huge hollow shadow in the evening light. Wend's shadow was even bigger as he stood up to meet them.

Seeing him, Maewen relaxed from a watch she had not realized she was keeping. Safe at last! she thought. Wend was Undying. He had the power to keep her safe. Most of her weariness dropped away. She realized it had been a smoke screen her mind had put up to disguise how terrified she had been that someone would jump out from behind a hedge and try to kill her again. She was so glad to see Wend that she leaned down from her horse and wrung his hand.

Wend was surprised, but she could tell he was very

flattered, too. His face looked like that of a normal human person who was glad to see friends again. "There's a good camp in a mile or so," he said.

It was a very good camp. It was a green lawnlike place set back from the road, spread beside a pool from a cascading stream. There were rocks to sit on and a small wood of rowans and silver birches leaning over the place. "Protection," Wend said, patting a graceful silver trunk.

"Libby Beer?" Mitt asked.

Wend looked at him. "You know her?" he asked sharply.

"You might say so," Mitt said. "We've met once or twice."

Wend stared at him gravely for a moment, as if he were reappraising something. Then he turned away, looking puzzled.

The fresh, safe feeling in the camp revived everyone. They all bustled about, seeing to the horses and making a fire. When Hestefan crawled out of the cart, rubbing his eyes and saying he didn't know what had come over him, he was greeted with jokes and laughter from everyone. There did not seem to be much wrong with Hestefan. He helped Wend fill Wend's hat with wild strawberries as energetically as Mitt and Moril were hunting mushrooms farther upstream. Among them they provided quite a feast.

Maewen kept looking at Mitt, wondering if he was still feeling bad about Hildy. She simply could not tell. The fact was, Mitt had no idea himself. At times, while Navis was giving Wend and Hestefan the story of all they had missed in Gardale, he thought that if only someone would give him definite proof that Hildy and Biffa were safely on the way to Ansdale, he could forget Hildy entirely—almost with relief. Trouble with me, he thought, watching Wend's straight, fair face turning to Noreth in alarm, I'm like a stupid dog that asks to be kicked.

"Twice?" said Wend. "Lady, I must ask you not to go down from the green roads again. The paths can keep you safe."

"But did you get the cup?" Hestefan asked.

"Navis did," Moril said. He was still sore about it.

"Please show us," Hestefan said politely to Navis.

Maewen forgot Mitt. This was going to be alarming. Nervously she watched Navis feel in his pocket and pull out the bundle of silk handkerchief. It was twilight by then and greenish. As the handkerchief fell aside, the firelight made mild dancing gleams on the silver of the cup. Navis bowed to Maewen from his seat on a boulder. "Your cup, Noreth," he said, handing it to Mitt to pass over to her.

Mitt was not expecting Navis to hand him the cup. He came out of his thoughts with a jump and fumbled. The handkerchief unrolled. For an instant the green light and the flicker of the fire just vanished, over-whelmed in blue fizzling light. *"Ouch!"* said Mitt. While everyone blinked and saw yellow dazzle, he hastily rewrapped the cup and passed it to Maewen. "Careful. There's a strong hex on it."

Maewen took the bundle. This was worse than the ring. They were all expecting her to unwrap it and take hold of it and she was probably going to be electrocuted. But, she told herself, swallowing hard, if I *had* been electrocuted, Wend would have mentioned it in the palace. Here goes. Pulling away the handkerchief, she said, "Look, everyone. This is the Adon's cup." She took firm hold of the lopsided silver bowl of it and held it out.

To her huge relief, nothing fizzed. Everyone's dim faces were turned to the cup. After a moment or so Maewen realized they were looking at the way her hands looked dark against it, darker than natural. The cup seemed to have grown brighter. Yes. It had. It was filling with a spreading gentle blue glow, shining like a blue lamp in the near dark, making her hands look bloodred against it. It was so beautiful, and so welcome, that her eyes filled with tears.

Several people let breath out noisily. "It is the cup," Wend said. "It knows you as it knew the Adon."

Well, thank the One! Maewen thought as she wrapped the thing up again.

Under the friendly rustling of the rowans and birches, they all slept well. But toward dawn, around the time when the pouring of the stream began to sound less soothing and more like a noise, and people began to turn and shift because the grass was flat and the bones of the earth came through, Mitt had a strange dream. There was danger in it, and wonder, and the two were mixed up confusingly.

It began with him looking down on the camp from above. He saw the silver cup glowing and another, yellower glow nearby. After a while he knew the yellow glow was from the golden statue. It was very important. Mitt looked at it and thought, Noreth won't need it so much now. I can have my share. But that was not why it was important. Mitt puzzled over this, until his attention was distracted by finding he could see the green roads winding away from the camp. While he was looking at them, he dreamed he was back in the camp, lying under his blanket, dreaming he was looking at the green roads.

He dreamed and looked at the roads with interest. They went in all directions, snaking among the mountains, linking place to place. He could see them all, right down past Dropwater to Kernsburgh and beyond that, into the North Dales and on into the South. Yes, there had been green roads that led through the South, but they were not kept up any longer. Things moved over them, keeping them hidden, dangerous things. But they had been meant to cover all Dalemark.

Mitt dreamed that he would have been happier about seeing it all if the roads had not kept coming back to him, lying under the rowan trees and in danger. Since the idea of danger made him impatient, he turned his attention out again, to the roads, gray under late yellow moonlight, and took a look at the people traveling on them. Quite a few people were up early or traveling through the night. Hildy was one. She and Biffa were riding, a long way over toward that smoking mountain, nearly into Ansdale already. Kialan was riding, too, well on the way to Hannart. This meant danger. That troubled Mitt, so he looked North, where the young Singer who was Moril's brother was up early and hastening toward Adenmouth. Beyond, and coming toward Dagner, there were more riders. These meant danger, too.

There was a black patch of danger centered on the camp under the rowan trees.

Mitt ignored it obstinately and kept watching the roads. He saw the Undying moving on them, too, unnoticed by ordinary people. They looked so much like ordinary people that Mitt wondered how he knew they were Undying. But he knew King Hern, coming down the King's Way to build Kernsburgh, though King Hern looked like a gawky boy only about Mitt's age, and he knew Manaliabrid, hurrying into exile with the Adon and a small boy who was the Adon's son. The Adon turned out to be a short man, much more like Navis than Mitt expected, and Manaliabrid had a strong look of Noreth about her. Wend was with them, to Mitt's surprise, looking much the same.

Now he knew he was dreaming. So it did not surprise him that the green roads were winding away into the past. He lay and marveled at the way they turned back and forth through history, up to the present, into the place where he lay in such danger, and then went winding and snaking on into the far future. The Undying went walking on, taking the roads through time, and history went with them, ignoring them, forgetting the Undying were making history. He watched the roads snake out again into the South, and battles, and other strange things. He would have enjoyed watching more, if the roads had not kept on winding back into the rowan trees and showing him Noreth was a danger.

"No," Mitt said to his dream. "She may be *in* danger, but she's not *a* danger."

And the dream kept telling him, "Not Noreth. You."

"Ah, come on! *She's* all right," Mitt told the dream. "If there's any danger, it's those earls."

Then he woke into white mist with gray trees like shadows in it, feeling very irritable and rather frightened.

Everyone else seemed annoyingly refreshed. When Wend asked Maewen, "Where to next, lady?" she answered cheerfully, "To get the Adon's sword."

"Then we go toward Dropwater," Wend said.

When the road branched at the next waystone, they took the right-hand branch and found themselves almost at once in the stony bottom of a vast valley. It dwarfed everyone. Sweeps of hill rose on either side, barren, and curved tight as a wind-filled sail. Mitt supposed he was put in mind of sails because the wind streamed in this valley, with a sour sort of whistling, as hard as he had ever known it at sea. Like wind at sea, it kept sweeping bands of misty rain across them, which made the barren hills look even more harsh and empty. They look stretched, Mitt thought, staring up at the bare yellowness, through little itching raindrops. A vision came to him of the One, immeasurably huge, taking the hard rocky edge of this land and pulling until it was so tight it would stretch no more. Rivers, rocks, and creatures went tumbling and rolling as the One pulled—

Mitt shivered and hunched into his jacket. He had a dim memory that he might have seen something like this in his dream. He put it, and the idea of danger, resolutely out of his mind. It did no good to get nervous fancies.

It was a drear day's ride and a cheerless camp that night, which could not have been more of a contrast to the camp under the rowan trees. The wind came from all directions. The flames of the fire blew out raggedly, making more smoke than warmth, and the smoke seemed to follow you about wherever you sat. Everyone, even Moril and Hestefan in the cart, rolled themselves in all the coats, cloaks, and blankets they could muster, but nobody slept very well. The wind seemed to get in everywhere. Mitt was so cold that he got up almost before it was light. It had rained again, and everything he had was damp. Since it did not seem to matter how much colder or wetter he got, he went off to wash in the stream beyond the pile of boulders where the horses were. It was a cheerless little stream, clattering down through gray stones with a sound like teeth chattering.

The sound of his going woke Maewen. She rolled up into the gray day, moaning. She had never been so cold or so damp in her life. The one good thing was that her stomach had stopped aching. As if the green roads cured you, she thought as she stumbled off to the latrine beyond the horses. She came back to find everyone else huddled in dead heaps. This was depressing. She went back to the boulders and started to attend to the horses.

She was alone. The deep voice spoke to her at once. "I have considered," it said. "Your way is now clear before you."

"Is it indeed?" said Maewen. "Welcome back. Where were you when I needed you to warn me about the *other* man with a knife?"

At the stream Mitt discovered that it *was* possible to be colder. The water was icy. It must have been snowmelt from some high mountain out of sight from here. The bits of him he could bear to dip in turned blue. He washed in a hurry, with great splashings and snortings, and put his clothes back on quickly. The sun was up by then. It was no wonder he was cold, Mitt saw. The stream was in deep blue shadow. But there was misty yellow sunlight on the boulders. Shivering all over, Mitt went over there to get warm.

He could hear Noreth talking on the other side of the rocks, and a deep voice answering her. So Hestefan or Wend was up. Mitt went cheerfully round the boulders.

"You were in no danger. Help was at hand whether I warned you or not," the deep voice said.

Mitt stood, confounded. Noreth was brushing Navis's mare and entirely on her own. He could see Wend, still asleep by the dead fire in the distance. Navis was the other hump. And Hestefan was just crawling out of the cart.

She said the One spoke to her, Mitt thought. But I never really believed it till now. He backed quietly away behind the boulders so that Noreth would not think he was prying and stood in the sun there. But he could still hear both voices.

Maewen said, "I'm not going down into the dales anymore. I'm staying up on the green roads. Wend says I'm safe here."

"You are not safe here," said the deep voice.

There was a pause. "Why not?" came Noreth's voice. She sounded quite calm. Mitt was not to know Maewen was shaking all over. He was thinking he had better back away some more, out of hearing, when the deep voice answered.

"The Southern youth you call Mitt," it said, "is the worst danger you have encountered yet. You must kill him before he destroys you."

After this Mitt could no more have moved than he could have flown.

"But Mitt *rescued* me from the second murderer," Maewen protested.

"For his own ends," said the voice. "And this Mitt will not be easy to kill while the man Navis is alive. Navis will defend Mitt for *his* own ends. For this reason I advise you to kill them both at the same time."

"You can't mean this!" Maewen said.

"After you have found the Adon's sword, both of them are expendable," said the voice. "Stab them as they sleep, the night before you reach Kernsburgh."

"Really?" said Maewen. "And what about Wend and Moril and Hestefan? Are they expendable, too?"

"I told you," the voice replied imperturbably, "you will need the Singer-boy to find you the crown. After that, he will be as much of a liability as the Southerners, and you may stab him as soon as you have an opportunity."

"You're asking me"—said Maewen; she was trying not to giggle, even though it was not funny at all—"you're asking me to arrive at Kernsburgh with nothing but a pile of corpses."

"You will be joined there by a sizable army. Display the bodies as the bodies of traitors and explain that all traitors to the crown must suffer the same fate."

"Thanks a bunch!" said Maewen. "That's quite a program!"

"Do as I say," said the voice, and the deep notes of it made both Mitt and Maewen shudder, "or fail, and die yourself."

There was silence then. Mitt stood where he was

until he heard vigorous horse-grooming noises from the other side of the boulders. Then he did his best to walk casually over to the camp. Nobody there seemed to notice that he was shaking all over. But they were all cold and all shivering.

Breakfast was nasty. There was no decent bread. The outsides of all the cheeses had gone moldy. Almost the only thing eatable was the pickled cherries, and Mitt discovered that he hated them by now.

They moved on up the stretched and windy valley, and neither Mitt nor Maewen spoke to anyone much that morning.

Maewen's thoughts were chaos. *Was* it the One who spoke to her? Or was it just a time-confused part of her own mind, reacting with violence to the violence she had met in Gardale? There was no doubt she had been in danger from *someone*. Or if it was the One, he was angry. Those he had singled out—Mitt and Moril had tried to steal the cup, and Navis had taken it. She had known during the song that Navis had done something awful. It might be because of the cup. But it did not really matter *what* spoke or why. It hurt. Maewen's head was now full of nasty suspicions of Navis, Mitt, and Moril. Right back at the beginning of this ride, she had seen that each of them had come to follow her for their own secret reasons, and Mitt and Navis had shown her some of those reasons in Gardale. It was Hildy who was important to them. That hurt.

Oh, I want to go *home*! Maewen thought this so

strongly that she almost said it aloud. In fact, she did utter a sort of noise, which caused Hestefan and his mule, who happened to be alongside her just then, both to turn and look at her. But no sooner had she almost said it than she saw she did not quite mean it. She wanted to find out what had happened to Noreth and to try to change history, even though she knew now that one of those three was going to do her some terrible harm. Correction. *Mitt* was going to do her some terrible harm. Navis was a cool customer, Moril was a deep one, and he had that cwidder, but Mitt was the one who did things. The knowledge made her throat ache, as if Mitt had tried to strangle her—and maybe he *had*, at the inn in Gardale.

Mitt kept thinking, This is a *laugh*! The One was playing games with him. Or he had it in for Mitt, which was much more likely. Mitt wanted to ride away from the whole mess. It would be lovely to settle down on a farm, somewhere near enough the South to be like what he was used to, and leave the One to stew. But he needed his half of the golden statue for that, and Noreth was not likely to part with it now. Not now she knew Mitt had been told to kill her. Anyway, he had to stay with her until Kernsburgh. If Hildy was safe, Ynen was not, and Kialan might not manage to bring Ynen there after all. He would have laughed at the mess if he'd felt like laughing. Meanwhile, he had to warn Navis and Moril somehow. And talking of warnings, that dream had been a warning, hadn't it just!

Mitt came out of his thoughts to find he was warm—more than warm, almost too hot, for a wonder. He undid his jacket. There was light, white rain steaming over them, but he was too warm to care. This makes a change! he thought. It must be almost record heat for the North.

They had come out of the stretched valley and were now following the green path across a high gorse-grown heath. The mountains had melted to white-purple distance, and the one behind, Mitt saw, peering through the misty bands of rain, did indeed have snow on the top of it.

"Where is this? Why is it so hot?" he said. It was the first thing he had said since breakfast.

Moril grinned at him. "Welcome back. It's the Shield of Oreth."

"It is a large upland that opens toward the South," Hestefan explained from beside Moril on the driving seat. Schoolmaster again, Maewen thought. The warmth was making her feel better. "We'll be having the warm air from now until Kernsburgh. This used to be fine land. Even in the Adon's day it was full of people."

Hang on! Maewen thought, coming properly out of her misery. If this was the Shield, she had looked out the train at it. There had been farmlands and factories, trees and towns. But Hestefan could be right. Up among the gorse and heather on either side there were piles of stone in faint, broken squares, which could have been ruined houses.

"Where did all the people go?" she asked.

"Fled in the wars after the Adon died," said Moril.

"Who owns it now?" Navis asked, looking out over bracken and heather beyond the gorse bushes as if he would not mind owning some of it himself.

As Hestefan went into a complicated account that suggested that Hannart or Dropwater might have a claim, but nobody wanted this land, anyway, Maewen frowned. She rather thought Navis would be owning some of it before long. The Duke of Kernsburgh owned the big brewery here in her day. Would she dare change history to the extent of cutting Navis out of it? *Could* she? No, of course not. That was a relief. But that did not apply to Mitt or Moril, who were not really in history at all.

She looked sideways at Mitt. He was turning his head to watch a slightly bigger pile of stones with an old apple tree drooped over them. I could farm here, he thought. It would take a deal of hard work, but I reckon it would be peaceful.

The rain blew away into the mountains, leaving a tearful sort of blue sky overhead. Everyone steamed in the heat. And the cart went along in its own cloud made of wreathing spirals of steam. Flies came out of the heather and circled the horses. They made the Countess-horse restive, but Mitt rode along with his chin down, hardly noticing. That dream was nagging at him. Farming had not been in it anywhere. Something was wrong.

By this time they were seeing occasional small farms built of gray stone, with square fields around them scratched out of the heather. The Shield was not quite as derelict as Maewen had thought. The farms grew bigger and more frequent as they went on. By midday, when they stopped to eat, there was farmland all round, and walled lanes leading to distant farmhouses on both sides of the green road. There were even a few trees. They stopped to eat under a mighty old ash on a corner by a lane.

Navis reveled in the heat. While the horses crowded into the shade with Maewen and Hestefan, Navis sat against the drystone wall in the sun and stretched both arms out. "This is more like it!" he said to Mitt.

"It is and all," Mitt agreed. "First time I've been warm since I came North. I'll be back in a moment." He picked up a couple of pickled onions—better than those cherries—and a handful of the manky cheese and set off up the lane. That dream was now mixing in his mind with what he had heard this morning, and he wanted to be alone to think. Something was badly wrong.

He almost wondered whether he might not simply walk away. He came to another lane and turned into it because it was narrow and had no walls and he felt freer there. He climbed higher with it, until he was walking in the warm wind between low hedges with a field of grain on either side. Gray-green both fields were, like the sea over sand in dangerous shallows.

:∥ 16 ∥:

Mitt's head snapped up. A tall golden man came walking along the lane toward him and bent his head in a solemn nod of greeting as Mitt looked. At this season Old Ammet had a face that was neither young nor old. He could have been the same age as Navis, except that the long golden hair blowing about his head and shoulders made him seem young.

"Now it's you," Mitt said. "Why do you Undying keep pushing me about?"

"It's not our fault, Alhammitt," Old Ammet answered. "The times are pushing *us*. And I should remind you that when you chose the wind's road, you chose the green road, too."

"I know, I know," Mitt said. "Once I got on, there's never been a moment I could have got off. But I keep having to choose all the same! And every time I choose and try to get right, things turn round on me and try to make me go the other way. The One told Noreth to kill me this morning—and Navis and Moril. You tell me what I'm supposed to do about that!"

Old Ammet looked at him gravely, in a way that reminded Mitt of Wend all of a sudden, except that Old Ammet was blowing and rustling in the wind. "I am not here to tell you what to do."

"No," Mitt said bitterly. "You Undying never do give a straight answer. You just push."

"It is not my place," said Ammet, "to question our Grand Father, whom they call the One. His law is that we do not tell his mortal family what to do. That is to make people into puppets."

"Then the One just broke his own law," Mitt said.

"I am here to tell you to think about that," said Ammet.

There was a silence full of the warm wind and the rustling and streaming of Ammet's white-blond hair, while Mitt digested this. "I don't get it," he said at last. He found Old Ammet looking so kind that it made him feel terrible.

"I should remind you that we gave you our names to say at need," Old Ammet said.

Mitt nodded. He felt his face screw up. There were indeed four names, the greater and lesser names of Old Ammet and Libby Beer, tucked away in the corner of Mitt's mind. That part of his head always felt like a sore tooth, where you kept putting your tongue even though you knew it would hurt. "You mean, I could say your biggest name at her?"

Ammet laughed. It felt as if the wind had turned to a warm gale. "That name is not to be used that lightly.

: 268 :

It will be many a long year before you will need to say my Great Name. But you have three other names. I am here to tell you that if you use those names properly, the Shield of Oreth can be covered again with fields like these."

His hand spread to show Mitt the surging barley and the stiff rustling wheat. Mitt looked wistfully, thinking of that farm he might have. "You'd like that, wouldn't you?" he said.

"We would, Alhammitt," Old Ammet agreed. He smiled at Mitt, rather sadly, over his shoulder among his flying hair, as he walked away round a turn in the lane.

Mitt stood looking a moment. The lane ran straight as a ruler through the two fields. Then he sighed and turned to go back.

Moril was standing a few yards down the hill. The two of them simply stared at one another for a moment. Then Moril licked his lips and cleared his throat. Still, his voice came out scratchy with awe. "Wh-who was that?"

"Old Ammet," said Mitt. "The Earth Shaker." His voice was not in much better shape. "What are you doing here?"

"You forgot to take any bread," Moril said.

"It was like a flaming gray rock this morning," Mitt said. "There'll be critters in it by now."

"Well, anyway, I brought—" Moril started to hold out the bundle in his hands. And stopped and stared at it. Then he unwrapped the cloth and held out a crusty new loaf. Mitt could smell the newness of it on the wind. He looked ruefully down at the cheese and onions he had not yet bothered to eat. The onions were the same but the cheese was now a fresh pale wedge. It smelled as wonderful as the bread.

He held it out to Moril. "Want some?"

Moril nodded. He arranged the cwidder on his back and sat down by the hedge. As Mitt sat down beside him, it occurred to him that this cwidder was as much of a sore place to Moril as those names were to him—and more of a nuisance, too. Moril had barely let go of the thing since Hestefan had threatened to take it away.

They tore the crusty fresh loaf in two, broke the cheese in half, and ate like wolves. "All the same," Mitt said, going back to what Moril had first said, "it's not like you to run after me with bread."

"I wasn't spying," Moril said, with as much dignity as someone who is crunching a pickled onion can. "I only *saw* him. I didn't hear a word he was saying. And he must have known I was there, because of the bread."

"So?" said Mitt.

"Something's wrong," said Moril. "This morning I was on top of the rocks, trying to get warm. I heard that voice telling her to kill us."

Mitt felt his appetite go. "And?"

Moril swallowed the pickled onion as if it was a lump in his throat. "I heard it before. I heard it tell her to find the Adon's gifts. It seemed all right then."

Mitt went on eating although his appetite had gone. If you had once been poor in Holand, you never wasted a chance to eat. "So what do you think?"

Moril was eating in the same dutiful way. Singers met hard times, too. "I think," he said, "that it isn't the One that speaks to her."

Mitt knew this was why Old Ammet had looked kind. It was something he did not want to think about. "Who is it then?"

"Kankredin," said Moril.

So it was out. Mitt nodded. "I think you're right. You know what this means, then?"

"He started talking to her when she was young and worked her up to this gradually," Moril said, thinking about it. "He's disembodied, so he could pretend to be the One."

"Probably, but I don't mean that," Mitt said. "Just stop and think what it means if she got to be Queen. *She* may be all right, but she'd go everywhere with this voice telling her to do what Kankredin wants. And she'd do it, too. She does."

"But," said Moril, "this morning she was sounding sarcastic, rather the way your Navis does."

"Maybe, but she'll do it in the end," Mitt said. "Don't you see? He works her along, like you said. He tells her she's got to be Queen and she's the One's daughter, and she sets out to ride for the crown. For all we know, she's got no claim at all. Alk thought not. It means this whole ride is a load of old crab apples."

"So what should we do?" Moril asked.

Mitt smiled his most unfunny smile. "It looks as if I better do what the Countess and your Keril wanted in the first place. Kill her somehow. It's a laugh!"

It was a horrible thing to say. Mitt almost choked on it, thinking of Noreth's nervous, freckly look—which seemed to get to him more now he knew her so much better—and how plain frightened she had been when that man attacked her in the Lawschool. He was still surprised at how *very* frightened she had been. She would be the same, or worse, when she found Mitt after her.

He was fervently relieved when Moril said, firmly and quietly, "No."

"But she's got to be stopped," Mitt protested hopefully.

"Yes, but if she's dead," Moril said, "won't Kankredin just move on to somebody else? Somebody who's more—you know—ruthless?"

Like Navis, Mitt thought. That would be worse. The idea snapped his brain clean out of the bind Keril and the Countess seemed to have put on it. "Then it's Kankredin we ought to go after." This was the way Old Ammet had been trying to make him think, he realized. "Can this cwidder of yours do anything there?"

Moril put his chin on his knees and twiddled the last crust of his bread while he thought. "It's got to be truth," he said. "I think, if we could catch him talking to her again, I could make him appear in his true shape. Would that be enough?"

"Could be just right!" Mitt said. "I've a name or two up my sleeve I could use as long as I know where he is."

Moril put the crust of bread in his mouth. "I hoped you might have," he said, munching it. "There are stories about you."

They got up and dusted off crumbs. "Don't give Kankredin any kind of hint," Mitt said.

"What do you take me for?" said Moril. They smiled at one another, conspirators, but not at all happy about it.

Mitt thought, as they walked back between the rustling corn, The worst of it is, if it goes wrong. I might have to kill her, anyway. The hot sun seemed to weigh on him. He felt as if he was in mourning already.

The others were waiting impatiently under the ash tree. They said, almost in chorus, "Where *were* you?" The rest of the bad gray bread had been tipped into the ditch. Mitt and Moril looked at it guiltily.

"We got lost," Moril said. "I think we ought to stop at a farm for more bread."

"Teach your grandmother," said Maewen. Mitt could see her, as they mounted and rode on, looking from him to Moril and wondering what they had been plotting. She had her nervous, freckly look. He knew he ought to do something about it, but the Countess-horse was balky in the heat and kept Mitt busy wrestling with it all through the long, blazing afternoon. Despite his warning to Moril, Mitt kept wanting to tell the horse, Cheer up! Come Kernsburgh, you could be carrying my dead body! He could see himself, too, dead hands trailing on one side, limp boots swinging on the other, and the whole thing starting to smell in the heat. He had to keep biting his tongue not to say it.

Maewen and he did not say one word to each other until they were camped that night—in a proper field with cowpats in it, near a farm. While Wend and Navis were away at the farm, buying bread, and Mitt and Maewen were doing the horses, Mitt took a deep breath and said, "Are we not on speaking terms or something?"

She jumped and turned to him gratefully. "Yes. Probably. You didn't have to wait under that tree and listen to Navis and Hestefan being sarky to one another."

Though Mitt knew there was much more to it than that, he said, "If you shoot someone's horse, he's not likely to love you. Mind you," he added, watching Hestefan fussily washing down the wheels of the cart, "if that Hestefan wasn't a Singer, he'd be teaching school and living alone in a house with the door barred."

"Yes! Wouldn't he!" Maewen said, quite delighted.

They chatted lightheartedly after that, until they saw Wend and Navis returning with cans of milk and armfuls of cheese and bread. Maewen said guiltily, "Oh dear. I bet Navis paid for it all. I hate the way we seem to be living off him."

Mitt's attitude to money was much more carefree. "Well, we can't hardly wave a golden statue at them," he said.

It was the wrong thing to say. She gave him a nervous, freckly look and went off to meet Navis. Mitt sighed. All the same, he and Moril took good care never to be far away from Maewen in case the voice spoke to her again. But nothing happened that night.

When they went on next morning, they found the farms thinning out again, giving way to more and more bracken and tumbled rocks. The Shield here descended slightly in a series of waves, downward toward Dropwater and the coast, and the green road went with it, up and over and down, up and over and down. The warm, itchy rain came over in waves, too. You could look back and see each white shower traveling back along the way you had come, up and up and up, like a ghost going upstairs, until it was lost in the high green distance.

In the middle of the afternoon Mitt was looking back after the latest shower, having watched it as it came climbing up and swept over them, when he thought he could see a darkish blot, right up at the top, where the road and the rain went out of sight. Next time he looked, the blot was more definite, wavering forward in the high distance.

"Ay-ay," he said. "Looks like there might be a troop of horses coming down behind."

Heads snapped round. Hestefan and Moril leaned

out on either side of the cart. It was what everyone had been dreading.

"Looks to be at least twenty," Wend said.

"In good order," said Navis. "Quite a body of hearthmen, I would say. Can anyone see what livery?"

"Too far off," said Hestefan.

"But coming quite fast," said Moril.

"And they must have seen us," said Navis, "if we can see them." He turned to Wend. "Is there anywhere we can get off this road while we're in a dip and they can't see us?"

Wend's solemn face twisted anxiously. "Not for some miles."

"Then get in the cart," said Navis. "Let's get there as fast as we can."

Wend took three running strides and heaved himself over the tailgate of the cart. Hestefan whipped up the mule. The cart set off rattling up the next rise, and the rest of them kept pace. It was maddeningly slow to Maewen. The mule was trying, but the cart was heavy, and it slowed down over every long, undulating rise. She grew a crick in her neck from looking back. The horsemen were gaining steadily. Every time she looked, there were fewer hills between them. Before long, they could tell that there were, in fact, only about fifteen of them. But as Mitt said, that was quite enough against six.

"Perhaps they aren't after us at all," Maewen said hopefully.

"Would you bet on that?" Navis asked. "Between us we have stolen a cup and a ring and attempted to start an uprising. I *wish* I could see the livery. That would give us a clue."

And stolen a horse, Maewen thought guiltily, looking at the patient ears of the horse she had hoped was Noreth's. Would someone ride all the way from Adenmouth after a stolen horse in these days? She wished she knew.

"And someone may think we sneaked Hildy along," Mitt said, with his head turned back over his shoulder. "Are they Hannart?"

The rain was blinding over in white clouds. It was never possible to see the horsemen except as a wavering dark blur, but they saw them most of the time. When the cart was down in a dip, the blur was cresting a rise, and as the cart labored uphill, the pursuers had already been down in the next dip and were wavering into sight again. They came closer and closer.

Navis was looking off into what could be seen of the countryside. It rose steeper and steeper to the left and not so steep to the right. Most of it was covered in head-high bracken. If they did go off the road, the cart would make tracks in that bracken that a blind man could follow. "How much farther?" Navis snapped at Wend.

"Just down to the river," Wend said anxiously. "Not far."

By the time they came down the last slope to see a

small river cutting across the green road, the horsemen were only three hills behind. They were almost invisible in what seemed to be a final cloud of rain. As the cart splashed into the moist edge of the river, weak sunlight traveled after the rain and made everything golden white.

"Stop a moment," Wend called. He leaned out of the back of the cart. "Will you play your cwidder now?" he asked Moril.

Moril leaned out to look at him. "Does it matter what?"

"Yes." Wend jumped down into squashy turf. "Play anything you can think of about the witch Cennoreth," he said, going to the mule's head.

Moril wrenched the cover away from the cwidder and hurriedly plucked out the chorus to "The Weaver's Song":

> *Thread the shuttle, throw the shuttle,*
> *Weave the close-bound yarn.*

As he moved on to the tune of the verses, Wend led mule and cart in a half circle, with much splashing and swaying, until it was facing up to the left, along the riverbank.

"Follow me upriver," he said to the others, under the music.

They rode after him along the wet grassy verge, none of them very hopeful. The light was brighter and more golden than before. Mitt looked at the tracks of the cart and the prints the horses were leaving and thought that even in another shower of rain the riders behind could hardly miss them. Maewen wondered if Moril had got the music wrong in his hurry. She knew "The Weaver's Song," and she had never known it had anything to do with the witch Cennoreth. Navis rode trying to look back up the green road, but the rise of the land cut off the view almost at once.

"This is going to take a miracle," he murmured.

The lawnlike riverbank turned into a proper track, leading easily upward among bracken and rocks. As the cart clattered onto the higher, rockier part, they all distinctly heard the drumming of several dozen hooves, mixed with the rattle of tack and mail, and a few voices. Navis stopped his mare and, in a resigned way, fetched out his pistol and cocked it. Above, the cart went on, and Moril continued to play.

To everyone's amazement, the drumming of hooves barely paused. It slowed and broke into separate noises, but that was mixed with the splashing of water and the *clack* of rolled stones as the party crossed the river. Then the regular drumming took up again and faded off into the distance.

"Missed us!" Mitt said. He could hardly believe it.

"Let's hope they don't come back before we're out of sight," Navis said, turning his mare back to the path.

Above the rocky section, the river was a mere stream, flowing out of a fair-sized lake, cupped inside steep black crags. The banks were squashy with marsh, but the path avoided it by mounting higher, among clumps of tall rushes. Maewen could not resist leaning sideways to trail her hand in the feathery heads. They were the scented kind of rushes. Clouds of strong pollen filled the air with a lovely smell, like nothing else she knew. Mitt sneezed. Navis pushed through the rushes in clouds of more pollen and caught up with the cart. Moril had stopped playing by then.

"Are you sure this is safe?" Navis asked Wend.

"Of course, sir," Wend said. "This is Dropthwaite where my sister's croft is. No one can find us here." He smiled in his pent-up way and pointed out into the lake where a number of fat white ducks were swimming beside a patch of white-flowering weed. "Those are my sister's ducks." The way he smiled, Maewen thought he and his sister must have some private joke about them.

∷ 17 ∷

T HEY CAME THROUGH the rushes to find a small ragged field with a stone trough in the middle. Hens wandered there. Two goats were tethered farther off, and there was a vegetable garden beyond that. The croft was a low stone house built against the crags, among fruit trees and lilacs. Everything was warm and fragrant because the rocks went round the holding in a high horseshoe and cut off all but the west wind.

Wend walked through the orchard with long strides and knocked at the house door. It was opened almost at once by an old woman leaning on a stick.

"His sister?" Navis said, watching the two talking eagerly together.

"More like his granny," said Mitt. "Still, we might get a bed for the night out of it." And a bedroom had a door you could bar, in case Kankredin persuaded Noreth to do her killing now.

Oh yes! Maewen thought. And a *bath*!

Navis looked nervously back down the path. "They won't find us here," Moril said to him. "Promise."

Navis looked at Moril's cwidder, but not as if he was convinced.

Wend came striding back. He seemed almost as carefree as when he had taken charge of the cwidder. "She says you're welcome to camp in this field here," he said cheerfully. "And if the young ones like to go to the door when the horses are seen to, she'll have milk and eggs and cheese ready for you." Whistling a little tune, he untethered the goats and led them away round the side of the house.

Bother! Mitt and Maewen thought, though both for different reasons.

"The old lady likes her privacy, I see," Hestefan said glumly. Evidently he had been hoping for a bed, too.

"It's not a very big house," Moril said as he unhitched the mule. Apart from Wend, he was the only one who was happy with the arrangement. Navis continued to watch the path, and he insisted on setting up the camp where it could not be seen by anyone coming up from the lake. This meant a long trudge across the grass to the trough, which Mitt felt was unnecessary. He was the one who fetched the water. The trough fascinated him. Clear water bubbled up in it the whole time, but it never, for some reason, overflowed.

When the horses were rubbed down and feeding, Moril jerked his head toward the house. Mitt winked and left Navis to see about the rest. They were both a little put out to find Maewen coming with them through the orchard trees. They did not consider Noreth as one of the young ones. Maewen saw it. But she had come along almost without thinking, and it seemed a little late to go back now. Besides, she was curious about this sister of Wend's.

Wend opened the door to them. "Come you in," he said. "This way."

He led them quickly through a kitchen-room and opened a door to the back of the house. Maewen looked around curiously, but all she had time to see was a scrubbed wooden table and a banked-up fire of smoky peat, with a copper kettle singing on it. The room at the back of the house was even harder to see at first. It had only one window, which was half blocked by a big loom with woolen cloth being woven on it. It smelled of warm wood and, even more, of slightly oily wool. The ceiling was low and beamed. The walls were dark from being paneled in old wood—very beautifully carved, in a mass of half-seen designs—and the rest of the dim space was nearly full of stack upon stack of tall, chubby wooden things. These things were where the wool smell was coming from. Large bobbins, they seemed to be, wound with woolen yarn of every conceivable color.

Wend's sister got up from her seat at the loom and edged through the bobbins toward them. She was tall, and she moved very spryly. When she was near enough to be seen clearly, all of them had a moment when

they thought the old woman who answered the door
must have been Wend's old mother. Then they realized
she was the same lady. But she looked much younger,
though older than Wend. Her face was thin and only
a little lined, and her hair was white, mass upon mass
of it, wriggly and curly and pinned back with combs
that glittered black among the white. Mitt thought
there was just a look of the Countess about her, but a
kinder look than the Countess's. Maewen, too, found
this lady reminded her of someone, but she could not
place it. She thought she must have been stunning
when she was younger, when all that hair was surely
flaxen fair. The lady's eyes were still stunning, huge
and blue-green.

"I'm pleased to meet all of you," she said. Her voice
was much more educated than Wend's, and that reminded Mitt of the Countess, too. "I hear you're looking for the Adon's sword."

"Oh, did Wend tell you?" said Maewen. "Yes. We've
got his cup and"—she held up her hand with the ring
on its thumb—"this."

"Then one of you is truly riding the royal road,"
the lady said, looking from Maewen, to Moril, to Mitt,
with very strong interest. "At last! I thought no one
would ever get round to it again! Very well. The sword
is here. You'd better see if you can get it down."

"The sword is *here*!" Moril was so astonished that
his voice went up into a squeak.

The lady swung round on him. "What makes you
so surprised?"

"Well," Moril said awkwardly, "I heard . . . the Singers say . . . that the Adon's wife—Manaliabrid—hid his sword when she went back to the Undy—er, her own people."

"And so she did," said Wend's sister. "My poor daughter. She'd thought her Adon was of the Undying, too—and as I told her, so he might have been for all we knew, but when a man sets himself up as King, he puts himself in the way of assassins, and sooner or later one of them will strike lucky. There are many ways to kill the Undying, though we don't die easily."

"Manaliabrid," said Moril, "is your daughter?"

"That's right," said the lady. She folded her arms and looked amused at the awe in Moril's face. "And the name you'll have heard for me is Cennoreth. Am I right?"

"Then you're a witch," said Mitt.

"You're the Weaver," said Moril.

Both of them turned to look at Wend. "My sister is both," he said.

"So I should hope!" Cennoreth snapped.

"But you—" Moril said to Wend.

"Tanamoril," said Cennoreth, energetically making her way between the piles of bobbins, "Osfameron, Oril, Wend, Mage Mallard—when a person lives a long time, names tend to pile up. Now, do you want this sword or not? Here it is."

There was a fireplace at the end of the room opposite the window, made of stone as beautifully carved as the wooden walls. Hung on the wooden panels above the stone was a long dark thing. Maewen and Mitt both took it at first for a stuffed fish. But when they had edged over there along the narrow path between the bobbins, they saw it was actually a sword, probably quite a plain one, in a blackish leather sheath. The reason it was so hard to see in that dim room was that it was tied to the wall by innumerable long strips of leather. The leather thongs had been knotted to about a hundred rusty nails hammered into the paneling above and below the sword, and then knotted and overlapped and knotted again, until the sword was in a kind of basket of leather strips.

"Hey, Moril!" said Mitt.

Moril was still over by the door, looking across his shoulder at Wend, full of awe and amazement. Mitt could hardly blame him. This was the man Moril had been named after, twice over, the hero of half the stories the Singers learned to tell, and Moril's own ancestor into the bargain. Wend was shifting about self-consciously, as if—just like a normal person—he had no idea what to say. He was obviously relieved when Moril switched his attention to Mitt.

While Moril was making his way through the bobbins, grinning and going like a sleepwalker, Wend said awkwardly, "These things happen—if you live long enough. You should think nothing of it—or not too much."

"Think nothing of it!" Moril said, looking up at the sword and its thongs. "That's asking a bit much! Those pieces of leather are knots and crosses. There has to be a catch."

"Quite right." Cennoreth stood by the hearth with her arms folded. "You're an observant boy. You must understand that none of it is my doing. My daughter nailed it up there. Remember she was mad with grief—though I suppose you're all too young to know how that feels—and try to forgive her. She was disappointed in her children, too. She expected too much of them, but there you go, I'm only her mother, and it didn't matter what I said. So she set this sword up, knots and crosses, like redhead said, for the children of her blood and the Adon's. That's rather a lot of people these days, but that's another thing she wouldn't listen to, when I told her how it would be if enough time passed."

"So what's the catch?" Mitt asked.

Cennoreth shrugged. "The knots must be undone without touching sword or scabbard, and the sword must be drawn before it touches wood, stone, or earth. My daughter," she said, "expected too much of her children's children, too, if you ask me, but I wasn't consulted."

They all stared up at the sword in its cat's cradle of leather. The thongs were black with age, and there was dust all over them. Maewen could see that each knot, beside being pulled fiercely tight to start with, had shrunk and hardened over the years—how many? two hundred?—and must by now be nearly impossible to undo. Just to think of the lasting fierceness of the misery that did this was appalling. Could one wet the leather and loosen the knots that way? "What happens if you break the rules?" she asked.

"She didn't say," said Cennoreth.

"Though you may take it that you won't get the sword, lady," Wend added from the other side of the room.

They stared up at the sword again. It was high above Maewen's reach. *I suppose if I knelt on the mantelpiece—the leather could just be old enough to crumble away when I touch it. Anyway, I don't really* need *this sword—though it seems a shame, when I've got the ring and the cup.*

Moril thought awhile. Then he sat down on the nearest pile of bobbins and started taking the case off his cwidder.

"What are you doing?" Mitt asked him.

"The leather was straight to start with," Moril said. "The cwidder could tell the truth and make it straight again."

It could, too! Mitt realized. Things unfolded with a crisp *snap* inside his head, and he saw that he and Moril had been so taken by surprise that they had not thought this through. *Why don't I* think? he asked himself angrily. If Kankredin was talking to Noreth, and Noreth had listened to him all her life, then even if he and Moril could do for Kankredin—which was a stupid thing to plan when even the One could not do it—then the last thing either of them should do was to help Noreth become Queen. That meant the whole country under Kankredin. So—break the rules, quick.

Mitt was the only one tall enough to reach the sword. "No. That's going at it the slow way," he told Moril.

Moril's fingers went slow and fumbling on the cwidder. As Mitt turned away and pulled out his knife, he knew Moril had seen the danger, too. Mitt pushed between Maewen and Cennoreth, reached up, and, quick as he could, slashed along the length of the sword, between the multitude of knots.

"Get ready to catch it!" he cried out merrily.

He had meant to call out too late. But to his annoyance, not all the age-hard thongs parted. He was forced to slash again, and again after that. Even then only the pointed end of the scabbard came loose. Mitt watched it with satisfaction, descending slowly to the mantelshelf, tearing the other thongs as it came.

Maewen yelled out, "Careful!" and flung herself forward with both arms up at full stretch. She was just in time to catch the tip of it. The cwidder resounded as Moril set it hastily down and jumped forward to pretend to help her. He grabbed hold of the scabbard above Maewen's hands and blundered artfully around her. But Maewen hung on grimly. All Moril managed to do was dislodge a long iron-handled hearth brush from beside the grate. It fell among their legs with a clatter.

Bother! Mitt thought. Hadd's *pants*! He took hold of the sword's hilt, thongs and all, and pulled. That ought to bring it down *and* make sure it touched the wall or the fireplace on the way.

The hearth brush seemed to set off an avalanche. Fire irons went on falling, with mighty clangs: ladles, toasting forks, a slotted spoon, shovels, two pokers, a mighty black roasting spit, a set of hooks for cauldrons. Cennoreth seemed to have a whole blacksmith's worth of implements in her hearth. Maewen and Moril stumbled on a firedog. Mitt found long tongs between his legs and reeled aside. This burst the last of the thongs. Maewen and Moril crashed backward onto Cennoreth's feet, both trying to save themselves by hanging on to the scabbard. Mitt was left holding aloft a naked sword.

It was indeed a very plain blade, he saw. "I reckon we broke all the rules there," he said in mock regret.

"You touched at least half a dozen knots," Moril gasped hopefully.

There was a strange look on Cennoreth's face. Possibly she was trying not to laugh. "No, he didn't," she said. "I was watching quite carefully. Which of you is supposed to be having the sword?"

"She is," said Moril.

"Then please give it to her and then clear up my hearth," Cennoreth said. "I think I'd better look at my weaving."

Maewen got to her knees and held the scabbard out. Mitt slithered the sword inside it with an angry flourish. It looked ceremonial, done that way. Mitt had not the slightest doubt that Manaliabrid would consider that Noreth had won the sword. He turned away disgustedly to help Moril collect fire irons and prop them in noisy bundles by the grate. *Clatter*. It was not that simple to defeat Kankredin's plans. *Clang. Boing.* Well, it wouldn't be, would it? Kankredin was of the Undying, and that meant strong. After all, Old Ammet was so strong that just saying one of his na— Oh flaming *pants*! Mitt stopped with pokers bundled to his chest and looked up at the dangling, broken thongs and torn-out nails. *This* was why the Earth Shaker had reminded him of those names! And he had never even thought of using one. *Clatter*—flaming—CRASH. There.

Dejectedly Mitt followed Moril and Maewen over to the window. Wend was standing, leaning on the loom, watching Cennoreth smooth and smooth at the most recently woven end of her cloth. You could see the likeness between them now, Maewen thought, although Wend looked so smooth and young. But she also saw another likeness. That dreamy, devoted way Cennoreth was smoothing at her weaving was like Mum's, when Mum was on a new statue. They were rather the same shape, though Mum's hair was straighter and darker. Cennoreth clicked her tongue and shook her head as she stroked the cloth, again like Mum. A comb fell out of her hair, and she rammed it back impatiently. That was even more like Mum. "This is a pretty snarl!" she said.

It was odd cloth—even odder than Mum's sculptures, which Maewen secretly considered quite mad. At first sight it looked as if the witch had used every color off all the bobbins at random, changing color so often that it all went down to reddish brown muddle. But after you had looked at it awhile, letters seemed to appear in the weave, small and close and almost making words. Then just as you thought you had found a word, you found instead patterns, large patterns and small ones, rambling and winding all over the cloth in various bright colors. The pattern Cennoreth was smoothing at was a rusty orange that suddenly turned into bright red. Indeed, it had turned red so suddenly and recently that the scarlet yarn was still in the shuttle, hanging down from the half-woven edge in a row of other shuttles, ready to be used in the next line.

"There's no need to stare," Cennoreth said. "My grandfather asked me to go on weaving. It's not my fault it comes out as it does. Just look at this! I can't think what you're doing with my son-in-law's sword, young woman. You're not who you should be at all. What's your real name?"

Their four faces stared at Maewen, and the shock on three of those faces was lurid in the low light from the window. Moril's mouth came open. Wend was white. He and Mitt both edged back from Maewen, and Mitt frowned, calculating and enlightened, as this cleared up several mysteries he had not properly considered before.

Maewen backed, too, clutching the sword. She felt she might have dissolved with horror without something to hang on to. "M-Maewen," she said. Cennoreth looked at her. Under those accusing blue-green eyes, Maewen found she had to correct herself. "Er, Mayelbridwen Singer, really."

"Hmm. That sounds like an outlandish version of my daughter's name," Cennoreth said. "Where are you from?"

"The present—I mean, your future," Maewen confessed.

Everyone was startled. "That can't be *possible!*" Wend said.

"Oh yes—or at least, it's quite true," said Cennoreth. "That red snarl is from no bobbin here in this room. I was planning how to get that color dye, but I haven't done it yet—though I suppose I will in time. I *thought* it felt strange when I threaded the shuttle the other day, but there's been a fog, and the light wasn't good. I didn't really see it till now."

Wend seemed completely shattered. His face looked older than his sister's. "Unpick—unpick it!" he burst out. "Before it's too late, Tanaqui—unpick!"

"Don't be silly," said his sister.

"But you've unpicked before!" Wend said.

"Not often and not for centuries," she retorted. "And only when the One has asked it of me."

"But *I* asked you last time!" Wend cried out. He seemed quite desperate. "Don't you remember? I asked you when that slimy traitor killed the Adon. You unpicked then!"

"Duck, that was unpicking a death," she said, very seriously. "You wouldn't want me to unpick a living person."

"Why not?" Wend demanded. "She's an impostor. Unpick! Send her back! I don't want her here!"

Maewen clutched the sword and stared from one to the other. Wend must be mad, after all. "But you *do* want me!" she said. "You sent me here! You told me in the palace you wanted me to take Noreth's place!"

Wend rounded on her, so angry and tall and so full of queer power that she backed away again. "I do not want you! Why should I send you here?"

"Because," Maewen faltered, "because the real Noreth disappeared and you know I look—"

"*Disappeared!*" Wend shouted. His eyes were not mad, Maewen saw, but so full of grief and shock and anger that they glared as if he was not really seeing her.

"I thought you knew," she said. "What you said, you know, by the waystone—at Adenmouth—"

"*What!*" said Wend. "For so long?" He rounded on his sister. "Where is Noreth of Kredindale?"

Cennoreth ran her finger down the rust-colored pattern, and on down the scarlet twist of wool, until she came to the thread hanging off in the shuttle. "It's not here. That part isn't woven yet." Wend made an angry noise. "Don't you understand, Duck? I don't know *either.*"

Maewen could have sworn that Wend was crying as he swung round again and glared at the boys. "And do *you* know?" Moril and Mitt shook their heads. "You wouldn't!" Wend said disgustedly. "You only think of yourselves. Don't you understand? All my hopes were on Noreth. There could have been a Queen again!"

"No, there couldn't," Maewen said unwisely. "There was a Ki—"

Wend swung round and shouted at her. "What do you know about this? You're not Noreth! You're no one! *You're* not the one I've kept the green roads for, all these years! You can go hang, and the green roads with you! Not one step more do I go with any of you!"

He turned and stormed through the room, going from space to space between the bobbins in enormous strides. The door to the kitchen-room slammed behind him.

Very shaken, Maewen looked at Mitt and Moril. She was afraid they were going to be as angry with her as Wend. What she saw growing on both their faces was simple, devout relief. Mitt even gave her a shaky grin as he asked Cennoreth, "He do this often, your brother?"

Cennoreth was frowning out of the window, at the rocks and apple trees there, busily and absently attending to her weaving, tying off a thread of dark green yarn beside the hanging scarlet shuttle. Very like Mum when something upset her, Maewen thought. At Mitt's question, Cennoreth gave a start and looked down at what her hands were doing. "Oh dear," she said. "You must forgive my brother. There are times when he feels that every mortal soul just lets him down. He *can* behave like this when his heart is very much in something. I expect he has gone to look for the real girl." She sighed. "I think you'd better go and collect the supplies I promised you; they're on the table in the kitchen. Your friends will be waiting."

She turned back to her loom. Mitt and Moril nodded at one another, and the three of them worked their way through the bobbins to the kitchen door. There was no sign of Wend in there, but on the table stood a crock of milk, butter, a bowl of eggs, and a round of cheese. Maewen looked up from wondering if Wend had put them there, to find Mitt and Moril facing her meaningly across the table. Here it comes! she thought.

"Who *are* you, really? You said Singer," Moril asked her.

"That's a surname," Maewen explained. "My dad said we had Singer blood. Believe it or not, he was showing me some of our family tree the night before I left, but the part from this time was really confused, and I've no idea whether I'm related to you." It felt so good to be able to be herself again that she could have chattered on for minutes. "I may be called Singer, but I can barely sing a—"

"How *long* into the future?" Moril said.

"Oh. Er—two hundred years, I think."

Mitt and Moril looked to one another. "That long!" said Mitt. "Then you'll know what's going to happen here—right?"

"Not really," Maewen confessed. She was rather dashed to find that what they were really interested in was their own future. She had wanted to amaze them about planes and computers and television. "History doesn't tell you about the Undying or the green roads or anything," she explained. "It's mostly kings and politics. Noreth didn't come into any of the history I learned, but I'll tell you who does: Amil the Great. I'm almost sure he's almost now."

"*Who?*" said Mitt.

"Amil," Moril said, rather accusingly. "That's not a king's name. It's one of the names of the One."

"What about him? Tell," said Mitt.

Maewen racked her brains. "Well, there was a big uprising, and Amil the Great took the crown and united all Dalemark. He reigned for ages and rebuilt Kernsburgh and changed the whole country."

"Ah," said Mitt. This sounded good. Let him and Navis only get in on that, and Earl Keril and the Countess could go whistle. "When is this uprising going to start?"

"I can't remember the date," Maewen confessed— which was *stupid*, considering how often she had heard it in the palace—"but it can't be more than a year away now. I've been thinking all along that I've only got to keep going until Amil comes."

"Then *where* does he start?" said Mitt. He needed to know where to make for.

Maewen flogged her brain again, feeling quite resentful at being released from her imposture only to

stand up to a history test. She would have told him
so, too, if she hadn't thought she owed it to them. The
trouble was, what she remembered was a muddle. "I
think it began in the South, down on the coast— No,
because I seem to remember that the North Dales and
Dropwater came into it, too. And Kernsburgh, I think.
Yes, I'm pretty sure that some of it began near Kernsburgh."

"Kernsburgh." Mitt and Moril looked at one another
again. She could see that both their minds were hard
at work. "Kialan's bringing Ynen to meet us at Kernsburgh," Mitt told Moril. "If he can."

"Kialan," said Moril, "would make a good king."

"My money's on Ynen," said Mitt. "I grant you that
Kialan's kingly, but Ynen's got the character." Both
boys looked at Maewen. "I reckon," Mitt said, "that
our job is to go along there and hand over that sword
and that ring and the cup, to one of them."

"Yes," Moril agreed. "I don't think we can stop.
The One's got an interest in it. You can tell from this
king's name." He frowned down at the little white
goat cheese in front of him on the table. "But I don't
understand. What's *happened* to Noreth?"

This was the part Maewen had been dreading. Both
of them were eyeing her, picking out the features that
did not match their memory of Noreth—or, maybe,
wondering if she was a murderess. "I don't know," she
said. "Honestly. She was gone when I got here. I
found her horse—at least I suppose it's her horse—

wandering about by the waystone. I thought maybe one of the earls might have kidnapped her."

Again Mitt and Moril exchanged looks. "It could be," Moril said. "About the only earl in the North who won't want to stop her is Earl Luthan."

Mitt said, "Then we'll look for her . . . after."

There was a silence, filled with the soft singing of the kettle on the banked peat and clacking from the loom next door. A memory teased at Maewen, now she had space to think. "I remember! Wend told me, back in the palace when he was tricking me into coming here, that Kankredin had got to Noreth somehow."

Both of them pounced on this. "The voice," said Moril.

"Now we'll tell you something," said Mitt. "That voice that talks to you. You think it's the One, don't you?"

"But it's not," said Moril. "It's Kankredin."

"How do you know?" Maewen said guiltily.

"By what it tells you—mostly," Mitt said.

"But I'm the only one who can hear it!" Maewen protested.

"We've both heard it," Moril told her. "And we know it's Kankredin."

He and Mitt looked at one another again. "If he's got rid of Noreth," Mitt said, working it out, "he got you instead because he thinks you'll do what he wants. *Do* you want to?"

"No!" Maewen said fervently. "If you heard— No!"

"Then don't let's talk about it outside this house," Moril said.

Maewen looked up from the bowl of eggs, big pale blue duck eggs and brown hen eggs mixed, which she had mostly been staring at, and gazed round the kitchen. Low beams with strings of onions hanging from them, copper pans, chairs with knitted cushions and a wall of shelves with glass jars on them, holding colored mixtures that may have been dyes—it all belonged to Cennoreth. It made sense that Kankredin could not hear them here, even if he seemed to be everywhere else. She shuddered. That voice. She knew it was Kankredin now. It was the same voice that had so frightened her from the old man in the train—the way it had not seemed to come from a person—but she had not realized, because there had not been a face to connect it to.

"No," she said. "I won't say a word. You know I— Secretly, I was afraid I might be going mad!"

"Not you!" said Mitt. "So we'll keep him thinking we don't know it's him. Right?"

"Right," said Maewen.

They were all suddenly jolly with relief. Maewen felt like a person who has long had a splinter festering under a fingernail, after someone has come along and pulled the splinter out. Mitt laughed as he picked up the bowl of eggs and the cheese. "One thing," he said. "I bet you got that idea about the miners from history books, didn't you? Telling them to go on smash."

"Strike," said Moril, and he laughed as he picked up the crock of milk.

This left Maewen free to snatch up the loaf and rush out of the door, crying out, "Wallop! Smash! Strike!" She raced through the trees, waving the sword in one hand and the loaf in the other. "We got the sword!" she shouted.

Mitt and Moril were forced to follow more slowly for fear of spilling milk and breaking eggs. Moril had gone sober again. "Penny for them," said Mitt.

"She never heard of Noreth," Moril said. "So what happens to *her*? She can't be in history either."

‖ 18 ‖

NAVIS HAD EVIDENTLY decided that the meadow was safe. Maewen caught him in the act of dressing after a bath in the stone trough. As she dashed across the field, Navis was scrambling into clothes, in time to behave as if nothing at all unusual had happened when she reached him. Hestefan left off polishing a row of cwidders and ambled across to look. By the time Mitt and Moril reached them, Navis was saying, "Antique, certainly, and worth devoting half the evening to, no doubt. We had more notable blades in the armory in Holand, but if we *are* to have an uprising, I suppose every weapon counts. And is Wend staying the night with his sister?"

"Didn't he come out here awhile back?" Mitt asked.

"We haven't seen him since he went away with the goats," Hestefan said. "Should we have done?"

"I'm not sure," said Moril. "He may have left."

There was no sign of Wend that night. When he had not appeared by nightfall, Mitt and Moril shared the buttered eggs they had set aside for him. Maewen was chiefly relieved that Wend had not rushed out and denounced her to Navis and Hestefan. She thought Navis might not have taken it too badly, but Hestefan would have been outraged. Navis, however, took Wend's absence as a sign that they were not safe and rigged up a trip wire across the rushes some way down the path.

There was no alarm in the night. They woke to a gray morning to find that the meadow cupped in the crags was smaller and more ragged. There was no garden and no fruit trees. Maewen discovered this first, when she went to have a bath in the stone trough before the rest were awake. The trough had gone. Where it had been, there was a muddy hole in the ground. She looked for the house. Where it had been, there was a thicket of crab apples and wild cherries against the rocks, overgrown with brambles and dog roses. Inside the thicket she could just see the broken walls of a small stone house.

"No hens either," Navis said, coming up beside her. "It was improvident of us to eat all the eggs." By this time the others were coming across the field in a dismayed straggle. Navis slid an eyebrow up at Mitt. "Would you say the Undying have deserted us?"

Mitt shrugged unhappily. "No idea."

Hestefan stood by the muddy hole and looked slowly round, stroking his beard. "I know this place now," he said. "This *is* Dropthwaite, and this"—pointing to the mudhole—"is the source of the river Dropwater.

I have camped here before. It is said that the Adon once lived in hiding in those ruins over there."

"Then that serves to authenticate the sword," Navis said, and went briskly off to inspect his trip wire. It took him a long time to find it. The rushes had been replaced by thistles and brambles. When they did find the wire, it was lying loosely a long way up the hill. From there they could all see that the lake of yesterday was now only a large green pond.

Hestefan stared at it gloomily. "This change is the worst of all possible omens."

"Oh come on," Maewen said, forgetting how Hestefan seemed to dislike her. "We got the sword."

Hestefan turned his gloomy look on her. "The City of Gold is always on the most distant hillside," he said. Before Maewen or Mitt could ask him what that was supposed to mean, he said, "I believe we should all now disperse on our separate ways."

Moril gave a short protesting "Oh!" and Mitt said, "Well, Navis and I can't, and that's final."

"But you may disperse by yourself, by all means, Singer," Navis added.

Breakfast made no one feel much better. Hestefan was, if possible, even gloomier, when they set off, to find that the path was mud and marsh, with hardly room to get the cart past the pond. As they came slowly down the bank of the river, Navis murmured, "The Undying make quite a difference."

Everyone was glad when they came to the place

where the green road crossed the river and found it just the same. They could even see the place where the pursuing horsemen had trampled through the spongy turf, in and out of the water.

"Go cautiously," Navis said, "since the pursuit is now ahea—" He turned round in surprise as the cart came splashing through the river, too, with water whirling from its wheels. "I thought you were leaving us, Singer."

"There are only two ways to go," Hestefan pointed out. "I chose not to turn back."

This seemed to be Hestefan's way of saying he was not going to leave them after all. They went on together, the same party, apart from Wend striding alongside, and the river Dropwater went with them, too, sometimes winding in the distance, sometimes skirling along beside them, and growing steadily larger. A long way farther on, they came to the place where the band of hearthmen had camped for the night. There was not much to see, merely hoofprints and the cold ashes of their fire, but it sent Navis very cautious again. From then on he was either watching for prints in the green road or scanning the distance on either side.

It was empty distance, all green sheep runs and faraway dark peaks, but there were sheep and, once or twice, a shepherd a long way off. Maewen found herself staring every time they saw a shepherd, expecting him to come striding toward them and turn out to be Wend. But no shepherd did more than turn and look at them. She was quite surprised to be missing Wend so much.

When they camped that night by the river, Navis insisted that they find a place a long way back and hidden from the road. Hestefan drove the cart after him along the riverbank just as if he had never threatened to leave, remarking cheerfully, "We've made good time without a walker to slow us down. We'll be at Dropwater tomorrow."

As they dismounted, Moril hopped off the back of the cart and came over to Mitt. "That's a relief," he said. "I wouldn't have known what to do if he'd decided to leave. I'm sure he's not well."

Maewen led her horse into the river, still thinking about Wend. She had been sure he would get over his anger and come back, but now she began to see that he was not going to. It was Noreth he followed, not her. So what was she going to do? She had, she saw, been relying on Wend to get her back to her own time. Perhaps she never would get back. She thought of Mum and Aunt Liss and Dad and felt a touch of fear—but only a touch. She was surprised not to be much more frightened.

"The Wanderer is no loss," said the deep voice. "You never needed him."

Maewen jumped and shuddered, wondering if it—he—could read her mind. "Didn't I?" she said. "That's a weight off my mind!"

Sarcasm always seemed to pass Kankredin by—if it was Kankredin. The voice went on imperturbably, "From now on, look for an opportunity to stab the Southerners. The danger from them is growing."

"Anything you say!" Maewen told it bitterly.

It was a great relief to her over supper to hear Navis arranging with Mitt for the two of them to keep watch that night in turns. Those pursuing hearthmen had been a blessing in disguise. Kankredin could not expect her to try to kill them tonight. But she was terrified of what might happen when he found she had no intention of trying.

They went on again next day through the same rolling green country, with Mitt yawning and Navis red-eyed. Maewen was inclined to be sorry for them until Mitt said, "I'm used to it, and Navis is one of those who just get sharper for it. Mind you, I've only seen him lose four nights of sleep, but he never turned a hair then."

She realized Mitt was right when Navis spotted the faint marks where the party of hearthmen had turned off the green road to the left, to follow a disused-looking path that led toward the mountains. Navis pounced on it like a cat. "Where does that lead?" he asked Hestefan and Moril.

"You can cut through to the North Dales that way," Moril said.

Navis narrowed his eyes at the path and then raised them to the mountains. They were nearer here. Ahead they curved inward and seemed to stand right over the green road. "And can horses work their way round through the tops to come back to the road?" he asked.

"Possibly," said Hestefan. "But the river goes down to Dropwater there." He pointed to the craggy eminences ahead. "We only have to go down into the valley to be safe."

"If they don't reach us first," Navis said.

From there on he rode with his pistol ready in his hand. When, around midday, they reached the crags, and the road wound in among them, Navis's eyes were continually flicking to the skyline above, watching for an ambush. Mostly he watched to the left. But if there was a heathery dip in the crags above the Dropwater, which now roared beside the road as a wide wild torrent, Navis was sure to check that, too.

Half a mile farther on, the Dropwater suddenly spread wider still, into an immense flat sheet of racing water, and seemed to plunge off the edge of the world into vague blue distance. The road curved so that they could see where it fell and fell and fell, nearly a mile of falling white water, in smoky rainbows and wet thunder. The noise was enormous.

"Quite something, isn't it?" Moril yelled.

Maewen turned to shout back and saw a squad of armed men running toward them from farther up the road. Her hands leaped to the Adon's sword, lying crosswise in front of her saddle, and then fell away. Navis swung round with his pistol ready. She saw him lower it. There were so many armed men. They were all wearing dark red and blue livery, except for the man in front who seemed to be waving at them, and she was sure she had seen those colors before— Oh. Maewen looked down at herself. She had grown so used to her clothes that she had thought of them as just clothes. But she was wearing the same dark red and blue. The man in front was in expensive scarlet silk and red leather, and he was definitely waving to her.

Maewen slid down from her horse. This was like Kredindale, only possibly worse, she thought, as she went hesitatingly to meet him. To her gratitude, Moril realized she would need help and hopped off the cart to come with her.

"Who *is* he?" she half shouted, under the roar of the falls.

"Luthan!" Moril yelled in her ear. "Earl of Dropwater. Noreth's cousin. He's been her hearthlord these last two years. Don't nod at me! Smile at *him*!"

Maewen stretched her mouth into a grin. At least, she thought, this saved them from any ambush.

The Earl of Dropwater pelted up and stood in front of her panting and smiling. "Cousin!" he bawled.

"Hearthlord!" Maewen shrieked back. He was awfully young. She took him for her own age at first sight. But as he laughed and seized hold of both her hands, she saw he was older than that, maybe at least eighteen. He was one of those people who have pretty pink and white faces, all curves. As he laughed, he tossed back glossy black hair.

"At last!" he shouted, fluttering long dark eyelashes Maewen truly envied him for. "Where have you been? We expected you yesterday at the latest."

He clearly had no idea she was not Noreth. Well, you see what you expect to see, Maewen thought. "How did you know when to expect me?" she bawled back.

Luthan put an arm round her shoulders and led her up the road, past the people who had been running with him, and among masses more. There was what looked like a small army strung out along the way, and horses for them standing in patient rows under the crags. "There's less noise along here. We can hear ourselves speak," Luthan said.

Mitt looked at Moril, who nodded and scampered off beside Maewen. Mitt slid to the ground and hurriedly led Maewen's horse and the Countess-horse along behind them. Navis looked at him questioningly and then rode up behind Luthan.

Luthan turned round, surprised. "Noreth, who are these?"

"My followers, of course," Maewen said. They came to a moist green ground beyond the rocks where Luthan had a fine tent set up. The noise of the waterfall was cut off by crags in the way. Maewen could speak normally as she said, "This is Navis Haddsson, and this is Mitt. This is Moril Clennensson."

Luthan's curvaceous face lit up. "The Southerners who came on the wind's road? I've heard of you. And of course, I've met you, Moril, now I think—though I knew your father better. My cousin certainly knows how to pick her followers." He smiled at Maewen and really seemed to mean it. She felt like a beast deceiving him. She felt worse as numbers of men and women in Dropwater livery came crowding round to smile and say hello. They were probably Noreth's personal friends. And all she could do was smile back and hope they did not think she was behaving oddly.

"Now, to business," said Luthan. "You were awfully secretive when you left, Noreth, but I guessed what you were up to. You're riding the King's Road, aren't you? Well, the whole North knows you are. What made you think I wouldn't follow you?"

Maewen found herself thinking, Flaming Ammet! She seemed to have caught that from Mitt. Here was the army she had been trying to avoid having. "It—it's going to be very dangerous," she said lamely.

Luthan swept that aside. "Danger—nothing! I court it! I intend to follow my true Queen!" He meant it. Maewen squirmed. "But I won't keep you guessing about how I knew. They sent word down by sea from Kredindale. They told the whole coast. All the coastal dales are ready to come to you as soon as you give the word, and of course, I got ready at once. You'll need my help. There's worrying news, too." Luthan's curved brows set in a serious line. "My agent in Hannart sent a carrier pigeon. Earl Keril has set out for Kernsburgh, and it looks as if he wants to stop you. I was going to invite you down to the mansion, but in view of that news, I think we'd better break camp and be on our way."

"You mean you're coming, too?" Maewen said. Oh flaming Ammet, oh *bother*!

Luthan smiled meltingly. "My Queen, what do you think I've been telling you? I am coming, and all my hearthpeople with me."

Navis coughed. "When did the Earl of Hannart set out, and how long will it take him to reach Kernsburgh?"

Luthan blinked his beautiful eyelashes. "Er. Um. Yesterday. He'd be there tomorrow evening if he rode hard."

"Yesterday." Maewen could see Navis thinking that it was not Earl Keril's band that had been after them, then. "And Dropwater is on the other point of a triangle, am I right?" Luthan nodded, in another flutter of eyelashes, and turned back to Maewen. "Then," said Navis, forcefully, "if you would be good enough to strike camp at once, my lord, I think we must ride through the night."

Luthan all but sprang to attention. "Oh. Yes. At once, sir." He ran away, waving his arms and shouting orders. Moril snorted. He butted his head into Mitt, and both of them bent over, howling with laughter.

"It's not funny!" said Maewen.

"Only some of it," said Navis. "But allies are allies."
He watched the Dropwater people running about for
a while, and he sighed. "These children have no idea
they are about to fight a war. And," he added, "no
idea how to hurry either. Mitt, stop giggling and come
with me. I'll need a serious aide." He shook his mare
into motion and rode into the confusion. Mitt popped
his eyes at Maewen and legged after him.

It was like magic. The confusion stopped as soon as
Navis took over. He seemed to know just which gaggle
of people to speak to and which to leave alone. And if
two or more inefficiencies happened at once, Navis
had only to nod to Mitt, and Mitt was at one of them,
sorting it out as quickly as Navis. Maewen was impressed. Barely half an hour later they were ready to
go. There was even a spare horse for Moril. Navis
came riding up with it himself. "Because I take it you
are ready to leave us now," he remarked unlovingly to
Hestefan.

Hestefan's beard jutted at him. "If you recall," he
said, "sir—Navis Haddsson from Holand—I told you
a long way back on the road that where great events
are toward, a Singer must needs be there. But by all
means remove my apprentice. I'll follow at my own
pace."

"As you please," said Navis, and he murmured as
he wheeled away, "*Crawl* behind, if you like. I don't
know what it is," he remarked to Mitt as soon as they
were well away from the green cart, "but I can't abide

: 313 :

that fellow. He sets my teeth on edge—rather the way my brother Harchad always used to."

Mitt shuddered. "That's a bit steep, isn't it? Your brother Harchad only killed a few hundred folk each year and terrified the rest. Hestefan's a Singer, Navis. Maybe it's the beard reminds you."

They rode. The cart was soon only a green smudge behind. They rode under Navis's direction as fast as they could without exhausting their horses. They stopped to breathe them and rode again, on over the green undulations of the Shield, rising now, toward the high plateau that held Kernsburgh. Before nightfall the more distant mountains had wheeled into the blue jagged shapes Maewen remembered seeing from Dad's apartment. The peaks of the North Dales, Dad had told her. They set off again into the sunset to ride some more.

The Countess-horse had had enough by then. It stopped with all four feet planted and tried to bite Mitt's leg while Mitt cursed and bounced and shook the reins. Navis looked. He beckoned with a trim, gloved hand. One of the Dropwater hearthwomen instantly rode up with Earl Luthan's spare horse for Mitt. Nobody seemed to object that after that Mitt rode on a mare that was almost as good as Navis's own. When Maewen next saw the Countess-horse, it was in the rear carrying someone's baggage. She was impressed all over again. This was the kind of thing, quite certainly, that was going to get Navis made Duke of Kernsburgh during the next year or so.

Otherwise she did not enjoy the ride. At least the actual riding was a pleasure. It was good not to have to keep to the pace of Wend or the cart. It was Luthan she did not enjoy. He was beside her far too often, and he would keep reminding her, with significant smiles, of all the things he and Noreth had done together. "Do you remember the Harvest when we threw plums?" he said, and Maewen had to pretend to remember. Or, "You know that time with the lawbooks? Ham the Markinder still hasn't got over that." This was bad enough. But Luthan's smiles grew more and more melting. Finally he sighed and said, "Noreth, it seemed an age, an endless age, after you had gone. Dropwater was empty. Empty and void."

This is *dire*! Maewen thought. Moril, jogging on the other side of her, thought so, too. "But," he said, "Dropwater *isn't* empty. It's full of plum trees and people."

Luthan was not at all embarrassed. He smiled meltingly again. "You know what I mean. Lovers are allowed to say these things."

Maewen gave up trying not to hurt Luthan's feelings and lost her temper. "Stop being so silly! I am *not* your lover!" Then she bit her tongue. For all she knew, Noreth was very fond of Luthan—though if she was, Maewen was beginning to wonder why.

Luthan sighed, and laughed a little. "Oh dear. Have I overstepped again? I never know where to have you, Noreth. I think I've won your heart, and then you bite my head off."

So that was all right. But it did not stop Luthan. When Mitt was relieved of the Countess-horse, he rode Luthan's spare mare firmly up between Luthan and Maewen. Whenever Luthan said anything sighing or melting, Mitt grinned, grinned like a death's-head. It was soon too much for Luthan. He gave up and rode on ahead. But then, as far as Maewen was concerned, it was almost worse. Moril and Mitt could not seem to stop teasing her about it.

"Your handsome lordly lover got it bad for you!" Mitt said.

"Every lady's dream!" Moril sighed. "An earl in red silk!"

"With eyelashes," said Mitt. "Don't forget the eyelashes. All bat and flutter, this dream lover!"

Moril giggled. "Now he's gone off to write a poem about you."

"No, he hasn't. Even he's not that much of a wimp," Maewen said.

"He *is* writing a poem, you know," Moril said. "He's dictating it to his scribe. The poor man's got real trouble, trying to write it down on horseback."

Maewen refused to look, so she had no idea whether this was true or just Moril's idea of a joke. Besides, it grew dark then, too dark for poems—or so she hoped. They stopped again, and ate and drank, and then went on. After that Mitt and Moril were too tired to tease her. They just rode.

Eventually, far into the night, Navis consulted Luthan and the Dropwater armsmaster and decided they could afford a longer stop. Everyone saw to horses, ate food they did not feel like, and fell down and slept for three hours. Then Navis had them all up and on their way again.

"Flaming Ammet!" Mitt groaned. "Is this necessary?"

"Yes," said Navis. "We have to be in a good defensive position before the Earl of Hannart arrives."

"Because of Ynen?" Mitt yawned.

"Not entirely," said Navis. "You and I have necks we need to save, too."

Mitt puzzled about this as he yawningly mounted Luthan's mare among all the blue-brown shadows of other people mounting, too. It seemed tremendous cheek for him and Navis to use the Earl of Dropwater's hearthpeople just to save their necks. Noreth was the excuse, of course. But somehow he did not think this quite accounted for Navis's urgency. Navis had something else in mind which Mitt was too sleepy to work out.

Dawn came as their small army set off again, whiteness pouring down the sky and blueness rising from the ground to meet it. Then the blueness was ripped open to the left by a dazzling bar of orange. In seconds, the grass was green again and the riders turned from brown shadows to solid, colored shapes.

There were more solid shapes advancing down the green road to meet them. The orange dawn flashed on gold braid and threw turning glints from steel and leather. It was a smaller group than theirs, but everyone in it was orderly and very well armed.

"It looks as if Earl Keril got here first," Maewen said.

"No," Mitt said, squinting up his eyes to look. "That's not Hannart colors, it's— Flaming Ammet! It's Alk! What's *he* doing here?"

:‖ 19 ‖:

ALK WAS RIDING an enormous horse. Mitt knew it
well. It was about the only one in Aberath which was
up to Alk's weight. By the horse and the hugeness Alk
was unmistakable, as he gestured to the rest of his
party to halt and rode out ahead of them alone. Though
Mitt knew Alk would be wearing his own special armor
under his pale leather clothes, he still thought this was
very brave—or very foolish—of Alk. Luthan's people
had guns and crossbows. They might be tired, but
after the way Navis had worked them, they were
jumpy as cats.

"Nobody fire!" Navis called sharply. Fifty weapons
were up.

Luthan came awake with a jump. "That's right, Navis. Hold fire, everyone. We've no quarrel with Aberath."

Speak for yourself! Mitt thought nervously as Alk
came to a ponderous halt halfway between the two
bands.

"Good morning," Alk called. "I need to speak to

some of you. Here's my list: Navis Haddsson, Alhammitt Alhammittsson, Hestefan the Singer, Tanamoril
Clennensson, and a lady known as Noreth Onesdaughter, if she's with you. I'd be grateful if they all
came out here and the rest of you went back a bit. I
need to talk to them in private."

They exchanged mystified looks. Mitt and Moril had
been yawning. Maewen's eyes had been nearly shut.
But they were all suddenly wide awake. "I suppose
we should see what he wants," Navis said. "We *are*
four to one."

"That doesn't count with Alk," Mitt said. "I've seen
him throw a *horse*."

Navis bowed politely to Luthan. "We'll try not to
keep you waiting long," he said. Luthan gave him a
polite, bewildered nod. Navis edged his mare out of
the throng, and the other three followed him.

Alk looked them over as they approached. Mitt had
never seen him look so glum and grim. "Where's Hestefan the Singer?"

"Following behind," said Navis. "His mule couldn't
keep up. Are you likely to detain us long, my lord?"

"My lord." Alk rubbed his chin. It rasped. Behind
him Mitt could see a cluster of faces he knew well from
Aberath. All of them had a weary, fed-up look, and
none of them greeted him. "My lord?" Alk repeated.
"Now, I reckon you're at least as much of a lord as I
am, Navis Haddsson. My reading is that when you
call people that, you don't mean any respect at all. So

don't call me that. As for how long we'll be, this'll take as long as it takes. You all gave me the slip once, when I'd nearly caught you up at Dropthwaite, and forced me to get ahead of you. I've been hanging around for you, up and down the green roads, for a day and a half now, so now you can just wait for me, Navis Haddsson. That reminds me—" Alk's glum manner vanished. He turned to Mitt. "This is something you'll appreciate, Mitt. I'd been in Aberath such years that I'd forgotten what these green roads were like. Lovely level runs, you get on them—bends beautifully cambered, not a sharp curve among them—and never a steep gradient anywhere! It would only take a little tinkering and filling in, and I could lay tracks and run my steam engines all over the North!"

Maewen had been watching Navis look as put down as she had ever seen him, but this snatched her attention back. So *that* was why there were no green roads in her day! They were all railways! "So that's—" she began, and stopped herself.

But the small noise caught this huge man's attention. "And who are you, young lady?" Alk asked her.

"Noreth Onesdaughter," she said. "You asked to see me."

"With respect, young lady," said Alk, "I don't think you can be."

He was terrifyingly grim about it. Mitt and Moril gave her looks that were plain frightened. As for Navis, he looked at her, narrowed his eyes, and looked again, in a way that made Maewen feel as if she were dropping fast through the earth, leaving sun and grass and friendliness behind. "Wh-what makes you say that?" she managed to ask Alk.

"The reason I came after you all." Alk settled himself stonily upright on his huge horse. "Four days," he said. "Four days after Mitt set out for Adenmouth, Lady Eltruda of Adenmouth arrives in Aberath. Came herself. Asking for justice. On a charge of murder. She brought the murdered corpse with her, because the victim was her niece. Noreth of Kredindale. The girl's throat had been cut."

"I don't believe this!" Navis burst out. His face had drained to a blue-white, except for his eyes, which were rimmed with red. "Does Eltruda—the Lady of Adenmouth—suspect that I—"

"You're on her list," said Alk, "though I can't say she likes the idea."

Navis sagged. There were big, deep lines on his face that had not been there a minute before. He's really fond of her! Mitt thought wonderingly. That little, loud lady. Who'd have thought it?

"It seems," Alk continued, "they didn't find the girl's body right away because whoever did her in killed her in the stables. Then shoved her in an empty stall and piled straw over her. It was only luck they found her. I reckon the killer hoped it would be longer than that before they did."

His eyes wandered over all four of them, bleak as

stones. Mitt shivered. He had never seen Alk like this. This was Alk the lawman. Seeing it, Mitt had an inkling at least of why the Countess had married Alk. Like this, he must have frightened even the Countess.

"Lady Eltruda," said Alk, "ought to have been a law-woman. She did a fine job. Everyone in Adenmouth she's accounted for, and had them all prove where they were and what they were doing. She has it narrowed down to everyone who went off on Midsummer morning. You'd better believe this. I do. I suspect you all, plus"—his eyes traveled to Maewen—"you. I've seen the body. You could be her twin sister, but you're not her. She looked older." His eyes traveled to Moril and on to Navis. "*You* told Fenna you'd sworn to follow Noreth, and *you* promised Lady Eltruda you'd look after her. But when you both went off, she was already dead." His eyes went to Mitt and, if possible, were bleaker still. "And you came and made promises to me in Aberath, so you could get that ring for someone who wasn't Noreth. Did you know she was dead then?"

"I didn't— I didn't know. I swear—" Mitt stammered.

"Nor did I," Moril whispered. "I was with Hestefan all—"

"*All* the time?" said Alk. "You went and talked to Fenna, up in her bedroom, and after that you were running around, no one knows where, looking for your cwidder."

Moril wilted. Navis said nothing. Maewen put her hands to her face. The poor girl. And here was I cheerfully thinking she'd just been kidnapped. Maewen knew, too well, what Noreth's last moments had felt like. Grabbed round the throat. The knife coming round. Or maybe Noreth had been glad to see the killer and turned round smiling—oh, are you coming, too?—and then she saw the knife. Tears came rolling down her face. Poor Noreth.

"This gets us nowhere," Alk said. "I came for justice, not playacting. And I made inquiries as I came. When Karet came back up from Gardale with the news that the Adon's cup had gone from the Lawschool, I thought, Can you believe anything that Mitt says? You stole it, didn't you?"

"No," Navis said. "I did."

Alk stared at him in genuine surprise. After blinking a bit, he said, "Then where is it?"

Navis answered by fetching the cup from his pocket, still wrapped in the handkerchief. Alk stared at it for a moment. He considered. Then he nodded at Maewen. "Give it to her. And you," he said to Maewen, "take hold of it without that wrapping and tell me your name is Noreth of Kredindale. Go on."

Maewen wretchedly took the cup and just stopped herself from wiping the tears off her face with the handkerchief. "My name is Noreth of Kredindale," she said, "Why—"

"Quiet," said Alk.

Maewen obediently shut her mouth. The man had

a personality as huge as his body, she thought, wiping her face with her sleeve. You did what he said.

"Now say your real name," said Alk.

"I'm Mayelbridwen Singer," Maewen said sadly. She was still thinking of Noreth. She saw everyone staring at the cup before it occurred to her to look at it herself. It was shining blue all over its lopsided shape. Even in the gold haze of dawn it was bright. And at the end of her long shadow, stretching away on top of her horse's longer shadow, right out across the grass and bracken, there was a blue haze where the shadow of the cup should have been. She saw Alk's followers turning to look at it.

"Marvelous!" said Alk. "Clever work! When I was a boy at the Lawschool, I heard they used it for truth telling in evidence." For a moment, in spite of their anxiety, all four of them had an irresistible vision of Alk at grittling. His side must have won every time. Even Navis nearly smiled. "But I never saw it at work before this," Alk said. "Now tell me another lie, young Mayelbridwen."

Maewen's mind would not come up with a lie at first. Then her horse sidled, no doubt puzzled by the blue light on its back, and she caught a glimpse of scarlet, where Luthan was standing, patting his horse's nose and staring at the cup. She said, "I'm in love with the Earl of Dropwater." The blue light went from the cup as if someone had turned a switch. Moril gave an unhappy chuckle.

"Now another truth," Alk commanded.

Maewen nearly began, "I'm in love with—" but she swallowed it down and said, "Oh—er—we found the Adon's sword. It's behind my saddle."

"Did you indeed?" said Alk as the cup lit blue again, like a small sheeny moon. "I thought no one knew where that sword really was. Well, well. Now pass the cup to the Singer-lad." Maewen reached across and handed the cup over. As Moril's hand closed round it, the blue light went again. Alk nodded. "You say your name," he said to Moril.

"Osfameron Tanamoril Clennensson," said Moril. And the cup was alight and blue again. He stared at it wonderingly.

"Untruth," commanded Alk.

"I—er—I can't play the cwidder," Moril said. And he was holding a simple silver cup.

"Now say— Did you kill Noreth of Kredindale?" Alk said.

"*No!*" said Moril, and again the cup flared blue. Moril screwed his eyes up at it as if he might cry.

"Now pass it to Navis," Alk ordered. When Navis had stretched out and taken the cup and it was once more a mild silver, Alk said, "And did *you* kill Noreth Onesdaughter?"

"I most certainly did *not*," Navis said, and screwed his eyes up like Moril when the cup shone blue in his hand.

Mitt waited anxiously. Alk was leaving him till last because he thought Mitt was the guilty one. He could see that. It was a wretched thought. But the cup itself was beginning to worry him just as much. If it was behaving as it was supposed to with the others—and from Alk's look as he tested it, it was—then it had behaved all wrong with Mitt, spitting blue sparks at him both other times he touched it. Mitt suspected the thing disliked him. He did not trust it not to prove him guilty out of sheer malice. He could see the faces of his onetime friends in Aberath behind Alk, shut away from him, sure he was a murderer.

"Now to him," Alk said to Navis.

Navis held the blue-glowing cup out to Mitt. That, and Mitt's worry, made his new horse turn round restively, giving him a sight of Luthan and all his people staring. Ammet only knew what *they* were thinking.

"Take it!" Navis snapped.

Mitt spared a hand for the thing. *"Ouch!"* It was like nettles, squirting blue rays between his fingers. He had to let go the reins and hang on to the cup with both hands or he would have let it fall. It hurt. It crackled blue streams round his wrists and knuckles. The cup clearly hated him as much as the Countess-horse did. *"Ow!"* And Luthan's spare horse did not help, bucking around in fear, until Navis grabbed it and pulled on the bit.

"Can you bring yourself to tell a lie?" Alk said, watching callously.

"You being . . . sarky is . . . all I need!" Mitt said with his teeth clenched. "Burn you! I— I— You don't make steam engines!" The blue rays faded inward between Mitt's fingers and vanished. The prickling lasted an instant longer, and then that went, too. Mitt shook the plain silver goblet he was now holding, and the other hand as well. The relief! "Burn you, Alk! This thing hates me! I won't dare tell the truth now, I warn you!"

"I dare you," said Alk. "Did you kill Noreth of Kredindale?"

"*No!*" Mitt spat, hunched against another assault from the cup. It spat at him again, with a sharp sizzle, but, to his surprise, it was nothing like so painful. More like a tingling. The blue rays reaching through his fingers were almost glorious. "Ah. Calmed it down," he said.

"Turn it off, turn it on. I thought that might do it," Alk said. He looked smug, like someone who had won a bet. As Mitt thankfully passed the cup back to Navis, he said, "Then I declare you all clear of the charge of murder. Now," he added to Maewen, "let's have a look at that sword, young lady."

"But why?" said Navis.

"It might do to swear some more on," Alk said.

Navis looked harrowed. "Please," he said. "I have to get to Kernsburgh in case my son, Ynen, is there."

Maewen hurriedly scrabbled the sword loose, knowing Navis was right.

Alk grinned. "It's just curiosity, really. I love clever metalwork. Just draw the sword and show it to me, young lady, and then you can all go."

Maewen tried to draw the sword in the same hurry—too hurriedly. She jammed it sideways somehow, and it refused to emerge. "It's stuck!" she said, hauling uselessly at it. Mitt and Navis leaned over to help. They both wanted to get going. Both their horses, and Maewen's with them, got the wrong idea and started to move and were pulled back. All three surged round in a circle, and Moril's horse joined in. Alk calmly moved his own horse back, where he sat watching the confusion. It was only resolved when Navis seized the leather scabbard Maewen was waving about and planted the hilt end on Mitt's saddle. Both pulled. The sword came loose with a slithery clang.

"There," said Mitt. He rode over and pushed the sword under Alk's nose. "Satisfied?"

"I'll say!" Alk looked it over admiringly. "It may look plain and a silly old fashion, but it's better work than any of us could do today. I'd give an eyetooth to meet the man that made it. He'd have taken a year and a day to do it, you know. No one bothers to take that sort of trouble today. All right. Put it away, and let's all get to Kernsburgh."

"All?" said Navis. He was more depressed than Mitt had ever seen him. "I've no more patience for jokes."

"No joke," said Alk. "I said I'd come to Kernsburgh with the rest of you. Keril listens to me."

"I don't think you understand," Navis said wearily. "You have just removed my pretext for dragging the Earl of Dropwater there with me."

Alk's eyes went to Maewen. "Is that so? Who heard

me do that, apart from you and two lads who knew, anyway? Didn't you?" he asked Moril.

"Kankredin might have heard," Moril said.

"All the more reason for going there," said Alk. He turned his vast horse round to join his hearthmen.

"Just a moment," Navis said. He seemed to have revived wonderfully. Alk stopped and turned his head questioningly. "If I have no pretext," Navis said, "you must have one."

"Must I?" Alk lifted his helmet and scratched his head. "I suppose it stands to reason," he admitted, "that if I pull the rug out from under you, you'll need somewhere to stand." He grinned. "Let's say I've got the same pretext as you have."

Navis laughed and wheeled round to ride back to Luthan.

"What did he mean?" Maewen asked as their three horses shimmied about, glad to be moving again.

"Not to tell Luthan you're not Noreth, I think," Mitt said, although, knowing Alk and Navis as he did, he was not at all sure.

She made a face. Moril laughed. "Don't look now. Luthan's on his way to ask you all about what Alk wanted."

Maewen naturally looked. Luthan was mounted again, trotting up the road with an eager, tender, questioning look. "What shall I *tell* him?"

Navis reached Luthan first. He spoke quickly and quietly to Luthan, and whatever it was he said, it seemed to satisfy Luthan entirely. He shot Maewen a look of deep understanding and rode gravely beside Navis as their party joined Alk's.

The two groups together made quite an impressive force, Mitt thought, as he rode in the midst of it. This ought to show Earl Keril they meant business—if this *was* what Navis and Alk had in mind. Since he was not sure, Mitt found himself thinking about Noreth instead, dead before she set foot on the King's Road. Kankredin must be angry about that. Wend had fooled him, and everyone else, by sending Maewen in her place. Except that Wend hadn't seemed to know what he was doing. Mitt was anxious about that. Wend had withdrawn his protection from Maewen, and she could well be in danger if Kankredin turned on her. Mitt decided not to let her out of his sight.

He was surprised, and a little ashamed, to find that when he thought he was thinking of Noreth, it was Maewen he was really worried about.

About an hour later they reached Kernsburgh. At least, it was where Alk and all the Dropwater people said Kernsburgh was.

"It is. Honestly," Moril assured Mitt and Maewen.

They had halted in a half circle three or four riders deep, facing an ordinary small waystone. Beyond it the green turf rose and fell in a hundred humps and hummocks. And that was all.

"City of Gold," Alk said genially. "Always on the hill beyond."

Navis beckoned Mitt and cantered among the grassy mounds to organize his defense. Everyone followed slowly, Maewen among the last. This felt weird. Where they had first stopped could have been the space which Kernsburgh Central Station was going to fill, except that the waystone was all wrong. Those low mounds were where she had last seen shops and office blocks, and the slightly higher hummocks ahead, up which Navis was riding slantwise, were where the Tannoreth Palace would be someday soon. The green crease she was following, full of hoofprints and horse droppings, was probably King Street. And instead of cars and lorries, there was a much quieter confusion of riders in two different liveries. Maewen could so little believe this was really Kernsburgh that she had to look up toward the distant hills to make sure. There she saw the blue jagged shapes she saw from Dad's apartment, the North Dales Peaks. But the oddest part was the way there had obviously been a city here once, under all these lumps. She felt as if time had stood upside down and she really was in the far future, looking at the remains of the Kernsburgh she had known.

A great shout jerked her attention back to here and now. Mitt was down from his horse, leaping across the hummocks, yelling. Maewen shook her own horse to a fast trot and arrived at the top of the palace mounds in time to see Mitt delightedly greeting two newcomers. The tall, curly one was plainly Kialan. Navis had his arm round the shoulders of the small pale boy with

Kialan. They were alike enough for Maewen to know that this was Ynen. There were two weary-looking horses in the hollow behind the two. It looked as if they had ridden all night as well.

"I'm sorry we kept out of sight," Kialan was saying. "There was a big troop of horsemen in war gear on the road last night. We had to leave the road to avoid them. We couldn't see who they were in the dark, but we didn't think they should see us."

"It was probably Alk," said Navis, "but we'll take precautions."

Maewen was watching Ynen frisk round Mitt like a terrier puppy round a greyhound. I'm so glad! she thought. He *likes* Mitt! I don't think I could have borne it if he'd been like Hildy. Ynen was so unlike Hildy that she thought maybe he was a bit of a softie. Then Ynen looked up at Maewen, and she knew he was not soft at all. He smiled at her uncertainly, not knowing who she was.

"Are you Noreth?" Kialan asked her. Lordly, Maewen thought. He reminded her of the boys at the sixth form college.

"We all thought so, but apparently not," Navis said. "Mayelbridwen, I believe, is the name."

Just then, there were agitated noises from Luthan a little way off. Mitt went haring over there to see what was wrong. Maewen found she could not face the puzzled looks from Kialan and Ynen, and she followed Mitt.

In another hidden hollow Luthan was standing over an immense heap of mixed bread and grapes. There was another heap beyond that looked like oats. "Where did all *this* come from?" Luthan demanded.

Mitt narrowed his eyes at the stuff. The loaves were the kind plaited into a wheat shape which he had last seen in the Holy Islands. The grapes were the sweet green Southern kind. He grinned. "A present," he said, "from the Earth Shaker and She Who Raised the Islands."

"You're joking," Luthan said uncertainly.

"I am not," Mitt said.

However it arrived, the breakfast was very welcome. By the time Navis had the place organized, everyone was glad to sit down and eat at their posts. Alk's people, and most of Luthan's, were posted hidden behind mounds in a great circle. Kialan and Ynen were sent to help pass a loaf and a bunch of grapes to everyone, while Maewen and Mitt were busy pouring a pile of oats in front of each of the horses picketed in the middle. Luthan's hearthwomen were standing by a third of the horses to mount a cavalry charge if necessary.

"There's still quite a heap of bread and grapes left," Kialan said as he arrived at the horses with an armload for the hearthwomen.

"As if they might be expecting more people," Ynen said, following Kialan with his arms clutched round loaves and grapes dangling from his fingers. "I got these for us."

Mitt wondered about this as they went to eat in the central hollow. What did the Undying think was going to happen? He had a sense that this was a lull before things got frantic. And once things got frantic, he knew they would go on that way for quite some time.

Before Mitt could mention this feeling to the others, Navis arrived with Alk and Luthan. "There," Navis said. "That should stop anyone interfering while we look for the crown. Has anyone any idea where it is?"

Everyone shook their heads. Wend would know, Maewen thought. Oh, bother the man!

Luthan broke apart a loaf. "They say," he said, "that the crown is buried in the ruins of King Hern's palace. You may be sitting on it," he added, with a melting smile at Maewen.

"Then it's going to take digging to find," Alk said, sitting on the slope with a loaf in each hand.

"Long, careful digging," Kialan agreed. "They took six weeks' digging to find the second spellcoat up above Hannart."

"I doubt," said Navis, "that we have six hours."

"Then we think it round another way," said Alk.

Moril arrived then, with his vaguest look, and was introduced to Ynen. Ynen was delighted. It turned out that he had met Moril's brother, Dagner, in Hannart, who had told him a great deal about Moril. The two of them chattered as they ate. They were the only ones talking. Everyone else was wondering how to find the crown, except Luthan, who kept giving Maewen such melting looks that she wanted to tell him to start digging. But he won't, she thought. It would spoil his scarlet suit.

"This won't do," Mitt said at last.

"No," Kialan agreed. He nudged Moril with his boot. "Moril, do the Singers have any sayings that might help us find the crown?"

Moril looked up. His face was full of a kind of nervous awe. "You want to go and get it now?"

Everyone stared at him.

"I've been walking around," he said, "trying to work it out. I *think* the cwidder will do it. We have to go to the waystone."

Everyone sprang up. "Why didn't you *say?*" Ynen cried out.

"I second that," said Navis.

"Leave him be," Kialan said, as they all raced down the hummock. "He's like that. One of us should have asked him before."

They raced past the hobbled horses, where the hearthwomen were fixing bayonets to long guns. Mitt knew how they felt. Every one of the women was trying to pretend this was just a training exercise, and very much hoping that was all it would turn out to be. As they ran on, more hearthmen sprang up alertly from among the green humps and then subsided, seeing they were not being attacked. Further heads reared up from across the green road and disappeared, as the eight of them gathered round the waystone.

"What do we do?" said Kialan.

"Go through," said Moril. "I think." He knelt down and carefully put his face to the impossibly small hole in the middle of the waystone.

"Look any different through there, does it?" Mitt asked hopefully.

"No," Moril said, crawling away backward. He slung the cwidder round to the front of him and stripped off its cover, thinking hard.

"I don't wish to cast a blight, lad," said Alk, "but not even young Ynen is going to get through there."

Moril frowned. "I know. I wish I could think how—"

"Wait a minute," Maewen interrupted.

As she spoke, there was a yell and a splatter of gunfire from the mounds over to the right. Here comes the frantic bit, Mitt thought.

"Uh-oh," said Alk.

Luthan's curvaceous face went a little less pink. "My sector," he said and went dashing away.

"Good," said Maewen. "Moril, in the time I come from, this waystone is as tall as a house—and I think the hole is lower down. Does that help?"

Moril's white face lifted to her. "Yes. That's a truth." He put his fingers to the strings of the cwidder and bent his head. Mitt, now he knew a little about the working of the cwidder, could feel Moril concentrate and the power begin to build. He knelt beside him, as if that could help.

There was another shot and a great deal of yelling, fierce and strident, from over to the left. Alk flinched in that direction and turned back. "I'd better go," he said. "That's my part. Here, Mitt. Here's a keepsake for you. Catch." He tossed Mitt something small and round and heavy.

Mitt was just in time to catch it. "What's this, then?"

"Told you I made a copy of the Adon's ring," Alk called over his shoulder. "Put it on. I may have a hole in me like that waystone when you see me next."

Mitt gave the ring a distracted look and shoved it on his nearest finger. Moril had begun to play, rippling music like waves from a stone dropped in water, expanding and expanding, and rippling again. The waystone looked no different, but Mitt could feel the solid booming beneath the ripples, and strange, shrill stretching sounds buried in it, that told him that something was happening. Counterpoint against the music came more shots and clamor, this time from behind.

Navis looked over his shoulder. "Now I must go. You young ones find that crown, and we'll cover your backs."

"But you'll need me," Mitt said, half getting up.

Navis put a hand on his shoulder and held him down. "Not yet. You go. Luck ship and shore."

A strange thing to say, Maewen thought. She looked back at the waystone and saw the impossible sight of Moril stepping through the hole in the center, carefully holding his cwidder. The waystone looked no larger.

Moril looked no smaller. Yet he stepped through, and there was no sign of him on the other side. Ynen hopped eagerly through after him, and he disappeared, too. Then Kialan stooped to follow. He was so much bigger that Maewen held her breath. But Kialan stepped through as calmly and easily as if he did this impossible thing every day. Mitt went next, in a gawky scramble of elbows and long legs. By this time the yelling and the gunshots were coming from all round. As Maewen bent down to follow Mitt, there were white puffs of smoke coming from every mound she could see. She saw the hearthwomen in the center grimly getting on their horses.

A strange voice behind her yelled, *"Charge! Come on, charge them!"*

Maewen had no time to think that the hole was too small. She simply scrambled through it, and was barely surprised to find that it was easy.

∷ 20 ∷

MAEWEN HAD A GLIMPSE of Kialan and Ynen following Moril down a silent golden street, casting blue-black shadows as they went. There was a warm sun and a feeling of humming peace in this place. But Maewen could clearly hear screams and shots and crashing in the distance all round. The battle was only a hair-breadth away. She knew it could come bursting through Moril's paper-thin enchantment any second. When someone came at her sideways in another long indigo shadow, it was just like Gardale again. She put her hands to her face and screamed.

"Hush!" Mitt said, giving her a shake.

It was only Mitt, who had waited for her. Maewen knew this, but still she whimpered and sobbed.

Mitt shook her harder. "Will you hush! Moril made this out of *sounds*, don't you understand! You're going to break it if you carry on. What are you, a baby?"

Maewen pulled herself together. "Of course I'm not a baby. I'm thirteen. It was just the battle out there."

"Thirteen? Really?" Mitt found this wonderful and

remarkable. He had been thinking of Maewen as the same age as Noreth, and here she was younger than he was! It seemed to turn everything round. As they set off to follow the others, Mitt slid his hand carefully down Maewen's arm and took hold of her hand. It was the most momentous and the most exciting thing he had ever done in his life.

Click!

"Snap!" said Maewen, as Mitt swung their joined hands up to see what the noise was. They both laughed. On Maewen's thumb and Mitt's forefinger were two identical gold bands and two identical gloomy profiles carved out of what seemed exactly the same kind of red stone. "Alk's copy?" Maewen asked.

"Yes. He made it to fit himself by the size of it," Mitt said.

After that it became a more normal thing to hold hands. They walked on, following the square gold-yellow stones of what seemed to be a street. Everywhere was misty, white mist with the sun in it, and the other three were out of sight ahead by then. But there seemed nowhere else for them to have gone except along the street.

At first there appeared to be houses on either side, though these were fuzzed out above the first story by the mist. But after a while they seemed to have come into a garden or a parkland. There was a feeling of openness. Delicate trees spread green-gold branches in the mist, and others were spires and blocks of gold-dark. It seemed moist underfoot. Maewen thought she could hear birds, but when she listened, they were somehow out of hearing. Seabirds? Mitt thought. Land birds? There were smells, too, delicately scrawled on the air. Mitt's head came up at the smell: the peat smell of the North, of a distant farm, the hot tang of the South, water lazily running, and even, amazingly, the far-off salt of the sea. This was a smell he had once thought of as home. Nearby, willows were budding.

It can't be this wet here! Mitt thought. But it was, secretly. The scent was conveying him the secret that under Kernsburgh the rock was porous and riddled with channels of water flowing down to the sea. Then they can sink wells, he thought with some relief. It had worried him slightly that Kernsburgh did not seem to have a water supply. He found himself saying to Maewen, "There's going to be war and fighting for the next two years."

"They can't do much rebuilding till that's over," she agreed.

"They can make a start. That's not what I meant," Mitt said. "I meant it was all building to war when I left the South, and I get the feeling I'm going to have to be part of it, but I don't like to think of you getting hurt in it."

"I don't want to be left out," Maewen said.

"But you don't like war," Mitt pointed out. "What I mean is, you might stay here and start the building."

"Only if you promise to come back and see me after

the war," Maewen said. "I'll come after you if you don't."

"All right," said Mitt. "I promise. In two years." In the strange scented gold mist it did not seem ridiculous to talk of these things.

"I'll hold you to that," Maewen said, laughing.

They wandered on. Shortly they came out into a wide golden courtyard where they found the other three, none of whom seemed to notice that Mitt and Maewen must have come by a side way. Ynen was pointing to a statue on a pedestal.

"Ours are the only shadows, here," he said. "Look."

He was right. All their shadows were long and blue-black. The statue ought to have laid a zigzag shadow up a flight of stairs, but it did not. Moril stumbled on the stairs because they were so hard to see. Kialan caught his elbow to stop him falling, all in a crisscross of inky shadows, and accidentally jarred the cwidder. It sang out melodiously. The sound seemed to shake the entire place. Everything blurred. For a moment, even the inky shadows were faint. Nobody dared breathe. They all stood still until the sound died and the faint golden buildings came back.

The tall building at the head of the steps, though it was lost upward into mist, was remarkably like the Tannoreth Palace. Like, but quite unlike, too, Maewen realized, staring up at it while the others tiptoed gently up the steps. It had almost no windows, and its roof was supported on mighty pillars shaped like buds—

long whorled buds, like the ones on magnolias—and yet it had the same shape and gave her the same feel as the palace she knew. She climbed the difficult steps on cautious, whispering feet and joined the others in the long gold-stone tunnel.

They trod forward as gently as they could, all horribly aware that this palace of gold was only the most fragile illusion. The stony air from the tunnel made both Ynen and Mitt want to cough. Neither of them dared make that much noise, and they had to keep clearing their throats as gently as they could. Then the tunnel branched.

"Where to?" Moril whispered.

"Follow your cwidder," Kialan breathed.

Moril seemed to consider this meant straight on. They tiptoed after him, deep into the heart of the palace. Now they seemed to be in a corridor whose golden stone roof was only an inch or so above Kialan's head or Mitt's. Both of them ducked when Moril led them under a heavy lintel and down misty steps into a warm oblong room. It was not a big place. It had stone benches along each side and a large stone seat at the far end. The first thing they all noticed was that this seat had a strange gap underneath, as if something that was meant to go there was missing. The second thing they saw was a thick golden circlet on the seat of the chair.

They all knew this was the crown. Everyone waited for everyone else to go forward and pick it up. Before any of them could sort out the courage to do it, a young man jumped up from the right-hand bench.

"At long last!" he said. He was very glad to see them. He strode joyfully over to the stone seat and picked up the crown. "I thought I would never do this again!" he said as he turned round, holding it in both hands.

Everyone stood very still. He was a tall young man, with rounded shoulders wider than Kialan's or Mitt's, and there was a sort of gawkiness to him that reminded them all of Mitt. His face, when he turned sideways to look from Moril, along the line to Maewen, was like Ynen's. He had the same nose, long and pointed. When he turned full face, to look at the whole group of them in a puzzled way, he reminded Maewen of Wend, though everyone else was reminded of Maewen, with a fleeting likeness to Moril and Kialan. And Mitt was reminded of Old Ammet, too, because the young man had the same flying white hair.

"What's the matter?" said the young man. "Why don't you speak?"

"Is it all right? It won't shake the place apart?" Moril whispered.

The young man laughed. "Not here. This part has to be more solid. It used to be my strongroom."

"Er—then, who are you?" Mitt asked. "If you don't mind being asked."

"My name's Hern," said the young man. "I used to be King here a long while ago."

All five of them gasped, and then drew breath, one after another, to ask the King if he was of the Undying—and then let the breath go, not quite sure. He had the same unshadowed golden look as the rest of the palace. If you caught him out of the corner of your eye, bright rays seemed to stand out from him, and across him, that almost canceled him out of sight.

Hern laughed again. "Don't be afraid. I'm only here because I asked the One on my deathbed if I could present the crown to the new King."

"Whatever possessed—" Kialan, Moril, and Ynen all began together.

"—me to do such a stupid thing?" Hern asked. "I know. What you ask the One for, you get."

"Then you *are* of the Undying," Mitt said. "In a manner of speaking."

Hern looked at him. His face was bleak and ribby as Mitt's face had been in Gardale. "In a manner of speaking is right. I was afraid all my life that I was going to turn out to be of the Undying. And because of that, I was always very careful never to let anyone make a picture or an image of me—that's how the Undying are bound into godhead, you know—and then I go and ask for the wrong thing, and my reward is this half-life." Mitt opened his mouth to say something, but Hern shook his head. His face relaxed and went businesslike. "No. Let me first ask who claims this crown. All but one of you have a perfect right to it."

Nobody answered. Each of them shot dubious looks at the others.

"Oh come on!" said Hern. "Isn't this what you came for?"

Maewen cleared her throat. "Yes. But I think we were supposed to get it for Amil the Great."

Hern shrugged. "That's news to me," he said. He came toward them, carrying the golden circlet. All of them made a move to back away and then stood, feeling cowardly. But it was alarming. Hern was misty and shot with beams of light, but his personality was as strong as it must have been when he was a King. As if that was the main thing left of him, Mitt thought. And the crown itself was thick, real, and solid between Hern's misty hands, of such pure gold that it shone orange in the golden light.

Hern halted in front of Moril. "Do you claim this crown?"

Moril gulped. The others could see him thinking that his answer would really be addressed to the One, and he had Hern's example to show him that he had better say exactly the right thing. "No," he said, "I don't want to be King. I want to be a new kind of Singer—a very good one, if I can."

Hern nodded and moved on to Ynen. "You?"

Ynen licked his lips. He was whiter even than Moril. "No, not me. I—I want to be a sailor, and they wouldn't let me if I was King, because I might get drowned."

Hern said nothing. He simply moved on to Kialan. "And you?"

"I—" said Kialan. He had to stop and try again. "I know I have a claim, and it isn't because of the way my father would hate it, it's— Well, I don't feel *big* enough. Inheriting Hannart's quite enough for me, honestly."

Hern frowned at this, which made Kialan flush bright red and then stare unrepentantly. But Hern said nothing again and moved on to Mitt. Mitt had expected Hern to pass him by. He backed away. "You're not including me in this?" Mitt said.

Hern nodded.

"Then include me out," Mitt said. "I'm not fit, I'm common and—and—" He searched for the feeling he had just now in the strangely scented parkland. "Listen, I don't mind helping in the war. The country needs a change. But all I want out of it is a bit of peace and maybe a farm somewhere."

Hern frowned at this, too, and Mitt looked as unrepentant as Kialan. Hern turned to Maewen. "I can't offer the crown to you," he explained, "because you are not really born yet. I'm sorry."

"I understand," Maewen said, but she knew she sounded wistful. "The only thing I really want is to be allowed to stay—" She caught herself up. The One alone knew what Mum and Aunt Liss would feel, but this was what she *wanted* and she knew, like Moril, that she had to phrase it right. "Stay in Mitt's time, I mean."

Mitt turned and gave her a smile that warmed them both. Hern, meanwhile, retreated, still holding the crown. When they looked back at him, he was sitting in the stone seat, looking exasperated.

"Let's get at this another way," he said. "We have eliminated one of you. We know that the one who accepts this crown will be King. Let's call him King— for the sake of argument—Amil, since that is the name you seem to have brought with you. Who will be Amil?"

"If you like," Ynen offered, "we could take the crown and give it to my father."

"Yes, or mine," Kialan agreed.

Hern gave them that bleak, ribby look again. "You didn't attend to what I said at first. I am to hand the crown to the next King. That means to one of you, since no one else is here to claim it." He let them think about this, uneasily, for a moment. Then he said, "When I made my unlucky request to the One, what I had really wanted was to give the new King the benefit of my advice, but since I didn't ask that, that is something I am not allowed to do. Instead I shall ask you what advice you would give to this new King Amil. Think carefully. You may be advising yourself."

There was utter silence. Nobody could think of anything.

Hern laughed. "I shall start you off. How about: People's *idea* of what they can do is even more important than what they *can* do?"

"Oh, I know that!" Moril said. "It's in the King's Sayings. The Singers all know those."

"There, you see?" Hern said. "I couldn't give you that saying if it hadn't been out in the world already. I said it at the battle with Kankredin. This is why I can't give advice to the new King. The One knew, though I didn't, that a dead man's thoughts stop with his life. Listen to the Singer. He'll tell you my thoughts."

"Yes, but I didn't know they were *yours*," Moril said.

"Hang on a minute," said Mitt. "What do you mean, you can't give advice? You just gave us a whole load of it!"

"Did I?" said Hern.

He said it perfectly neutrally. This made Kialan say, almost exasperated, "You did, you know. He's right. You warned us straight off to be careful what we said, or the One would take us at our word."

"Roundaboutly," said Mitt. "Using yourself."

"A King should always set an example," Hern said. "That's in my Sayings, too, isn't it?" he asked Moril.

Moril nodded. "And," said Kialan, "you told us to attend to your exact words."

But Mitt broke in across Kialan. "No, before that! Didn't you listen? There was that about not being bound like the Undying."

The two of them were leaning forward eagerly. Hern's face was intent. Oh I see! Maewen thought, from her standpoint as a nonqualifier. We're in Round

Two now. Ynen seemed to have dropped out. He was staring sadly at Hern. Maewen saw Mitt notice Ynen's sadness and wonder about it as he spoke.

"Then you made a song and dance about your sayings being dead and over with," Mitt said, "just so we'd notice they weren't."

"Yes, the exact opposite of what you seemed to be saying," Kialan agreed. "Your thoughts *have* gone on after you."

"That's not new," Moril put in. "It's in a song by Osfameron."

Moril would be disqualifying himself, Maewen thought, if he went on sticking just to what Singers knew. Perhaps Moril did not mind. Maewen had thought she did not mind, but now she knew she felt sad and alone and left out.

"I'm glad it's not new," Hern said. "I have no business having new thoughts. It wouldn't be reasonable."

Mitt could not help grinning.

"What are you smiling at?" Hern asked.

"You," Mitt said, "must have been a regular eel in your day. Not reasonable, my big toe! You keep turning up new ideas."

A slight, enjoying smile bent Hern's mouth. "I was always very hot on reason," he said. "If I had been able to give the new King advice, I would have told him never to rely on things being reasonable. I did, and it caused me no end of trouble."

"There you go again!" said Mitt.

Kialan laughed. Hern's smile grew slightly. "I defy you," he said, "to discover any other new thoughts I've shown you."

"Well," said Kialan. "You *can* have new thoughts. Osfameron may have written that song about thoughts flying on, but you were dead when he wrote it."

Hern shook his head. "Won't do. Osfameron is my brother."

Kialan looked very dashed at this and turned to Mitt for help. "He said *shown*," Mitt said. "And he did tell us to listen to every word. Let's see." He looked at Hern. "You've shown us what comes of asking for the wrong thing, and then shown us yourself getting round that, and giving advice like you meant to. That's how to keep the rules and break them, too. I like that. It takes a cool head. But there's more," Mitt said, thinking aloud, which was the way he always thought best. "Maybe this was what Kialan was driving at. Yes— you're still at it. You're not beat yet. You're showing us that."

"*Is* it a new thought, then, to say, 'Keep on, there's always hope'?" Hern said. "I thought that was a very old saying."

"Yes, but you're the first person *I've* met who's still saying it when he's *dead*," Mitt answered. "That has to be new."

Hern laughed and stood up. "I believe you. Bend your head, Alhammitt, so that I can put this crown on it."

"*What!*" Mitt backed away in horror. "Now, look. I told you. And I was only saying what Kialan said."

Hern looked at Kialan. "Was he?"

"Not really," Kialan admitted.

"Tidying it up, then," Mitt said pleadingly. "Take the thing away. I'm not qualified."

"Yes, you are," said Hern. "*I* told *you*. Your right descends from the Adon's son Almet, who went to live in Waywold."

"Pretty sideways, I'll bet!" Mitt said.

"Only as sideways as direct descent, from father to son," said Hern. "If that was not so, why does the Adon's ring accept you?"

Mitt looked down at the Adon's seal, snugly above his knuckle. "This is just a copy."

"No," said Hern. He nodded toward Maewen. "Hers is the copy."

Mitt shot a disbelieving look from Hern to Maewen and rapidly tried the ring on his little finger, then on his thumb. Each time it slid over his lump of knuckle and fitted as if it had been made for him. "This is plain ridiculous!" he said. He turned round. For a moment it looked as if he was going to storm from the room.

"Wait!" said Hern. It was the voice of command that Navis was so good at using. Mitt almost stopped. But he shook his shoulders and put one foot on the steps. Hern said quickly, "Accept the crown, and you may ask the One one favor."

Mitt turned back. "You mean that?"

"I do," said Hern.

"Now?"

"Crown first," said Hern. "Bend your head."

Mitt sighed and bowed his head down. "Extra bit of advice," he said, looking sideways at Kialan. "Kings drive a hard bargain."

Hern chuckled as he settled the thick gold band carefully over Mitt's lank hair. "A King should have a sharp mind," he said. "That may be in my Sayings somewhere. I am sorry that I cannot give you the kingstone as well as the crown. The stone is in the South. A man in Holand called Hobin knows where to find it."

Mitt stared at him from under his own forehead. "Hobin? Gunsmith? He's my stepfather!" He straightened up slowly and put one hand uneasily to the crown, thinking it might slip, but it seemed steady enough. Like the Adon's ring, it was an exact fit. "Hobin!" he said. "You Undying really got me hemmed in, haven't you?"

Hern nodded as he stepped backward. "It was the same for me. Now you can ask your favor."

"All right," said Mitt. "Then, do you really have to sit here, century after century, waiting for the next new King to come along?"

Hern went very still. "This I know is in the Sayings of the King," he said. "Never be beguiled by pity. Are you talking pity?"

"No," said Mitt. "You've been showing us you're

stuck here and you don't like it from the moment you first spoke."

"Mercy, then?" asked Hern. "This sits well on a King."

"No," said Mitt. "Flaming Ammet, I don't know what it's called! I'll have to take a leaf out of your book and *show* you. Take a look at Ynen. He's miserable because all he can think of is that you have to sit here, year in and year out, waiting for a King that may not come. Only he doesn't like to say so because the One made you sit here. Isn't that so?" Mitt asked Ynen. Ynen went pink and nodded hard. "See?" Mitt said to Hern. "I don't know the word for what I'm doing, unless it's having the cheek to say things no one else dares to say. Is that kingly?"

Hern did not answer. He laughed.

"Laugh away," Mitt said. "I'm going to ask the One to take you off duty."

Hern went on laughing, but the sound was confused now and fading. The beams of light, which had half hidden him if you looked at him sideways, came to cover him however you looked, crisscrossing and elongating confusingly. He was like a candle seen through tears. Then the beams separated and slid away. Each silvery streak carried a dim piece of Hern's shape with it, as if he were dissolving underwater. Mitt set his teeth and clenched his hands until the Adon's ring bit into him. This was exactly like his worst nightmare when he was small. He had been fairly sure this would happen, but it had seemed worth asking all the same. He made himself watch until Hern had rippled away into nowhere.

The rippling did not vanish with Hern. It remained as a green-goldness, like air shaking in heat. The stone seat, and that whole end of the room, wavered as if they were under clear, shallow water. Mitt's hands remained clenched. The scent he had recognized outside, of peat and farm, willows budding, and slow, deep river flowing to the far-off sea, was back again, stronger and more potent. And the rippling had formed a shape, a huge gold-green shadow with a profile like Hern's or Ynen's. Mitt had no doubt, nor had any of the others, that there was a presence standing behind them, casting this shadow, but it was beyond any of them to turn round and look.

When the One spoke, the voice came from behind them. "Hern has long ago gone down the River to the sea."

Mitt relaxed. Ynen murmured, "Oh good!" Maewen wondered how anyone could mistake Kankredin's voice for the One's. This voice was like the whole land speaking, the settling of rocks, the grind of water through granite, the slow shift of earth, and the wind blowing, and it burred in your ears in the same way as the low string on Moril's cwidder.

"It is not easy," said the One, "for my mortal children to speak with me face-to-face."

This was true. All of them were aching to turn round

and see the One, and all of them knew it was quite impossible.

"Witness this, all of you," said the One. "You have a new King."

No one was sure what to do, until Moril led them in a ragged chorus. "We witness we have a new King."

"I thank you," said the One.

The rippling shadow stooped then. It was as if the One bent to have a private word with each of them, all at the same time. Maewen heard the great voice at her ear, saying, "I cannot promise you what you asked. Too many imponderables lie in between. I am sorry."

To Mitt the One said, "You have been offered the name of Amil, which is my name. Before you choose between that name or your own, you must know that I have sworn to root out Kankredin from my land. If you take my name, that will be your task, too. What name do you choose?"

Mitt knew it was a real choice, even if Maewen had told him which way he chose. He weighed it up. Alhammitt was a good name, except that it was the name of half the men in the South. Amil was a name no one else had, but it carried the One's burden with it. Well, Mitt had carried burdens all his life. Kingship was another one. One more seemed to make no difference on top of that. "I'll take Amil," he said.

Then he turned round, like someone waking up, wondering what the One had said to the others. The rippling shadow was gone, and with it, most of the golden mistiness. He could see they were standing in a place that was no more than an oblong trench, with walls made of big blocks of yellowish stone that were broken off at about waist height. Beside him Maewen was fiercely blinking back tears. Moril looked much the same. But Ynen and Kialan both looked happy, in a stunned kind of way.

"I think we have to go back through the stone," Moril said.

∷ 21 ∷

W HEN THEY TURNED ROUND, they found three stone steps the color of oatcakes leading into a green-gold landscape of humps and hillocks. Had it not been for the silence, and the mist still clinging to the near distance, they would have thought they were back in the Kernsburgh outside the waystone.

They walked, slightly downhill, through a dip on the gold-green turf. The humps of Hern's palace were small behind them. Ruins were like that, Maewen thought. Buildings, even palaces, seemed to take up far more room than they really did.

At first they were very silent and sober. Everyone kept glancing at Mitt, walking in the midst of them with the crown gleaming orange against his hair. He seemed taller. Nobody knew quite what to say. At last Maewen decided that someone must say something.

"Do you want us to call you Your Majesty?" she asked.

"Flaming Ammet!" said Mitt. "Don't you dare!" He grabbed hold of her hand. "Don't any of you treat me different," he said. "I'm going to need you all around for sanity."

Everyone broke into relieved laughter. After that they were able to talk together quite normally until Moril said, "Hush a moment."

His cwidder was humming, and humming louder for every step they took forward. Something dark was rising out of the mist ahead. The cwidder was almost growling as they reached it. It was the waystone, but it was not small any longer. It towered in a mighty arch above them, even bigger than the one Maewen remembered outside the station.

Moril murmured, "Wider than the world, or small as in a nut." It must have been a quotation. Kialan recognized it and grinned at him as they all stepped through the waystone together, with Ynen, who was last, almost treading on Moril, who was just ahead of Kialan.

They were back on green grass under a gray morning. The waystone was waist-high behind them, and they were in a battle.

The fighting was noisy, it was vicious, and it was all round them. Everywhere they looked, people ran and struggled and hacked at one another. Riders and loose horses galloped and screamed. They had a glimpse of Luthan, still on horseback, furiously hacking at someone in a wavy helmet and shiny armor that gave him a chest like a pigeon. Luthan's face was bright with blood that clashed with the red of his clothes.

One of his arms was the wrong red, too, and the mail was dangling from it in strips. They just had time to see this before the horses and fighting swirled and both Luthan and his opponent vanished. The air was full of drifting puffs of white smoke, shouts, clangs, and the slurring whisper of crossbow bolts, which were even crueler than the guns, because you could barely hear them coming.

Kialan threw himself behind the waystone. "Get down, all of you!"

The waystone was a tiny piece of cover, but it was the only one available. The rest crowded up against Kialan, kneeling or crouching, Mitt on one knee with one hand steadying the crown.

"What's going on?" Moril gasped. He was doubled protectively across his cwidder. "Those look like Southerners! That armor!"

Ynen took a look through the hole in the waystone. "They are, too! I *think* they look like Andmark."

"Earl *Henda*!" Mitt exclaimed. Everyone except Maewen bobbed up for a hasty look. "Hundreds of them," said Mitt. "Where have they all come from?"

"It must have been *them* we heard in the night— Ynen and me," Kialan said, doubled over his own knees. "I remember thinking I heard supply wagons."

Mitt bobbed up again to look through the savage smoky confusion. He bobbed down again, almost at once, and a speeding crossbow bolt whizzed above all their heads, but he had had time to see a row of big black wagons drawn up some way beyond the green road. "They're using the wagons for cover," he said. "The ones with guns."

"Who do you think's winning?" Kialan asked.

Mitt shook his head. It felt heavy with the crown. The battle had obviously gone long beyond the stage where you could tell what was going on, but there had looked to be far more Southerners than Northerners. He had a feeling the Northerners were getting beaten.

There was another noise now. It was hard to pick out among the din. Mitt thought he had noticed it only because he seemed to feel it in his bones as much as his ears. For a moment, he wondered if he had accidentally said the name of the Earth Shaker. The earth seemed full of drumming.

There was a tremendous shouting behind.

They all whirled round to find a wall of horsemen galloping down upon them. The world seemed full of thousands of pounding horse legs, flying divots of turf and hollow drumming thunder. Kialan spread his arms out and pulled the four of them into a tight bundle in front of him. *"Down!"* he yelled, and fell forward on top.

Even so, they all ducked and flinched as the horsemen swept up to them. Horses were all round them, all over them. One rider actually hurtled over their heads, leaping the five of them and the waystone, too. The ground shook in earnest.

"O great One!" Kialan groaned, with his head up to follow that particular rider. "That was my father. Now we're in the soup whatever happens!"

The noise of fighting suddenly doubled. They could almost feel the riders from Hannart crash into the battle. Beyond the edge of the waystone Maewen saw a horse rear, screaming and gushing blood. Something else tumbled into view, with a clothy *thwump*, and she saw it was the rider, thrown down like a broken doll in a strange position. He was not moving, but his horse went on screaming, and so did others she could not see. She nearly screamed herself. She wanted to be sick. Her eyes felt twisted and hot. Mitt had been right to say she did not like war. It was horrible. And the worst of it was that she had helped cause it by riding the King's Road instead of Noreth. The only reason she did not scream and kick and beat the grass with her fists was that it would be letting Mitt down. She crouched, swallowing.

A bullet went *whang* on the edge of the waystone. That nearly hit me! she thought. Beside her Kialan yelled out an extremely filthy word. Maewen jumped round to find him clutching his arm. There was a slice of granite standing out from his sleeve and blood was trying to flood out around the slice. His sleeve was soaked red already. Kialan repeated the filthy word and took hold of the piece of granite to pull it out.

"Don't do that!" Mitt shouted at him. "Stop the bleeding first!"

"But it hurts," Kialan said. There were gray-green smudges of shock under his eyes.

Maewen could see how much it hurt. And Kialan had had his arms spread out to keep them from being trampled. He didn't deserve this. She wanted to do something to help. She bobbed up. The fighting was a frantic seething out beyond the green road. The space in between was full of loose horses and quiet, doll-like dead people. One of the horses wandering there was her own—or Noreth's, except that poor Noreth would never have any need of it now. Here was something she could do.

"I've got a roll of bandage in my saddlebag," she said, and jumped up to get it.

Mitt and Moril both screamed at her to come back, but there were scarcely any bullets now. The fighting had rolled back again and was now around that line of black wagons. Maewen covered the space to her horse in perfect safety and told herself she was being brave at last. The horse stood docilely. She heaved and fumbled at the straps on her baggage roll. Quick, quick, before Kialan bleeds to death! It seemed to take a hundred years just to undo two buckles.

Then the voice spoke to her. "There is a loaded pistol someone has dropped on the ground at your feet," it said. "Take it and—"

"Oh shut up!" Maewen told it. "Kialan's hurt."

"Moril!" said Mitt.

"I know. I heard him." Moril bent hurriedly over

his cwidder, trying to make the power gather. Mitt could feel it was slow and difficult to gather again so soon, and the screams and roaring of the battle did not help.

"I made sure the Adon was injured," the voice told Maewen smugly. "These are my instructions. Shoot the Southerner with the crown first, and then—"

"I said *shut up!*" Maewen screamed. The buckles were undone. The bandage was—where? *Where?* Oh, here it was. She took the roll and backed away. Pistol? Oh yes. There, almost under the horse's feet.

The voice rose to a blare. *"Pick it up, you stupid girl. Shoot them all and take the crown!"*

"Quickly!" said Mitt.

"No," said Maewen. She aimed her boot at the pistol and deliberately kicked it as far away as she could.

Mitt groaned. Moril put all his fingers under the lowest string and plucked, desperately. The cwidder responded with a deep brassy *twang*, as if Moril had struck a gong instead.

The horse in front of Maewen drifted away sideways. Although it seemed like a solid horse, it behaved just like smoke and shredded into the air, in brown wisps. In its place was the ghost of a man, twelve feet high or more, bell-shaped and robed, bent over to glare at Maewen with human eyes under fat eyelids. He was hollow. She could see the empty space in the middle of him, and somehow this was the most horrifying thing about him. I was riding *that!* she thought.

It did not seem to bother Kankredin that Maewen could see him. He blared, "I am the One! You must do as I command!"

Mitt made a movement to stand up. The ghostly fat-lidded eyes caught the movement. The vague hand in the hollow sleeve made a small gesture, as Maewen said, "No, you are *not* the One. And you never fooled me for a moment." She was shaking, but she was glad to find she could be brave in this way at least.

The towering shape bent toward her. The sheets of wriggly hair on both sides of its face fell forward, and the huge, vague hands reached. Mitt found he could not move his legs. Beside him Moril's hands seemed to be stuck to the cwidder, in crooked shapes. But Mitt did not need to walk. He drew breath and shouted.

"YNYNEN!"

Then he moved, in spite of not being able to, and took off like a sprinter. Somehow he covered the distance between himself and Maewen, just in time to knock her over and fall on top of her before Ammet answered his call.

There was a howling wind, full of chaff. They were peppered with stinging grains of wheat, first from one side and then from everywhere. It made them both cringe. But in spite of that, in spite of grain coming at them like hailstones, and flying straw and blinding chaff dust, Maewen and Mitt both craned round to see the ghost of Kankredin spinning in a spinning trumpet shape of wheat-filled wind.

It was over almost as they looked. The ghost drew tatters of itself together and dissolved away backward. The trumpet shape unraveled and streamed away across the green land, carrying chaff and grain far and wide.

"Did you get him?" Maewen asked.

"Not sure." Mitt dragged himself to his knees. There was no sign of Kankredin. The gong note Moril had evoked from the cwidder was still in the air, sounding on and on. If Kankredin was near, he would be visible. "Had a feeling Ammet only got part of him," Mitt said regretfully, "but I think he's gone."

Maewen scrambled up with the bandage. The crown had fallen beside her. She picked it up, thick and orange and heavy, and it left a bare oval shape in the grain that covered the grass. "I *knew* there was something strange about that horse," she said as they went back to the waystone among drifting chaff and pattering grain.

Moril looked up as they came. Mitt nodded. Moril put one hand on the throbbing string to stop the sound, and then flexed both hands as if Kankredin had cramped them. Behind Moril, Kialan had Ynen's belt buckled round his arm to stop the bleeding. He was holding it tight for Ynen while Ynen tore pieces off both their shirts to bandage the place where the slice of stone had been.

"Rather a waste of two good shirts," Kialan said. His face was a better color. He looked up at Mitt. "What happened to the crown?"

Maewen realized that she was holding it. "Bend your head down," she said to Mitt.

None of them noticed that the noise of fighting had all but stopped. As Mitt bent his head and Maewen fitted the crown carefully over his hair, Earl Keril came crunching toward them over the scattered grain. He was a little disheveled, but he barely looked as if he had been in a battle. He hooked his thumbs in his sword belt and watched Mitt and Maewen. "Well, now," he said pleasantly. "I had five possible outcomes in mind when I sent you to Adenmouth, but this was one that I confess never occurred to me."

Mitt straightened up. He was slightly taller than Earl Keril. "Get me hanged and make sure there's no uprising," he said. "Right?"

"Hanging you may yet be the solution," Earl Keril said in the same pleasant way. "Let me put to you my point of view. The North had been agog for some years with stories that Noreth Onesdaughter"—he bowed pleasantly to Maewen—"would take the royal road the year she was eighteen. Then, all of a sudden, *you* arrive in Aberath in a manner which fulfills every prophecy ever made, and all the common people are hailing you as the new King come at last—"

"I never knew that," Mitt said. "I had no idea. If you'd let me alone, I wouldn't be here now. But you set me on to murder Noreth."

"Naturally I hoped that the two claimants would cancel one another out," Keril agreed. He looked at

Maewen again. "Rather than the one crown the other. But we were prepared for other outcomes, too. To that end the Countess took you in and educated you, and I took steps to make sure you would remain under the sponsorship of Hannart and Aberath—"

"Sponsorship is one word for it," Mitt said. "Nice try."

"I asked you to see my point of view!" Keril snapped. "When I was young and ignorant, I took part in an uprising. I know better now. I would go to greater lengths than this to stop another. People die in uprisings, by thousands, most horribly."

"When *I* was young and ignorant," said Mitt, "I lived in Holand. People died there all the time, only slowly. And the rest were too scared to help. There needs to be an uprising. One that works this time."

The two of them stared at one another unlovingly. "If this is your attitude," Keril said, "I shall see you hanged at Harvest. There are plentiful grounds."

Moril, Kialan, and Ynen surged to their feet, Kialan saying, "Listen, Father—" and Ynen protesting, "Don't undo the belt yet!"

"Be quiet!" said Keril. "I'll deal with you two later. What I want to know—"

Hasty feet crunched over the grain, and Alk and Navis arrived, one on either side of Keril. Alk's leathers were torn all over, showing battered links of mail underneath, and he had a streak of blood on his chin. One side of Navis's face was black with powder. He looked tired to death, but he spoke to Keril with the utmost courtesy. "My lord, we have to thank you for your timely intervention."

Alk grinned. "We were goners without you, Keril."

Keril turned his unloving look on them. Navis said, "Is there some trouble, my lord? May we assist?"

"Yes," Keril said grimly. "I want to know how this Mitt of yours contrived to have a Southern war band to meet him."

"I did no such thing!" said Mitt.

"Those are Henda's men, my lord," Navis said. "As you surely know, Henda can be trusted to respond to anything that might be a threat to his earldom entirely on his own."

"But how did he know?" Keril said. "Did you tell him, Navis Haddsson?"

"Oh come now, Keril," said Alk. "You saved Navis's life yourself. You heard the Southerners calling him traitor."

Keril hitched his shoulders irritably. Navis bowed to him. "As to how Henda knew, my lord, since I had heard of Noreth Onesdaughter at least two years ago, I can only suppose Henda's spies told him at the same time." Mitt stared. This was news to him. "One of those secrets," Navis said to him, "that my brother took good care not to have known on the waterfront in Holand."

"So I am to understand," Keril said to Navis, "that Navis Haddsson commandeered the hearthmen of

Dropwater and Aberath to fight Henda, knowing that Henda would oppose Navis Haddsson's candidate for the crown."

Navis's eyes went to the golden band round Mitt's forehead. He smiled slightly. "My lord, I did not expect Henda. I expected you. But you are right to believe that I hoped Mitt would be King."

"Why?" Keril asked icily.

Navis shrugged. "Aside from obvious personal wishes, my lord, one of the pictures in my rooms in Holand was a portrait of the Adon. My impression is that you, too, my lord, were struck by Mitt's resemblance to the Adon. I thought about it much of the time we sailed North. But I would have waited a few years to do anything about it. You forced our hands."

"I'm glad I did," said Keril. "Your candidate is not of age and has no right to that thing on his head."

Alk had been exchanging looks with Moril. Now he said, "Right, Keril. Why don't we ask?" And he nodded at Moril.

Moril stood forward. "The One called us to witness just now," he said, loudly and formally, "that we have a new King. The One gave Mitt the crown and his own name of Amil."

"I hereby witness this as lawful," Alk said. "Come on, Keril. Accept it."

Keril still seemed entirely unwilling. Moril, carefully and meaningly, arranged his fingers on the cwidder. "I could summon the One," he said.

Keril looked uneasily at the cwidder. "You always were a bit of a mystic, Moril," he said. "But this is a reasonable age—"

He was interrupted by howls and yells and catcalls in the distance behind him. "Traitor!" they heard. "Traitor! There's the traitor!" The shouting was coming from hearthmen in all three liveries. It seemed to have something to do with the row of supply wagons beyond the road. Navis set off that way at a run. Alk and Keril followed. Mitt pointed a thumb at Keril's back. "Never rely on things being reasonable," he said.

"Sayings of the King," Moril said, laughing.

They jogged toward the wagons, with Ynen and Kialan following more slowly. As Mitt reached the crowd milling round the wagons, Navis waved. People fell back respectfully to let Mitt through. Everyone's eyes for a moment fixed wonderingly on the crown. "What is it?" said Mitt.

"We invite you to look at this," Navis said. And, with a smooth stare at Keril, he added, "Your Majesty."

He waved again. Several hearthmen hauled on the dark weatherproof covering of one of the wagons. As they dragged it away, the trim green-painted cart underneath came into view.

Hestefan was on its driving seat. When he saw Mitt, Maewen, and Moril all staring at him, he writhed away backward. "I didn't do it!" he said. His fine Singer voice cracked into hoarseness. "I was made to! They forced me to come along!"

"What do the Southerners say about it?" Mitt asked.

Alk nodded to the nearest person from Aberath. "Go and fetch the Andmark captain to the King."

The Southerners were sitting in a large huddle a little way off with their hands on their heads. Luthan and his hearthwomen were walking round and round them with their bayoneted guns. Luthan's clothes were ruined, and his arm was in a sling. He looked warlike and efficient as he nodded at the message and beckoned someone from the midst of the Southerners.

The man was most unwilling to move. In the end Alk strode over and brought him out of the huddle, almost dangling from his big fist. "Here we are, Majesty," he said. "One captain."

The prisoner looked at Mitt and looked puzzled. "It was supposed to be a woman we had to ambush," he said. "What's going on?"

"Never mind that, Captain Fervold," Navis said. "Just tell us what this Singer had to do with it."

"Never forget a name, do you, Navis Haddsson?" said the captain. "It must be ten years since—"

"Twelve years," said Navis. "Tell."

"Simple enough," said Fervold. Alk let go of him, and he straightened up, looking relieved. "Orders were to land secretly at Cressing Harbor, come up by night to the green road, and rendezvous with the Singer at dawn, and he would show us where Kernsburgh was.

Then we were to ambush the, er— Anyway, get to them before they got the crown. And we'd have got you, too, if you hadn't been a day late. But we missed the green road in the dark both nights, and the Singer didn't turn up to put us right until well on in the morning. What did he do? Give us away? Our information was we'd only find five folk here."

"Your bad luck," said Alk. "So Hestefan was working for the South?"

"Has been for years," said Fervold.

At this Hestefan cried out, "They made me! I tell you, they *made* me!"

Alk turned to him with his lawman's look. "And did they also make you murder Noreth of Kredindale?"

Hestefan straightened up and jutted his beard. "What nonsense is this? How could I have done? Look. She's standing there!" He pointed at Maewen.

"I'm not Noreth," Maewen said. It was embarrassing to say it in front of all these people, but a great relief, too.

"And I have seen Noreth's murdered corpse," said Alk. "The others who might have killed her are proved clear. I accuse you in law and before the crown of cutting Noreth's throat."

"Never," said Hestefan. "On my honor as a Singer. Never."

"Better get that cup out," Alk said to Navis.

Maewen had a different idea. She tugged at Mitt's sleeve. "This may not be right, because it was Kankredin who said it, but if he did kill her, he may have stolen a golden statue."

"That statue!" said Mitt. "You know, that clean slipped my mind! Where would Hestefan hide something really valuable?" he asked Moril.

He had to nudge Moril and say it again. Hestefan was saying, "A Singer is honorable. Our word is our bond. We are sworn to speak true and purvey no lies. Nor do we do dirty deeds and dastardly acts. This accusation soils all Singers."

Moril was staring at Hestefan as if he could not believe what he was hearing. "Sliding panel under the cart at the back," he said colorlessly, and went on staring.

Mitt whispered to Alk. Alk passed the cup back to Navis and, leaving Hestefan still ranting, he strode round to the rear of the cart. It heaved. There was the sound of wood splintering. Alk came grimly back with gold shining in one massive fist. "Shut your mouth, Hestefan. Where did you come by this?"

Hestefan gaped at the statue. His face had gone gray and piteous. "I tell you I did not kill her! The woman is of the Undying and cannot be killed! I took that statue—yes, yes, I admit—the first time I tried to cut her throat, but she was alive again half an hour later on the green road. I had no choice but to go with her and kill her again. And as I knew she would not die, I sent word in Kredindale to Henda's agent there to send a boat South for an armed band to cut her in pieces. And sure enough, she did not die, though I killed her twice in Gardale." He rocked about on the seat of the cart. "I had to do it. I had to do it for Fenna!"

"Deranged, I think," Navis said, leaning wearily on the nearest wagon.

"How come—you did it for Fenna?" Mitt said.

Hestefan looked at him and did not seem to see him. "Fenna is in Earl Henda's dungeons. The Earl will kill her painfully if I do not do as he wants."

"Oh nonsense!" said Navis. "You and I both know that Fenna is in Adenmouth recovering from a cracked head."

"That," said Hestefan, "is not my Fenna. That Fenna is the daughter of Henda's court musician. He sent her with me so that no one would know I had lost my daughter."

"You think this is true?" Alk asked Navis. "*Is* it true?" he said to Fervold.

"No idea," said Fervold. "But knowing our Henda, it could well be."

"True or not, the man's confessed to murder," Earl Keril said, stepping in to take command. He nodded to some of his hearthmen. "Take him down to Dropwater—it's nearest—and ask Earl Luthan to see him hanged."

Mitt could see that Keril had stepped in because it was what he was used to. Keril was thinking of himself as the senior Earl here. It made him angry. In spite of all that had been said, Keril was simply discounting the crown on Mitt's head. And it made him even angrier that Keril had done to Mitt himself exactly what Hestefan said Henda had done to him—and Keril had not even seemed to notice.

"*Wait* a minute!" he said. "You can't hang him. We need him. Singers can go where other people can't."

Keril stared at Mitt with his lips pressed together hard. He glanced round and saw that everyone else, including the hearthmen he had nodded to, had turned respectfully to Mitt. He pressed his lips together harder still. But he said nothing.

"Hestefan," said Mitt. Hestefan looked up, still not really seeing Mitt. "Hestefan, I want you to go and tell Henda that you carried out his orders. Tell him Noreth is dead. Can you do that?" Hestefan nodded, blinking, as if he were beginning to be able to see again. "But," said Mitt, "you're to go to Andmark through Holand. You're to go to Hobin the gunsmith in Holand—got that?—and tell Hobin that I've got the crown and he's to bring me the kingstone. Understand?"

"Well . . . yes . . ." Hestefan said slowly. "But if Henda hears I did that—No, no! I can't!"

"Oh yes, you *can*!" Moril said. "My father did that kind of thing all the time! *Do* it!" Hestefan turned to Moril, shivering so that his beard juddered. This made everyone look at Moril. Moril was as white as a person can be, so white that he was lurid, and the look of betrayal on his face made everyone look away again quickly. "Do it," Moril said, "or I'll curse you, Singer's curse, with the power of this cwidder, so that the curse will follow you beyond your grave! You've betrayed all Singers!"

"Ah no." Hestefan held up a shaking hand against him. "I only did what any man—"

"You aren't just *any* man!" Moril shrieked at him. "You're a *Singer*! I thought you were a good one. I trusted you. I know better now. So go to Holand. Go *now*!" He turned his back on Hestefan, looking as if he was going to be sick.

Keril turned to Mitt. "And what about our Southern prisoners?" he said, with a politeness and sarcasm that outdid Navis. "Are you finding a use for them, too?"

This was enough to make Mitt find a use for them on the spot. "*Of* course! This crown is the crown of all Dalemark. I'm going to need an army that comes from the South as well as the North. They can all swear to me on the Adon's cup, and the ones it doesn't shine for can flaming well stay here under guard. I don't want word out round the South until Hestefan's got through to Hobin."

"And what will they do here? Sit with their hands on their heads?" Keril asked.

Mitt laughed. "No. They'll be digging. They can start on the foundations for the palace I'm going to build here. After that they can go on and flaming well rebuild Kernsburgh."

"That's the stuff!" said Alk. "I'll be the guard. Want me to make some drawings for the buildings? That's much more my line than fighting. Let's see—Luthan's scribe had pen and paper." He looked at the statue in his hand and then looked round for somewhere safe to put it. "Seeing you thought to look for it," he said to Maewen, "just hold it for me while I do some sketches."

He passed her the statue. As soon as her hands were on it, she was not there any longer.

PART FIVE

Kankredin

:‖ 22 ‖:

SHE WAS NOT THERE any longer. She was back in the museum gallery of the Tannoreth Palace, in exactly the same spot where she had been standing when she left. Wend, who was in the act of locking the golden statue away again, jumped round and stared at her.

Wend was as neat and trim and handsome as ever. Maewen was instantly aware that she was dirty, and moist all through with showers of rain she had given up noticing days ago. Her mail smelled of rust. Her boots were filthy. The livery of Dropwater smelled of wet wool, horse, and person. Under the little helmet her hair felt damp and clotted.

"You're back!" said Wend.

"Yes." The animal wariness she had acquired in those days of journeying told Maewen that Wend had not expected to see her again. It was in every line of Wend, as he carefully placed the statue on its shelf and locked the glass front. She noticed it, even though she was distracted by her hearthwoman's clothes dissolving away from her, leaving her again in grubby shorts and shirt. Her hair tumbled back to her shoulders, and it still felt damp and clotted. She was even more distracted by the shrill beeping of the radio clipped to Wend's uniform, but she still noticed.

"What happened?" Wend casually rattled keys, but that wariness showed Maewen he was, underneath, very eager to know.

"Hestefan the Singer murdered Noreth before she even set out from Adenmouth," she said. She was ashamed of the wariness—it showed her Wend was full of fury and frustration, carefully hidden—but she could not help knowing it. They all had this wariness: Moril, Mitt, Hestefan, Navis, everyone. It was the way you lived in those days.

"I'd thought it was . . . one of the others," Wend said, across the *wheep-wheep-wheep* from the radio on his chest.

Thought it was Mitt, you mean! Maewen thought. The wariness again. The noise from the radio was getting on her nerves, so she said, "I think you ought to answer that."

Wend unclipped the radio and flipped the switch. "Orilson here. Over."

Major Alksen's voice blasted from it like someone talking into a tin. "About bloody time! Wend, get down into the front court soonest. There seems to be something going on in Amil's tomb—animal or something shut inside. Over."

"Coming, sir," said Wend. "Over and out." He

clipped back the radio, forced a smile at Maewen, and said, "Tell me about it later."

Maewen watched him hurry away down the gallery. Tanamoril, Osfameron, Mage Mallard—he was all those heroes of all those stories, and he could be one of her own ancestors, too—and he had come down to this, a museum attendant in league with Kankredin. She knew how Moril had felt about Hestefan. It made a bad taste in your very bones. Playing the good guy on the train so that she would trust him. Yuk.

It was like knowing the answer to a crossword clue by instinct and then working out the clue after that. That photograph. Aunt Liss had sent it to Dad. Wend had seen it and known she was like Noreth. It had to be Wend. How would Kankredin know to look?

Maewen looked at the golden statue, a buttery shine from behind the glass. She was fairly sure that if she hunted along the cases, somewhere she would find a lopsided silver cup and a ring with a big red stone that had the Adon's profile on it—maybe two rings—but she had not the energy to look. Her boots had dissolved into sandals again, showing her toes outlined in brown dirt. She needed a bath. She had to wash her hair. She looked at her thumb. There was a clean white band round it where the false ring had been. Yes, there would be two rings. The One had turned everyone's cunning schemes round—Wend's, Kankredin's, Earl Keril's, that Earl of Andmark's, Maewen's own ideas—and used them against themselves. Maewen herself had not been able to change history; she had just helped it happen as it should.

She really had to have a bath.

Instead she set off round the gallery, very slowly, toward the line of huge windows that looked over the front court. She did not mean to look in the cases as she went, but she could not help seeing the sword. It seemed to throw itself at her eyes, in spite of its dark color, in its dingy, somber sheath. Maewen took a step back, having almost walked past it, and read the label:

ONE OF SEVERAL SWORDS REPUTED TO BE THE ADON'S. LEGENDS CLAIM THAT ONLY THE RIGHT-FUL MONARCH CAN UNSHEATH THE ADON'S SWORD.

That's true, she thought. I couldn't draw it. Mitt had to do it both times. She dawdled toward the windows, with heaviness on her heart. Ordinary life was so very ordinary. Everything was *over*.

When she came to the first window, she looked cautiously out from one corner of it. There was the wide cobbled yard, with its paved patterns and the absurd onion-domed stone tomb in the middle. A very fine example of Amilian stonework. There was Major Alksen, too, and all his people, Wend included, in a cautious circle all the way round the tomb, slowly moving inward. What did they think was in there?

Whatever was in there squealed, a long, descending *hee-hee-hee*. Maewen could hear it quite clearly even through the glass. Horse. Something began banging in her throat, and she felt her face go pale as she realized *which* horse. It had not whinnied much, but Maewen knew horses, and she knew this one only too well. She wanted to lean out of the window and scream to Major Alksen, *Don't go near it! That's Kankredin in there!* Wend must know. He was letting them all move in on it, not knowing what they were up against. Major Alksen was right beside the tomb now. He was putting his hand on the grille over its door.

There was a disturbance in the air over the little domes of the tomb's roof. Major Alksen did not see it. It was very faint, like the ghost of the trumpet-shaped whirlwind Mitt had summoned, but the new wariness in Maewen had prepared her to expect it. She was looking right at it as it went spiraling up to hover level with the roof of the palace. She saw Wend's head tilt slightly as he saw it, too, but his face was expressionless and he did not say anything to anyone. Meanwhile, Major Alksen threw open the grille and then the door, and his lady helper threw open the ones at the other end at the same moment. They went in. They came out. They walked with blank, puzzled, irritated movements. Nothing there. All the other people in the circle moved uncertainly, let down, but ready for some kind of trick.

Maewen discovered she was watching this in glimpses, mostly with her back to the wall so that the hovering cloud of Kankredin would not see her. Her throat pounded harder and her legs felt weak as she caught up with the way her new wariness was making her behave. He's come for me! she thought. He's not going to forgive me in a hurry! Had Wend summoned him? Or perhaps by the action of coming and going back over two hundred years Maewen herself had opened the way for Kankredin. Or again, with One-like cunning, maybe Kankredin had used the force Mitt had thrown at him to help him take that open way through time. It could not be coincidence that Kankredin had arrived just as she had taken hold of the golden statue. It just could not be.

She was very frightened indeed.

This was worse than any time on the green road. It was more horrifying than being attacked twice in Gardale. Why? At first Maewen thought it was because that had only been Hestefan, and this was Kankredin. But she had not known her attacker was only an elderly Singer in Gardale. No—it was because this was her own time. This was modern life, when things like this were not supposed to happen. And worse still, she was alone. All the friends who might have helped her had been dead for two hundred years.

That was when it hit her. Dead. Two hundred years. It was Mitt's tomb she had been looking at, down there in the court.

Grief thundered down on her, hard and continuous as the waterfall at Dropwater. Maewen fled under it, round the gallery, and up the stairs, and upstairs again to her father's apartment. There she ran a bath. Even with both taps full on, the water did not pour as fiercely as grief poured on Maewen. She sat in the bath and she washed herself and she washed her hair without, for a single instant, thinking what she was doing. Instead her mind was going through, going through that entire journey from Adenmouth to Kernsburgh. She found she remembered things about Mitt she had not even known she had seen until now.

When the water was cold, she noticed it was with a dull sort of jump, and got out and dried, and dried her hair. By that time she had been through everything twice and was starting round again. She even laughed in several places—that time when the ring stuck, for instance. By then the grief had stopped pouring and set into a full ache, so that her throat hurt, and her chest, as if she was full, full of sorrow as a person could get. Her hair dried wild and floating and fluffy, as it always did. It was a good inch longer. Aunt Liss would have noticed, but she was fairly sure that Dad never would. There was more than a touch of Cennoreth's wriggliness to it—or Kialan's, or Kankredin's. She put on her nicest dress. That was not to let Mitt down when she had to face Kankredin alone. She looked quite good in the mirror.

I might have been the Queen, she thought, in an experimental way, watching herself. And watched herself shake her head. Somehow that was never a possibility. So I might have been feeling like this, anyway, even if I never touched the statue and Alk passed it to someone else, she told herself. She did not believe that either. Whatever she believed, there was no point to might-have-beens. *Now* was enough—and bad enough.

Mitt had left her a legacy, although he did not know it (at the word *legacy* Maewen had a moment when she thought she was going to cry, but she did not seem to be able to cry; she was hard and dry inside). She had heard the word Mitt shouted to bring that whirlwind, and she had no doubt it would work for her, too. She could use it on Kankredin—and Wend—if need arose.

Out on the leads the pigeons were landing, taking off, circling uneasily. They knew. Kankredin was hovering as a nearly invisible cloud somewhere near. But before she went into battle, there were things she wanted to do.

Maewen let herself out of the apartment again and raced downstairs, down, and on down, until she came to the old part of the palace where the pictures were. She had spent too long in the bath. The art students were all there, and she had to edge round their easels and step over them as they lay on the ballroom floor, in order to look at the paintings on the walls and the ceiling.

She shook her head at the fair-haired Amil in his purple trousers. Whoever painted that had not had a clue what Mitt looked like. Or *had* he? she wondered, remembering King Hern. *Was* it deliberate? she thought, looking up at the battles in the ceiling. Navis was up there, and a huge man who was supposed to be Alk, and a fierce-looking woman. Was she the Countess? She did look a bit like a horse. And now Maewen knew whom to look for, she could spot Kialan and Ynen, neither of them much like themselves—and the young man with red hair, carrying a cwidder and half hidden behind a troop of horses, was surely intended to be Moril, and that was nothing like him. She still had no idea who the savage type in fur was, down in the South.

There was no real portrait of Mitt, she knew that now. All the same, she went on into the polished room where the pictures hung. It was full of people, large men from Haligland, who all looked a bit like Kialan, talking foreign talk and wearing silly national-dress kilts and badges—a convention of some kind. Maewen pushed among them with urgent curiosity. Here were the two old, old portraits of the Adon—quite right: One said it was from Holand, the other from Aberath—and both were startlingly like Mitt, or rather, like Mitt painted by someone who had not got it quite right. She could see why Mitt might not want his portrait painted. That bony, ill look. Or was that the reason?

But here was Navis as Duke of Kernsburgh, staring keen and haughty over his shoulder. The artist had got Navis to the life. And round here was Moril. Moril looked more than betrayed. He looked heartbroken. Maewen wondered whether he ever got over what Hestefan had done. She rather thought not. It was funny, though, because it was not that Moril had been so enormously *fond* of Hestefan. No, she thought, as her eye fell on the cwidder in the picture; it was because they were both Singers. If you were a Singer, there were things you just did not do.

Maewen pushed between two broad backs from Haligland to look at the real cwidder in its glass case. Yes. It really was Moril's. And it had looked so much newer and more used when she last saw it. Shame that a thing of such power should lie crumbling in a glass case. But though her name was Singer, Maewen knew she had not the least chance of using it as it could be used. Shame. Waste.

She backed away and worked her way out to the exit. And caught the eye of another portrait, one she had never bothered to do more than glance at before. A woman. A thin white-faced woman with black hair piled up high and an angry little frown between the eyebrows. Hildy. O great *One!* Misery came thundering down on Maewen again, more than she had thought possible—and here she had thought she was as full of it as she could be. Memories came with the misery: Mitt brushing at the damp patch of her tears in the Lawschool; the straight, greasy feel of Mitt's hair when she put the crown back on him; the incredible knuckliness of Mitt's hands. . . .

Maewen caught up with herself to find she was racing upstairs again, pushing past a big party of tourists and then another, and then hammering on upward alone. By the time she flung through the doorway of the palace office, she hardly had breath left to pant. She leaned against the wall to recover, watching the usual frenzy, people rushing all over, papers being passed, typing, telephones ringing. Dad sensed she was there. He put down a telephone to turn to her over his shoulder and raise his chin inquiringly.

That pose! *Now* Maewen knew whom Navis had all along reminded her of. Both of them were short men. And just like Dad, Navis was in his element giving orders and attending to a thousand things at once. No wonder Mitt had made Navis a duke and let him organize the kingdom! Dad saw she needed something and came over to the door. That was like Navis, too.

"What's the matter, Maewen?"

Nothing, she wanted to say. I'm only in love with a King who died over a hundred years ago. Stupid. Keep your mouth shut. "Dad, who did Amil the Great marry?"

He raised an eyebrow, although unlike Navis, he could not do it without raising the other eyebrow slightly, too. "Is this important? All right, I see it is. Well, she was never very prominent. She seems to have been rather a retiring character, because very little is known about her apart from the fact that she was very tall, and I believe she was also very kind-hearted—"

"Her *name*, Dad!" Maewen said. "Not a lecture."

"Didn't I say?" He was surprised. "Enblith—though she is *not*, of course, to be confused with En-blith the Fair."

"Thanks."

Fancy that! Maewen thought as she ran away downstairs. Biffa! *Biffa!* Well, Mitt had shown some sense, at least! And it was really a very good choice, she thought, patrolling round the museum gallery while she waited for Kankredin to show himself. Biffa was nice—so nice, in fact, that it was entirely likely that Mitt had lived happily ever after. Maewen tried to feel glad. But in moments she was saying, "I expect he forgot about me entirely after a day or so. I don't suppose he thought about me *once* in the rest of his life."

Her voice rang out, peevish and hurt. Don't be so ridiculous! she told herself. Kings have to marry. Besides, he *had* to remember you in order to get the waystone changed to a huge one, like I told Moril it was. And—well, the waystone was not really a message, since it *had* to be there—but Maewen stood suddenly stock-still, wondering if Mitt might not indeed have left her a message, buried in history. She was on her way upstairs again, before the idea had had time to be fully formed.

"Dad!" she said from the office doorway.

Dad was reading a bundle of papers, but he came over to her. "Yes?"

"Dad, how did the Tannoreth Palace get its name?"

"Amil named it," Dad said. "I'm sure I told you the first day you were here. Nobody knows quite where he got it from. The first part, *tan*, is the old word for 'young' or 'younger,' and we assume Amil was thinking of Hern's old palace, which may have been on the same site."

"And the *noreth* part?" Maewen asked.

"Nobody knows. It seems to be just a name—Maewen, forgive me, but I *must* get this read before the Queen's Office phones me."

Maewen galloped away downstairs again, thinking, Young Noreth—no, the *younger Noreth*! Not Noreth, but the one who was younger. Great One! He named a whole palace after me, and I'll never be able to say thank you! It made her eyes prick, and it warmed the heavy hurt inside her without making it any better. She walked twice round the gallery, hugging Mitt's message to her. Then there were other things that she just had to know. Upstairs she dashed again.

"Dad!"

She forgot how many times she rushed up to the office or quite what order she asked the other questions in. Each time Dad was surprisingly patient—like Navis, if you really needed something. Or was it, in some confusing way, that Navis had had some kind of family feeling for Maewen? One of the first things she asked was, "Dad, who did the Duke of Kernsburgh marry?"

Dad frowned. "I really don't remember the name of his first wife. But his second wife was the widow of the Lord of Adenmouth." He clicked his fingers. "What *was* her name? Eltruda, that was it!"

"Thanks, Dad." Noreth's aunt. It all fits. And downstairs again to patrol round the gallery.

Upon one of her reappearances in the office, one of Dad's young ladies handed her a cheese roll, saying it was lunchtime. Maewen had no appetite. She carried the roll about as she patrolled. She was carrying it when she saw Wend coming and fled from him up to the office again. There she had to stop and eat the roll, chokingly, for fear of offending the young lady.

"Dad, who did Hild—er, the Duke of Kernsburgh's eldest daughter marry?"

"Hildrida. Dear me. That family seems to be an obsession with you," Dad said. "I really can't remember. She certainly *did* marry, because her descendants are still Wardens of the Holy Islands, but— Not that Hildrida ever spent much time in the Islands. Amil was there far oftener, and so was Hildrida's brother, Ynen, building up our navy. That was when Dalemark first became a big sea power, you know. Ynen tried out the first steamships there."

Bless Dad and his lectures! Maewen thought. You always got twice the answers you asked for. Sometimes on her visits to the office she got more than she wanted, like the lecture she got when she asked who Hobin was. That lecture started, "You mean Bloody Hobin of Holand? He was the center of the uprising in the South at the start of Amil's reign. Like so many revolutionaries, he got quite out of hand. . . ." Maewen did not attend to this one much, because it was all about Hobin and nothing about Amil.

But there were times when she got next to nothing, as when she asked, "Moril the Singer, Dad? Does history say anything about him?"

"No," Dad said. "I never heard of him."

"Hestefan the Singer, then?"

"Nope," said Dad. "You must remember that things changed very fast in Amil's reign. Singers were right out of date by the time Amil died."

Poor Moril. Next time Maewen charged upstairs, she asked, "Earl Keril of Hannart, Dad. Was he a great nuisance to Amil the Great?"

Eyebrows up, like the image of Navis, Dad said, "Are you writing a historical novel or something? Far be it from me to discourage such a venture. But let it be accurate, please. Earl Keril supported Amil, like most earls of the North, but he never seems to have been very deep in Amil's confidence. Historians usually put Hannart's decline down to this period."

"Thanks." Oh. So history had Keril as just a politician who backed the wrong move. Right, in a way, but so wrong, too.

Maewen went thoughtfully away. She was tired. Today had literally lasted two hundred years. But even if she could have borne to sit and wait for Kankredin, Maewen's misery would not let her keep still. She patrolled wider and wider, through most of the palace by the afternoon.

Halfway through the afternoon the loudspeaker outlets crackled all over the palace. Here it comes! Maewen thought, and stood stock-still where she was, between two state bedrooms.

"Attention. Your attention, please." It was Major Alksen's voice. "A bomb has been reported concealed on the palace premises. I repeat. A bomb has been reported somewhere in the palace or grounds. I must ask everyone to leave as quickly and quietly as possible. This applies to all visitors and staff alike. Please leave the palace and its grounds as quickly as you can. Doors and gates have been opened front and rear. Please leave by the nearest exit you can find. Please do not return until the bomb is located. Attention, please . . ."

The message went on and on, repeating.

The palace resounded softly as hundreds of people's feet hurried through rooms and down stairs to find the doors. Presumably Dad and his ladies were on their way out, too. Maewen wanted to know. Once more her feet took her on the familiar journey to the office. But the stairs were blocked by the office staff pouring down them.

"Your father, dear?" said someone, barely stopping. "Mr. Singer's gone down to Security. He'll probably stay with them until the bomb squad gets here. You come down with us."

Maewen hung back and let them pass until the stairway was empty. Dad was not safe, but there was nothing she could do. She went softly down again. The palace was weirdly empty, much emptier than she had ever known it. Maewen went on a zigzag course, quite unimpeded, from back windows to front ones, and then back windows again, as she went down. She saw people pouring out through gardens at the back and through the court at the front. Nothing would happen until everyone was gone. She was sure of that. Kankredin was after *her*. Maybe he would also destroy the palace as a belated revenge on Mitt, but he would not blow up all the tourists. Kankredin valued power over people, and you could not have that if all the people were dead.

She went on down, checking windows. By now she had come to the floors that opened onto the cloister balconies at the front. The windows were big glass doors, and Maewen had to go through those, into a roofed space held up by thin pillars, and then lean over the parapet to see into the front court. When she did this at the highest balcony, there was still a scatter of people hurrying away through the court and out under the arched gateway. At the next floor, everyone had gone. Everywhere was empty and still— No, it was *not*!

Maewen leaned on the parapet and did not dare move. Over the multiple domes of Amil's tomb, a big cloud of something nearly invisible rolled and coiled on itself. She could see it mostly by the way it distorted the wall and the city buildings beyond, in ugly, glassy waves. It was not person-shaped—yet. Kankredin was busy assembling himself. Maewen licked her lips.

There was so much of it. Kankredin seemed to have brought more of himself from somewhere. The ugly shimmer was easily five times the size of the ghost thing that had been her horse. She supposed she ought to shout that word, but she had a feeling that the thing hovering there was too big to be dealt with like that.

On the other side of the court the gates in the big main gateway were softly closing, switched by remote control from Security, shutting her in with Kankredin. But Dad was inside, too. She had to do *something*.

Before the gates had quite swung closed, a man in an old leather jacket slipped between them and pushed them shut with his back. He must be the bomb disposal expert. Maewen had heard that bomb men were daredevils who dressed all anyhow and enjoyed risking their lives. The trouble was, he was not up against a bomb. She saw him realize. He stood as still as Maewen, staring up at the heaving, invisible cloud. Then his head switched— There was something odd about— There was somebody else in the court, running. Maewen could hear running footsteps. Then see who. It was Wend, racing toward Amil's tomb.

The man by the gate gave a great shout. "GET BACK, YOU FLAMING FOOL!"

That was Mitt's voice! Maewen was head down, leaning far out over the parapet, without knowing she had moved. She *knew* she was right. Except it couldn't be true. The man was not gawky enough—was he?

Above the tomb, the coiling movement, which had

been bunching and bending over itself ready to move down on the man by the gate, now swayed round and turned to face the movement Maewen had made. She saw—no, *felt*—eyes in its midst. Eyes that knew her. Eyes that hated her. Fat-lidded eyes she knew.

Mitt's voice yelled a word. It was not the word Maewen knew. This was a word that made your brain clench and then prefer to forget you had heard it. It was a word that dragged shivers from deep, deep under the earth. A word that shook the palace. The invisibleness above the tomb coiled hurriedly round to throw itself at the shouter.

In the act of coiling it was caught, and held, and thrown high, high in the air, mixed with and part of a tremendous jet of water, a huge tsunami. Water burst from the tomb in a giant dark horn, throwing pieces of building aside like a card house. Maewen stared, with her neck twisted, at the immense column of water hanging into the sky, darker and darker with dissolving shreds of the coiling cloud, and all spouted to yellow froth at its distant top.

Then it fell.

Maewen threw herself flat beside the parapet. Even so, she was soaked. The open balcony bucked under her. Salt water stung her eyes. Salt? And the roar of falling tons of water was more deafening than any bomb. It went on and on, mixed with the crashing of stone. Maewen scrambled up in the midst of it, unable to care that she was deaf as a post. Three pillars that held up the balcony were missing nearby, and there was a gap in the parapet where she had been leaning. Unable to care about that either, she walked over balcony that swayed and grated until she reached the nearest whole pillar. Clinging to it, she stared at the courtyard awash with angry, gray, leaping waves. The gate was down. The gateway was mostly rubble. Water was roaring out into King Street. The salt that ran on Maewen's face was partly tears. No one could have survived that.

But he had. He must have been swept over to the side wall. She could see him, nearly out of her view, where it was blocked by the ragged edge of the balcony, clawing himself along the wall, first shoulder-deep, then, very quickly, only waist-deep. The water was rushing away all the time, going back underground. Maewen could dimly hear the surge and growl of it running away. But she was staring at the man's soaking, lank hair. It *did* look like Mitt's.

Then he had clawed himself out of sight. Maewen had turned to dash away down into the court when she heard him speaking, right under the balcony. "Come on, get up, you fool. Walk." It was Mitt's voice, no doubt now.

Wend's voice answered. "Let me go. I deserve to drown."

And then Mitt's voice again: "If that was true, the Earth Shaker wouldn't have left you alive. Come on, stand up."

Maewen heard splashing, and coughing. Wend said, "Don't you understand? I was working with Kankredin."

Mitt answered, "Well, you had the sense to phone and tell me when you realized how much of him he'd collected here. He's an expert in blackmailing and tempting and all that. Stop kicking yourself. What I want to know— Watch it! These steps are all broken." There were flounderings, and the sound of wet stones rolling and splashing. Then Mitt's voice came from right underneath, where the palace door was. "What I want to know is how did he persuade you?"

"Noreth," said Wend. Maewen could tell he was crying. "My daughter Noreth! All these years I thought you were the one who'd killed her."

"Of all the idiots!" Mitt answered. "There were several hundred people you could have *asked*!"

Maewen found she could wait no longer. She had not dared believe it was really Mitt until now, but this proved it. She dashed back through the open windowdoors and sped through the ballroom to the nearest stairs. Halfway down she found herself pausing—with an impatient skip, because of the vanity of it—to look at her draggled self in the grand mirrors: wet, salty hair, tear-stained face, damp rag of a best dress. Well, he's seen me look just as bad, and he knows I'm only thirteen. But, as she sped down again, she found herself repeating, Only thirteen. He's two hundred years old. I'm only thirteen. Over and over.

Across the slippery grand hall she sped. Rubble rolled under her racing feet, and she splatted in pools of seafoam. And there was the open door at last, open onto heaved-up paving stones and steaming water. A gust of sea scent blew in through it. Maewen hurtled out of it and stopped. There was only Wend, leaning against a pillar, soaking wet. In the distance, across uprooted cobblestones strewn with seaweed, bloodred and olive green, Mitt was just climbing over the rubble that had been the gate.

"*Mitt!*" she screamed.

He heard her. He stopped. She could see him think about it. He turned round and gave her a cheerful wave before he jumped off the pile of rubble and walked away down King Street.

Maewen was left gazing. Between her and the remains of the gate there was a scummy, odd-shaped pool, turgid with tainted waves, draining away into the ground as she looked at it. That was where the tomb had been, of course. That tomb must have been one of Mitt's biggest jokes. By the time he had had it built, he must have known he was of the Undying. No wonder he made it so absurd. Maewen almost smiled, in spite of her misery. *He's two hundred years old. I'm thirteen.*

She turned to Wend. Wend was staring straight ahead, dripping. "I owe you an apology," he said.

"Yes," Maewen agreed. "Did you take this job at the palace to wait until I turned up?"

"No," said Wend. "I was never sure where you came from. I took the job for something to do. There's so much time, you know."

He said it very drearily. Maewen could see time stretch on and on, before and behind him.

"Why did you tell Noreth she was the One's daughter?" she asked.

"I didn't. That was an idea her mother had," Wend said. He laughed, a nasty hacking sound, like a bad cough. "The One told me she would ride the royal road. He lied."

"Are you sure that wasn't Kankredin?" Maewen asked.

Wend turned and stared at her, as if this had never occurred to him. Beyond him she saw Major Alksen in the distance, followed by Dad, gingerly picking his way toward the empty slot that had been Amil's tomb.

"Come with me," Maewen said to Wend. "I've got an idea about you." When Wend did not move, she took his chilly hand and dragged. "You ought to get into dry clothes, at least."

"No problem," Wend said. His clothes began to steam as if he were out in hot sun. But he made no protest when Maewen dragged him, in a trail of steam, through the rubbly hall and to the stairs. Thank goodness, she thought. For what she had in mind, it would be better that Major Alksen and Dad were busy outside. But why am I doing this? she wondered as she towed Wend upstairs. He thought he was sending me to be killed. He knew he was sending me to Kankredin. Am I trying to be worthy? But she knew why, really. She knew how Wend felt.

She dragged him through the ballroom and round into the smaller room where the pictures hung. She pushed him in front of the glass cabinet where the old cwidder lay.

"Get that out," she said. "Play it. It's yours, anyway."

"Oh no," Wend said. "I gave it to my son. And it's the Queen's property now."

"Is it?" said Maewen. "I think Moril gave it to Mitt, not to Amil, and as Mitt's still alive, it's *his*. I know he won't mind you having it in the least. It's wasted, lying there."

"Maybe," Wend said. He looked down at the old beautiful instrument as if he were very tempted. "But someone will notice if I take it."

"You are beginning to annoy me!" Maewen said. "From all I've heard, you're one of the greatest magicians there ever was. Surely you can make it *look* as if the cwidder's still there? Nobody's going to try to play it, after all."

"True." Wend stared down at his uniform, now dry and trim. In a hopeless, fussy way, he picked a piece of dry seaweed off it. For a moment, he stared at the red-brown spray of weed as if he had never seen such a thing before. Then he smiled. He took his keys out, unlocked the cabinet, and raised the glass lid, tossing the seaweed spray inside as he did so. Then he picked up the cwidder. To Maewen, it looked as if he drew the ghost of the cwidder out of itself. There was a cwidder lying in the cabinet, fat, mellow, and glossy. Wend had an identical cwidder in his hands and was hitching the strap over his shoulder.

"You'd better replace that strap," she said. "It's awfully frayed."

Wend smoothed the strap. "I know. I made the strap, too. It'll hold." His face already looked different. It was newer and happier. It became serious-happy as he turned the pegs and brought the strings into tune. And it changed to a dreamy pleasure as he picked out a little tune. The cwidder hummed, almost purred, with happiness. "Forgive me," Wend said. He looked up at the portrait of Moril, as if Moril was really there.

"He will," Maewen said. "It was always a burden to him."

Wend sighed. "Yes, and that's odd. Or perhaps not. It was my power I put in the cwidder—a good half of it." He strummed another hasty tune. It made him stand in a different, easy way, and he looked stronger. "I should never have passed that power on," he said, and looking as dreamy as Moril often did, he turned and walked out of the room.

"Oughtn't you to tell my father you're leaving?" Maewen said.

"A message is on his desk now," Wend said, conjuring a small waterfall of notes as he walked off. His

uniform had gone. He was wearing a shabby leather
jacket, rather like Mitt's.

He was really going. Maewen hurriedly called out
the selfish part of why she had done this. "Wend! How
can I get in touch with Mitt?"

Wend paused. "Through Cennoreth, I suppose."
Then he turned and looked at her over his shoulder,
like Navis in the portrait behind her. His face had
gone beyond happy to become the face of a man of
power. Oddly enough, that made him look kinder.
"Mitt gave me a message for you. I'm sorry—I'd forgotten until now. I've no idea what he meant. He said,
'Tell her to make it four years, not two, to allow for
inflation.' Does that mean anything to you?"

It certainly did. Maewen almost laughed as she
watched Wend walk away. Four years! No way! She
was going to get the train to Dropthwaite tomorrow,
and somehow, she was going to find Cennoreth there.

A Guide to Dalemark

Aberath, the northernmost earldom of North Dalemark; also the town on the north coast, situated on the Rath estuary at the mouth of the river Ath.

Aden, the small river running north to the sea at Adenmouth, thought by some to be all that remains of the great River of the spellcoats.

Adenmouth, a small town and lordship in the extreme northwest of North Dalemark, and part of the earldom of Aberath.

Adon, a name that seems to mean "High Lord" and has several applications:
1. One of the secret names of the One.
2. The name or title of the heroic King of Dalemark about whom there are many songs and legends. The Adon was an Earl of Hannart who married Manaliabrid of the Undying as his second wife and went into exile with her and the Singer Osfameron, during which time he was murdered by his jealous half brother Lagan and brought back to life by Osfameron. He then became King, but on his death his two children disappeared, leaving Dalemark without a King and riven by civil war.

3. The title of the eldest son and heir of the Earl of Hannart.

The Adon's gifts, the legendary gifts Manaliabrid brought to the Adon as her dowry. These are:

1. A ring said only to fit the finger of one with royal blood.

2. A cup which was believed to acknowledge the true King and also to shine in the hands of anyone telling the truth.

3. A sword which, it was said, only the true King could draw from its scabbard.

"The Adon's Hall," one of the old-style songs composed by the singer-mage Osfameron, in which Osfameron seems to be thinking not only of the Adon in exile in a ruinous hall but of his own cwidder and of the Sayings of King Hern.

Al, the most common short form of Alhammitt, the commonest name in South Dalemark. The name of a castaway picked up by the yacht *Wind's Road*.

Alda, the wife of Siriol; a confirmed alcoholic.

Alhammitt

1. The true name of the Earth Shaker.

2. The most common man's name in South Dalemark.

3. Mitt's actual name.

Alk, a lawman from the North Dales who took office under the Countess of Aberath and shortly married her. His status then became that of Consort of Aberath, with the courtesy title (which was seldom used) of Lord. Alk devoted his time to inventing steam engines and eventually, almost single-handedly, brought about the industrial revolution of Dalemark.

Alksen, Major, the head of security at the Tannoreth Palace.

Alk's Irons, the name given by the people of Aberath to the steam machines invented by Alk. The most notable of these were a plow, a hoist, a press, a pump, and a locomotive.

Alla, the elder daughter of Alk and the Countess of Aberath.

Allegiances, the personal ties of primitive Haligland. A man or woman would be born into one clan, sent as foster child to a second, swear friendship to a third, and marry into a fourth. This formed a network of friendship and obligation which you were bound to tell to a stranger when you told your name. Allegiances defined you as a person. If you did not tell, or had no allegiances, you were either a criminal or a social outcast.

Almet, the son of the Adon and Manaliabrid, who declined to be King after his father.

Amil, one of the secret names of the One, which appears to mean either "Brother" or "River." It later became the name of the line of kings that began with Amil the Great.

Ammet, a straw image thrown into the sea every year at the Sea Festival in Holand in South Dalemark, which was said to bring luck to the city. Small images were also made and sold for luck. Even greater luck was supposed to come to any boat that found Ammet floating beyond the harbor and brought him aboard. The name is a corruption of Alhammitt, one of the names of the Earth Shaker. See also **Poor Old Ammet**.

Andmark, the earldom in the center of South Dalemark which was probably the wealthiest in Dalemark. Henda was Earl of Andmark until he was killed in the Great Uprising.

Anoreth of the Undying became the wife of Closti the Clam. The name means "unbound."

Ansdale, a remote valley east of Gardale. The birthplace of Biffa, whose family kept the mill there.

Arin, a senior lord of the (Heathen) invaders from Haligland and chief warrior-minister of Kars Adon.

Armor was markedly different in the two halves of Dalemark.
Southern soldiers wore helmets and breastplates with exaggerated curves designed to deflect bullets, over tough leather, with knee-length boots and big gauntlets. Many carried guns as well as swords, and foot soldiers carried pikes.
Northern soldiers still used chain mail under sleeved jerkins of leather or tough cloth. The mail was long enough to protect the wearer to the wrists and knees, and the helmets were round, coming low enough in the back to protect the neck. Gloves were leather with mail or studs on the backs. Weapons were usually crossbows, swords, and daggers. Guns were few and could only be spared for picked hearthmen.

Arms inspectors were employed by all the earls of South Dalemark to keep strict watch on gunsmiths, armorers, and weapons makers, who were not allowed to work without the inspectors' seal on all their equipment. The earls rightly feared that the craftsmen might otherwise sell weapons to the common people or make weapons for the earls that were deliberately flawed. Despite the inspectors, many armorers seem to have done both these things.

Arris, a rough spirituous liquor brewed throughout South Dalemark from discarded grapes and sprouting corn. All that can be said in its favor is that it was much cheaper than wine.

Ath, the river that runs north into the sea at Aberath. It is thought to be one of the remnants of the great River of prehistory.

Autumn Festival, the usual name in the South of Dalemark for Harvest, the feast that celebrated the gathering of crops.

Autumn floods in the prehistoric Riverlands were as regular as spring floods but never so large. They were due to the rains that fell in the autumn storms.

Autumn storms were a regular feature in Dalemark. In historic times they reached as far north as Gardale and could be very severe. The worst lasted for days, with the gale swinging from northwest to southwest. With a shorter storm the winds tended to gust even stronger but not veer so much. If the gale was southerly, the storms came repeatedly for several days.

Bad luck gave rise to many superstitions all over Dalemark. Those which require explanation are:
1. Giving. It was considered disastrously unlucky to give, or promise to give, something and then not give it. This is why Ganner was forced to give Lenina to Clennen and also why he seems to have been certain she would one day come back; he had not incurred bad luck by refusing to give her away.
2. Festivals, feasts, and ceremonies. Enormous bad luck was incurred if anything happened to interrupt these. Note that the Heathens interrupted the One's fire ceremony; that both Mitt and Al interrupted the Sea Festival; and that Fenna interrupted the Midsummer Feast by fainting.
3. A death brought great bad luck and could only be countered by a marriage on the same day. Lenina and Ganner take advantage of this belief.
4. Speaking a falsehood to the Undying brings more bad luck than any of the foregoing.

5. An unlucky person can bring bad luck to others. Gull was considered to be doing this, and Kialan believed he was such a person.

6. A person or group can carry their own cloud of bad luck around with them and nothing will go right for them until the cloud passes away.

Barangarolob, the full name of the horse that pulled Clennen the Singer's cart. Clennen, who loved long names, named him after the Adon's horse Barangalob, with the inserted superlative particle *ro* meaning "youngest" or "much younger."

Barlay, Lawschool slang. "No barlay" means "no quarter given."

Beat the water, as part of the Holand Sea Festival in South Dalemark. People pretended to beat the sea with garlands of fruit and flowers. The ancient aim seems to have been to subdue the sea for the following year.

Beer was drunk throughout the North of Dalemark instead of water, wine, or coffee until near the end of Amil the Great's reign. One of Navis Haddsson's many profitable enterprises was to set up a large brewery in the Shield of Oreth, but the best beer came from Hannart and still does. The lager brewed in Kinghaven is to be avoided at all costs.

Bence, captain in chief of the fleet of the Holy Islands and commander of the *Wheatsheaf*. Bence was not a Holy Islander. He was born in Wayness in the earldom of Waywold.

Besting, Lawschool slang for best friend.

Biffa, pupil at the Gardale Lawschool, a native of Ansdale and best friend of Hildrida Navissdaughter. The name is a shortened pet-name form of Enblith.

Big Shool, one of the larger of the Holy Islands.

Black Mountains, the highest range of mountains in prehistoric Dalemark. It is possible, though not certain, that they were thrown higher in the mountain-folding at the start of the reign of King Hern, to become the Black Mountains of historic Dalemark, in which case the name may refer to the large deposits of coal to be found there.

"Both hands cut off . . ." refers to the law of primitive Haligland, whereby any member of the High Lord's (King's) family who was suspected of treason could be legally deprived of both hands, not as a punishment but as a precaution against a threat to the throne.

Bradbrook, a lordship on the coast of Waywold in South Dalemark.

Brid, daughter of Clennen the Singer and sister of Moril and Dagner, who fled North with Moril. Soon after her arrival Brid went to Gardale and trained as a law-woman, and thence to a professional appointment in Loviath. After the Great Uprising she became Countess of Hannart and eventually the first head of the Royal Dalemark Academy of Music, which she helped her brother Moril to found.

Bull, the most usual form in which the Earth Shaker appears. For this reason bulls' heads are carried in the Holand Sea Festival. It is said that the Bull is most frequently seen in the Holy Islands.

Canden, the younger of two brothers from Waywold in South Dalemark, devoted to freedom fighting. He moved from Waywold to Holand, where conditions were much worse, deliberately to foment rebellion. In Holand he joined the secret society of the Free Holanders and shortly proposed the firing of one of the Earl's warehouses. The older Free Holanders refused and stayed at home, while Canden led the younger ones to the warehouse. There he found that they had been betrayed and that soldiers were waiting for them.

Canderack, the earldom on the west coast of South Dalemark, where the best wine was grown. Until the reign of Amil the Great, Canderack owned a fleet that rivaled Holand's.

Canderack Head, south of Canderack Bay, an important landmark for shipping on the South Dalemark coast.

Carne Bank, a mudbank at the far east of the prehistoric Rivermouth, notorious for quicksands and shallows.

Cenblith, a queen of prehistoric Dalemark who first took the One for her lover and then bound him to the will of mortals, apparently either by forcing him to make the great River or by carving an image of him.

Cennoreth, one of the Undying, known in legends as a witch and often called the Weaver. It was said that whatever she wove became truth. She was sister to the legendary King Hern and mother of Manaliabrid, wife of the Adon.

Chindersay, one of the outer ring of the Holy Islands, notable for the dark color of its rocks.

Cindow, a village northeast of Markind in South Dalemark.

City of Gold, King Hern's lost city of Kernsburgh, which gave rise to the saying "The City of Gold is always on the most distant hill," meaning that your ideal is never *here*, under your hands, but always out over *there*.

Clans, the tribe families of the Heathens of Haligland. The clans are very large and contain all classes, from aristocrat to lowborn. For instance, Kars Adon and Ked both belonged to Clan Rath, but Kars Adon was King while Ked was lowborn and had no real relation to the royal family.

Clennen Mendakersson, one of the most famous and characterful of the old-style Singers, a musician, composer, and teller of tales. He married Lenina, niece of the Earl of the South Dales, and was the father of Dagner, Brid, and Moril. He was murdered near Markind in South Dalemark on suspicion of being a spy, and bequeathed to Moril a cwidder with strange powers, which he claimed had been handed down to him from their ancestor Osfameron.

Climbers, Lawschool slang name for the cloistered court with steps.

Closti the Clam, father of Tanaqui the weaver and a native of Shelling in the prehistoric Riverlands kingdom of Dalemark. He was called the Clam for his extreme uncommunicativeness, which may have been caused by the early death of his wife, Anoreth, or perhaps by the command of the One. He was killed in the invasion of the Heathen Haliglanders before he could tell his children many very important facts.

Collen, one of the two Southern forms of the name Kialan; a name fairly common in Markind.

Collet, the steward of the King of the Riverlands, whose duty was to memorize the King's debts for lodging and provision.

"The Color Song," composed and sung by Dagner Clennensson.

"Come Up the Dale with Me," an apparently innocent love song from South Dalemark which was actually urging rebellion. It was banned.

"Come with Me," a song being composed by Dagner Clennenssen, which Clennen objected to on the ground that it could be seen by spies as urging rebellion.

Coran, a townsman of Derent in Waywold in South Dalemark, later well known as a freedom fighter.

Countess
    1. A female who is earl in her own right, like the Countess of Aberath.
    2. The wife of an earl.
    3. Mitt's name for his bad-tempered horse, which was not even female.

"Cow-calling," a traditional patter song to a lively tune. Each verse is two lines longer than the last, until the singer is addressing the whole herd of cows.

Crady, a large town in the south of Andmark in South Dalemark.

Credin, the tidal wave which, at certain seasons, runs up the river Aden from the sea. A lesser wave usually runs up the river Ath at the same time. It is thought the name derives from memories of the mage Kankredin.

Cressing Harbor, a small fishing port to the northeast of the Point of Hark. It was the nearest landing for ships from South Dalemark and much involved in smuggling goods and people from both sides.

Cruddle, one of the traditional instruments played at the Holand Sea Festival, a sort of triangular fiddle with three gut strings. The player held the cruddle under his chin and scraped the strings with a loose horsehair bow. Cruddlers were seldom musicians. Their sole aim was to make as much noise as possible.

"Cuckoo Song," a comic song with rather indecent words composed by Clennen the Singer.

Cwidder, a musical instrument rather like a lute but with some of the properties of an acoustic guitar. Cwidders are found in all sizes, from small trebles through medium-sized altos and tenors to large bass and deep bass. Moril's cwidder was a large bass, but it could be used as a tenor. Cwidders were much used by Singers because they were both versatile and easy to carry.

Dagner, the elder son of Clennen the Singer and a noted composer. Dagner became Earl of the South Dales very early in his life but was so reluctant to leave his life as a traveling Singer that he only took up his earldom after fifteen years, at the urgent request of Amil the Great.

Dalemark, the fifteen earldoms of Aberath, Loviath, Hannart, Gardale, Dropwater, Kannarth, the North Dales, the South Dales, Fenmark, Carrowmark, Andmark, Canderack, Waywold, Holand, and Dermath, with the so-called King's Lands (the Holy Islands, the Marshes, and the Shield of Oreth), that, together with their peoples and history, make up historic Dalemark. For prehistoric Dalemark, see **Riverlands**.

Dapple, the mottled gray horse belonging to Hestefan the Singer. It was blind in one eye. There was usually something amiss with Singers' horses because they could only afford to buy them cheap.

Dark Land, the place where the souls of the newly dead gather before they make their way to the constellation of the River and on to oblivion.

Dastgandlen Handagner, the full name of Dagner Clennensson, who was named for the twin brothers of the Undying encountered by the witch Cennoreth. It was said that Clennen could not resist long names.

Derent, a prosperous town in the northeast of the earldom of Waywold in South Dalemark.

Dermath, the earldom in the extreme southeast of South Dalemark.

Diddersay, one of the Holy Islands.

Dideo, a fisherman of Holand in South Dalemark, one of the older members of the Free Holanders, who knew how to make bombs. Dideo put this knowledge to use for Mitt, and again in the Great Uprising, when he had a hand blown off by one of his own bombs, but he survived this and ended his days on the City Council of Holand.

Dike End, the birthplace of Mitt, farmed by his parents for the first six years of Mitt's life. The name comes from the situation of the farm and the nearby village at the end of the great Flate Dike, quite near where it runs into the sea about ten miles west of the port of Holand.

Doen, one of the Holy Islands.

Doggers, Lawschool slang for top of the game league.

Doreth, second daughter of Alk and the Countess of Aberath.

Dropthwaite, a secluded valley at the source of the river Dropwater where the Adon is said to have hidden as an outlaw. A center of tourism in modern Dalemark.

Dropwater, after Hannart, the richest and most influential earldom of North Dalemark, situated facing southwest astride a wide fjord that is ideal for shipping, and sheltered by the mountains from the normal harsh weather of the North. The chief riches of Dropwater come from wool and leather goods, but it was mostly famous for its strong plum brandy and, above all, for the spectacular giant waterfall at the head of its dale.

Duck, the pet name of the youngest son of Closti the Clam, who later became famous as Mage Mallard.

Duke of Kernsburgh, a new title created by Amil the Great and bestowed upon Navis Haddsson. It was designed to ensure that Navis outranked all the earls.

Earl
1. The aristocratic ruler of one large segment of Dalemark. In the old days, prior to the reign of the Adon, earls held their places as officers of the King but, when Dalemark ceased to have kings, each earl became a small king in his own right, with absolute authority over everything in his earldom. Many misused this power, some brutally, and all went to great lengths to keep it.
2. The title of a clan chief among the Heathens of Haligland. This later became the modern title.

Earldom, a division of Dalemark ruled by an earl. It was said that earldoms came into being when King Hern divided his kingdom into nine and set nine men in charge, whom he called earls after the name of the clan chiefs, to govern under him. These divisions he called marks. Later six more marks were added in the South when Hern's conquests had reached that far. The system worked well, provided the King was strong. The common people traditionally regarded the earls as only the officers of the King and continued to think this way even after there were no kings.

Earth Shaker, the title of Alhammitt, one of the elder Undying, who had become the god of corn and of the sea. The title might describe the sea, but it possibly also refers to what happens if any of the Earth Shaker's secret names are spoken.

Edril, the younger grandson of Amil the Great and one of Maewen's ancestors.

Egil, a hearthman in the service of Earl Keril of Hannart.

"The Eighth March," the last of a set of marching songs usually called "The Seven Marches," and only sung or played in North Dalemark because the words were offensive to the South.

Eleth of Kredindale, the mother of Noreth, who died soon after Noreth was born, declaring to the end that her daughter was the child of the One.

Elthorar Ansdaughter, keeper of antiquities at Hannart in North Dalemark in the time of Earl Keril, a law-woman of great learning who gave up the law in order to study the history and prehistory of Dalemark. She was present at the discovery of the spellcoats and translated them, sometimes rather inaccurately.

Eltruda, the Lady of Adenmouth, wife of Lord Stair, and younger sister of Eleth of Kredindale. Being childless herself, Eltruda brought Noreth up when Eleth died. On the death of Lord Stair, Eltruda married Navis Haddsson and became a considerable force in Dalemark politics and almost legendary for her quarrels with her stepdaughter, Hildrida.

Enblith the Fair, Queen of Dalemark some hundreds of years after the reign of King Hern, daughter of the Undying and said to be the most beautiful woman who ever lived. The musician-mage Tanamoril found Enblith living as a pauper in the woods and tricked the King into marrying her.

Falls

1. In prehistoric Dalemark the great River rose as a waterfall said to be half the height of a mountain. This was the site of Hern's battle with the mage Kankredin.
2. In historic times the falls at the head of the dale of Dropwater, where the river Dropwater fell nearly three hundred feet to the floor of the valley, were among the most admired sights of North Dalemark.

Fander, a revolutionary in Neathdale in South Dalemark a grocer by trade, who provided the family of Clennen the Singer with bacon, lentils, and, for some reason, a large bunch of rhubarb.

Farn, the southernmost of the Holy Islands.

Fayside, one of the dormitory houses in the Lawschool at Gardale.

Fenna, the daughter and apprentice of Hestefan the Singer.

Fenner, Ganner Sagersson.

Fervold, captain of Earl Henda of Andmark's private army.

Fire, a ritual bonfire which had to be lit for the One every spring as soon as the River ceased to flood. The fuel had to be specially arranged with the image of the One at its center and kindled with coals from the hearth of the officiators. The lighting of the fire was celebrated with a feast. When the fire died down and the One was revealed in the ashes, only the eldest male of the family was allowed to remove the image.

Firepot, a clay pot with a lid and cunningly placed vents in which a fire could be kept alight and carried until needed. Until the invention of the wheel-and-flint tinderbox, firepots were in use all over Dalemark and continued in use by Singers and traveling traders until some time after the reign of the Adon.

Fishmarket, a broad thoroughfare in Holand in South Dalemark where fish was sold until the days of Amil IV.

Flags were considered potent symbols in Dalemark from prehistoric times onward:

1. In the old Kingdom of Riverlands flags were religious symbols and only carried in the holiest ceremonies to honor the Undying.
2. To the Heathen invaders from Haligland flags were equally holy as expressing the honor and status of a clan. They were carried at all times and defended to the death in battle.
3. In historic Dalemark flags were nearly taboo. They were only flown at Midsummer Fairs and by ships at sea. No earls and few kings dared fly flags until Amil the Great designed the royal standard of the crowned wheatsheaf. To this day only the monarch flies a flag.

"Flaming Ammet!," an oath peculiar to Holanders and a favorite of Mitt's. Since Ammet was an image of the Earth Shaker made of wheat straw, the notion of it on fire amounted to blasphemy.

Flapper, Ganner Sagersson.

Flate, the general name for the flatlands surrounding Holand in South Dalemark, most of which were at, or below, sea level.

Flate Dike, the main drainage ditch for the lowlands around Holand. It was wider than most roads and ran dead straight for nearly fifteen miles, the water in it flowing like a river to an outlet ten miles west of the port of Holand.

Flate Street, a street in a poor but respectable district to the west of the city of Holand in South Dalemark, where Earl Hadd provided Hobin the gunsmith with a house and workshop.

Fledden, a small town to the north of Andmark in South Dalemark, the birthplace of Earl Henda and one of the few places where Henda could rely on absolute loyalty.

The inhabitants held the curious belief that the color
yellow was unlucky.

Flennpass, the last of the passes open in the mountains
between North and South Dalemark. It was said that
the musician-mage Osfameron had closed the other
three passes at the time of the Adon.

Flind, a common name in South Dalemark.
1. A vintner outside Derent in Waywold, who brought
Kialan and a supply of wine to Clennen the Singer.
2. A nonexistent person mentioned in a password as
part of Siriol's plans for Mitt's escape.

Flower of Holand, the boat belonging to Siriol on which
Mitt served as apprentice, part of the fishing fleet that
sailed regularly from the port of Holand in South
Dalemark.

"Follow the Lark," a song about bird catching whose
secret meaning was "overthrow the earls," composed
during the last rebellion before the Great Uprising.

Fort Flenn, the fort at the northern end of Flennpass, in
the hands of the North and designed to hold the pass
against incursion from the South.

Fredlan, one of the Singers, who traveled in a cart with
his family, giving performances all over Dalemark.

"Free as Air and Secret," a song pretending to be about
the delights of the countryside which secretly urged
rebellion, composed during an early uprising in South
Dalemark.

Free Holanders, one of many secret societies of freedom
fighters in the city of Holand in South Dalemark, the
one to which Mitt belonged from the age of eight. Its
members were mostly fishermen who believed ardently
that they should free South Dalemark from the tyranny

of the earls but who could seldom agree how this should be done. However, when the Great Uprising finally came about, all the Free Holanders were active in it, both in the fighting and in the reshaping of the government afterward.

Gander, Ganner Sagersson.

Gann, a great hero in the legends from South Dalemark who performed many great feats with his sword, Soulmaker, which was forged for him in secret by the Undying smith Agner while both were captives of the mage-king Heriol. Some stories give Gann as the brother of the witch Cennoreth. See also **Gull**.

Ganner Sagersson, Lord of Markind in the earldom of the South Dales, who had been betrothed to Lenina Thornsdaughter as a young man. When she left him for Clennen the Singer, Ganner did not, despite pressure from his household, marry anyone else. He seems to have expected Lenina would eventually come back to him (see **Bad Luck**). Ganner was a just and efficient administrator and one of few Southern lords to survive the Great Uprising untouched. He became regent for the South Dales on the death of Tholian.

Ganter Islands, a cluster of three islands in the Holy Islands.

Gardale, a prosperous valley, town, and earldom in the southeast of North Dalemark, site of the famous Lawschool.

Garlands of apples, corn, and grapes were worn by all those taking part in the Holand Sea Festival and afterward thrown into the sea.

Golden Gentleman, the name given by the King of the Riverlands to the image of the One when he finally found it in the keeping of Robin Clostisdaughter.

Gosler, Ganner Sagersson.

Gown, the distinguishing garment of the mage among the Heathens of Haligland. The gown had spells woven in it which appeared as words and, once put on by a mage, was never taken off, even for washing.

Grand Father, the most respectful of the titles of the One, possibly derived from the fact that most kings and many earls claimed to be descended from the One.

Great Girl (or boy), Lawschool slang for the pupil who comes top in the oral examinations held just before Midsummer.

Great Ones, the term for the Undying in the Holy Islands.

Great Uprising, the name for the countrywide revolution in Dalemark which brought Amil the Great to the throne. The Uprising began in the North around Kernsburgh and, almost simultaneously, in the South in the city of Holand, where a mob stormed the palace of the Earl and then had to fight a bloody battle with soldiers hastily sent by Dermath and Waywold. In the North a number of lords and earls who did not at once side with the rebels were killed or forced to go overseas.

Green roads, the system of highways said to have been made by King Hern. They remained for many centuries, being remarkably well engineered, never steep, despite running through the peaks of North Dalemark, and deliberately grassed for ease of travel by horseback. Many people believed that the Undying made and maintained the green roads, particularly as they continued to exist long after the main centers of civilization had moved down to the valleys. The roads were used as drove roads and by those who wished to travel quickly from dale to dale, until Alk took them over as railways in the reign of Amil the Great.

Gregin, Alk's valet in Aberath in North Dalemark.

Grittling, the traditional ball game of the Lawschool at Gardale.

Guilds, organized companies of craftsmen and merchants in South Dalemark. Most guilds were formed at the time of the Adon, when the men of many trades realized that the South was becoming increasingly estranged from the North, while the Southern earls grew ever more powerful. Almost every trade, including the Singers, took hasty steps to obtain the protection of the law, usually by petitioning the Adon for a Royal Charter, so that in after years the earls could not easily disband them. The guilds generally kept a low profile, looking after their own members and the widows and orphans of members, training apprentices, educating children, saving money, and paying taxes promptly. They had considerable power and were suspected by the Southern earls to be quietly financing the various uprisings, though nothing was ever proved.
In the North guilds were almost unknown.

Gull, eldest son of Closti the Clam and Anoreth of the Undying, the only one of Closti's sons to go to the wars. Gull was captured early in the fighting by the Heathen invaders and interrogated by the mage Kankredin, who returned him to his own side little better than an idiot. Gull is thought to be the same person as the Southern hero Gann, and if this is the case, it seems that Gull did eventually recover from Kankredin's treatment of him.

Guns were invented at the time of the Adon but never much used in North Dalemark. The South used guns extensively, although they were forbidden to all but earls, lords, and their hearthmen. The early guns were clumsy and inaccurate and used mostly for sport until Hobin invented the rifled barrel, which had a spiral groove down the inside that caused the gun to shoot far more accurately. There was then a rush to buy guns. Waywold and Canderack drove a thriving trade smuggling guns to the North.

Gunsmith's Guild, to which Hobin belonged, together with all other gunsmiths, was a very sober and respectable body of men who, in fact, spent the majority of their meetings laying careful plans for the Great Uprising.

Hadd, the angry and tyrannical Earl of Holand in South Dalemark who, after a lifetime of injustice, quarreling with Earl Henda, terrorizing his family, and overtaxing and suppressing his subjects, was murdered at the Sea Festival by an unknown marksman.

Halain, a spy for the Earl of the South Dales who had infiltrated the freedom fighters in Neathdale in South Dalemark.

Halian Tan Haleth, Lord of Mountain Rivers, is an old name for Tanamil. A legend about him was woven into the rugcoat given by Anoreth to Closti on their marriage but is otherwise unknown.

Halida, the wife of Keril, Earl of Hannart, who was born a poor relation of a lord in Canderack in South Dalemark. When Keril was taking part in an uprising in South Dalemark as a young man, Halida helped him escape capture and fled North with him.

Haligland, a country on the other continent, peopled by emigrants from prehistoric Dalemark several centuries before the reign of King Hern. Once in Haligland, they developed a clan system, a science of magery, and a religion of the One. Modern Haligland is an oil-rich republic, still with a clan system and a fanatical religion, but one which denies vehemently any connection with the uncanny.

Ham, the partner and mate of Siriol aboard the *Flower of Holand*. Ham's full name, like so many in Holand, was Alhammitt. He was a large, good-natured, unintelligent man who was killed in the violence following the storming of the palace in Holand during the Great Uprising.

Hammit, a South Dalemark name, one of the many abbreviations of Alhammitt.

Hand organ, a musical instrument with pipes, bellows, and keyboard, like a very small church organ. It had a sweet, piping tone, strong enough to be heard above the noise of a crowd. The player carried the organ on his or her right arm and pumped it with the left hand while playing the keyboard with the right.

Hands to the North, an unknown group of secret freedom fighters in Holand in South Dalemark. They were quite possibly invented either by Harl Haddsson as cover for his attempt to assassinate Earl Hadd or by Harchad Haddsson as an excuse to pull down buildings to give *his* assassin a clear shot at Earl Hadd.

"The Hanging of Filli Ray," a popular ballad about a young outlaw who was hanged for having the temerity to court a lord's daughter. The version sung in the South concluded with the arrival of the Earl, who reveals, too late, that Filli Ray is his son. In the North it is the King who arrives too late.

Hannart, the leading earldom of North Dalemark, famous for its music, its flowers, its buildings, and the frank, outspoken nature of its people, and reputed to be the first civilized area of Dalemark. Certainly some of the buildings in the town of Hannart itself are thought to date back to the days of King Hern. Throughout much of history Hannart stood for freedom, justice, and opposition to the South and its ways. Its heyday was from the reign of the Adon to that of Amil the Great, when it was also a center of learning, but it became steadily less important from the time of the Great Uprising until it passed by marriage into the royal family and was adopted by the Crown Prince as his country retreat. Nowadays Hannart is mostly famous as a beauty spot and for the remains of the giant steam organ at the north end of its dale.

Harchad, second son of Earl Hadd of Holand in South Dalemark, head of Hadd's secret police and master of his spies, said to be the cruelest man in Dalemark.

Hardimers, the name given to disciplinary officers at the Gardale Lawschool.

Harilla Harlsdaughter, eldest girl cousin of Hildrida and Ynen and betrothed at an early age to the Lord of Mark by her grandfather, Earl Hadd.

Harl Haddsson, the eldest of the Earl of Holand's three sons, a fat and seemingly indolent man, who became Earl of Holand for a year following the death of Hadd, during which time Holanders took to saying that Earl Hadd was preferable. He was killed when the mob stormed the palace in Holand during the Great Uprising.

Harvest, the Northern term for the Autumn Festival.

Headman, the leader or chieftain of a village in prehistoric Dalemark. The office combined the functions of major, priest, and judge and was usually handed down from father to son.

Hearthmen, a privileged band of soldier companions sworn to a lord or earl and personally responsible to him only, who lived in their hearthlord's mansion with him and formed a private army when need arose. A lord was also said to be the hearthman of the earl who was his overlord if he had sworn to follow the earl to war. In the South of Dalemark hearthpeople were always men, but many lords and earls of the North swore in women, too. The maintaining of hearthpeople was forbidden by royal decree in the reign of Amil II.

Heathens, emigrants from Haligland who invaded the prehistoric kingdom of Dalemark and eventually intermarried with the natives. They brought with them their women and children and the mage Kankredin and his college of lesser mages, intending to settle, and introduced to the country both the worship of the One and many magical practices that were previously unknown. Their main, disastrous invasion is described in the spellcoats, but it seems certain that small boatloads of Heathens had been arriving for decades previously, compelled by the harsh conditions in Haligland to find better living and possibly inspired by legends of their former home in the Riverlands.

Henda, Earl of Andmark in central South Dalemark, a violent and paranoid man who spent much of his time quarreling with the Earl of Holand and lived in constant dread of plots from the North. He was beheaded by his own hearthmen during the Great Uprising.

Herison, Lawschool slang meaning "the right to start grittling until the next full moon."

Hern, the second son of Closti the Clam and Anoreth of the Undying, who became the first known King of Dalemark. Most of what is known of him is legend, like the story of his defeat of the mage Kankredin, but numerous laws, customs, and sayings are said to be his,

and it is fairly certain that he founded the city of Kernsburgh, moving the seat of the throne there from his early base in Hannart and constructing the system of roads now known as the green roads or the paths of the Undying.
The name Hern means "heron."

Hestefan, one of the traveling Singers, of whom little is known beyond the facts that he befriended both Dagner and Moril Clennensson and became a follower of Noreth of Kredindale during her bid for the crown of Dalemark.

High Mill, a village twenty miles northeast of the port of Holand, on the rising ground toward Dermath, well known as a beauty spot.

Highside, the dormitory house at the Gardale Lawschool to which Hildrida Navissdaughter belonged.

High Tross, one of the islands of the Holy Islands, so called from its high and rocky outline.

Hildrida Navissdaughter, one of the company who sailed North to Aberath in the yacht *Wind's Road*, granddaughter of Hadd, Earl of Holand, betrothed to Lithar, Lord of the Holy Islands, at the age of nine. After spending several years at the Lawschool in Gardale, Hildrida was able to annul this betrothal, and practiced as a law-woman in the North Dales until Amil the Great appointed her Warden of the Holy Islands upon her marriage. Hildrida seems to have preferred living in Kernsburgh, however, where she became a leader of fashion and notorious for her quarrels with her stepmother, Eltruda.

Hildy, the pet name of Hildrida Navissdaughter.

Hobin, known as Bloody Hobin, the elder of two brothers devoted in different ways to freedom fighting. He was born in Waywold in South Dalemark of a family which seems to have been secret hereditary guardians of the kingstone, and he became a brilliant and innovative gunsmith, highly respected by his guild and much in favor with the earls of Holand, Waywold, and Dermath. He then moved to Holand, where he married Milda, Mitt's mother, and bided his time, building up a hidden stock of weapons and an organization of sober revolutionaries like himself, until word came from the North that Amil the Great had seized the crown. Hobin sensed the time was ripe and at once led a massive revolt in Holand, which spread to Dermath and Waywold and rapidly became a bloodbath. Hobin killed so many people, many of them innocent, that Amil himself was forced to intervene. It was said that Hobin shot himself rather than submit to a King. This may be true, but the story that he shot his wife and daughters at the same time is probably a fabrication.

Hoe, a village on the rising ground west of Holand in South Dalemark.

Hoe Point, the second major landmark for ships sailing northwest out of Holand. Sailors took care to know it well because a strong current flowed northward from there.

Holand, the leading earldom of South Dalemark, a sizable city, a flourishing seaport, and the seat of Earl Hadd, situated in the extreme south of Dalemark.

Hollisay, one of the Holy Islands, named from the number of holly bushes that grow there.

Holy Islands, a scatter of islands in the bay between the Point of Hark and Carrow Head, famous as a haven for shipping. The islands are home to a strange, fey people and full of legends of the Undying. They are part of the

King's Lands and owe no allegiance to any earl, but in the long interregnum between the Adon and Amil the Great they were regarded as part of South Dalemark and claimed by whoever was the strongest earl. Amil the Great rectified this by appointing a Warden of the Islands and spent much time there himself helping Ynen Navisson build his new fleet and experiment with steamships.

Holy Isle, the centermost island of the Holy Islands and rightly named. Only those who are meant to go to it can find it.

Honker, Ganner Sagersson.

Horsehair drums, traditional crude drums made of horsehide with the hair still on it, beaten loudly at the Holand Sea Festival, probably because Old Ammet was thought to govern the wild horses of the sea.

Horses of the sea were said to belong to Old Ammet and to appear galloping round a ship that was doomed.

Hurrel, Lawschool slang for a big push at grittling, a real scrimmage.

Incantation, a measured alliterative way of speaking, passed down from Singer to Singer and only used on the most solemn occasions.

Irana Harchadsdaughter, one of Earl Hadd's many grandchildren, cousin of Hildrida and Ynen, betrothed at an early age to Agnet, third son of the Earl of Waywold in South Dalemark.

"I sent the hidden death . . . ," one of Kankredin's two chief mages, who seems to have had no name apart from the boastful spell woven into his gown.

"I sing for Osfameron, I move in more than one world" are the words inlaid in Moril Clennensson's cwidder in the old writing, by which the cwidder describes itself. Compare Tanaqui's weaving. It is possible these words cause the cwidder to behave as it does.

Island people, the inhabitants of the Holy Islands who are something of a race unto themselves, being small and brown, with dark eyes and pale hair. Their sing-song accent is unlike any other in Dalemark. They are said to be remnants of the first people ever to settle the country.

Isle of Gard, the ruling island of the Holy Islands where the Lord's mansion and the main fleet are.

"I tortured the beast . . .," one of Kankredin's two chief mages, known only by the words woven in his gown.

Jay, herald and captain to the King of the Riverlands. Jay seems to have started as a minor, though trusted, herald, but he distinguished himself in the wars with the Heathens, when he lost an arm and endeared himself to the King by his cheerfulness, and became the favorite of the King in exile.

Jenro, a Holy Islander, coxswain aboard the flagship *Wheatsheaf.*

"Jolly Holanders," a sea shanty that was known and loved all over South Dalemark.

Justice, an essential part of the corrupt legal system of South Dalemark before the reforms of Amil the Great. A justice was appointed and paid by an earl and did the earl's bidding, sitting as a magistrate and hearing only such cases as interested his employer or could bring the justice himself a bribe. The South had no access to the Lawschool of the North, and justices seldom had any legal training. They had to rely on their clerks, who were equally corrupt, to tell them what the law was.

K at the beginning of a personal name was only used in
North Dalemark. In the slurred and softer dialect of the
South a *K* becomes either *C* (pronounced *KH*) or *H*. For
instance, the Southern form of the name Keril is Harl; or
there are sometimes two forms of a Northern name, as
in the name Kialan, which appears in the South both as
Collen and as Halain.

Kanart, an Earl of Dropwater killed in battle during the
Adon's wars.

Kanarthi, the conjectured Northern form of the name
Cennoreth.

Kankredin, an evil magician, sometimes called the mage
of mages, who accompanied the Heathen invaders from
Haligland, intending to use them to help him usurp the
power and position of the One. Kankredin was himself
of the Undying and had increased his powers by
magically passing through death, which made him
virtually impossible to kill. Though legend claims that
King Hern overthrew him, Kankredin appears again in
stories long before the time of the Adon and was later
said by the North to be the cause of all the evils in the
South. It is claimed that Amil the Great frustrated an
attempt by Kankredin to take over the North, too.

Kappin, Lawschool slang for fighting to hold the team's
position.

Karet, a hearthman of Aberath.

Kars Adon, son of Kiniron, who became clan head and
High Lord after his father died in the invasion of
prehistoric Dalemark. Though Kars Adon was barely
fifteen and crippled from birth, he was held in great
honor by all his subjects. This was partly due to the
custom of the clans, but mostly to the character of Kars
Adon himself.

Kastri, the Adon's son by his first wife and ancestor of Earl Keril of Hannart, who accompanied his father and Manaliabrid into exile.

Ked, a lowborn member of Clan Rath, aged about eight, who had a bad reputation as a liar.

Keril, Earl of Hannart, descended from the Adon and generally considered the most influential man in North Dalemark. As a young man he had high ideals and set out to free the South by helping in an uprising. The rebellion failed, and Keril had to be rescued and smuggled North by Halida, whom he married. He arrived back in Hannart to find his father dying and himself with a price on his head in the South. This seems to have given Keril a strong distaste for revolution of the violent kind. As an earl he supported the Southern freedom fighters surreptitiously, with money and advice, apparently hoping for a peaceful political solution, no doubt with himself as chief negotiator, for he possessed a lively and devious political mind. Unfortunately this same deviousness caused him to miscalculate gravely in the case of Navis Haddsson, and he had, as a result, to watch the gradual fading of Hannart as a power in the land.

Kern, the Northern form of the name Hern.

Kernsburgh, the capital city of Dalemark, situated nearly at the center of the country. Kernsburgh was founded by King Hern and flourished for many centuries until the kingship shifted to Hannart, Canderack, and elsewhere, after which it fell into ruins. At the time of the Great Uprising it was little more than grassy humps in the ground. Amil the Great's first act as King was to rebuild Kernsburgh, and from then on the city grew continually, to become the seat of government, center of commerce, and international metropolis it is two hundred years later.

Kestrel, the husband of Closti the Clam's elder sister, Zara, an old man who married late in life when Zwitt refused to marry Zara after Closti had jilted Zwitt's sister. Kestrel, it seems, did not wish to see Zara suffer through no fault of her own.

Kialan, younger son of Keril, Earl of Hannart, and later his heir.

King of the Riverlands of prehistoric Dalemark. Tanaqui never gives his name, perhaps out of respect, or perhaps because she never knew it. She clearly shows that he was not the correct man for dealing with the Heathen invasion, although he seems to have done his best at first, until his family was killed and his spirit broken.

Kinghaven, in the earldom of Loviath, the main port city of North Dalemark and otherwise notorious for brewing bad lager.

King's Sayings, a collection of proverbs and wise thoughts memorized by all Singers and supposed to be the words of King Hern himself.

King Street, the main thoroughfare in Kernsburgh.

"The King's Way," a traditional song with a rousing tune which celebrates the customary journey of the new King down the green roads of North Dalemark to Kernsburgh to claim his crown. This song was banned in the South, where the earls did not wish to remind people there had once been Kings.

Kiniron, the younger brother of the King of Haligland who led the main invasion of the clans to prehistoric Dalemark, where he died of wounds from the fighting.

Kintor, Lord of Kredindale and cousin of Noreth Onesdaughter.

Knots and crosses, one of the oldest and most potent charms of binding and, of course, the basic pattern of a net. See also **Nets.**

Konian, the elder son of Keril, Earl of Hannart, executed in Holand in South Dalemark after a travesty of a trial.

Korib, son of the miller in Shelling and an excellent shot with the longbow.

Kredindale, a valley, town, and lordship in the extreme northwest of North Dalemark where deposits of coal were found very early in history. From the reign of the Adon, mining became the main occupation of the valley until the mines were closed in the reign of Amil III. Kredindale was the birthplace of Noreth Onesdaughter. Its name is thought to be derived from Kankredin.

Labbard, King of Dalemark prior to the Adon, an indolent and incompetent man who openly declared that he would rather sit and drink cider than rule the country.

Ladri, one of Kankredin's mages, whose task was to collect the souls caught in the soulnet.

Lady, the wooden image of a woman which the family of Closti the Clam kept, according to the customs of prehistoric Dalemark, in one of the niches reserved for the Undying.

Lagan, the villainous half brother of the Adon, a student of sorcery and, some legends say, a pupil of Kankredin. Lagan seems to have been consumed with jealousy both of the Adon's status and of the Adon's love for Manaliabrid. Having conspired to have the Adon sent into exile, Lagan then followed him, disguised himself by sorcery, and stabbed him to death. The Adon was recalled from death and later killed Lagan.

Lake, a large body of water in the center of prehistoric North Dalemark, which must have been extensive even when the River was not flooding, to judge from the petrified remains of freshwater life to be found all over the central peaks. By historic times this lake had shrunk to a row of small tarns, the largest of which is Long Tarn.

Lalla, housekeeper at Lithar's mansion in the Holy Islands and an aspect of Libby Beer.

"Lament for the Earl of Dropwater," an old ballad song composed during the Adon's wars, mourning the death of Kanart, who was one of many earls who opposed the Adon.

Lathsay, one of the Holy Islands.

Lavreth, a coastal town northwest of Hannart in North Dalemark.

Lawman, a position of great power and prestige in North Dalemark. Lawmen served earls, lords, and town governors as advisers, justices, or planners for the future and in many other ways, often for very large fees. Quite a few lawmen married into the families of lords or earls. Since the law was open to everyone, however lowborn, training as a lawman was a favorite way to rise in the world.

Law of the sea was very largely unwritten but was held throughout Dalemark waters to be much more binding than the law of the land. It stated, among other things, that all ships must go to the assistance of any boat in trouble.

Lawschool at Gardale in North Dalemark, the only such school in the country until the reign of Amil the Great, very famous and much sought after. It took only those pupils who could reach a very high standard in its oral entrance exams, but a pupil could join the school at any age from nine to fifteen and then be assured of the very best education, both in law and other studies, and nobody ever failed to get a job after graduating. The Lawschool was well endowed with funds and gave quite a number of scholarships to poor students every year. Students entering the school found it a world in itself, with many strange customs and words that were not found anywhere else.

When Amil the Great founded lawschools all over the country, the status of the Gardale school diminished. In the reign of Amil III it became simply a part of Gardale University.

Law-woman, a female lawyer, had even more prestige in North Dalemark than a lawman and could command an even higher fee.

Lengday, Lawschool slang for Midsummer Day.

Lenina Thornsdaughter, niece of Earl Tholian of the South Dales, wife of Clennen the Singer, and mother of Dagner, Brid, and Moril. Lenina was brought up as an aristocrat in the Earl's household in Neathdale in South Dalemark and left there when she became betrothed to Ganner Sagersson. Clennen saw Lenina at the betrothal feast and persuaded her to marry him instead.

Libby Beer, the name of the image made of fruit that was yearly thrown into the harbor in Holand in South Dalemark at the Sea Festival. The name is certainly a corruption of one of the little-known names of She Who Raised the Islands, the Undying mother of fruitfulness and wife of the Earth Shaker.

License, a legal document with the seal of an earl attached, showing that the holder was allowed to exercise his or her trade anywhere in South Dalemark. Licenses were expensive. Their main value was the unspoken assumption that the holder was allowed to travel between the South and the North. Without a license, a traveler would be arrested at the border.

Liss, Maewen's aunt, who ran a livery stable near Adenmouth in the north of Dalemark.

Litha, a woman of the prehistoric Riverlands who was killed by the Heathen invaders from Haligland.

Lithar, Lord of the Holy Islands, who was of special value to the earls of South Dalemark, both because of his fleet and because, as lord of the onetime King's Lands, he was not the subject of any earl. He was betrothed to Hildrida Navissdaughter when he was twenty and she was nine years old.

Little Flate, a village on the slightly rising ground southwest of Holand in South Dalemark, which was the first landmark for ships sailing out of Holand. Sailors gave it a wide berth because of the shallows just offshore.

Little ones, the name Holy Islanders give those mortals under the special protection of the Undying.

Little Shool, one of the Holy Islands, barely yards from its neighbor, Big Shool.

Lord, a lesser ruler under the earls, who owed allegiance to the earl in whose earldom his lordship was, paying taxes and providing fighting men when his earl required him to. A lord was also supposed to obey every other command from his earl, but not all lords did so. Otherwise a lord lived in his mansion, kept hearthmen, and ruled his subjects just as an earl did, but on a smaller scale.

Lord of Mark, lord of the northernmost lordship in South Dalemark, a plump and middle-aged widower, betrothed to Harilla Harlsdaughter when he was thirty-eight and she was ten years old.

Lovely Libby, one of the big merchant ships sailing out of Holand in South Dalemark. Like most of the tall ships of Holand, she was named from the Sea Festival for luck.

Loviath
1. The earldom on the northwest coast of North Dalemark.
2. The name of Maewen Singer's physics teacher.

"Luck ship and shore," the ritual reply to the traditional greeting "The year's luck to you" at the Sea Festival in Holand in South Dalemark.

Lucky ship, any ship sailing out of Holand that could retrieve the image of Poor Old Ammet from the sea. The yacht *Wind's Road* was doubly lucky from having accidentally brought the image of Libby Beer as well. Anyone noticing this fact had to be a Holander.

Luthan, Earl of Dropwater and cousin of Noreth of Kredindale. Because of his almost accidental support of the King's side in the Great Uprising, Luthan—and Dropwater with him—became extremely important in the reign of Amil the Great. Luthan was made chancellor and was twice elected prime minister.

Lydda, Siriol's daughter, a plump, good-natured girl who married a sailor from the merchant fleet of Holand. Her husband later took over Siriol's boat and business.

Maewen Singer, a teenage girl hijacked from modern Dalemark to take the place of Noreth of Kredindale. See also **Mayelbridwen**.

Mage Mallard, the Undying musician-mage, youngest son of Closti the Clam and brother to the Weaver and King Hern. See also **Duck.**

Mages were fairly common in primitive Haligland and much respected because much feared. No one dared insult a mage of any kind, but the greatest fear and respect were reserved for the so-called college of mages, which was always made up of fifty of the strongest and most experienced enchanters in the land. When Kankredin came to head this college, he seems to have made it a condition that every mage should have passed ritually through death before he joined, which was not the case before his time. College mages were always male, but female mages also existed, with a coven of fifty of their own.

"A man came over the hill . . .", a rhyme woven into the skirt of Robin Clostisdaughter by her sister Tanaqui, but hopelessly garbled. As far as can be understood, the rhyme seems to be about the meeting of Closti with Anoreth, or else it refers to a much older but very similar story.

Manaliabrid
    1. The Undying wife of the Adon, daughter of Cennoreth the Weaver.
    2. The full second name of Brid Clennensdaughter (her first name was Cennoreth).

"Manaliabrid's Lament," a song in the old style, said to have been composed by Osfameron after Lagan killed the Adon. It has a tune of strange broken phrasings, so unlike the usual style of Osfameron that many consider that Manaliabrid may have composed the "Lament" herself.

Mansion, the large semifortified house of an earl or lord, always the most prominent in the area. Besides housing the lord's family and many servants, the mansion had to be big enough for a band of hearthmen, advisers, lawyers, clerks, and numerous other assistants.

Markind, an area in the very south of the South Dales, the lordship of Ganner Sagersson, and notable for its

Diana Wynne Jones

many little hills and valleys, which are, in fact, the worn-down remnants of volcanoes.

Marks, an old name for the fifteen divisions of Dalemark that later became the earldoms.

Mark Wood, a large forest at the northern edge of the third and highest Upland in the earldom of the South Dales, part of the lordship of Mark. It was full of clearings stockaded against possible invasion by the North, where wood was cut and charcoal was made. The inhabitants hated the North heartily and put up the stoutest resistance met by the army of Amil the Great at the start of the Great Uprising.

Marriage by proxy, a custom among earls of holding a wedding without the bride's being present. Her place would be taken by a woman who was married already. The practice probably originated to save the nobly born bride the trouble and expense of a journey, but it was widely used if the bride was unwilling, or a child, or both.

Marshes, a huge area of volcanic swamp to the east of Dalemark. Throughout historical times the Marshes were considered worthless, remarkable only for curious plants and birds, and they became King's Lands because nobody else wanted them. When, in recent times, oil was discovered there, they remained the property of the crown but added considerably to the wealth of the country.

Mattrick, chief among the freedom fighters in Neathdale in South Dalemark.

Mayelbridwen, a form of the name Manaliabrid from Fenmark; Maewen Singer's full name.

"May the clay purge from you . . . ," the start of the ritual spoken when the image of the One was put into its yearly fire. The speakers of this invocation had, for generations, no idea that what they were uttering was a spell for the unbinding of the One.

Medmere, the valley where Clennen the Singer was murdered. The round lake in the middle is the center of an old volcano.

Middle vokes, Lawschool slang for the second stage of the training course.

Midsummer flags, traditional bright banners flown at Midsummer Fairs all over Dalemark. The devices on them—the Eye, the Sheaf, the River, et cetera—are versions of the Old Writing. The flags are thought to be the debased remnants of flags once carried in religious ceremonies.

Milda, the mother of Mitt and afterward the wife of Hobin the gunsmith, who was the father of her two daughters. Sadly, neither Milda nor her daughters survived the Great Uprising. Though there are several highly colored stories about their deaths, the most likely theory is that they perished in the terrible violence and confusion after the mob stormed the Earl's palace in Holand, when the earls of Dermath and Waywold sacked the city in reprisal.

Mitt, short for Alhammitt. Mitt was born at Dike End in the earldom of Holand in South Dalemark, on the day of the Sea Festival. He moved to the city of Holand as a child, where he became a freedom fighter and was forced to escape to the North to avoid arrest. After just under a year in Aberath, in training as a hearthman, he left to follow Noreth of Kredindale in her bid for the crown.

Modes, Lawschool slang for a progress report on the term's work.

Moril, younger son of Clennen the Singer. Clennen bequeathed to Moril a cwidder said to have belonged to the minstrel Osfameron. After the death of his father, Moril went to Hannart in North Dalemark, where he briefly joined Hestefan the Singer before leaving to take part in the Great Uprising. He played a considerable part in the Uprising and afterward became court musician and chief architect of the Royal Dalemark Academy of Music, collecting traveling Singers from all over Dalemark and gathering them together in Kernsburgh. This caused such changes and improvements in the making of music that by the end of Amil the Great's reign the old traveling Singers had ceased to exist.

Mount Tanil, a very tall volcano on the edge of the Marshes southeast of Gardale, thought by unlearned people to be the home of the One.

Mucks, Lawschool slang for gloved hands, the gloves often weighted by being stuffed with metal or stones.

Natives, the term given by the Heathen invaders to the prehistoric inhabitants of Dalemark, who were mostly dark and squarely built. After the invasion many of these people went South, where they intermarried with the settlers there to give rise to the average Southerner, pale-skinned and brown-haired. Those who stayed in the North interbred with the invaders to produce the brown-skinned, light-haired Northerner.

Navis Haddsson, third son of the Earl of Holand, a brilliant and efficient soldier and a ruthless politician, who was forced to escape North from the palace plots in Holand (he was disliked by both the old Earl and the new for having shown too much sympathy for the plight of the common people of Holand). He spent nearly a year as a hearthman in Adenmouth before leaving to follow Noreth of Kredindale and to take part in the Great Uprising. It was probably thanks to Navis that the bloodshed was not greater. Early in the reign of Amil the Great, Navis was made Duke of Kernsburgh, partly in reward for his services and partly because he then outranked the earls it was now his job to control. A year later he married Eltruda, widow of Lord Stair of Adenmouth.

Neathdale, a large market town in the South Dales, the seat of Earl Tholian. Because it was the last major town before the North, Neathdale flourished both on legal trade and by smuggling goods and people in and out of North Dalemark. The earls' spies and security forces were particularly active there, which led to the Siege of Neathdale during the Great Uprising.

Nepstan, a country in the far South.

Nets, a potent item of magecraft, akin to weaving. The netmaker, working with power, could design his net to perform various tasks. Kandredin's soulnet, besides trapping departing souls, was intended to draw Gull's soul to him *and* to bind the One. Tanamil's nets likewise had several purposes: concealing the army, blocking the mages, and forcing them to assume their true shapes.

New Flate, the drained flatlands some miles west of Holand in South Dalemark, where Halain, grandfather of Earl Hadd, was supposed to have had dikes dug and drained the sea marsh. In fact, the New Flate was probably older than that. It was very fertile farmland but was denied prosperity until the reign of Amil the Great by the ridiculously high taxes imposed by the earls of Holand.

Noreth, known as Onesdaughter, of whom it was said that the One spoke to her all her life, telling her she was to take the crown when she reached the age of eighteen. She was born in Kredindale to the Lord's unmarried daughter, Eleth, who died soon after Noreth's birth, declaring that the child's father was the One himself. If this was true, it gave Noreth the strongest possible claim to be Queen. She was educated first in Adenmouth, where she was left in the care of her aunt Eltruda, and then at the Gardale Lawschool, from which she graduated early, then spent the next two years at Dropwater as junior law-woman to her cousin Luthan. The Midsummer after her eighteenth birthday Noreth returned to Adenmouth, where she formally declared her intention of riding the royal road to claim the crown.

North, the seven earldoms of Hannart, Gardale, Aberath, Loviath, Dropwater, Kannarth, and the North Dales, all these being north of a line drawn east and west from the Point of Hark. This was the earliest part of the kingdom of Dalemark and also the most mountainous, where the people, though generally poor, had a long tradition of independence and freethinking. The earls of the North quickly learned that injustice was not to be tolerated (quite a few earls lost either their lives or most of their subjects to the mountains while this lesson was being learned), and the laws of the North were therefore fair and lenient, applying to earl and commoner alike. From well before the reign of the Adon, the North was known as the place of freedom. It was also, perhaps because it was the oldest-settled part of Dalemark, renowned for strange old beliefs and even stranger happenings.

North Dales, the earldom immediately to the north of South Dalemark. Though it was cut off from the South by a range of high mountains, the people there were used to dealing with the South (often as smugglers) and were in some ways more akin to the South than to the North.

Northern Cross, the most noticeable constellation in the night sky at all seasons, invaluable to sailors because it revolved around the true north. Other well-known constellations are Enblith's Hair, the Flatiron, the Big Cat, the Kitten, Hern's Crown, and the River. Astronomy was not much studied in Dalemark until the reign of Amil the Great, so that although it was known that the world was round and circled the sun, little account was taken of the planets. Sailors called them the Unreliable Stars, for always moving about, or the Unchancy Ones.

Old Flate, the flatlands toward Waywold in South Dalemark, part of the earldom of Holand which had once been drained and farmed but allowed to return to marsh in the course of the two centuries before the Great Uprising because of the ruinous taxes imposed by the earls of Holand. The Old Flate became the haunt of snakes, criminals, and disease.

Old Man, the highest mountain in Hannart, at the south end of the dale, thought to be named for the One.

Old Man of the Sea, a seeming priest who appeared to certain people in the Holy Islands, an aspect of the One.

Old Mill, across the River from Shelling in prehistoric Dalemark, where the first spellcoat was completed and the second begun. It had become a forbidden place for the villagers after the marriage of Closti and Anoreth. Some said it was haunted by the ghost of a woman, others that it was the abode of bad spirits, and still others that the River had cursed the place. As the King's men found mussels being cultivated on a system of ropes in the millpond, it appears that not everyone in Shelling believed these tales.

Old Smiler, Mage Mallard's derisive name for the King of the Riverlands.

Old Writing, a system of syllabic signs in use before letters were developed, which came to be thought of as magical. It was often used in spells or for inscriptions intended to be potent.

Olob, the shortened name of Barangarolob, Clennen the Singer's horse, which Clennen often said he would not part with for an earldom.

Ommern, one of the Holy Islands, the greenest.

Ommersay, one of the larger of the Holy Islands.

One, the greatest of all the Undying, whose face could not be looked upon and whose names could not be spoken. The One was said to have fathered the human race by his union with the witch-queen Cenblith, at which time he made the great River of prehistory and was for centuries bound by magic at its source. He was at length unbound by the Weaver and shook the country into its present mountainous state when he defeated the mage Kankredin.
The One was worshiped as a god by the invaders from Haligland and for a long time remained a god in the North of Dalemark, where many beliefs and customs about him still remain, but he was almost unknown in the South. Nowadays he is regarded simply as an old superstition.

Or, er, ro, a particle inserted into a name to give the meaning "younger" or most often "youngest." Compare Barangalob and Barangarolob, Tanamil and Tanamoril, Osfamon and Osfameron, et cetera.

Oreth, one of the secret names of the One, the least known, meaning "he who is bound."

Orethan the Unbound, the name by which the One was known after the Weaver released him from the spells of Cenblith and Kankredin. This name is almost never spoken.

Oril, one of several names taken by Mage Mallard to disguise the fact that he was of the Undying.

Orilsway, a town which grew up at the junction of the green roads in the far north of Dalemark, possibly taking its name from Mage Mallard in his guise as the Wanderer. When the green roads were abandoned as highways, Orilsway fell into ruin and was only rebuilt and resettled after the coming of the railways.

Osfameron, one of the two names taken by Mage Mallard in his guise as a minstrel and meaning "Osfamon the younger." It is not known who Osfamon was. Under this name Mallard became the friend of the Adon, whom he raised from the dead, and also created the cwidder with which he is said to have made mountains walk, later bequeathed to Moril Clennensson.

Palace of Earl Hadd in Holand in South Dalemark. Most earls, even in the South, lived in much humbler mansions, but Earl Hadd, perhaps because he insisted on his entire family's living with him, enlarged and renamed his dwelling. The palace was largely destroyed in the Great Uprising.

Pali, a prison guard in Neathdale in South Dalemark who was a secret freedom fighter.

Panhorn, an intricately curled horn with four mouthpieces and eight valves, very difficult to play.

Paths of the Undying, a name for the green roads of North Dalemark used by those who believed that the Undying created and maintained them.

Peace-piping, a very difficult form of musical magecraft in which the mage must first use his pipes to echo the anger of combatants and then reduce their feelings to calm and shame. Moril Clennensson unwittingly used a form of peace-piping on Tholian, Earl of the South Dales.

Peelers, Lawschool slang for willow wands with the bark peeled off.

Penner, Ganner Sagersson.

Pennet, a village between Waywold and Holand in South Dalemark.

Piper, the name most often used, from the time of the Adon onward, for Tanamil of the Undying, onetime lord of the Red River. It was said that being released from bondage at the same time as the One, Tanamil went to the Holy Islands, where his piping may still sometimes be heard on calm evenings.

Point of Hark, the high rocky peninsula that divides North from South Dalemark waters.

Poor Old Ammet, the full name of the image made of plaited wheat decorated with fruit and flowers and ribbons which was thrown into the harbor in Holand in South Dalemark each year at the Sea Festival. Opinions vary as to whether this ritual echoes some personal sacrifice by one of the Undying or is simply a charm for improving the harvest, but what is certain is that any boat which picks up Poor Old Ammet beyond the harbor has good luck ever after. This is rare; the tides and currents have to be exactly right. Usually the image sinks in the harbor.

Portable organ. See **Hand organ**.

Porter, the main spy for North Dalemark, operating under the noses of all the earls of the South, and the most wanted man in the South. He reported to Hannart almost everything the Southern earls wished to keep secret, organized freedom fighters, and ran a rescue service for wanted men and women. The Porter was operating for most of the eleven years prior to the Great Uprising.

Prest, one of the Holy Islands, large, with high crags.

Prestsay, a small rocky island in the Holy Islands.

Proud Ammet, a big merchant ship based in Holand in South Dalemark, where Earl Hadd's assassin seems to have been when he fired. Like all the big merchant ships, this one was named from the Sea Festival.

Ratchet, a cat found by the children of Closti the Clam on their journey up the great River, named from the sound of her purring.

Rath Clan, sometimes called the Sons of Rath, the royal clan of primitive Haligland into which Kars Adon and Ked were born. The clan colors, which appeared on banners and in clothing, were red and blue.

Rattles, rotating wooden rattles, where the noise is produced by a wooden flange meeting a ratchet, which are traditional at the drowning of Old Ammet in the Holand Sea Festival. The rattle users are always small boys dressed half in red and half in yellow.

A Reader for the Poor, a book designed to teach working people to read. It was written by a clerk in Carrowmark who had little imagination. A typical page begins, "Ham beats the cask. He knocks in five nails. Will that make it hold water?"

Red One, one of the names for Tanamil the Piper.

Riss, a seaman aboard the flagship *Wheatsheaf* in the Holy Islands.

Rith, a boy's name, fairly common in North Dalemark.

River, the mighty prehistoric watercourse which flowed north through Dalemark from a source somewhere near Hannart. It was said that the One made the River, and that the River was both the One and the soul of the land, and that it was the path of souls on their way to the sea. The River was destroyed by the One when he shook the land to rid it of the evil mage Kankredin. It only remains nowadays as two small rivers, the Ath and the Aden, and in the belief that the souls of the dead travel down the constellation of the River to oblivion in the sea of the universe.

Riverbed, the spirit land behind the great River, otherwise called the River of Souls.

Riverlands, the correct name for the prehistoric kingdom of Dalemark.

Rivermouth, the place where the great prehistoric River of Dalemark ran out into the sea in the north, through a delta of marsh, quicksand, and changing tides and currents. Its remains can be seen today in the bay between Aberath and Adenmouth, where there are still treacherous currents and constantly changing shoals.

Robin, the eldest child of Closti the Clam and Anoreth of the Undying, whose birthright was knowledge. Unlike her brothers and sisters, Robin passes clean out of all history and legend after the narrative of the spellcoats. It is possible that stories about her have been lost or attributed to her more spirited sister, Tanaqui.

Royal road, the green roads of North Dalemark between Adenmouth and Kernsburgh. Tradition said that each new monarch should make this journey on the old roads before claiming crown and kingstone at Kernsburgh.

Rugcoats, the poncholike garments of woven wool worn by men and women over their other clothing in prehistoric Dalemark.

Rugcoats for weddings were presented by a girl's family in prehistoric Dalemark to a husband-to-be as a sign that the two were officially betrothed; the groom then wore the rugcoat at the wedding. These rugcoats were always of specially fine weaving, usually with words all over. It was believed that the coat brought luck to the wedding, and possibly children, too. If the bridegroom did not wear the coat at the wedding, it was a sign that the bride would soon be either deceived or a widow. If the groom gave the coat back before the wedding, the betrothal was broken off.

Rushing people, the souls of the dead that hurry along the Riverbed toward the sea.

Rush mat, woven by Mage Mallard to deceive the King of the Riverlands. Weaving in any form is a potent spell.

Rusty, a ginger tomcat found by the children of Closti the Clam on the journey up the great River.

Sailing in grybo, Lawschool slang for being in the clear, without black marks.

Sard, a trusted soldier of the King of the Riverlands—trusted because he enjoyed killing.

Scap, Lawschool slang for the spring solstice.

Scarnel, a pipe made of pea or bean stalks, hollowed and varnished, traditionally played at the Sea Festival in Holand in South Dalemark by any number of amateur players. The sound is indescribably horrible.

Sea Festival, celebrated in autumn and called the Autumn Festival or Harvest elsewhere in Dalemark and peculiar to Holand in the South. Two images, one of straw and one of fruit, are carried down to the harbor in a procession of men clothed in red and yellow, draped with garlands and wearing traditional hats, accompanied by music from traditional instruments and by other lesser images; at the harbor with solemn words the two greater images are thrown into the sea. This is followed by feasting.

"The Second March," one of seven tunes used by soldiers to march to all over Dalemark. "The Second March" has a jaunty tune and is generally more in favor in the North.

Sein right, Lawschool slang for the right to start grittling. The team with sein right could choose weapons and set up the first move.

Sending Day, at the Lawschool, the day on which pupils returned home for the summer. Pupils' families were asked to attend the closing ceremony before they removed the pupils.

Sessioning, the Lawschool word for school term.

Sevenfold, a merchant ship based in Holand in South Dalemark which had the good luck to pull Poor Old Ammet out of the sea. Every man aboard was said to have made his fortune subsequently. *Sevenfold* herself was sold when she became old to a merchant in Waywold who renamed her *Fair Enblith* and was not particularly lucky with her.

Sevenfold II, a merchant ship sailing out of Holand in South Dalemark, so called when the first ship of that name was sold. Her cockboat was found by the yacht *Wind's Road.* Like most Holand shipping, both *Sevenfolds* were named from the Sea Festival.

"The Seven Marches," the set of lively tunes to which soldiers marched in both North and South Dalemark. Each march had well-known words.

Shelling, a village much like other villages on the west bank of the great River of prehistoric Dalemark, the birthplace of Closti the Clam and his children.

Shelling River Procession, held once a year at Midsummer to honor the River as a god. This was one of four yearly ceremonies in which flags were carried, and probably gave rise to the custom of flying flags over the stalls at Midsummer Fairs all over historic Dalemark.

She Who Raised the Islands, the most common term for the lady of the Undying who, as wife of the Earth Shaker, has power nearly equal to his but is, on the whole, more benign. As Libby Beer she provides fruit and nourishment, but in her stronger aspects she is the earth itself and the only one of the Undying able to control the Earth Shaker. She is adored particularly in the Holy Islands, where she takes the shape of a beautiful red-haired woman dressed in green.

Shield of Oreth, a mountain plateau in the southwest of North Dalemark that faces the milder weather of the sea. The name is from the least known of the secret names of the One, and it should perhaps be noted that at least three of the Undying and the Adon's sword were to be found there. In early historic times the Shield was well farmed and populous, but it fell into wasteland during the Adon's wars. Navis Haddsson was given ducal lands here and was fond of saying that of all his achievements, the one which gave him most pleasure was the restoration of the Shield to farmland and prosperity.

Singers, a race of men and women, most of whom claimed descent from Tanamoril or Osfameron, who traveled the country of Dalemark singing, playing music, and telling stories. Because Singers were among the few people able to move freely between North and South, they also carried news, letters, and often fugitives. Some even acted as spies, but this was rare: Singers had their own rigid customs and standards, chief among which was always to tell the truth and never to perform a vile or a violent act. They also passed down by word of mouth innumerable old customs, sayings, beliefs, and incantations, many of which were lost when Moril Clennensson disbanded the Singers in the reign of Amil the Great.

Siriol, the owner of the *Flower of Holand*, a fisherman and a prominent member of the Free Holanders, the society of secret freedom fighters to which Mitt also belonged. Mitt was apprenticed to Siriol for a while until his indentures were bought out by Hobin the gunsmith. Siriol greatly distinguished himself during the Great Uprising and afterward became first a councillor and then semipermanent Mayor of Holand.

Six steps up to a front door were standard in Holand in South Dalemark, where the land is only inches above sea level and there is constant danger of flooding, particularly during the autumn storms.

Skreths, Lawschool slang word for the cloister to the east of the school.

Small Western clan, any of several minor clans that sailed from Haligland to prehistoric Dalemark during the years before the main invasion.

Soulboat, a small skiff specially enchanted to hold the souls of the dead once they had been retrieved from Kankredin's net.

Soulnet. See **Nets**.

Souls of mortals were believed until quite recently to be the prey of witches and sorcerers, whether joined to a body or not. The mages of primitive Haligland claimed to be able to steal a man's soul while he slept, and Kankredin is said to have been able to take someone's soul at any time he wished. Souls of the Undying and those descended from them were a different matter because they were believed to be combined not only with a body but with the entire country, too.

South, the eight earldoms of Dermath, Holand, Waywold, Canderack, Andmark, Carrowmark, Fenmark, and the South Dales. This part of Dalemark has a warm climate, a rich soil, and few high mountains. In early historic times it was very wealthy, but it became steadily poorer under the oppressive rule of the Southern earls, until, shortly before the reign of Amil the Great, the South was actually often poorer than the North and only ruled by fear. The North regarded this regime with disgust; the South was deeply suspicious of the North; and each considered itself superior to the other. The South, in fact, was noted for a number of virtues not seen in the North: efficiency, coolheadedness, perseverance, and clear-sightedness, combined with a strong sense of humor.

South Dales, the earldom closest to North Dalemark and in many ways not unlike the North in climate and geography. But being this close to the freethinking North had a bad effect on the earls of the South Dales: They were the most tyrannical, warlike, and unjust of all the Southern earls.

Spannet, a stablehand in Adenmouth in North Dalemark.

Specials, guns made secretly by Hobin of Holand in South Dalemark which he sold only to a chosen few. Each gun had some unusual feature, and all were better than any of the weapons he sold in public.

Spellcoat, a poncholike garment woven with word pictures that either told a story or stated facts. The garment, in the weaving, became the spell that made the story or fact come true. See also **Weaving; Words.**

Spirits were thought to be everywhere and to govern everything in prehistoric Dalemark, and it was necessary to please or soothe them every day. Some of the more powerful spirits almost had the status of gods and were confused by many with the Undying. The unusual thing about Closti's family is that they did not share this belief. Hern, in fact, rejected spirits out of hand as "unreasonable."

Spring floods, as a result of the snow melting in central Dalemark, are extensive even in modern times. In the uncontrolled River of prehistoric times there was always much flooding, which not only devastated homes but also brought fertile silt, driftwood, and fish. This violent mixture of destruction and benevolence caused many people to regard the River as a god.

Square rigging, the old type of sail which is simply a sheet of canvas hung between two yards across the mast and swiveled at both ends to catch the wind. South Dalemark very early gave this up in favor of the far more efficient fore-and-aft rigged triangular sail, but the North still clung to the old rig right up to the reign of Amil the Great, when Ynen Navisson reorganized all shipping to form his fleet.

Square-topped pillar, a waist-high primitive altar only found in the Holy Islands.

Squarks, Lawschool slang meaning "being too bumptious."

Stair, Lord of Adenmouth in North Dalemark, a confirmed alcoholic.

Stapled, Lawschool slang meaning "to be posted on a notice board as a wrongdoer." Any pupil who was stapled lost certain privileges for a month.

Steam organ, at Hannart in North Dalemark, a huge music-making machine built into the side of the mountain, operating like a church organ but powered by steam. It was said to have been the brainchild of the Adon and brought sightseers to Hannart from the moment it was built. It is clear that the people of the Adon's time knew all about steam power two centuries before the industrial revolution but considered it only worthwhile for providing entertainment.

Stirring, Holy Islands dialect for rowing a boat.

Stork, the totem standard of the King of prehistoric Dalemark, where birds had a significance and potency which it is now hard to define. No one but the King or his accredited agents dared carry the Stork. Thus the people of Shelling knew at once that the messengers were there by royal decree.

Surnam, Lawschool slang for the one who spearheads an attack at grittling.

Sweetheart, a black cat rescued from an island by the children of Closti the Clam on their journey up the great River.

Sweetrush, a pet name for Tanaqui the weaver.

Talismans, charms for keeping the soul in the body made for King Hern's army by Tanamil the Piper. Many centuries later Dalemark people still call pebbles found with a chance pattern of cross-hatching piper's pieces.

Tally, the Lawschool term for its list of prizes.

Tan, a particle added to the front of a personal name to mean "the younger," as in Tanabrid, Tankol, Tanamil, et cetera.

Tanabrid, the daughter of the Adon by his second wife, Manaliabrid of the Undying, who married the Lord of Kredindale after the death of the Adon.

Tan Adon, Young Lord, one of the names for Tanamil the Piper.

Tanamil, one of the elder Undying, whose name means "younger brother" or "younger river." It is said that Tanamil was enslaved by Cenblith at the same time as the One and forced to create the Red River. There are many legends about him, some of which confuse him with Tanamoril, the mage-musician. Tanamil, however, is earlier than Tanamoril, for he is said to have played a major part in King Hern's defeat of Kankredin, after which he is said to have gone to the Holy Islands, where he can sometimes be heard playing his pipes at sunset.

Tanamoril
1. Moril's full second name. He was called after his famous ancestor.
2. The name taken by Mage Mallard in his earliest disguise as a minstrel. Under this name he assisted Enblith the Fair to become Queen because, according to some stories, she was his daughter.
3. The name means "youngest brother" and also refers to both Mallard's and Moril's position in their families.

Tanaqui
1. The second daughter of Closti the Clam and Anoreth of the Undying. She was a skilled weaver who made the two spellcoats which were dug up from the hillside above Hannart in North Dalemark. Her name is a punning one, meaning both "scented rushes" and "younger sister." There has been speculation as to whether Tanaqui is herself of the Undying and, if so, is to be identified with Cennoreth the Weaver, but this is probably without foundation: Tanaqui was plainly a real person. See also **Weaving**.
2. The scented rushes that are nowadays rare, growing only in certain habitats in North Dalemark.

Tankol, otherwise known as Young Kol, head foreman of the mineworkers at Kredindale in North Dalemark.

Tannoreth Palace, built by Amil the Great in Kernsburgh at the start of his reign, to Amil's own design, and still the royal palace although the present monarch seldom lives there. Amil appears to have invented the name Tannoreth himself (as he invented so many other things in the course of his long reign). It means, if anything, "the younger Noreth."

Tanoreth, the "young bound One," a name for Tanamil the Piper.

Tears, a potent magic. When Mitt weeps on an image of Libby Beer, he unknowingly invokes her protection.

Termath, the southernmost port in South Dalemark, the seat of the Earl of Dermath.

"The year's luck to you, " the ritual greeting between Holanders on the day of the Sea Festival.

"This is my will," a form of words used by a dying King to name the next King. These words had the force of law. King Hern, having named his son Closti as King, is said to have continued, "and it is my will that I name all Kings after you."

Tholian, the name of several earls of the South Dales. After the last Tholian perished in an abortive invasion of the North a year or so before the Great Uprising, the name was discarded as unlucky.

"To tide swimming . . ., " the ancient charm of invocation to the Earth Shaker and She Who Raised the Islands, spoken as part of the Holand Sea Festival. Any who doubt that this is indeed a charm should note that the words *go now and return sevenfold* are thrice repeated in it.

Trase, Lawschool slang for a team attack at grittling.

Trethers, Lawschool slang for roll call, for which all pupils had to be present to answer their names.

Tross, one of the largest of the Holy Islands.

Trossaver, one of the Holy Islands, held to be the most beautiful.

Tulfa, the Southern spelling of Tulfer Island.

Tulfer Island, a large island some eight leagues off the coast of Dropwater in North Dalemark, closely allied to Hannart by marriage.

Undying, immortals. There are three kinds:
1. The gods and closely related spirits of prehistoric Dalemark, whose images were kept in niches by the hearth and worshiped and placated daily.
2. The Elder Undying, who had the status of gods and whose souls were supposed to be enmeshed in the land. They were worshiped in numerous rituals throughout Dalemark which still remain as fragmentary customs and superstitions, particularly in the North. Though there never was any organized religion and only a few buildings were dedicated to the Undying, it is clear that everyone in early historic times, from the King downward, joined in rituals of worship or invocation to the Undying at certain times of the year. The Elder Undying can be distinguished by their ritualized names—e.g., the One, whose names are not to be spoken; the Weaver of Fates, et cetera.
3. People who live forever. There seems to be a gene of true immortality in the blood of Dalemark. Such people—for instance, Tanamoril or Manaliabrid—are born rarely, possibly one every three or four centuries, but do seem to exist. They nearly always

possess unusual powers or abilities and often claim descent from the Elder Undying. It has been said that these immortals are the same as the Elder Undying, except that the Elder Undying unwisely allowed themselves to be bound into godhead by mortals wishing to worship them, but there is no proof of this theory.

"Undying at Midsummer, " a very ancient tune of invocation to the One at the time of his greatest power.

Updale, a small village in the center of the second Upland, north of Neathdale in South Dalemark.

Uplands, the most northerly section of South Dalemark. The land here rises in three steep escarpments to meet the mountains of the North.

Virtue, power, life force, or magic.

Wailers, mourners, women who traditionally sit over a dead person making sounds of grief. The sounds have strict rules, which have to be learned. Wailers are usually elderly women or those without children who have had time to learn the rules.

Wanderer, the one of the Undying who walks the green roads of North Dalemark, keeping them in good repair. He is the patron of all travelers and invoked even in the South at the start of a journey.

Warden of the Holy Islands, the title bestowed on Hildrida Navissdaughter by Amil the Great.

Warm Springs, mentioned in the spellcoats, halfway along the southern stretch of the great River and certainly of volcanic origin. Dalemark lies across two tectonic plates, and the land has always been prone to earthquakes and volcanic upheavals. Most historians believe that the shaking of the land by the One was in fact caused by the colliding of the two continental plates. There is evidence in Markind of a much earlier upheaval accompanied by massive volcanic activity.

Wars in Dalemark were frequent, but three only need concern us:

1. The prehistoric invasion by Heathens from Haligland.
2. The Adon's wars when the Adon claimed the crown, one of the few civil conflicts in which earls from both North and South appeared on either side.
3. The Great Uprising, when Amil the Great took the crown, which ended in the establishment of modern Dalemark as one kingdom.

Watersmeet, in the prehistoric Riverlands, the junction where the Red River flowed into the great River.

Waystone, a flat, round stone with a hole in the middle, set up on its narrow edge to mark the start of a green road in North Dalemark. It was the custom to touch the waystone for luck at the start of a journey.

Waywold, the earldom next door to Holand on the south coast of South Dalemark.

Weaver, the lady of the Undying who weaves the fates and fortunes of mortals. She is said by some to be the same as the witch Cennoreth.

"The Weaver's Song," a well-known nursery song that may originally have been an invocation to the Weaver.

Weaving was always to some extent a magical skill and not simply to do with making cloth. In early historical times each pattern woven was held to have significance. Note that Tanaqui takes it for granted that whatever she weaves will contain at least some words, usually at the hem or wrists of the garment, but quite often in bands throughout. See also **Words**.

"Welcome aboard, Old Ammet, sir!," the traditional greeting from the crew that found Old Ammet floating in the sea, showing respect proper to one of the Undying.

Wend Orilson, assistant curator at the Tannoreth Palace in Kernsburgh, who claims to be one of the Undying.

West Pool, the second harbor of Holand in South Dalemark, shallower than the main harbor and protected by walls and gates, where the rich have always kept their pleasure boats. Harbor dues here are very high.

Wheatsheaf, the flagship of the Holy Islands fleet.

Wheatsheaf crest, the badge of Holand in South Dalemark, much feared in the time of Earl Hadd, when Harchad Haddsson gave each of his paid spies a small gold button stamped with this crest.

"Wider than the world, or small as in a nut," a quotation from a song by the Adon, sung by Kialan on the road north. The song is called "Truth" and, at one level, describes the working of the cwidder bequeathed to Moril Clennensson.

Wind's Road
  1. An archaic term for the sea, used in spells and invocations.
  2. The name of the yacht in which Mitt and his friends escaped north.

Wine, made all over South Dalemark. The best vintages, red and white, are from Canderack, and the worst from Holand, and there are one or two superb reds from Andmark. The Holy Islands make a strange sparkling white and a brandy so good only earls can afford it. Apart from this, everywhere north of Markind tends to make cider instead and distill from it the spirits called gley. The main drink of the North is beer, except in Dropwater, where they make a sort of plum brandy.

Winthrough, Lawschool slang for a scholarship student.

Wittess, one of the Holy Islands, low and green.

Words, a term used by Tanaqui and Kankredin for the clusters of woven signs in the spellcoats which only the learned or the initiated could read in the cloth. These signs not only formed words in the normal sense but were also potent ingredients of a mage-weaver's spell.

Wren, the headman of an unknown village in prehistoric Dalemark who led his people northward, fleeing from Kankredin. He was the first man to swear allegiance to King Hern.

Yeddersay, one of the outer ring of the Holy Islands.

Ynen, son of Navis Haddsson, who became Amil the Great's admiral in chief. Ynen not only experimented with steamships but built the conventional navy up to the extent that Dalemark quickly became an important sea power.

Ynynen, the lesser of the Earth Shaker's two Great Names. Readers are strongly advised not to say this name beside the sea or in a boat.

Young One, the red clay image of a smiling young man which the family of Closti the Clam kept in one of their fireside niches reserved for the Undying.

Zara, the sister of Closti the Clam, who was to have married Zwitt, the headman of Shelling, if Closti had not jilted Zwitt's sister. Zara was then forced to marry Kestrel or remain a spinster. Zara never forgave Closti or his family for this, though she seems to have retained a strong fondness for Zwitt.

Zwitt, the headman of Shelling beside the great River of prehistoric Dalemark. When Zwitt was young, he was betrothed to Closti the Clam's sister Zara, while Closti was betrothed to Zwitt's sister. Closti, however, fell in love with Anoreth and married her instead. Zwitt, in revenge, refused to marry Zara. This caused continuing bad blood between Zwitt and Closti's family.